ANDE TREMBATH

LECTOR HOUSE PUBLIC DOMAIN WORKS

ANDE TREMBATH

MATTHEW STANLEY KEMP

9 789354 200984

ISBN: 978-93-5420-098-4

Published: 1905

LECTOR HOUSE LLP
E-MAIL: lectorpublishing@gmail.com

ANDE TREMBATH

ANDE TREMBATH
A TALE OF OLD CORNWALL ENGLAND

BY

MATTHEW STANLEY KEMP

Author of "BOSS TOM"

1905

TO MY FRIEND
THE RIGHT REV. CORTLANDT WHITEHEAD, S.T.D.
BISHOP OF PITTSBURGH

IN MEMORY OF PLEASANT HOURS SPENT TOGETHER
AT "BURGTOWN."

CONTENTS

LIST OF ILLUSTRATIONS

ANDE TREMBATH

CHAPTER I

A CALAMITY AT THE MANOR

"Never before in the history of the Manor have deeds like these been perpetrated," said the squire, his genial, rubicund countenance turning pale with anger.

"Prithee, prithee, cool thyself; look at the affair calmly and you will speedily discover the rogue," replied the parson.

"Cool myself!" replied the squire, in some heat; "it is easy enough to talk, but this is the third offence in a week. Last Monday the tulip beds and shrubbery were trampled and ruined; Wednesday, the fish-pond drained and the best fish secured; and last night, the unknown miscreant killed poor, faithful Borlase. It is becoming unbearable," —and the squire, with angry features and the semblance of a tear in his eye, knelt down by the body of the English mastiff to convince himself again that the life of his canine friend was extinct.

The scene was in a remote corner of the gardens of an old Cornish manor estate. Some distance away, looming up above the nodding heads of trees, were the gables and chimney pots of the squire's residence. Near a clump of shrubbery was the kneeling form of the squire, with flushed face and unsteady hand, for his soul was trembling with indignation, examining the head of his slain, four-footed friend. The parson, with dignified step, was closely scrutinising the ground between the squire and the road-side hedge.

"Ah! Here, do you see? Here is where the missile struck him." It was the squire who spoke, for he had found a long deep gash near the right ear.

"From what I can see," said the parson, who was a keen observer, "the rogue was making for the hedge, the most natural deduction, the hedge being the nighest escape from the dog. Then," he continued, with homiletical precision as if outlining a pulpit theme, "since the dog followed him, he must have hurled some missile at him. What more natural missile than a stone, and what more natural place to secure it than from the hedge? Now the missile must be around here somewhere. Ah! Here it is," and Parson Trant picked up a good sized stone from amidst the shrubbery. "There is blood upon it; proof, number one; now let us discover its place in the hedge."

The squire arose and accompanied the parson to the hedge and, after a minute examination, the stone's former location was discovered.

"So far, good," ejaculated the parson. "Now what servants would be most likely around the gardens last evening?"

"Tut, tut, you would never make a barrister, parson. To suspect any of my servants! You are well versed in theology, and no one knows better how to preach a sermon, but in matters of law and trespass we, magistrates, must take the precedence."

Now at times Squire Vivian could be as genial and pleasant as the sun on a June-tide morning. Kind-hearted, generous, frank, bluff, with a rough veneer of the old-time courtesy was the old squire, and yet with a choleric spirit underneath all, that would sometimes burst forth into passionate invective, to the scandal of his friends and to his own aftertime regret. Add to this a dignified opinion of his position as a landed magistrate and the squire of Trembath Manor is evident. He had a goodly amount of hard English sense and in managing his estates and finances had been tolerably successful, but in sharp penetration of character and shrewd judgment in other affairs, he was lamentably deficient. His frank and open nature had not given him much chance to develop these talents, even had he ever possessed them, and, like many persons whose positions require talents in which they are lacking, or at best but meagrely gifted, the squire felt vexed when his little magisterial keenness was surpassed.

"Tut, tut, parson, you are losing your judgment if you suspect the servants. There's old George Sloan, the hostler, and Ned Pengilly, the gardener, the only two persons likely to be on the grounds at that time, and they loved old Borlase,—ay,—even better than they love his master. No, no, parson, you are at fault there."

Parson Trant smiled, for he knew one of the chief failings in the squire's character.

"No, I did not suspect them, but they, being on the grounds, can no doubt enlighten us and bring to view more evidence. The most learned and keen-sighted judge, at times, profits by the evidence of common labourers and country parsons, who are far beneath him in the knowledge of law and criminal investigation."

"To be sure, to be sure," said the squire, somewhat mollified, "but here comes Sloan."

An old man, whose erect form and sturdy step belied his grey hair and wrinkled brows, was seen approaching from the direction of the stables.

"Canst tell us anything more about this outrage, Sloan?"

The hostler was now close at hand and had removed his cap in deference to the gentlemen near him.

"A bad job, beant it, squire, as I was a-telling nephe Bob this morning. No, sir, I can't say as Hi knaws much. I 'eard Borlase barking savage-like last night, and I ups and slips quiet-like down from my room o'er the stables, and run through the paddock just in time to see the rogue on the other side of the 'edge. It was dark, squire, and I 'aven't the heye-sight I used to 'ave, and so I couldn't make un out who 'e was. This marning I looked around and found poor Borlase a-lying there and brought you word. That's all I knaws, only I 'opes the villain will be caught and 'anged."

"And did you see no person around the grounds late in the afternoon, George?" asked the parson.

"None, sir, except my nephe Bob, who comes hover to the stables to 'elp me in my work, now and then, but 'e always leaves afore evening. Now—as I think of it, Bob was a-telling me 'e 'ad seen Ande Trembath nigh the Prospidnic road gate, as 'e was going 'ome last night; 'e may 'ave seen the rogue and could tell you summat."

Blackness as of a thunder-cloud rolled across the old squire's features, and a purple stream of blood mounted and flushed his temples.

"Spawn of the traitor! He shall smart for it!"

"What a horrible oath! Squire, you are beside yourself," said the parson, with gentle, chiding reproof.

"Well, damme, parson, what's a man to do? Here's all these outrages, and it's perfectly clear to my mind, now, that that traitorous son of——"

"Tut, tut, fie, squire!"

"That that traitorous son of a traitor, knowing that I have the possession of the manor of his ancestors, which the King—God bless him—took from their family on account of their treason, that boy—don't interrupt me, Parson Trant—that boy is the culprit, and damme—I'll have him arrested for malicious mischief and trespass."

"Not so fast, squire. What evidence do you have except your own suspicions and the fact that the lad was seen nigh the Prospidnic road gate? If I know aught of law there's not sufficient evidence."

"There, there, you talk of law—as if a magistrate didn't know the law."

"Well, the evidence is lacking," said the parson, gently, though firmly, for he would not allow the squire to shake his confidence in his best pupil. "The lad has a good reputation, is a bright scholar in my parish school, and——"

"Well, well, we'll get more evidence," interrupted the squire, a little testily. "George, see that the dog is buried, and—here, hitch up the black mare for Mistress Alice; she's going out this morning."

The hostler paused, fingering his cap.

"I'm feared, squire, Queeny is a little huntrusty; she's been standing in the stall some time."

"What!———"

The presence of the parson restrained the squire from saying more, but his flushed countenance spoke volumes. George saw it and, touching his cap, hastened off to obey.

"Here's a pretty pass things are coming to! Outrages committed daily, and my own servants in open rebellion, disputing my word."

"Come now," said the parson, gently, "he meant no harm and no disrespect, I'm sure. Suppose we go down to the lodge and see Pengilly."

Squire and parson wended their way across the gardens to the broad carriage-way and thence down to the main entrance of the manor estate, the latter talking and the former keeping down his temper as best he could in silence, until he became of a more quiescent frame of mind. In truth, the squire was inwardly regretting his outburst of temper, and the violent language he had used in the presence of his friend, the parson.

"Such a thing is possible but not probable. Ande has been the best scholar in the parish school and a model boy, so the master assures me. We must not condemn him too hastily and without being heard. His mother is a noble woman and has inculcated high principles in her training of the lad."

There was silence for a moment unbroken save by the crunch, crunch of the gravel underfoot and the twitter of bird overhead. Then the squire, sufficiently calmed, spoke.

"All very true, but envy and malice crop out even in the very best of characters; especially is it true in those who, having been deprived of high position, see others occupying that which was formerly theirs. They are apt to allow their feelings to bias their judgment."

"And are you sure that you, my old friend, are not doing the same thing?" said the parson, with a winning smile, referring to the last remark of the squire.

Squire Vivian flushed at this rejoinder.

"Well, we'll give the lad a fair chance; perhaps I was a trifle too hasty, but you well know, parson, that next to my Alice and you, I was extremely fond of Borlase, and naturally feel angry at his loss. I secured him when a puppy from an old friend, one of the Borlases of Borlase at St. Just. You know, to be sure, Dr. William Borlase, the scholar and antiquarian?"

"Aye, I have studied his works with interest."

"Well, I named the mastiff after him; the intelligence of that dog, parson, was phenomenal. Ah, here we are at the lodge."

The drive-way terminated at the entrance gate, a large affair of massive iron bars, fancifully and artistically wrought at the top into intricate curves and flourishes. Huge square pillars of Cornish moor-stone surmounted at the top with the Trembath arms—a Lyonnesse warrior galloping amidst ocean waves—flanked the gate on either side and gave it desired support. Why the squire, or his father, had not removed the arms of his predecessor, replacing them with his own, is hard to tell. The whole gateway stood out like fret-work upon the background of the squire's woods beyond the highway, woods and trees of ancient standing, as scrupulously cared for as the members of the squire's own household.

Within the gate and close on one side, lovingly environed by beds of blooming gilli-flowers and marigolds, and almost concealed by enveloping masses of English ivy that affectionately embraced its walls, was a small, neat, stone cottage that bore the dignified name of "the Lodge." A man, still in the prime of life, was labouring assiduously over some strawberry beds in the rear.

"Ned, this way, please," shouted the squire, and Ned Pengilly, who acted in the double capacity of gardener and porter, dropping his hoe, hastened to comply. There was independence and respect for his master admirably blended in the demeanour of the gardener, as he stood before parson and squire.

"Ned, did you see Ande Trembath nigh the place of late? We want you to freshen up your memory and tell us when and how often you have seen him about the place of late."

"Well, I seed him going through the Manor woods—yesterday; 'e was whistling a tune, bright and cheery-like, and bid me the time of day as 'e passed the gate. We all likes young Squire Ande, as we calls 'im—no offence, squire, I 'opes;— we all calls 'im 'young squire' 'cause 'is grandfather was squire 'ere years ago, afore 'e turned for the French—which the lad can't 'elp."

"Which the lad can't help!" fairly thundered the squire, his wrath getting the better of him once more, no doubt fired at the term of young squire. "I suppose he couldn't help draining the fish pond? I suppose he couldn't help trampling the shrubbery? I suppose he couldn't help killing Borlase last night? Couldn't help— —"

The latter part of this ebullition of passion died away in a hoarse growl of something like "blood will tell."

The effect upon the porter of this news of the killing of Borlase was most striking.

"Bless m' well, squire! What! Borlase dead—killed! Good hold Borlase! 'ow fond we were of 'im! Dead!"

There was a curious working of the gardener's features and he hastily rubbed the sleeve of his rough shirt across his eyes.

"You must excuse me, squire—to blubber 'ere like a babby—but then you knaw 'ow I brought un, nigh ten year ago, from St. Just—a puppy 'e was then, and I loved un—ay—like—like—like a father. 'Ow 'e used to bark—just like the roar of a lion—ah was—and 'ow sensible 'e was too when 'e would come nigh me at work on the flower beds; 'e'd wag 'is tail and look on like a gentleman, as if saying, 'thas all right, my man,' and yet 'e'd ne'er put foot on a posy or stamp on my work. Dead! But bless'ee, squire, you can't suspect Ande. Why, I knawed Ande when 'e was only a hinfant, and I knawed him from then up, and a brighter, better, honester lad ne'er breathed. Soul of 'onour, 'e ez, sir! Ande! Why 'e wouldn't 'urt nothing, sir."

"I agree with you, Ned," said the parson. "Ande has too kind a heart to hurt any of God's creatures. His character is above suspicion in the matter."

"'Zactly so, so 'e ez," affirmed Ned.

"The principles and character of his father and grandfather were not above reproach. He's a chip of the old block," growled the squire.

"But, I am afraid the commonwealth is against you in your judgment of the lad. You know the old adage, 'a man's innocent until proved guilty,' squire," rejoined the parson.

"Aye, but in this case it's the Irish verdict, 'guilty, but not proven.' Ned, fix up the berry bushes and trim the shrubbery to-day. In the meantime keep an ear open, and report to me any news you may hear of last night's outrage."

The gardener touched his cap and returned to his labour, and squire and parson, still conversing, sauntered away through the grounds.

"A man shouldn't allow his feelings to run away with his judgment," said the latter, warmly championing the cause of his favourite.

"The days of the Stoics are past. You have a marvellous predilection for that lad, Parson Trant. Now, I shall just send the steward down to the village, this evening, and have him up here, not for a trial, but just for a private examination, and he shall have fair play. But going to other subjects, old friend,—what think you of young Master Lanyan?"

"Master Lanyan—um—a bright young man—bright beyond his years, I think. He will certainly make his mark in life if he keeps to right principles."

"Ah, exactly so," said the squire, rubbing his hands in the first satisfaction he had had for the whole morning. "I wanted to get your opinion and am glad you think so highly of him."

His companion shook his head.

"As to thinking highly of him—I don't know. He has a strong, subtile mind,—culture,—and a determined will, but he plays cards and——"

"Pooh! Pooh! Pish! Physician, heal thyself; you know that you and I engage in a social game at times."

"But we don't gamble."

"Only a few wild oats. That is natural to a high-spirited lad. He has culture, a strong head—a genuine gentleman," stoutly maintained the squire.

"Ah, but those things in my estimation are not the true requisites of a gentleman. I consider the foundation principles of a man's life."

"Yes, but the English gentry are supposed to be dominated by the highest principles," said the squire, earnestly.

"As a class, yes, but in reference to the individual, it is a supposition without the fact, frequently; and, if your statement holds good, how about my young friend, Ande Trembath?"

The squire flushed with angry impatience.

"Back again to that young villain! Well, parson, that family no longer belongs to the English gentry class, as you can readily see. Attainder of property and corruption of blood!"

It was the parson's time to "Pish! Pish! Pooh! Pooh!"

"Pshaw! Nothing of the kind. Does a plant cease to be the same when it is transplanted to another soil, or the king of the jungle cease to be a lion when surrounded by the bars of a cage?"

"Yes, to an extent. Environment has a large influence on life; at least so our parson said in last Sabbath's discourse." The squire laughed heartily, and thwacked the discomfited parson on the back with his large, broad hand.

The parson smiled and resumed.

"I am beaten with my own stick, yet, notwithstanding that you quoted me correctly, you are wrong. Environment is not a paramount influence. Man can conquer. Tertullian and Origen——"

Afraid of starting his friend on some long-winded discourse on ancient church worthies, the squire interrupted him.

"Your idea of a gentleman is——"

"My idea is that wealth, culture, position, etc., are the emoluments or adjuncts, and that high, sound, moral principles, a righteous heart and a noble soul, whether under the blouse of the peasant or under the silk vest of the prince, are the only badges of gentility."

"Well, well,—little did I think that my old, conservative friend would turn out such a radical."

"Not at all. My firm belief, that these, by training, education, blood, descent, are embodied more fully in the gentry class of England than in any other, has made me an extreme conservative. But, about young Master Lanyan?"

"Young Richard? Young Richard in a year or so will attain his majority. What think you of a match between the young Richard and my Alice? You see," added the squire, as he linked his arm in that of the parson, "I am getting old and I would like to see my only child well settled in life before I leave the earth. The Lanyan estates are nigh to ours and they will fall to Richard after his father's death. What better match than Richard? My Alice is worthy of being called 'My Lady' and Richard will be Baronet in time. Now, what think you, old friend?"

"You asked me two questions; let us consider one at a time. In reference to young Richard. It is not the playing of cards that I object to; it is the trait that his gambling reveals. You know of the schemes of his grandfather, and of his great-grandfather; the rage for speculation, the South Sea Bubble, and the hundred and one schemes that that family has engaged in. Blood will tell. Richard's gambling reveals that. He will either make or break his family. This mad rage for speculation is an evil thing. Some day either Sir James or Richard will overreach himself and should—but of that anon. He is determined and has a strong will, but should his will be thwarted might not the young Richard be like his grandfather, a man of no principle. I do not wish to misjudge the young man, but I fear me that he is one who will allow nothing to come between himself and his ends, and even to stoop to questionable and evil things to accomplish those ends. God forgive me if I have judged wrongly. Then he is proud and even supercilious at times, a disdainer of the commons. Should he be brought to poverty, the lack of principle which I fear is in him would hasten the degradation of his character. He may be different than I have said, but whenever I see him I have an undefinable suspicion of incipient evil within. Now in reference to Alice and this projected alliance. Alice is a good child and has commendable traits. No 'My Lady' will enhance her worth any more than it is now. Her happiness is no light consideration. I believe she can be happy with no man except one of high and noble principles. Then, in event of this alliance being consummated, there may be danger of Trembath Manor being involved in the ruin that may come upon Lanyan Hall. Has she been consulted? Would she offer no objection to this plan of yours?"

"Objection! No," said the squire, a little testily, for he had been listening impatiently to this advice of his friend. "Alice is a good child and will do as I say."

The parson had his own opinion, but said nothing.

The great gables and chimney-pots of the "great house," as it was generally called by the peasantry around about, loomed up in the distance and suggested to the parson that the hour was getting late. Taking out his watch — —

"I declare! I had no thought that the hour was so late, and Harriet will be waiting for me, too. I must go and we'll talk about the matter later on."

The squire tried to prevail upon his friend to stay for lunch, but, finding that it was unavailing, cordially shook hands and they separated, the former going on toward the Manor house, the latter hastening down to the entrance gates.

CHAPTER II

THE SON OF A TRAITOR

"Blithe bird of the wilderness, sweet is thy song,
Blithe lark of the wildwood, O, all the day long,
A-singing so cheerily in the green tree,
Thy anthem dispels gloom and sorrow from me;
Thou sayest in thy song, 'What can sadness avail?
Injustice shall fall and the good shall prevail.'

"Yet bird of the wilderness, sad is our lot,
Our home, confiscated, our name, a dark blot;
The Cornish chief, stricken at Prestonpan's fight,
Wounded at Culloden for King and the right,
And captured at Braddock's defeat in the glen,
Was branded at home by a sycophant's pen.

"Oh, bird of the wildwood, upon the green bough
Thy ancestor sang just as sweetly as thou,
He sang, as thou singest, that evil should fail,
Injustice should fall, and that good should prevail;
But surely the goddess of justice is blind,
When traitor is honoured and patriot maligned.

"Sing sweetly, O wild bird, upon the green tree,
And let me draw comfort and solace from thee,
Though home's confiscated, dishonoured our name,
And poverty adds a deep sting to our shame,
And father's departed,—yet, evil shall fail,—
Some day,—right shall triumph and good shall prevail."

Clear and sweet arose the melody, and yet with a plaintive element of sadness in it. The parson paused in his steps to listen. On one side of the highway stretched the woods of the Manor, their shadow etched darkly by the slightly slanting sun-rays; on the other side were the fields, yellow, ripe, all ready for the sickle of the reaper. A wood-lark, the sweetest of all English birds, arose in the air from the Manor woods and, still twittering, flew over hedge and field, no doubt seeking its home and mate.

A smile of pleasure lit up the saintly old rector's face and then merged into the thoughtful. He made a pleasing picture leaning on his silver-headed cane, his long skirted coat slightly open at the neck, revealing the white stock-cravat in its fluffy folds, his head slightly inclined as if not willing to lose a single bar of the song. Not until the song was ended did he venture forward.

"Most remarkable song and most remarkable sweet tenor voice—yes—a great deal sweeter than Penjerrick's. I must have that voice for our parish choir."

Arriving at the corner of the woods, the silence of the singer was explained in a single, brief, cursory glance. There, seated on the hedge that separated the woods from the road, sat the figure of a boy, tall, sinewy and strong, yet still a boy. His cap had fallen to the ground and the tangled masses of dark red hair lay deep on his brow. With melancholy, abstracted air, he was gazing across the fields as if in meditation.

"Why, Ande, you are quite a singer," said the parson, in a pleasant voice.

The lad, startled from his reverie, leaped down from the hedge, picked up his cap and coming forward gave his customary salutation, "Good-morning, Parson Trant."

The parson returned the salutation and then there was silence for a moment, during which the rector scrutinised him with his kindly, yet keen grey eyes.

The lad's face was both attractive and strong. His slightly aquiline nose revealed a sensitive nature; his prominent chin and firm lips, a resolute will; his high, rolling forehead—swept by the tangled waves of rollicking hair—intellectuality; the hue of his locks and the deep blue eye, a soul that, though kind and affectionate, could be fired by strong passions. At least so conjectured the parson, who thought he could read character in human lineaments.

But these thoughts did not occupy the latter long. It was the manner of the lad that disturbed him. With bright, cheery smile he had been accustomed to greet him heretofore. Now the youth stood before him almost with the air of a culprit. He shunned the rector's eyes, and seemed as if wishing to avoid that calm scrutiny. A fleeting thought possessed the mind of the pastor. Could the youth possibly be guilty of the misdemeanours committed at the Manor? Was he wrong in his judgment of his favourite pupil? The truth of the matter was that the youth had been crying over petty vexations. At least there were tears in his eyes and, like many of his age, he disliked to be seen thus.

"Well, Ande," said Parson Trant, breaking the silence, "you have a voice that ought to be in our parish choir. Now what do you say about coming in next Sabbath morning? Mr. Penjerrick will give you a little preliminary training Saturday afternoon."

"I—I would rather not come, sir, if you could excuse me. I—I don't sing in church."

"And why not?" asked the parson, kindly.

"Because I would be singing the praises of God when—when—I don't feel like it," responded the lad a little slowly, and with some effort.

"Why, Ande, you are a Christian lad—true, you have not yet been confirmed and united to the church—but still, you are a Christian lad. Are you not?"

"I don't know, sir," said the lad, and again relapsed into silence.

"My poor lad," said the good old man, as he put one arm over the boy's shoulder, affectionately, "there's something wrong with you to-day; you are not yourself. Come now, confide in me. Tell me about it and let me give you my advice in the matter. You have not done anything wrong, have you?"

Thus questioned by the good old rector, Ande, who loved him for his worth as a true man and a noble exponent of Christianity, could not help but respond. Flinging up his head and pushing back the masses of hair that would persist in falling over his eyes, he said:

"It is this way, Mr. Trant, I have made up my mind to leave the country. There is room for me on the sea or in foreign parts. I can't bear the taunts of some of the lads at the parish school. The master doesn't know and you don't know how mean some of the boys act. There's Bob Sloan, Dick Denny and some more of that stripe that are becoming unbearable."

"Why, what do they say?" asked the parson, kindly.

"They call me the ugly Dane or Deane and cast slurs upon my father and grandfather, saying they were traitors to the government."

"Ah, in reference to the first name, methinks, my lad, you are old enough to know that that old story of the Danes seizing the wives of Englishmen has no historical foundation; in reference to the second matter, time itself must clear up the truth or falsity of the accusation. It certainly shows a mean, petty spirit to vilify a son for the reputed deeds of a father."

"Aye, there's just the point about my not singing in church. The Bible says 'the sins of the fathers shall be visited upon the children,' and I think that's unjust. Here," said the boy with a trace of angry passion in his tones, "I am taunted, despised, looked down on, not only by the lads, but by some of the grown people as well. I believe, just as you say, that it shows a small spirit in lads, men and the Bible, to condemn a lad for the faults of his father. How can I sing then?"

The parson was dumfounded and completely silenced for a moment. He was grieved and dismayed to hear how his last remark was misapplied.

"And," continued the youth, rather bitterly, "I believe, and know you believe, that neither father nor grandfather were guilty of any treason, that there's a mistake somewhere. Yet—yet I have to stand all this. Squire Vivian looks upon me with an angry look. Sir James Lanyan looks upon me as if I was a dog. Master Richard called me a traitor's cub, because I happened to be in his way this morning, and if he hadn't been on horse-back I would have made him take it back— and—and—I hate them. I hate them all!" The lad's face was marked with passion, his fists clenched, and there was an angry tear in his eye that he could not conceal. "Why does God allow all this? Why—and—and—but I'm not going to stay here and bear it."

The parson looked grave and turned the conversation for a moment by asking the name of the author of the song he had heard.

"The Song of the Lark, you mean? That was made by my father, and my mother taught me to sing it when I could first finger the harp. The harp is the only thing we have now that used to belong to the Manor." There was a sad ring in the boy's voice that but indicated the feelings within.

"Do you believe in the truth of that song?"

"Yes," responded the lad.

"Well, why don't you put in application the thought?" and Parson Trant quoted the words:

> "'What can sadness avail,
> Injustice shall fall, and good shall prevail.'

Now, Ande," continued the parson, "I know the history of your family almost as well as you. Your grandfather was a faithful subject of the king. He fought with Gardner at Prestonpans, at Culloden, and also against the French in the American colonies. He disappeared after Braddock's defeat and was shot a year afterward by General Armstrong's troops, by mistake, no doubt. Now consider,—at the time he had on a tattered French uniform, with a commission as captain in the French army in his pocket. These things were brought to England and, through the instrumentality of Sir Richard Lanyan, father of Sir James, the attention of the authorities was directed toward them and the Manor confiscated. Under the circumstances was not the king justified in suspicioning his loyalty? Consider, too, that England and the Hanover dynasty had been threatened seriously, by the Pretender, with another invasion of French troops. Culloden was still fresh in men's minds. Cornwall was noted for her adherence to the Stuarts in the Cromwellian wars, and even at the time of the young Pretender many noted Cornish families sympathised with him and the Stuart claims. You know the story of Burnuhall[1], and how young Prince Charles, the Pretender, spent several nights there in concealment. Do you wonder at a ready ear being given to suspicion coming from this quarter? Blame not the king or your fellows, my lad. The suspicion was natural, although the friends of your family believe that there was a mistake somewhere. Hope for the best and bear up cheerfully, my lad. You misapplied my remark some moments ago about God being unjust and that therefore you could not sing His praise. My remark applied only to men and not to God. God is above our judgment. He cannot be measured by our standards. You spoke about playing the harp. It was hard work to learn, was it not?"

"Yes, sir, but mother kept me at it."

"Well, so God is trying to teach you some things. You heard my sermon last Sabbath. Can you tell me the text?"

"Part of the eighteenth verse of the Hundred and Fifth Psalm, 'He was laid in iron,'" responded the boy.

"I am glad you remember it. You remember how Joseph was treated, sold into

[1] Burnuhall—A fine old mansion near the English Channel in the parish of Buryan, Cornwall, England. Sheltered the young Pretender in 1746.

slavery, maligned, slandered, imprisoned. Yet he had done no wrong. Now is your case any worse than his? No, not nearly so bad, yet he didn't refuse to sing God's praise, although he knew God permitted him to be slandered and to be unjustly imprisoned. Now, what was it for? You remember the old Hebrew rendering that I quoted as the last thought, 'Barzel baah naphsho,' and its meaning iron entered his soul. You remember I said his soul was strengthened as with iron, on account of his suffering and dishonour, and that through that same discipline he gained the courage, wisdom, resolution and position of a prince, and became ruler o'er all Egypt. Now, Ande, God may be training you in the same way. You know Cowper's hymn, no doubt, by heart."

> "God moves in a mysterious way
> His wonders to perform;
> He plants His footsteps in the sea
> And rides upon the storm.
> Ye fearful saints, fresh courage take,
> The clouds ye so much dread
> Are full of mercy and will break
> In blessings on your head.
> Judge not the Lord by feeble sense
> But trust Him for His grace,
> Behind a frowning Providence
> He hides a smiling face!"

The beautiful hymn was quoted to the very end, and the good old parson, apparently filled with the glad, stirring thought, had a smile of exalted hopefulness on his countenance. Ande gazed at him and it seemed in that smile he read a happy augury of his own future. The parson had preached a sermon without realising it, but yet he could not fail to see the effects of his words on the youth at his side. There was a serenity on the boy's features and a new, hopeful light in the eye as he grasped the parson's hand with fervour, and said, "I'll not doubt God again, Parson Trant, and I'll not refuse to sing."

"And not hate Squire Vivian, Sir James Lanyan, or the young Master Richard?" asked the parson.

The parson had overreached himself. The youth's countenance flushed with anger and the hands were slightly clenched. There was silence.

"Perhaps it is a little too much to ask that now. That will come. Don't doubt God. Love Him and you will soon love men. In reference to the slurs of the lads, pay no attention to them and they will soon cease their annoyance. In reference to your name and the stain upon it, resolve to make a new name for yourself and your family by your own conduct. Can you think of anything more noble than to labour against unfavourable circumstances, against slander, encumbered by a stained name,—false though the accusation may be,—fighting against odds, and yet finally coming forth from the struggle, a victor, having made a new and honourable name for yourself and family? Can you, my lad?" Parson Trant gave the lad an affectionate pat upon the back.

There was silence for a moment.

"Yes, I can."

The rector was taken aback, for he had expected a different answer.

"And what is more noble?" he asked.

"I think it is better to clean the old name; and I'll do it, if I can." There was a steady light of purpose in the eye of the youth, as he replied.

The parson said nothing for a time and they walked on in silence and then — —

"Perhaps you are right, lad. You are very much like your father. Those were his words and sentiments. I trust you may be more successful, though."

Parson Trant, while giving vent to these brief, epigrammatic sentences, was thinking of another matter, — the depredations on the estate of the Manor, — and had just decided to broach that unhappy subject. They were standing near the village stocks and the parson, placing his arm again in that of Ande, began the subject in an indirect manner.

CHAPTER III

THE RUNAWAY

"And as the chariot rolled along the plain,
Light from the ground he leaped, and seized the rein;
Thus hung in air, he still retain'd his hold,
The coursers frighted, and their course controlled."

—Dryden's Virgil.

"Ande, my lad, if—"

His remarks were very unceremoniously cut short by a shout from the lad.

"Look out, Mr. Trant! A runaway!" and before he had finished speaking, he caught the old parson by the shoulders and gave him a shove to one side of the road. Now the action of the youth was so quick and with such vigour, that the parson had no alternative but to go in a very undignified manner. His shovel-shaped hat went into the hedge, and with coat-tails flying like the pennants of a man-of-war, the parson was following, but tripped on some obstacle and plunged very quickly and involuntarily into a bunch of stinging nettles and thistles by the road-side.

Nor was the action too quick, for down the road, galloping and plunging as if mad, her eyes flashing and nostrils distended with terror, came the squire's black mare, Queeny. A brief glance had sufficed for the youth's quick eyes. The bit had broken in the mare's mouth. The chaise in the rear rocked from side to side in a most frightful manner, but the plucky driver, Mistress Alice, with resolute will, though pale with fear, still held the lines, seeking in vain to restrain the maddened creature. There was a quick thud, thud, thud; the creaking of wrenched axle; a rolling cloud of dust; and through it all in the rear a strained face, beautiful, yet fear-stricken, with wide, dark eyes and a tumbling mass of curly hair as black as the clouds of a moonless night.

Then there was a leap and a vision of a flying, athletic, youthful form, and Ande was clinging with the grip of a vise to the black, flowing mane. With his right arm up over the animal's neck, supporting himself, with the other hand he grasped the mare by the nostrils, completely shutting off all air. Then there was a struggle for the mastery. The infuriated creature reared, plunged, until there was imminent danger of the shafts breaking, but the lad was too strong to be thus shaken off. There was a cry, almost a shriek, like unto a scream of human agony, from Queeny. On, on, on plunged the creature with its human burden, but there was a slowness of speed until some hundred yards from the parson's position, when the runaway was brought to a standstill, although trembling in every limb with fright.

"THERE WAS A VISION OF A FLYING, ATHLETIC, YOUTHFUL FORM— CLINGING WITH THE GRIP OF A VICE—"

The squire's daughter, only too anxious to alight after that mad ride, stepped from the chaise, and between her petting and speaking to Queeny and Ande's grip, that he still maintained, the mare was pacified.

"Now," said the lad, speaking for the first time, "please unbuckle those backing straps and unhook the traces."

The girl, though unaccustomed to be ordered in this manner, saw the necessity of complying, since her rescuer did not dare to leave his position at the mare's head.

"Now, let me have the halter in the chaise."

The girl produced it, and the animal thus secured was led out of the half-ruined shafts.

Parson Trant, in the meantime, had disengaged himself from the unwelcome embrace of the nettles and thistles. Picking up his shovel-shaped hat and dusting it with his handkerchief, he placed it on his head after first arranging his scattered locks, and then hurried forward to assist the squire's daughter. That young lady had, however, finished the work before his arrival.

"Well, well, well!" exclaimed the parson, as he came up, puffing with over-exertion and mopping the perspiration from his brow. "That was a narrow escape, Mistress Alice—thank God for it—also—this brave young man. Mistress Alice, this is Master Ande Trembath."

The parson in the midst of his hurry had neither forgotten his religion nor his courtesy that seemed inherent in his very nature, but he little realised the ludicrous figure he presented in that scene. His neckerchief was all awry; one coat-tail was sadly torn by the violence of his fall and was now hanging in a most melancholy manner by a few threads from his coat; his broadcloth trowsers were soiled and covered with nettle stickers and thistle down; and his hat, in the hurry of putting it on, was located on one side of his head in a most rakish and disreputable manner.

A silvery peal of laughter from the girl, which was joined by a hastily suppressed chuckle from Ande, caused the rector to notice his condition and he was much chagrined in consequence. There was a flush on his countenance that made both of the young parties regret their hasty merriment.

"Parson Trant, you must pardon my rudeness in pushing you aside, but if I hadn't done it we both might have been hurt."

"To be sure, to be sure—don't mention it, my brave lad. You did a noble action and probably saved my life as well as that of Mistress Alice," said the parson kindly, as he patted the lad on the back.

"And as for me, dear Parson Trant, I must beg pardon for my rudeness in laughing," said the girl with regret in her tone, and then turning to Ande she thanked him for his brave conduct. "And now you must both come up to the Manor for lunch, will you not? O do, please; father will be so delighted."

Parson Trant cast a rueful glance at his clothes, saying he was hardly presentable, and then his face relaxed into a smile that widened into a good-humoured laugh as he pictured himself seated at the squire's table in his present condition.

As for the lad, the invitation would have been acceptable, had he not thought of the squire's antipathy toward himself. He declined also, but accompanied the squire's daughter to the Manor gates, having first bid the kind-hearted parson adieu.

"I can't tell why it was that Queeny ran away. She never acted that way before. I was so frightened. It was very brave of you to stop her."

The lad was a trifle confused under these glowing tributes to his heroism and could make but little reply.

"Trembath — Trembath," continued the girl musingly, "why that's the name of the former owner of the Manor — that is, before my grandfather. They said he was killed in America, and you — —"

"He was my grandfather," said the youth with a sensitive flush on his face. "He was an honourable man."

The flush on the face of the youth was reflected on the countenance of the girl, for she realised that she had committed an indiscretion in referring to the death of his grandfather.

There was an embarrassed silence for a time and then the girl exclaimed,

"There's Ned Pengilly!"

It was indeed the worthy lodge-keeper who appeared at the gates. To him Ande consigned the animal that he was still leading and, receiving the thanks again of the girl, he turned and wended his way toward home. Within a short distance he paused and turned, watching the retreating forms of the girl and the lodge-keeper leading Queeny. Then, with a feeling he knew not what, he once more continued his journey.

CHAPTER IV

THE PRIMROSE COTTAGE AND TOM GLAZE

"Ande, laddie, thou art late to-day. Here it is almost one o'clock—and—why—what have you been doing? Hast been fighting? Why, your jacket has a rent of fully five inches and your trowsers look as if you had been rolling over in the dirt."

The scene was in the main living room of a little stone cottage. Indeed the cottage could only boast of having two rooms and an attic—but this room was the main living room. A primrose vine covered the house front and several roses that still retained their position, though late in the season, drooped on their stems over the small, diamond-shaped window panes, as if anxious to catch a glimpse of the speaker within. A fire of Cornish furze and sea coal was blazing brightly in a grate in the chimney. A tea-kettle, suspended from a crane o'er the fire, had been humming away for quite a time and mingling its tune with the steady tick-tick-tick of a great-grandfather clock standing in the angle of the stairs that led up to the attic. A harp, its gilded framework much tarnished with age, stood in the opposite corner near the dresser, a striking contrast to the humbleness of its surroundings. A few cheap prints of country scenes, one a scene of Wellington at the battle of Waterloo, and a picture in oils of a rugged soldier—an officer evidently—who had a striking resemblance to Ande, adorned the plain white-washed walls.

The room altogether presented a cosy appearance and just now was filled with the odour of steeping tea, fresh biscuit and a scrowled pilchard—most welcome indeed to a hungry boy.

A kind, motherly looking woman, who had not yet passed middle age, was busy laying a cloth on a small centre table. She had a pleasant, refined countenance, marred a little with care, a countenance classic with its profile and grey eyes. Hair, dark, mingled with a few grey streaks, fell down gracefully o'er the ears from a parting in the centre, lending a sweet, motherly appearance to the classic features. Though clad in an ordinary common house dress, a stranger gazing at her for the first time would say she must have occupied a higher station in life in her earlier years; and his estimate would be correct.

Mrs. Thomas Trembath, the mother of Ande, for it was she, was the daughter of William Borlase, a younger son of a young branch of that illustrious Cornish family. He had been a rising young barrister of Bodman town, and would have won fame in his profession had not death claimed the bright mind. His wife and child managed to live on a thousand pounds that constituted the bulk of his little fortune. It was to Bodman that Captain Thomas Trembath came, seven years after the war with the American colonies terminated. He had never married, partly because he had been engaged in the American war and had no time to think of matrimony; partly because one great thought absorbed his attention, the vindication of his family name; and partly, most potent reason of all, no doubt, he had found no lady of his rank willing to take upon herself a name so stained with treason as his own; and, as for marrying beneath him, he gave it not a thought. He was then approaching middle age and was thinking most seriously of the problem, when, meeting young Mistress Elizabeth Borlase, he mentally decided the question. For three years this soldier, who had the courage to face the American batteries and the charge of Washington's horse, attended the Borlase home before he had the courage to settle his doubts. The daughter accepted him, but when the consent of the widow was asked there was a stormy scene. She was much outspoken against it, alleging the difference in ages, the Captain being fully fifteen years older than his affianced bride. The truth of the matter was that the widow had resolved to secure the handsome middle-aged Captain as a mate for herself and was mortified to find it was the daughter and not herself he desired.

For ten years no children were born of this union. In the year 1805, however, a male child was born.

"We will call him Borlase Trembath," said the mother, "for he has the Borlase mouth; those lips are like his grandfather's. He will be a speaker and a good singer."

As if in testimony of his mother's opinion the babe set up a lusty wail, sometimes crescendo, sometimes staccato, then babbling recitando, flourishing his fists and kicking his limbs in animal spirit.

"Oratory enough to oppose a Pitt," said the Captain, with a grimace, and putting his fingers in his ears. "He will be a parliamentarian some day, no doubt. See, he is already beginning to gesture." Then, changing his bantering tone, "He has the nose, the forehead, the blue eyes, the hair of his grandfather, Squire Andrew Trembath, my father, and why not the name."

The wife saw the desire of her husband and acquiesced in the name. "He shall be called Andrew," she said.

The Captain, though much pleased with the comforts of home and the presence of his wife and child, still retained the passion for war and battlefields. He came of a long line of Cornish soldiers and the war spirit had become intensified in himself. Was there any truth in the old legend of the blood of the Danish freebooters mingled in his ancestors? He knew not and gave it not a thought. War called him, and he joined the Iron Duke in the Peninsular campaign. When the War of 1812 with America began, fired with the same old passion to redeem his family name from the stain of treason, he secured his discharge, with the rank of major, and was soon on his way to participate in that struggle. Here he disappeared after the defeat of Proctor, and his wife and son, Ande, were succoured from dire distress and want, into which this event plunged them, by the death of the widow Borlase. Her fortune of a thousand pounds, depleted somewhat, was by regular process of law conferred upon Mrs. Thomas Trembath. Such was the condition of affairs at the time our tale opened.

"Ande, laddie, hast been fighting?"

"Well, I had a bit of a fight with Bob Sloan—a great hulking bully 'e is—but the master parted us. He called father and grandfather names and said I was a coward, and I beant a coward."

"Laddie, why are you always picking up the insults of the lads, and how often have I told you about language. 'Beant' isn't good English."

Now before the parson and other dignitaries Ande was accustomed to use good language, but before the boys and at times before his mother, he drifted into a little of the vernacular.

"Well, I forget sometimes, mother dear, but my torn clothes are due to another affair and not the fight."

The lad recited the incidents of the runaway, while engaged in eating the lunch that had been so long delayed. The mother listened with bright eyes, attending occasionally to the wants of the table, and when the tale was fully narrated, she leaned over the back of his chair, kissed his forehead, and called him her "brave laddie."

"But, laddie, how rudely you must have treated Parson Trant! Was he not angry at his fall?"

"No, mother, parson saw that I did not mean to push him down, but only tried to get him out of danger, and he laughed afterward, too."

The lunch was ended and Mrs. Trembath was bustling around, clearing the table. Ande had a project in view that afternoon. It was a half-holiday and he had purposed going to the Loe Pool with some of his fellows to gather shells, and a swim in the lake or in the sea adjoining was a pleasure to his athletic nature. The Loe Pool had other fascinations for him also. What wonderful tales were related about it! A little sheet of water below Helston, kept full by the little River Cober, having no outlet to the sea except by percolating through the sandbar which Mother Ocean, inhospitably, threw up between herself and her child; yet was it not the remnant of the old harbour of Helston. He had heard of it from the old Droll Tellers, and loved to lie on the sandbar meditating, dreaming of the things that had happened there centuries before. He knew the Phœnicians had sailed over that sandbar with their ships and the Danish freebooters in later times. It was a pleasure highly anticipated.

"Well, laddie, I suppose you must hurry back soon to school."

"No, there's no school. The master gave us a half-holiday to-day; that is the reason I loitered some on the way home."

"Then thou canst cut the furze in the croft."

Submissive to his mother, not even mentioning his disappointment, with furze cutter o'er his shoulder, the youth sallied forth and was soon busy in the furze croft, a sort of high, rough land in which the furze grew. The prickly, shrubby plant grew around him in great abundance, some of them reaching the height of three feet. He paused for a moment during which he viewed with delight the abundance of its golden flowers, dappling the whole field with its starlike disks. It was a pity to cut them down, thought the lad, but then we must have something to burn, and what is equal to furze in a grate on a cold evening? With this thought he again wielded the cutter with a will, and the desired amount was soon bound in bundles, ready to carry to the cottage.

"Well, young squire, and how dost like the work?"

The remark emanated from a tall, muscular man, in shirt-sleeves, who, leaning on the hedge, calmly smoked a "bob" or short Cornish pipe. He was a little over the medium height but looked short because of the heavy shoulders and thick, muscular arms and limbs which nature and hard work had given him. The face was kindly, good-humoured, honest and open. By his general outline he was neither a hard eater or drinker. There was a suppleness and ease in this young man of twenty-six that made him admired by the whole country around, a suppleness demonstrated by the ease with which he placed one hand on the hedge and leaped lightly over.

"Pretty well, thank 'ee, Tom Glaze," responded Ande.

"I 'eard that thou and Bob Sloan 'ad a bit of a scrimmage this marning and that 'e was a bit too much for 'ee. Is that so?"

The welcome look died out of the lad's face and he flushed, angrily.

"There's no truth in that at all," he said, curtly.

Glaze laughed heartily and then, seeing he had offended his young friend, sought to soothe his spirit.

"Come now, no offence, I 'opes. There's no dishonour in your being licked by Bob, seeing as how 'e is both bigger and older. He 'as beaten you when 'ee were smaller, 'asn't 'e?"

"Yes, 'e has, but I would like to know why you are throwing the defeats at my 'ead, when you say they were no dishonour."

Tom Glaze laughed again and then seated himself boy-fashion on the turf, embracing one knee with his great arms.

"Let me tell 'ee a tale. There was once a great rogue elephant that lived in the jungles of Africey. He was a very bad 'un, 'e was, I can tell 'ee. He 'ad great long tusks and a great trunk and everybody was afeared of 'im because 'e was so large. He was mean, too. The other elephants banded together and drove 'im from the herd, and in spite 'e began to abuse all the other animals of the jungle. There was also a young lion that come that way one day. He 'adn't been long away from 'is mother's 'ome in the jungle, but he thought 'e was big enough to go forth to seek 'is fortune in the world. He was a-lying asleep in the path when Mr. Elephant come by. 'Out of my way,' bellowed the elephant. Young Lion reared up and says he wasn't going to move a step. With that Mr. Bad Elephant seized 'im with 'is trunk and flung 'im pretty 'ard into the bush and walked on. What did Young Lion do?

He went straight 'ome to 'is father and told 'im all about it and 'is father was pretty mad, but 'e didn't say much. He thought a bit and then 'e said: 'My son, 'ee need a few tricks of the lion trade.' And then he began to teach 'im some of the tricks, 'ow to spring and where to land. The next time Young Lion met Mr. Bad Elephant, 'e 'ad all the tricks of the trade and 'e just beat the elephant all around, clawed 'im up so that 'is best friends wouldn't know 'im. The animals of the jungle all come together and gave a public feast in honour of Young Lion and they thought 'e was a public hero."

Tom Glaze ceased speaking, and smiled again.

The lad said nothing.

Now this Tom Glaze had always inspired Ande Trembath with admiration. Tom had been a tin miner for years, but he also had another calling. Cornwall was and always will be noted for her wrestlers and boxers, and, though Glaze was not a champion, he was on the highway to that distinction. There were only three or four wrestlers in the whole country that he could not defeat. In addition to this he was an all-round athlete. Many a time Ande had seen him break the head of his opponent at the contest of quarter-staff at the county fairs.

"Now why do I tell 'ee about thy defeats? Why? 'Cause I've sized 'ee up, many a time, and says I to myself, that with summat of a training thee could do wonders. All 'ee needs is the tricks and the training."

"And could I beat Bob?" asked Ande, eagerly.

"Bob? Aye, and two like 'im, and I would like to see 'ee do it. Now thee art about through with furze cutting let me give 'ee a lesson or two."

Ande sprang nimbly to his feet and Tom having arisen, they set to work.

What tugging there was in the scrimmages! What dodging! At first it was slow work, but as the lad learned point after point he speedily put them into practice. With all his heart, with the remembrance of Bob's insults strong within him, with the consciousness of his strength yet undeveloped, and with the burning desire to avenge some of those insults to his family honour, Trembath was resolved to profit by the instruction of his teacher.

"Bravo! Bravo! That was finely done," exclaimed Tom, when the youth, having learned a new dodge and counter, put the same into practice in a way that delighted the wrestler.

"Now, I suppose we 'ad better go 'ome, as thy mother may be looking for 'ee. But, mind 'ee, my lad, doant'ee go a-telling of this. Doant'ee go a-telling. Why? 'Cause you want to take Bully Bob by surprise. Thee meet me 'ere every evening, and thee will soon knack Bob off 'is pins."

The good-humoured wrestler vaulted the hedge and strode lightly and rapidly away, while Ande shouldered his burden of furze and started toward the Primrose Cottage.

CHAPTER V

"THE BIG HA' BIBLE, ANCE HIS FATHER'S PRIDE."[2]

Burns has beautifully described the cotter's Saturday night, but that was the cotter of Scotland. Cornwall, too, has that beautiful and appropriate custom, not only of closing the week but also the day with the worship of God.

Supper is over in the Primrose Cottage. The sun is slowly sinking to rest in the watery bed of the western sea, flecking and streaking the distant blue into a variegated coverlet for its nightly repose. In a few hours twilight will come and then night with its darkening mantle. The main living room of the cottage is gilded by the slanting sunbeams that glisten through the small, diamond window panes and the open doorway. The floor of stone has been freshly sanded with white sea sand and raked and marked in neat figures. Ande Trembath is interested in a new tale that seems fascinating to him. It is Scott's "Lady of The Lake." Mrs. Trembath is seated in a comfortable rocking chair, knitting, for Ande must have warm stockings for the coming cold weather. The hour of worship peals out from the great clock in the corner of the stairs. Without a word, the lad places away the tale he has been perusing and picks up the worn gilded volume of God's word. The mother places her knitting on the small side table and prepares to listen, while her laddie opens the book with care at the One Hundred and Fifth Psalm. The reading of God's providence revealed there seemed to have additional interest for the lad, and he paused for a moment over the eighteenth verse and thought over the parson's morning talk. The Scripture ended, the mother and son kneel in prayer, using not only the prayer of ordinary evening worship, but that other prayer for the safety of those astray on sea or land, and as the mother reads reverently the latter prayer, the thoughts of both are concentrated on the dear one lost amidst the American wilds eight long years ago. Then followed the Lord's prayer, repeated in concert, until the part "forgive us our trespasses as we forgive those who trespass against us," where the lad's voice faltered, and ceased for a moment, resuming the prayer in concert with his mother when the phrase was passed.

The prayers were ended and the harp was brought forth with loving care. The lad handled it with reverence, for it was his father's, and his grandfather's, and he knew not how far it had dwelt in the annals of his family. Then came the strains of Bishop Ken's Evening Hymn,

"Glory to Thee, my God, this night,

---

[2] Burns' "Cotter's Saturday Night."

For all the blessings of the light;
Keep me, O keep me, King of kings,
Under Thine own almighty wings."

The worship was finished and the Word, the prayer book, and the harp replaced in their usual positions; Ande had returned to his "Lady of The Lake," the mother to her knitting. There was no sound for a time save the monotonous click, click of the knitting needles, keeping up a sort of recitative duet with the tick, tick of the clock.

"Ande, laddie, why is it that thou dost not repeat the whole of the Lord's prayer with me? I have noticed the last few times and have wondered."

The lad was silent for a moment and his face flushed.

"I cannot, mother dear," he said simply.

"Why, laddie?"

"Because there are some I cannot forgive, it seems. There's Sir James Lanyan and Richard, his son, Squire Vivian, and Bob Sloan, and—and—they treat a person mean. When I think of the Lanyans and Squire Vivian and how they or their people treated ours and took away the estate, and—and when I think to-day how they treat father's and grandfather's memory, I cannot feel like forgiving them and I can't say 'forgive us our trespasses as we forgive those who trespass against us,' for that would be asking God not to forgive me."

As Ande Trembath referred to the Lanyans there was an angry light in his eyes, which softened into gloom as he spoke of the Lord's prayer.

"Ande, laddie, we must pray to God to help us to forgive. 'If ye forgive not men their trespasses, neither will your heavenly Father forgive your trespasses.'"

The widow was silent. She felt as keenly as her 'laddie' the injustice done the Trembath family and there was a half-inaudible sigh from her lips. She had not that bitter, unforgiving spirit, but she knew the temper and spirit of her laddie. Will time ever remove the sting of an unjust act? she thought. It was of no use to urge the point now with her boy. She must think.

There was a clicking of the garden gate; a step was heard on the stone garden walk, and a figure appeared at the door. It was that of a man clad in livery dress—knee-breeches of nankeen, long stockings, and low shoes with immense silver buckles, and a coat of velveteen. In short, he was clad very much like a gentleman of the period fifteen years before, but inasmuch as the majority of the gentry had adopted the new costume of trowsers, the knee-breeches, low shoes, and long stockings generally indicated the servant. And such he was—Master Stephen Blunt, Squire Vivian's steward. Master Blunt doffed his cap and hesitated a moment. Mrs. Trembath paled a little, for the steward was scarcely ever the bearer of good news. He was a general factotum of the squire. He rented farms, collected the dues, was an officer of justice, the terror of small boys, and, in short, was a kind of constable, sheriff, and prime minister of the squire's little domain.

Concerning the rent there was nothing to fear, for the Trembath's had owned in fee simple as it was called, for many years, the Primrose cottage and the few fields adjoining.

Master Blunt was a silent man, not wasting many words.

"The squire wanted to see Ande a bit," he stated.

A new thought flashed across the mother's mind. It was her laddie's bravery in stopping the runaway in the morning. Yes, the squire was going to reward her laddie and a more favourable understanding was going to be established between the squire's people and theirs. She communicated her opinion to her boy in a whisper as she assisted in getting him ready. There was a smile of happiness on her countenance which Master Blunt, seated on the garden settle outside, did not observe.

Ande Trembath, however, was not so happy to go. Honour heaped upon him for an act that he considered only an ordinary matter-of-fact affair, and especially by one whom he considered in the light of an enemy, to be hated and to be hated in return, was distasteful to him; but he knew the necessity of going, as one did not dare disobey the squire.

CHAPTER VI

SQUIRE AND PARLIAMENTARIAN

Thud, thud, thud, thud.

Squire Vivian was riding at a smart pace on the solid roads. He was fond of horse-back riding, but long ago, having given up riding after the hounds, he was constrained to solace himself by daily trips over the turnpike. This was not exercise, however. He must see his old friend, Sir James Lanyan, about one or two things, and so, after a hasty lunch and a word of instruction to the steward, he mounted his fast-pacing cob and was off. His thoughts were not very pleasant as he started forth. He was thinking of the conversation he had had with Parson Trant just a short time before.

"The lad is guilty," he muttered, and then there was silence save for the rapid hoof strokes.

"He shall smart for it. The traitor's cub!"

The squire compressed his lips and the frown on his ruddy features boded ill to Ande Trembath. Then pleasant thoughts gained the upper hand. He had reached the confines of his estate and the fields and woods of Lanyan Hall stretched on either side of the highway. There were round hillocks nodding like Indian chieftains with their proud headgear, downs alive with cattle and sheep, farmhouses of stone—as short and thick-set in appearance as the sturdy farmers that occupied them. Yes, thought Squire Vivian, with a smile, these shall belong to Alice when she marries young Richard. My Lady Alice sounds as good as any other name with a Lady attached to it. The pleasant expression passed and a worried look came in its place. He was thinking of the Parson's disapprobation of young Richard. The vale was passed and Lanyan moor, as wild and uninviting as his thoughts—Lanyan moor, a high rough land of a few miles in extent, covered with a rank, rough grass, extended on either side. Under the influence of his surroundings and pressed by his thoughts, the squire spurred the cob into a gallop and after a few minutes the gables and tower of Lanyan Hall greeted his vision. It was a stately mansion, built partly in the Queen Anne style and partly in the style of previous times, one side being built during the Crusades, of Cornish moor-stone that lent a heavy warrior-like appearance to the whole structure.

The owner, Sir James Lanyan, a son of that Lanyan whose agitation in certain quarters of the government had produced the confiscation of the Trembath estates, like his grandfather, had devoted considerable time to politics and had been twice in Parliament; but failing of re-election he had turned the strength of his ambitious mind to the rebuilding of his fortunes, which were sadly shattered by the schemes and speculations of his grandfather.

His grandfather, in coöperation with Sunderland, the Premier of that time, had been unduly interested in the South Sea Bubble; but though Sunderland cleared his skirts in the gigantic swindle, Sir James, Sr., was entrapped. His estates were heavily mortgaged and his private fortune ruined. He died of a broken heart, bequeathing to Sir Richard, Sr., his son, the ancestral hall and its liabilities.

Sir Richard, Sr., was a rogue, with very little ability. Casting about by hook or crook to retrieve his father's reverses, he thought he saw an opportunity in the reputed treason of Squire Andrew Trembath. His covetous eye surveyed the rich farms and woods adjoining his own, and so, with the outward reason of loyalty to King George, and the inward hope of profit, he turned the keen eyes of government authorities upon the matter.

The name of the Stuart and France were still to be dreaded. The first tendency in that direction must be crushed and an example made. The fiat went forth, the estates were confiscated, but Sir Richard, Sr., instead of receiving them or even a money reward, received a flattering letter from London, a ribbon of honour and a star. With a muttered oath he flung the bauble from him and ground the letter under his heel. He knew what all men were to know in time, that neither Newcastle nor Pitt were as free-handed as Walpole.

The present Sir James, a son of Sir Richard, Sr., had inherited the bold, daring, scheming ambition of his grandfather, and was in every way superior to his father, Richard. At first, a great Parliament man, he gradually lost power with the electors, or rather they lost in terest in him; then he turned his attention to the task in which both his father and grandfather had laboured in vain.

On the day mentioned, the squire rode up the drive-way and with a sigh, for the gallop had wearied him. He slipped from the saddle, gave the cob into the hands of a servant, and mounting the veranda, raised the rapper and sent a peal through the old house that speedily brought to the door a footman, clad in green livery. By him he was ushered into the main living room—a large hall, its walls curiously and artistically panelled in wood. Here he reposed himself in a large armchair by the open fireplace and awaited, musingly, the coming of Sir James.

Yes, thought the squire, a fine old place—a fine old place—and my Allie will be one of the first of Cornwall. Then he mused on.

There was a sound of a soft tread on the floor behind him, and a smooth, liquid baritone voice broke the reverie.

"Well, my old friend, so you have decided to return my call."

The squire almost leaped to his feet, for, lost in his thoughts, the voice startled him.

"Zounds! Sir James, you come in like a spirit."

Perhaps there were not two men in the whole kingdom of such a contrast as Sir James and the squire of Trembath Manor. The latter was a perfect picture of the gentleman of the olden school. His hair, silvery white, curled in ringlets over his forehead. His face was a sturdy English one, smooth, round, rubicund and pleasant, and yet with a dignity peculiarly its own. He was stoutly built and as he stood switching his Wellington boots with his riding whip, a close student would say, "Here is a man easily imposed upon, but when that imposture stood revealed what a hot, indignant enemy he would make!"

Honesty, frankness, integrity, were stamped all over the old squire's frame.

Sir James was just the opposite in many respects. He was tall, dark, and sallow of countenance. A hooked nose, like the beak of an eagle, overhung a mouth that was firm and thin-lipped. His eyes, that were the strangest feature about him, were dark and had an unsteady, shifting light in them. He was clad in the conventional broadcloth tail-coat and trowsers of the same material. A man of the world, having felt the pulse of national life, he was generally cool, calm, and self-possessed.

With the remark above mentioned, he came forward and his own pale, slim hand was grasped by the strong, brown one of the squire.

"Welcome to Lanyan Hall. It is not often we have the pleasure of entertaining such an old friend of the family; and how are all things at the Manor? Mistress Alice, is she well?"

"My Allie is tolerable well, but of her—more anon. It is of other matters, not so well, in which I want your advice."

"Ah—and what is wrong? The rents not paid, failure of your tin mine, or has Midnight Jack been making some depredations on your hen roosts or sheep-folds?"

"Well," rejoined the squire, as he once more seated himself beside the fire, his friend having done likewise, "as to Wheal Whimble tin mine, things are moving steadily, but the new shaft is costing a heap of money. The rockmen dull six or seven jumpers before they can make much of an impression in drilling a hole, and though they receive ten pounds a foot, yet say they can't make a living. I don't see how I am going to come out of it. As to rents, they have all been paid but Farmer Samson's, but quite a few of his sheep were taken with the murrain, and one must give a man a chance when he's honest."

"And about Midnight Jack?"

"As sturdy a knave as ever lived, but he and his gipsy band have left the neigh-bourhood some time ago. I suspected him of stealing a sheep and threatened to have him hanged if he showed nigh the place. He knows well enough not to fool with me. I don't think we shall ever be annoyed with him again. There has been, though, some unknown miscreant lurking around the estate. I do not mind so much when a sheep is stolen, I can reprimand a man and threaten him as I did Midnight Jack, but when property is wilfully destroyed and faithful retainers killed—it is too much," and the squire flushed, angrily.

"Why, there has been no murder?" said Sir James, startled out of his ordinary self-possession.

"Aye, as good as a murder," rejoined the squire, and he related with flushed countenance and angry voice the incidents of the morning.

The master of Lanyan Hall interrupted him midway by asking him to the study, where they could talk at their leisure. They arose and passed from the main hall to a side apartment fitted up in elaborate style. There, surrounded by tomes of learning and every mark of ease and comfort, the squire and his friend were soon discussing the former's grievances and suspicions.

"Now, what I want to know is this, what does the law allow a man to do in such circumstances? You, Sir James, are well versed in law, have been to Parliament and can advise me. I confess I cannot find anything about it in the statutes."

"Well, the only thing you can do, having nothing but suspicion, is to have a private interview with the lad and worm a confession out of him," said Sir James, and there was a scarcely perceptible little smile of amusement that lingered around the lips of Lanyan.

"I am pleased to find out that I have acted wisely, for that was exactly my plan," said the squire, flushing with gratified vanity to think that his views and the learned parliamentarian's coincided. "And now what are your plans for reëlection to Parliament?"

"Reëlection. Plans—none at all, friend Vivian."

"Why, you are certainly going to stand for the section, are you not?"

"No, I think not; my interest is not strong enough with the classes. To tell the truth, squire, I am heartily disgusted with Tory principles, and were it not for the name I would become a Liberal."

"What! what!" said the squire aghast; "you jest, Sir James!"

"Jest! Not at all. It is this way. It matters not what talents a person may possess, he must stand in with a few of one's brother notables before election is possible. Our elections are nothing but a humbug. We have no representative house; the House of Commons does not represent the nation."

"Why, Sir James, you did not talk this way formerly, and I am exceedingly sorry to see one of our most distinguished parliamentarians so inveterately opposed to the system."

The master of Lanyan Hall said nothing in reply. Indeed he was inwardly debating with himself how far he should trust his honest friend with his own plans and schemes. The fact was that Sir James had lost his influence with the electors and saw no hope but in an extended franchise; he was politician enough to see that the times were getting riper and riper for reform. There was more hope of election for him in the future than at the present; he must bide his time. Now it was not any great affection for the people that induced him to take this stand. His political creed was James Lanyan—how can he become great and powerful, a creed dominant among politicians of all times.

"IT'S A COMPACT," SAID THE FORMER.

"Well, we must talk of that more anon. There is another matter pressing on my mind," said the squire, and with a little reluctance he began the topic. "Young

Master Richard has been paying some attentions to my Allie, and it is a matter that we fathers ought to talk about. There is nothing dearer to my life than my Allie, and I am anxious to see her settled in life before I leave the earth; but then you, Sir James, and I ought to have some understanding before matters go any farther. Our estates lie adjoining. What better thing than that they should be united after you and I pass away. I thought it better, though, to speak to you, so that we might have a clear understanding." The old squire fastened his clear, honest eyes on the master of Lanyan. The latter was silent and there was a gleam in the shifty light of his eyes as he thought. Then he spoke.

"A good thing, no doubt, if there are no objections on your part."

The master of Lanyan stretched out his hand which was grasped heartily by the squire.

"It's a compact," said the former.

"Aye, a compact," affirmed the latter.

There was a tap at the door and a servant entered to announce tea in the hall. Squire and parliamentarian adjourned their informal meeting and emerged from the study.

CHAPTER VII

TEA-TABLE AND POLITICS

There were three parties assembled around the tea-table, bluff Captain Thomas Lanyan, a brother of Sir James, a sturdy old widower; Mistress Betty Lanyan—a spinster and a distant relative of the family, and Master Richard—a young man in his last year in Eton and the perfect counterpart of his father, only much younger.

Mistress Betty was tall and angular, like Sir James, yet with a good supply of feminine sweetness in her features. The sole drawback to her countenance was her nose, that was neither a thing of beauty nor grace. It was of the large hooked variety, so common to the family. Yet so strange are the freaks of Madam Nature, that the eagle nose of Sir James was universally commended as giving him the commanding and dignified appearance of a statesman; while one of the same variety on the countenance of Mistress Betty was considered exceedingly derogatory and shrewish. Notwithstanding this detractive feature, Mistress Betty was a good-hearted soul. She always had, at least in company, that mellow smile on her face that gave a vivid reality to the stanza,

> "Full many a flower is born to blush unseen,
> And waste its fragrance on the desert air."

The Captain was moulded more like his mother's side of the house. Clear grey eyes lighted up a countenance that was rugged and weather-beaten, while the family nose was absent and in its place was the straight, plain variety characteristic of his mother's family. Over his forehead was a long, livid scar that ran from the centre of the forehead, obliquely, to the right ear, a cavalry slash of the battle of Waterloo. Mistress Betty always persisted in having this covered by the Captain's waving grey hair, but the Captain would just as persistently throw his hair up and to one side, revealing the full extent of his old wound. What Mistress Betty was ashamed of was the Captain's glory. Captain Tom lived in tolerable contentment on a government pension, and of all the family, none were upon such intimate terms with the squire as himself.

"Ah, Captain Tom, what cheer?" said the Squire as he cordially shook the hand of the veteran. "And Master Richard, you are quite a man and every inch like your father. And Mistress Betty, I hope I see you well," and the squire made a profound bow that would shame an old-time knight, at the same time grasping her small hand delicately with his own.

The salutations were returned and then, seated around the tea-table that was placed near the immense bow-window, the master of Lanyan requested his guest to pronounce the blessing. The squire, who was seated beside Mistress Betty, perhaps designedly, who knows, for that lady had not given up the custom of angling, proceeded according to his usual custom.

"We thank thee— —Oh! zounds and the devil!"

The latter part was like the explosion of a battery of artillery, and with reason. Mistress Betty's lap-dog, an unsightly brute, deeming himself insulted by the proximity of the squire, or perhaps jealous of his mistress' attentions to another—like many a human rejected suitor filled with vengeful spleen, or perhaps—kept waiting for his dinner—and seeing a fat limb much larger than the usual chicken leg near him, he decided to forage for himself. Whatever reason he had within him, the results were the same, for he fastened his teeth most vindictively in the squire's nankeen trowsers. Human nature was not proof against such an assault, and the victim gave vent to the above startling and most unseemly expression. He leaped up from the table, slapping and rubbing the affected part to relieve the pain.

The young Etonian had a grin on his generally calm countenance. Captain Tom with more zeal than wisdom grasped the poker and shoved it through the bars of the grate, saying that they had best have the wound cauterised at once. Sir James was profuse in apologies and Mistress Betty, much vexed, hurried the snarling brute into the library.

"This is out—outrageous," faltered the squire, in the midst of his pain; "such a savage brute, I wonder why you don't have him killed, Sir James."

"Cruel man, to abuse poor Cæsar so," said Mistress Betty, with a flash of the eye.

"Zounds, madam," replied the squire, but he went no further. His inherent courtesy to ladies, and the ap pearance of Captain Tom with the hot poker, caused him to beat a hasty retreat to the table.

With a smile of anguish he sat down, saying, "It is nothing, madam, nothing, Captain Tom—I do assure you—no need of cauterising—the pain has already gone."

Captain Tom very reluctantly replaced the poker, and soon they were all seated, chatting merrily, as if nothing had happened. The squire, occasionally slipping his hand beneath the table and giving the smarting limb a soothing rub, talked as cheerfully as the rest.

"And you won't stand for re-election," said the squire to Sir James.

"Not at present; the times are not yet ripe for reform and we must have a more extended suffrage before I can stand with success," said Sir James, helping himself to another lump of sugar and dropping it carefully into his cup with the air of a sage.

"Fudge," said Captain Tom, "the country doesn't need extended suffrage. Why, brother James, if your ideas go into effect the landed estates will be ruined. We have seen enough of those things over there in France. The people got extended suffrage and the king and the gentlemen got the suffering. Bah!" said Captain Tom in some disdain, "the landed estates must rule, pass out of existence, or give place to a Napoleon," and the Captain thumped the table emphatically with the sugar tongs.

"What a sage student of history you are, Captain Tom, and yet there are some things yet to learn. The revolution in France was not caused by their obtaining the suffrage, but by the retention of suffrage from them until they arose in revolt. A fortunate thing is it for the government that yields to the demands of the people and is not compelled to yield. When the proper form of government is in vogue, then there will be no occasion for the people demanding or of the government yielding. Government should stand halfway between the highest pinnacle and the broadest base of the populace."

"Why, Sir James, you surprise me!" ejaculated the squire; "you may as well turn American with those ideas! Tut—tut!" followed by a disapproving shake of the head.

"A vast discrepancy between Americanism and my ideal. Government in America stands upon a broad base, but is not as truly representative as our own government will become in a few years."

"You speak in riddles, Sir James," replied the squire.

"Well, let me explain. Strictly speaking, there is no real representative government. Even in America, women, negroes and Indians are not represented; neither among those that are represented is there any fair proportion of representation. Jefferson, their great sage, wrote the most foolish thing imaginable when he said 'all men are created free and equal.' It is evident that the opposite is the case. All men are different, different in physical strength, mental power, culture, attainments. Even in infanthood they are different. Equal ity is nowhere on earth, neither in the vegetable nor animal kingdom. It is a manifest injustice then to alter the plan of the Creator."

"Aye, aye, now you are coming around to our opinion," said Captain Tom.

"Not at all. Our present conservative system is wrong and unsafe. Government is resting on the highest pinnacle of the populace, from which position it may easily be deposed."

"Pshaw," said the squire, "I can't understand you; I thought you said our government was more representative than the American."

"No. I said it will be in a few years. In America the Church is not represented, neither are the institutions of learning—although they ought to have some special representation as well as the States. Now mark me well. In a few years, a decade at the most, the franchise will be extended to the humblest shop owner, house owner and tenant, and only the criminals and the utterly uneducated will have no voice in the government. Then we will have a more representative government and a more stable one than our American cousins. More representative, because colleges, universities, the clergy, and large and small property owners will have their respective portion of power; more safe because the roughest and lowest element of society will not have a controlling and dominating influence. How is it now, however? The landed proprietors and men of influence pack our House of Commons as they please. Everyone knows of Old Sarum—that it hasn't a single inhabitant, and yet it sends a member to the Commons, while Manchester, Leeds and Birmingham have no voice whatever in the affairs of the nation. We must have an extended suffrage. The people want it," and Sir James silenced his batteries.

"Well, so far as I can see," said Captain Tom, doggedly returning to the charge "the people are not demanding anything. Our people are comfortable and happy. Corn has arisen in price and our farmers are growing rich."

"Aye," said the squire, "so far as I can see, things are pretty prosperous. Corn has risen to fifty shillings per quarter."

"Ah," said Sir James, contemptuously, "what benefit is it for Cousin Jack in Cornwall to have a full stomach, and Tom in York and Devon to have an empty one? Fine national prosperity, that. Squire, you are interested in your own section, Captain Tom reads nothing but war news, and so both of you are blind to the signs of the times. The memory of the Blanketeers is still before the public and the pulse of the middle classes is mounting higher and higher. What signify the riots of last year and the affair of Peterloo?"

"A set of rebellious knaves, that need the hand of the Iron Duke to teach them their manners," replied Captain Tom, who was indignant to be accused of ignorance on national affairs. "A set of rebellious knaves, but where do you find gentlemen marching side by side in a cause with such a rabble."

"William Cobbet, the journalist," rejoined Sir James.

"Aye, a ploughman," sniffed Captain Tom, in some disdain.

"Aye, and more than a ploughman," added young Master Richard. "There's Sir Francis Burdette, Lord Brougham, the great Canning, Lord John Russell, Grenville, and Earl Grey—and Canning and Grey were Etonians." The last part was uttered with a little triumph in the tone.

"Ah, the young cock is beginning to crow," said Captain Tom, who knew not what else to reply.

Sir James looked pleased at this heavy broadside from his son and then again took up the reform cudgel, saying: "Very true, and even the younger Pitt over twenty years ago agitated the subject."

Here the squire thought it time to assist his friend, Captain Tom, and also show that he was not destitute of knowledge on national affairs.

"Tut, tut, that is a bad argument; Pitt abandoned his position as untenable, and——"

"Aye, he knew he couldn't hold the position and retreated as a sensible general should," interrupted Tom.

"Because of the excesses of the French revolution," replied Sir James.

The spirited debate went on with varying success to either party, Mistress

Betty participating, sometimes on one side, and at times on the other, always sympathising with the weaker party, as women generally do. Toward the close, Captain Tom and the squire being hopelessly put to rout by the combined wisdom of Etonian and parliamentarian, she faithfully adhered to the former side, until even Captain Tom was forced to admit that, though a woman was of no service in a battle, yet they made pretty fair tongue-soldiers.

"Well," said the squire, as he was preparing to go, "your remarks, Sir James, have convinced me of one thing, and that is your sincere disinterestedness in self and your love for old England and her welfare. You are a statesman, sir, and we shall soon see if we can't place you in Parliament; aye, Tory or Liberal,—what matter—so long as the man is honest and capable."

Now this was exactly what Sir James had expected, and he shook hands cordially.

"Hold on, squire, we must have James there as a Tory. I don't believe he is as much a Liberal at heart as he pretends. Don't surrender the standard, squire," said Captain Tom.

A servant was holding in readiness the squire's cob, and assisted him to mount. Raising his hat, gallantly, to Mistress Betty, and waving an adieu to the others he paced briskly down the drive and out on the highway.

"What a courteous gentleman, and young, though he is a widower," murmured Mistress Betty. "Did you notice how, out of respect for my feelings for Cæsar, he didn't utter any complaint."

"Fudge," said Captain Tom, "that was due to his brave spirit in enduring pain. What a soldier he would make!"

"Pshaw!" exclaimed young Master Richard, "the old gentleman thought more of the hot poker than he did of courage or courtesy."

"It was courtesy," reaffirmed Mistress Betty.

"It was courage," exclaimed Tom.

"It was hot poker," reiterated the Etonian again and again, until under a score of reproaches from Mistress Betty and Captain Tom,—the former emphasising the courtesy, the latter the courage of the squire,—he found safety in speedy retreat.

Sir James said nothing until after Master Richard's exit, and then he broached the squire's desire of an alliance between the families.

"It seems we'll get the estates of the Manor in our family after all, and by a much more honourable method than father tried. That deed always did make me half ashamed of our name."

"Captain Tom," said Sir James, with a little of asperity in his voice, "the plan that exposed a traitor was perfectly honourable."

"I have always had my doubts whether my old comrade, Major Tommy Trembath, was a traitor, or his father either. They were both too honest to be guilty of treason. Why, look at the record of old Captain Ande at Culloden and Prestonpans. He was a hero. There he stood with Gardner at Prestonpans, fighting gallantly until stricken down with overwhelming numbers, and there was Major Tommy in the Peninsular campaigns. Aye, the more I think of it the more am I inclined to disbelieve the report of their treason,—but circumstances were against them," and the old soldier sighed, and with a halting step, due to a wound—a relic of the Napoleonic wars,—he tramped once or twice up and down the veranda. When he ceased, the look of sadness was gone and a humorous twinkle was in his eye. Around his weather-beaten countenance there was the faint trace of a smile of merriment.

"However, it is a good plan,—this marriage—and—if Cousin Betty can catch the squire we'll have a double claim on the Manor."

"Why, Captain Tom, how absurd!" exclaimed Mistress Betty, blushing confusedly.

"A tell-tale blush! I'll have to tell my old friend, the squire, of his opportunities to capture the stronghold of ages, that has remained unconquered for——"

"How absurd!" exclaimed Mistress Betty, in mingled anger and confusion, as she beat a hasty retreat to her apartments.

CHAPTER VIII

"OFF WITH HIS HEAD."[3]

It was still twilight when the squire reached the Manor. Hastily giving the cob into the hand of Sloan, he hurried into the hall and seated himself by a large window, where was stationed a large oaken table littered with a motley array of books and papers. This was the squire's position when any petty case was brought before him. Whether the books were kept for show or use no one knew. The only time the squire was known to look at them was during a trial, and this he did with the air of a Lord Chief Justice, which air had a very perceptible effect upon the trembling culprit.

If the truth were told, the squire had a more intimate knowledge of fishing, hunting, farm and mine management, the origin of ancient village plays and customs, than about law. Law always was a perplexing study to him. But as a compensation for his lack in this respect, he more than made it up in the learned dignity of his demeanour.

There were approaching steps heard on the veranda, and then the opening of a door, and in a moment more Stephen Blunt and Ande Trembath stood before him.

The steward took the chair that he was accustomed to occupy, ushered to such position by a wave of the squire's hand, and sharpened his quill pen preparatory to writing. Ande, neither invited to sit down nor stand, remained near at hand. His mother in her fond delight, thinking that he was to be rewarded for his morning heroism, had determined that he should be dressed in a manner suitable for the occasion. He presented a very creditable appearance in his snow-white trowsers, neckerchief, and neat blue jacket. His feelings were not as pleasant as his garments. Since he was evidently going to be rewarded for his services in saving the life of Mistress Alice, he felt exceedingly out of place. He rested his weight on one foot, fidgeted with the other, and fumbled his cap in a nervous manner. He grew restless under the steady eye of the master of Trembath Manor, and his restlessness increased the suspicions in the mind of the latter.

"Master Trembath."

The lad felt relieved that the silence was at length broken.

"Master Trembath, you were nigh the estate of late?"

"Yes—s, sir. I frequently go through the Manor woods, sir."

"Note that down, Master Blunt."

[3] "King Richard III."

A bewildered look passed over the lad's face.

"You were nigh the estate last evening, and will you now tell us what you were doing in that place at that time?"

Ande grew more amazed and confused; amazed because he knew not what the squire was trying to ascertain, confused because he had been there and even in the gardens, but for a purpose he did not wish to divulge. A wave of crimson swept over his countenance, rivalling the sanguine hue of his locks.

"Take notice of his confusion, Master Blunt," and then in a stern voice to the lad, "You may as well out with it, we know all the facts of the affair."

Ande tried to answer, but his tongue clave to the roof of his mouth. His heart seemed to sink lower and lower in his chest.

"Sir, sir,—I—I——"

"You were in the gardens last evening," thundered the squire, his wrath getting the better of him. "You were in the gardens, were you not? Answer on your honour?"

"I was," falteringly.

"And for what purpose?"

"That I cannot tell."

"And why not?"

The youth was silent. He had the appearance of a culprit, and felt wretched and miserable. The squire continued to question and cross-question, but of no avail, and at length, growing nettled and peevish, he said, "I will state the case plainly to you, Master Trembath. You were in the gardens last evening, last Wednesday night and last Monday night. On Monday night you drained the fish-pond and stole the best fish; on Wednesday you ruined the shrubbery beds; last evening you took a stone from the hedge and killed my faithful mastiff, Borlase. What answer do you make to these accusations? Make a clean breast of it and it will be better for you, my lad."

The accusation, thus plainly stated, had a directly opposite effect upon the crestfallen lad. All his diffidence and confusion fell away from him like a garment. He flung up his head like a young lion cub, his blue eyes scintillated, and his red locks shook like the mane of a savage beast under rising passion. Blunt was alarmed and the squire was awed.

"What have I to say to these accusations? I say they are lies! They are false! I was not here on Monday or Wednesday. I never stole your fish or drained the pond, or trampled the shrubbery, or killed the dog. Who accuses me? Who, I say?" The lad advanced to the table, boldly, all his confusion gone, and the wild soldier blood of his ancestors coursing like molten fire through his veins. "Why am I brought here in the home of my fathers to be insulted? Have not you, Squire Vivian, and the Lanyans, done enough evil to our family but that you must charge me with being a thief, and——"

"Silence!" thundered the squire, who had been stirred up by the lad's charge of injustice. Ande stood silent, with heaving breast. The squire mastered himself before he continued.

"Your charge against me is not to the point. If you do not know, I will tell you that this estate was bought from the government by services rendered, which had no connection with your family. Your family affair, neither my father nor myself had anything to do with; that is between the Lanyans and yours."

Ande Trembath had heard for the first time that the Vivians had had no hand in the confiscation of the Manor, and there was a revulsion of feeling within him. The squire nor his family, then, were enemies of his. He felt, notwithstanding the accusation against him, a better feeling, and even a little gladness within his heart. Why, he did not know.

"I beg your pardon, your honour. I had never heard it put that way."

"That is neither here nor there," said the squire, sternly, "and has no connection with the case. You were seen nigh the grounds. You confess to being on·the grounds a short time before last evening's outrage, yet you say you are innocent of the charge."

"I am innocent."

"Well, why were you on the grounds?"

Again the lad flushed painfully and was silent.

"Now," said the squire, "since there is no direct evidence, but only circumstantial, I shall dismiss you with a reprimand, and a caution to be careful in the future and amend your ways, or Newgate will have you yet, and"—here the squire pushed his countenance into a large law-book, as if consulting reference—"and as to punishment, I will let you off lightly. Master Blunt, call Sloan."

The steward dropped his writing and left the hall, returning soon with the stout, old hostler.

"George, take Master Trembath out and put him in the stocks for one hour."

The old hostler opened his mouth slightly in amazement, as if to say something, but the frown on his master's brow checked him. Without a word, George Sloan and Stephen Blunt took the dazed lad out of the hall, down the garden avenue, and out through the gates to the very scene of his morning exploit, where was situated the village stocks. Resistance was out of the question, and so he submitted, as if his spirit was crushed.

"I am sorry for 'ee, my lad," said old George, "but us has to hobey horders. To think that the grandson of old squire shud be shut in th' stocks," and old George shook his head, for he felt the disgrace as keenly as the lad.

Stephen Blunt, who was not a native of the section, but had come in with the squire's father from the East, said nothing. The Trembaths were nothing to him, having never known them intimately. But old George Sloan, Ned Pengilly and others native to the soil, who had served with their fathers under the Trembaths, took great umbrage at the shabby treatment of the "young squire."

Ande thought of the misery of the disgrace; he, the best scholar in the parish school, condemned and punished as a common thief. He thought of his father and his grandfather. They were of the bravest gentry in Cornwall. None could show a better record in the annals of the county. They had taken their part in every prominent movement in the nation. The last of the line, branded as a thief, and, like a common vagrant, imprisoned in the stocks! He thought of his mother and her pride in him. He gave an impatient wrench to free his imprisoned ankles, but the framework was too heavy to be opened in his position. He thought of the parson's sermon of the previous Sabbath. Yes, he was like Joseph. The iron was entering his soul. He gave vent to his pent up feelings in tears.

CHAPTER IX

THE VILLAGE STOCKS

"'Allo! What 'as us 'ere?"

It was a coarse voice, half boy's and half man's.

Ande looked up and perceived, coming through the gloom, a long-legged, stout lad, about three years older than himself. He had just emerged from the Manor woods and was engaged in what he thought a manly occupation, smoking a short pipe—or Cornish bob. The prisoner did not recognise him at first, for the twilight had begun to darken into night, but as the newcomer advanced he saw the most unwelcome sight of his bitterest school enemy,—Bully Bob Sloan.

The recognition was almost simultaneous and the newcomer allowed his freckled face to relax into a grin of delight.

"'Allo, can't 'ee speak? What has tha done, boy, to git in they wooden leggins?"

"The squire did it, Bob, but I 'adn't done anything. Squire said I 'ad drained the fish-pond, but I didn't. Now, let me out of here, do, Bob."

This was said in a propitiating tone, for, thought the lad, Bob might help him. But he had not estimated Bob aright.

"Um," with a sage air and a shake of the head, "can't go against the squire's horders; and then I 'alf suspect 'ee'rt guilty, my lad, for I seed 'ee myself and told squire, or rather caused 'e to hear it, that I had seed 'ee a-lurking nigh the grounds. Ah, my lad, think what a fall ah be for 'ee, the best scholard in the school,—a criminal, a-sitting in the stocks; and by and by 'ee will be hung for more thieving and willainry. What a karacter! What a disgrace!" and Bob shook his head, in mock sadness. "And when I tell the master and the lads at school, 'cause I got to tell them to save they from associating with a thief, 'ow shocked they will feel. I expect, too, I 'ad better clear out myself, as my repertation might be a-hinjured a-talking 'ere with a criminal."

"Don't lad me," said Ande, in some wrath, "you're no more of a man than I am, and as for reputation, you've none to spare."

"Softly, softly, little lad; 'ow pretty 'e looks, a-dressed in 'is Sunday clothes, a-sitting in the stocks, and as I do live, the little lad 'as been a-crying. Aren't 'ee afeared 'ee'll spoil your pretty new jacket?"

Bob advanced a step or two, and placing the pipe again in his mouth at a dangerous angle, and grinning with Satanic pleasure, shoved his freckled countenance almost into Ande's face.

Now the stocks was an instrument of confinement in which the ankles were held securely, while the arms and hands were free. Bob had evidently forgotten the latter fact, but was made aware of it by a stinging left-hander, that sent the pipe flying and Bob likewise into the dust.

"Now, damme, for a traitor's cub, I'll eat 'ee up," exclaimed Bob in his wrath, as he arose from the dust, with bloody lip and vengeful eye. And he doubtlessly would have made some attempt to carry out his dire vengeance had not the sound of approaching footsteps and a cheery whistling in the distance been heard. Dreading some encounter with the Hall people, and with a threat of vengeance at some future time, he made off for the village.

The whistling came nearer and nearer. A tall, dark figure emerged from the gloom, walking with a quick, jaunty step.

"What ho, my Bob Cuffins, scragged in wooden leggins!" The white trousers and blue jacket caught his eye. "Well, a gentry cove." Dropping all dialect, his language became more respectful.

"And what hast done, lad, to be trussed up like this?"

Ande looked at the stranger, doubtingly. He was clad in a long rough coat, the skirts of which were slightly torn. His countenance was dark, but with a healthy bloom on it.

"Come, my lad, I look rather unprepossessing and rough, but mayhap I am better than I appear."

Ande, reassured, told his story briefly.

"And you're Squire Trembath's grandson, and you were accused of the mischief at the Manor?" said the fellow, and then softly whistled to himself. "I think I had better let you out for two reasons. First, because you couldn't have done the things said, since one of my partners did that. I don't mind telling you, as you can't prove your innocence otherwise, and as long as you don't tell the squire before a day or so, it won't hurt us. Then, in the second place, I like to pay my debts to friends. If you ever see your father, tell him that Midnight Jack returned his favour of over sixteen years ago."

With a quick movement, the tall gipsy chief leaned down, wrenched open the clasp of the stocks, and the imprisoned lad was free. He was gone even before the lad could thank him.

Burning with indignation at his disgrace, Ande hastened home with flying feet. His mother had already retired. In anguish of soul, he quietly stole up the little attic stairs to retire, but not to sleep.

CHAPTER X

REPARATION

Some days elapsed before Ande went near the village or the Manor. With a boyish burst of confidence, he related the whole affair to his mother, who was not only shocked, but highly indignant at the treatment accorded her "laddie." The lad refused to attend school and lost some of his old buoyant spirit. In these days, he spent most of his time working around the home place, meeting frequently Tom Glaze, in the furze croft, and profiting much by his training. Tom had heard of Ande's shameful treatment, and had given him much advice, that seemed phenomenal, coming from such a pugilistic character.

"See 'ere, my lad, doan't 'ee go a-moping around, looking as ghastly as a death's head on a mopstick. Thee might as well knaw there's no use a-fighting sarcumstances that way. The squire will discover his mistake some day, and will maake all right. When the lads tease 'ee a bit about the stocks, doan't 'ee take any offence. Doan't 'ee fight o'er little things."

"Aye, but the world treats a man pretty hard once when he is down, and what's a fellow to do?"

"Why, above all things, doan't 'ee be a great chuckle-head, but have some judgment," said Tom, at which Ande flushed angrily. "Now doan't 'ee take no offence. What I means is this. Did 'ee ever see a kicking donkey? Treat un kindly and 'e won't kick. Smile and duck your 'ead to the world and say, 'What cheer,' or ''Ow do 'ee do,' and the world will smile and bow or duck back and say, 'Pretty well, thank 'ee,' or 'Brave, thank 'ee.' Frown, and give the world the cold shoulder, and you gets the same. They say the Golden Rule is 'Do unto others as 'ee would be done by,' but the practical rule is 'Others do to 'ee as 'ee do by they.'"

"Well, Master Glaze, that doesn't 'old good in my case. Here I did good to Squire Vivian and received evil in return."

"Exceptions prove the rule. Anyhow, try my hadvice."

Ande did try Tom's advice, and was gratified to see that, with the exception of Bully Bob Sloan, all the village lads improved in their conduct toward him. The rescue of Mistress Alice was soon noised abroad, and he was considered almost in the light of a hero by the juvenile element.

One evening, as the lad was returning from the furze croft, he noticed a chaise and pony at his mother's door. It was the chaise of Mistress Alice, who had, since the affair with Queeny, betaken herself to the pony and chaise when desiring an airing. His mother had received her with a certain amount of cold dignity which her feelings would scarcely allow her to conceal.

There was a variety of emotions in the lad's breast as he approached. There was anger at Squire Vivian's indignity to him, a feeling of shame at the report of his depredations, and an emotion that had lived in his soul for quite a time, but which he had never fully analysed. From early childhood he had remembered the squire's daughter. He remembered, with all a youth's tenacity, how he was led to church by the tall, soldierly man, his father, and how rapidly he had to move his infantile feet to keep up with the soldier's tread. In the family pew he would sometimes turn his head to a nice dark-haired little miss of a few summers' age, seated in Squire Vivian's pew. Once she had shyly and demurely returned his look, then quickly turned away, as if displeased. He had asked his father afterward whether he didn't think the squire's girl a "pretty little maid," and he remembered the hearty roar of laughter with which his father responded. Since he had been attending the parish school, he had not seen her much. Indeed, he had never become acquainted with her before the affair of the runaway. He had always admired those dark elfin locks, and in church he had thought if he had one of them how he would cherish it, and then he had flushed crimson at what he thought almost a profanation. He had always admired her, but the feeling he had had for quite a time past could neither be admiration nor friendship. He had not analysed it. It was this strange sentiment that had led him frequently into the vicinity of the Manor, before the regrettable affair of the stocks. His appearance there on the evening of the killing of the mastiff was an incident of that kind. He had conceived a passion for flowers, and especially for the flow ers of a garden plot, watered and attended by the hand of Mistress Alice. Could he secure one of those blossoms? Now, Ande was the perfect soul of honour, but he had had a hard fight with himself to keep from appropriating what was not his own. The slightness of the offence, the intensity of his feelings, the heritage of his ancestors, all urged the harmlessness of the deed. He might have secured one by request, but he would have died before exposing his feelings to ridicule.

Ande stood near the threshold with a tumult of feelings within him, that made him look more like an awkward, country lout than the grandson of a squire.

"Master Trembath, I have come to beg your pardon for the hasty act of father."

Ande could not help noticing the slight colouring of her features, enhanced by the wealth of dark locks overhead. There was a sincerity and earnestness in her tone that made her a hundred times more attractive than he had ever seen her before. He mastered himself with a great effort.

"The apology comes from the wrong person, Mistress Vivian, and the deed being done, cannot be undone."

"It was a cruel injustice," said Mrs. Trembath, with some little warmth in her tone, "and I wondered how the squire could have done it, seeing how bravely my laddie acted in the runaway."

The young girl flushed at the charge of injustice.

"Indeed, father was not aware of Master Trembath's brave conduct; he was away all afternoon, and I was not aware of the judgment on Master Trembath until the following day. I was very much vexed over the whole affair, and when I told father, he, too, was chagrined, yet he said the circumstances were so much against Master Trembath that he didn't see how he could amend matters. I want you to accept these flowers, Master Trembath, as a token of my high esteem, and I trust that you will neither consider my father nor myself in any hard light."

She placed the large bouquet of flowers on the settle and turned to depart. Mrs. Trembath placed her hand on the dark, raven locks of the squire's daughter as she stood on the portico step.

"And may God's blessing attend you, Mistress Vivian, for your kind and charitable spirit, and may your father be imbued with the same!"

Ande accompanied her to the pony chaise. His righteous indignation against the squire was mitigated by this unexpected visit and by the flowers. He had coveted only a single blossom; here was a gorgeous bunch from her very hand.

They made a pretty picture, standing without the gate, in the rays of the setting sun. The pony stood patiently waiting near the hedge, occasionally nibbling a choice bit of herbage that seemed to seek safety from his investigating jaws in the rough rock crevices.

"I thank you very much; the flowers are very beautiful."

"And you will not think hard of my father."

The youth was silent and bit his lip; then avoiding the question, he answered:

"It was not the stocks, but the accusation and the condemnation, that has made all people look down on me."

"Oh, Master Trembath— —"

"Call me Ande; it's more natural to me; you were going to say— —"

"I was going to ask whether you could not clear yourself from being on the grounds at that time."

"No. I was there."

"After your having saved my life. I shudder to think of it— —"

"You shudder to think of my saving your life," said the youth, a little stiffly.

"Oh, no. How you misunderstand me!"

"You mean you are pleased," said Ande, brightening.

"Stupid!" said the girl, a little indignant. "Why don't you let me finish my sentence."

Ande was abashed at this rebuff.

"I shuddered at the accident that might have been, and I want to see you justified. Now if you could tell me why you were there I could inform father, and he, being the soul of honour, would make all right."

"No, I cannot tell my reason," said the youth, flushing painfully.

"And not even tell me, when you know I am so interested in having you brought out from under this cloud."

"If you knew you would not tell him either," said the youth, doggedly.

She gazed at him quickly. Somehow in her young woman soul she seemed to read his reason. Yes, in a moment, with that keen intuition, developed earlier in woman than in man, she read through this hesitation, this confusion. She knew.

"I can tell who did the deed, though," said the lad, for he thought of the information of the gipsy chief, and that now he was at perfect liberty to tell.

"Who?" asked the girl, eagerly. This youth that had so bravely saved her life should be justified.

Ande related the events of his rescue from the stocks and the tale of the gypsy chief. The girl listened with brightening eye and kindling cheeks.

"It must be so, for how could you have gotten forth from the stocks? No one would have dared to let you out but a person like that. I know how we all wondered when Stephen Blunt came in and told my father that the stocks were empty. But why did you not tell this before?"

"Because Midnight Jack told me it would not hurt them if it wasn't told for a day or so."

"I shall see that you are justified. You have been shamefully treated."

The squire's daughter mounted into the pony chaise, grasped the lines with her slender, gloved hands, and with a smile was gone.

"Poor lad! He has been shamefully treated and he shall be justified," she thought to herself. "How foolish I was not to see before. He loves me," she said softly. "He is good looking and tall and man-like for his age." Then there was a pause in her soliloquy, unbroken save by the pony hoofs. Then she drew her brows down with a slight frown. "Pshaw!" Then the scowl left her features and she broke into a slight, nervous laugh. "Absurd!"

The remainder of the drive was spent in silence, but there was heightened colour in her cheeks and a soft, pellucid light in her eyes.

Old Sloan took the pony and chaise at the entrance of the great house, and Mistress Alice tripped up the steps and into the hall. The old squire was seated by the hall fire, meditating apparently, for his chin was resting on his hand and he had his eyes fixed upon the flaming coals. His daughter bent over his chair, and lightly kissed his forehead; then drawing a stool near him she seated herself, leaning her head against him and waiting for him to speak.

But the old squire did not speak for a time; he placed his big, brown hand upon his daughter's dark locks, and still gazed into the fire. It was the daughter that broke the silence.

"Father, I have news to tell you."

"Well, Allie?"

"It was not Master Trembath that killed Borlase, or drained the pond; it was one of the gipsies." Then she poured forth the whole story of Ande's escape from the stocks, while the old squire listened, as he gazed into the fire. When she had finished he gazed at her.

"I know it, Allie. I had my eyes opened, and even saw the rogue, this afternoon, at Sir James Lanyan's. Sir James had him up for some offence and he confessed all, the rogue."

"And about Master Trembath?"

"Aye, that's what troubles me. I can't see what I can do to justify him. True, I can exonerate him, but to make reparation for the injustice of putting the lad into the stocks—I can't see what I can do. The lad is better than I thought, if he does have treasonable blood."

"We must exonerate him by announcing it in the parish school and at the church. We ought to reward him, too, for stopping the runaway. It ought not to be said that a Vivian received a favour of such kind, from any one, without doing something in return."

"Reparation shall be made!" exclaimed the squire, emphatically. Alice had touched him in his pride. She had also touched him on the side of his honesty and uprightness.

"We will have it announced in the parish school and church, as you say; the whole parish knew it when he was placed in the stocks, and the whole parish shall know of it—that he is not guilty—that—that——But we must do something else. That will be only common justice. We must reward the lad,—but how?"

The eyes of Mistress Alice became luminous; she was winning her case. With deftness she proceeded.

"He doesn't like to attend school, so Parson Trant says, and I was thinking how nice it would be to send him to the Helston Grammar School. Now, father, if you could make the offer?"

The squire brightened. He had found a way out of his difficulties. He kissed his daughter and called her a wise, little prime minister. He hastened away that very evening to the parson's house, and the old rector was delighted to be the means of Ande's reinstatement in popular favour.

After the departure of Mistress Alice from the Primrose Cottage, Ande had better thoughts of the squire and his people. Somehow or other he felt lighter of heart, but his mind was strangely confused. During the evening hymn instead of the sweet strains of Ken's Evening Hymn he was guilty of fearful, musical blunders.

As he lay awake under the eaves that night, his imagination still carried him back to the garden-gate scene. Yes, she stood before him just as attractive in memory as she did then. In impatience he tried to banish her face.

"Fudge," said he "I'll get Glaze to give me a skevern in the chacks that will knock some sense into my addled head."

He dreamed that night that he was under the walls of the great house, near Mistress Alice's window, and that he was playing on the harp of his fathers. Once he thought he saw her face—then it changed to the features of the squire—and, wonder to relate, a smile upon his rugged features—then over the squire's shoulders appeared the sardonic countenance of Sir James Lanyan. He changed the strains to the Hymn of the Lark, and Sir James paled and fled.

CHAPTER XI

DEFEAT OF BULLY BOB SLOAN

"I am the Valiant Cornishman
Who slew the giant Cormoran."

—Cor. Ballad.

"Ande, my lad, I have been thinking about you and your unfortunate experience, and have been pondering in my mind, for quite a time, what to do. Your education, already so advanced, must not be slighted. You do not feel like continuing school here?"

It was the parson who was speaking. Parson Trant with Ande was seated in the study room of the rectory, a pretty, half stone, half brick edifice, nearly concealed from the public road by masses of ivy and foliage. It was built for the express use of the parson, and, according to his desires, was as retiring from public notice as a mother bird ensconced in her nest amidst enveloping leaves.

"No, Parson Trant, I think not."

"I thought so; but your education shall not be neglected. Squire Vivian has come to me and realising how bravely you acted in the runaway, and how unjustly you were treated, proposed that you should go to the Helston Grammar School."

Ande's countenance flushed. The parson perceived it and continued.

"Now, Ande, lad, the ill feeling between the squire and you ought to cease. He is good-hearted in the main. He has made ample reparation for the offence of the stocks and he wishes to show his good will and thankfulness for the rescue of his daughter. It is a creditable action of his, and you are not receiving any favour, but a just due. I have talked to your mother of the matter and she is willing for you to go. I have written to the head and he will make room for you. You must not allow any hard feeling on your part to mar the happiness of your mother and the hopes of your best friends. Besides, it is not courteous to refuse to meet the overtures of friendship from one whom you have always esteemed an enemy, especially when that person meets you more than halfway. Your father would not have scorned to do so, and you desire to be as much of a gentleman as your father was."

The youth was won over by the earnest manner and words of his friend, the parson. There was quite a conversation as to the time of entrance, the necessary preparations, and the conclusion of it all was that Ande should go after the Christmas holidays.

His mind delighted with the prospect of attending the Grammar School, and with airy dreams of what that existence would be, he left the rectory and wended his way with light steps down the walk and out on the public road. The sun seemed to smile brighter upon him, the birds to warble sweeter, and all nature seemed to be tinged with the bright hues of his day dreams of the future. There were voices in the distance, boyishvoices, and with laugh and rude joke, a crowd of parish school lads, bubbling with spirits, surged around a neck of woods. The master had given them a half-holiday and they were bound to the Giant's Quoit, a huge rock said to have been used as a plaything by the ancient Cyclops of Cornwall.

"YES, GIVE THREE HOOTS FOR THE RED-'EADED DEANE AND ALL HIS TRAITOR HANCESTORS."

"'Allo, come along, Ande, will 'ee?" exclaimed Tommy Puckinharn.

"No, can't go," replied Ande, shaking his head. He must go home and talk with his mother over the great prospects of attending the Grammar School.

"Naw,—'e must ask 'is mawther fust," cried Bully Bob, with a great coarse laugh. The laugh and the reference to his mother stung Ande, but he pretended not to notice.

"'E's getting up too far now in society to 'sociate with we; 'e was calling on squire some time ago, and squire give 'im the seat of honour—fact," said Bob with a wink and a grin that seemed to bring forth additional grins upon the countenances of several of his satellites.

Ande stood for a moment, irresolute, then resumed his way.

"Les give three hoots for the red-'eaded Deane and all his traitor hancestors."

The last was too much for the impatient spirit of the lad to brook. Turning about and with a calm, steady voice, he cast his gauntlet at Bob in the shape of a few words in the dialect, equivalent to a challenge to battle the world over.

"Bob, thee'rt a great, ghastly coward, and thee knaw it."

A wave of redness swept over Bob's face, completely drowning the freckles with which it was freely sprinkled.

"'Ow's that! I 'ave a good mind to scat thee in the chacks for thy himpudence, m'lad." And then in a tantilising manner, as Ande approached, he continued, "Thee art a traitor, for thy faather and grandfaather were traitors. Everybody knaws they were traitors and cowards hout in blooming hold America."

The words had hardly emanated from his lips when—smack!—went Ande's hand on the mouth that had spoken this base libel. A thrill of expectancy passed over all the crowd, a thrill of amazement, awe, vivid interest.

"Damme," said Bob, as he spat his blood and froth from his lips, "I'll make 'ee think Saint Michael's Cormoran had 'ee when I get done weth 'ee. Wilt fight or must I knack 'ee down?"

There was no occasion to ask, for Ande, boiling with rage, was coming at him with a rush, when a deep voice from the side of the hedge cried, "'Old hard, there a-bit."

Tom Glaze vaulted the neighbouring hedge and strode forward into their midst.

"Now, I observed the quarrel and I suppose you 'ave got to fight un out, but 'ee must follow the regular Cornish rules. Thee, Ande, get thy second, and thee, Bob, get thine, wost tha, and I'll be timekeeper and referee."

Glaze led the way over the hedge and the crowd of lads followed, leaping the barrier like a flock of sheep. A circle was formed in true British style. Bob chose one of his satellites, and Ande chose Puckinharn to act as second. The crowd looked on with intense interest. Was not this to be the greatest fight they had ever seen? Who had ever dared to challenge redoubtable Bob before? And to make it additionally interesting, Tom Glaze, one of the most expert wrestlers and boxers of the Duchy, was to be the one in charge. It was of as much moment to them as the battle of Waterloo to their fathers.

The coats of the contestants were cast aside and their sleeves were deftly rolled up by the seconds.

"One, two, three," counted Glaze, and then the battle began.

With a roar, Bully Bob rushed as if to break every bone in his antagonist's body, and truly had the blow fallen the battle would have been a short one, for in age, height and weight Bob had the advantage. Now did Ande feel grateful for the training in the furze croft. Heretofore, it was stand up, take and give, but now, to Bob's intense amazement and disgust, his blow landed on empty air, and as he swept by, carried by his momentum, he received a fierce jab in the ribs that added nothing to his good humour. Observing, after one or two encounters like this, that he had no ordinary battle to fight, he began to be more cautious and his usual confident, sneering face assumed a doubtful air, but he still pressed the conflict. With his sledge-hammer fists he shot out blows that would have felled a much larger opponent, but they were either parried or fell on air. With the litheness and agility of a leopard his opponent was here, there, everywhere, side-stepping and putting in heavy body blows that made Bob gasp with something more than astonishment.

But Ande was growing too confident. Pushing his antagonist in turn, he sought to reach Bob's freckled countenance, fell short, and, to use his own expression, "received a skevern on the noase and eyes that made un see fire."

A yell went up from Bob's satellites. Bob had drawn first blood, and he now pressed the dazed Ande, showering on him a number of blows that he with difficulty avoided.

The mute silence of the crowd was broken by Bob's success. Whooping, yelling, they urged Bob on.

"Give it to the hugly Deane! Knack down the traitor! Hooray! Braavo-o-o!"

Only Puckinharn shouted encouragement to his principal.

"'It un in the ribs, Ande! Thee cussent reach 'is faace. Braavo! Braavo, now he's gurking."[4]

The latter was said in response to a crashing left jab in the ribs that made Bob lower his guard spasmodically. "At un, Ande; his faace now is like that of a roasted herring on a gridiron. Up and at un, lad!" Puckinharn's shouts were swelled by the voices of one or two others who had been silent before.

Bob now sought to end the battle in close quarters, and rights and lefts were freely exchanged. Ande wheeled and his friends were silent in dread for a moment, but only for a moment. Bob staggered back with a heavy elbow jolt in the small ribs, but not before he had given his opponent a blow that sent him to the ground, dazed. Ande's pivot blow had left a bad opening. Bob seeing his opponent down, was rushing in to finish the contest on the ground, apparently, no rules

---

[4] Gurking—weakening.

having as yet been devised against it, when Tom Glaze shoved himself between.

"Round's hup."

The boys began to cheer for Bob, thinking that the battle was over and that Bob was a victor, but that worthy silenced them with a growl.

"Shut up, will 'ee; 'e edent licked yet."

His crestfallen adherents were silent. In the meantime some of the crowd had brought water to bathe and refresh the youthful gladiators. An old horse trough was used by Bob and a battered field kibbel[5] by Ande. The first round was manifestly Bob's. He had drawn first blood and had knocked his antagonist down. His face was untouched, while Ande's was a bit drawn; but to judge by the many soft rubs that Bob gave his ribs, he had not come out of the first round unscathed.

As Ande rested on Puckinharn's knee, that worthy gave him sundry pieces of advice.

"Thee must keep on 'itting 'im in the ribs; 'e's taller than 'ee, and thee cussent reach 'is faace; 'e's sore and weak there now; 'e's gurking, I tell'ee."

"Time!" called Tom Glaze, and to the fray again they rushed.

Bully Bob, flattered by his adherents, had regained his confidence. He would finish the battle in close quarters, and rushed again and again, but his wily antagonist was as agile as an eel. Bob paused for breath and glared.

"At un, Bob! Eat un up!"

"I will," said Bob, "as soon as I catch un."

The fighting continued, Ande playing his old tactics—hitting in the ribs and getting away. Puckinharn grinned in delight. Round two was up and honours were equally divided. Bob was filled with wrath.

"See 'ere," he said to Tom Glaze, "I want to knaw if that is fair, for 'e to go running and dodging around like that? Us aren't playing fox and hounds. Why doan't 'e stand up and take and give like a man?"

He was reassured by Glaze, and Glaze's word was law.

"Thee didn't think it was unfair to crack to Ande when he was down, did 'ee,—thee great bucca," exclaimed Puckinharn.

A bucca was the highest title of reproach that Puckinharn had in his vocabulary.

"Silence," said Glaze; "the rules are that all dodging is allowed."

"And wrastling, too," said Bob.

"Aye, and wrastling, too," affirmed Glaze with a peculiar smile.

And so the rounds went on until the seventh, when

Bob being unwary, Ande seized his left guard, gave his ankle a queer, Cornish side kick, and sent in a blow on Bob's jaw that toppled the redoubtable bully over

---

[5] Kibbel—bucket.

on his back.

"Hooray! Braavo!" exclaimed Puckinharn, swinging his cap up in the air in his delight.

Bob was up the next instant and began to fight in a cautious, crouching attitude. His ribs, black and blue, he sought to shield by drawing his body back and shoving his head and arms forward. There was a better chance, too, for a wrestle, he thought. The small boys held their breath. This was the attitude Bob always assumed when meeting hard opponents. Rumour had credited him with throwing a sailor in this manner. The bully was at bay and would fight hard. Now, Ande, you have need of all your skill, so hardly earned in the practice bouts with Tom Glaze. There was no further chance at Bob's ribs, and his head seemed perfectly guarded. They circled warily around each other seeking for an opening. Then, like a flash came Ande's chance, the opportunity that he would not let slip. "If 'ee ever get that chance and take it, it will put thy opponent down and hout sure," Glaze had told him time and time again, in their practice bouts.

Bob made a slight pass with his left. The next instant his wrist was grasped in an iron grip. Up over his neck Ande raised Bob's arm, then bending his back he grasped with his other hand his opponent's right knee, and putting forth all his strength, Bob went up in the air as if hoisted with a derrick.

"A clinch! a clinch!" shouted some, and it was a clinch in which one did all the clinching.

Bob struggled manfully, but the grip that had stopped the squire's runaway mare could not be unloosened. Up, up, up, went Bob, and then with a heave the form of the bully, like a comet, went over his opponent's head and over the heads of the close-pressing ring-siders, his foot kicking off the cap of one of the lads in his involuntary flight. There was a thud and a cry. The battle was ended. Bully Bob had a broken collar-bone, and his prestige was forever terminated.

Trembath was the hero of the hour. Tom Glaze was jubilant and slapped the victor on the back.

"Thee did what I told thee, and I couldn't do un better myself. Thee'lt be champion of the county yet. Thee make off home now, for thy mother will be looking for 'ee, and I'll see to the tother chap."

Ande started homeward. The boys still remained around the fallen bully, or in little knots by themselves discussed the great battle. Then a short distance away were seen the approaching figures of the squire and parson, and the spectators melted away like magic, until only Tom Glaze remained.

"Ah, Tom, a bad day's work, inciting the young to fight," said Parson Trant, shaking his head disapprovingly.

"Well, lads will fight and sometimes it does them good," said the squire, who loved the old British game of boxing, and felt like supporting Glaze, who was a favourite of his.

"A bad thing, stirring up the worst passions," replied the parson.

"I doan't knaw about that," sturdily replied Glaze, encouraged by the squire's words. "This was a thing that 'ad to come off, and seeing as 'ow the little one 'as given the big un a much needed dressing down, — I think it proper, sir," and Glaze touched his cap.

"Another case of the valiant Cornishman and the giant Cormoran, eh, Glaze?" said the squire, laughingly.

"Aye, sir, 'tez so," said Glaze, as they passed on.

CHAPTER XII

CHRISTMAS AND CHRISTMAS PLAY

"Come, bring with a noise,
My merrie, merrie boys,
The Christmas block to the firing;
While my good dame, she,
Bids ye all be free,
And drink to your heart's desiring."

—Herrick.

There was bustle and activity in the parish. There was a chill in the air, the presage of the rapidly approaching Christmas time. House cleaning and baking occupied the time of the busy housewives. The small boy's eyes glistened as he watched the huge cakes, loaded with citron, currants, and coloured as yellow as gold with saffron, emerging from the oven and consigned, still steaming hot, to some secure place of retention. Then the bag-puddings—a most indigestible mass—yet sweet and toothsome, the pastries, pies, and fuggans, passed in regular order through the hands of the cook.

There is activity among the male population as well as among the housewives. Small lads run hither and thither crying shrilly, "Pennorths of Christmas," and exhibiting evergreen, holly and mistletoe for sale. The farmers are preparing bands for saluting the apple trees. Youngsters are planning schemes for watching the oxen kneel. Singers are practising, night after night, the Christmas carols or "curls." Youths are preparing for the Christmas play of St. George and the Turk.

Ande had been to Helston with the donkey and cart to purchase needed supplies, and in returning along the "Red Revver" road was allowing the animal to take his own gait.

"'Allo, Ande, we want 'ee for St. George in the Christmas play," said a voice from the hedge. It was Puckinharn.

"How art tha, Tommy! Up with 'ee and 'ave a ride. Who's in the company?" said Ande, all in one breath.

"We doant knaw as yet, but thee must be St. George, that's settled," said Tommy, as he clambered up into the cart.

"Well, if I'm to be St. George, we had better begin soon. Suppose we meet in our furze croft and get down to business this afternoon."

"The very place," assented Tommy.

The donkey was hurried on, while both lads planned and talked. That afternoon saw a crowd of the village boys assembled in the rough highland, "the croft," and after much debate the parts were assigned and practising begun.

Christmas eve came at length. The moon shone serenely from between broken clouds. The air was clear, crisp and cold, and made great coats a necessity to comfort. The trees had lost their leafy robe, and now stood shivering or shaking in envy of their evergreen brethren, while all the green hedges had aged into withered brown. There was a flash of light from the parish church tower, and then the single pencil of light was increased by another and another, until every window of the old structure was ablaze with illumination in honour of the coming birthday of the Nazarene. Light after light appeared in cottage of peasant and mansion of gentleman, as if an answer to the summons of the old church to do honour to Him who is the "light of the world." Then on the night air came the song of choirs and carol of singers, mingled with the strains of musical instruments. From cottage and hall sounded the merry noise of revelry, the hearty laugh and general good cheer.

Forth through the night, bubbling with good spirit and anticipated merriment, stalked the St. George Band of Christmas players, adorned in such a brave manner as even to make the redoubtable British champion, had he lived to see it, green with envy. What variable garments! What coats adorned with tinsel, red, and gold, and striped! What shields of brilliant paper or tin, spears of warlike hickory, and swords—not near so sharp as the Saracen blade, but still as sharp as wood could be whittled with a jack-knife; and caps of tall, many-hued tinsel; had the real St. George worn one of them the terrible, ripping, snorting, steam-breathing dragon would have bellowed in anguish, and have fallen down in a dead faint. But they were good enough for the occasion and their very form was sacred by ancestry.

House after house was visited and the fun grew fast and furious. At very few places were they not given a ready entrance and hearty welcome.

"Now les to the squire's!" exclaimed one, and the proposition was hailed with delight. The distance was not far, and the time was shortened by conversation and by a little warlike practice between St. George and his Mohammendan enemy, the Turk, in which practice the Turk received a terrific, broad sword slash, that made him pucker up his face like the picture of the Saracen's head at the village inn. The Turk was not gifted in the Turkish language, but made up for it by giving vent in broad Cornish dialect to his feelings.

"Damme, Ande, ef thee'rt going to cut my nose off my faace and scat my brains out, I'll be a Turk no longer," and Tommy Puckinharn flung down his sword in disgust, and stalked on ahead of the company. With one hand nursing his injured olfactory and the other thrust in his breast, and meekly followed by his fellows, he looked like Napoleon and army on the retreat from Moscow. Some one picked up the Turk's weapon and immediately a discussion arose. No one but a knight must carry a sword in the company. Sword bearing was the special prerogative of a knight and "tother chaps must carry spears." The sword bearer then pleaded to be made a knight, and if Tommy wouldn't be the Turk to install him in his place.

But that was what Tommy didn't want. He had no desire of being turned out of the second place in the company, even if he did throw down his weapon, and so he returned and indignantly protested. When a soldier loses his sword and another finds it, he ought to return it, was the Turk's argument.

St. George settled the affair by raising the sword finder to the rank of a squire. The bravery of the Turk in their late encounter, and his heroic courage on other occasions, merited that he should have an armour bearer, a squire, to be his constant attendant. The sword finder was elated and, somehow or other, the pain in the Turk's nose was healed by this new dignity that his valour had added to his reputation. There was no more practice in the warlike arts, for the Manor gates were passed and the great house was near.

The numerous chimney pots sent up various curling clouds of smoke that glistened palely in the moonlight. The diamond-shaped window panes gleamed and scintillated with the illumination within, except where a dark shadow of holly wreath obstructed the light. The broad verandas were festooned with ropes of evergreen. Up the broad steps strode the players and, after a few mute looks and a little whispered colloquy, the herald lifted the rapper and sent a peal through the old building that would have been certainly heard at any other time but Christmas eve.

Within there was the noise of frolick. The servants were haw-hawing in the kitchen department over some joke or amusement, and the occasional thump, thump of feet in measured time indicated a dance, perhaps between the cook and hostler. The squire's hall was replete with good cheer. Wreaths of evergreen inter twined with sprigs of holly were hung at regular spaces on the waxed, panelled walls. At one end was a large life-sized painting of George the Second. Squire Vivian had a great reverence for the king that had secured to his family the estate of Trembath. His father had served King George faithfully in the east, and there had ever been a strong friendship between the Vivians and the Hapsburgs. At the other end of the hall hung the picture of the squire's father and, although in warlike garb, yet had a friendly smile on his features as if in greeting to His Majesty, the King, on the opposite wall. In the centre of the side wall was the great open fireplace, the grate having been removed to make room for the great yule block that was kindled every Christmas eve with almost religious ceremonies, and near its warm glow was the form of the squire, seated in his great armchair. He looked the very impersonation of Father Christmas, minus the beard. Near him were two or three of his friends from the east, men of his own age, who seemed to enjoy his conversation and laughed as merrily as himself. A whist party was in progress on the other side of the fireplace, while down the long room, here and there, were scattered various groups engaged in various Christmas games. The hall floor was not carpeted, for the squire scorned such modern improvements as innovations and desired nothing better than the old-fashioned waxed floors. Neither did he see fit to remove any of the emblems of his father's predecessors, for above the flaming firelog stretched the high oak mantel, and carved in relief on its shiny surface was the figure of a Lyonnese warrior galloping amidst devouring ocean waves.

The squire was just chuckling over a young lady's mishap in getting under the mistletoe when the herald of the St. George company, tired of raising the great knocker, pushed open the door and entered the hall. There was a thump on the floor to demand attention, and then in as authoritative voice as he could command came the heralding of the brave gallants without.

> "Room, a—a—room, brave gallants, room!
> Within this court,
> I do resort
> To show some sport
> And pastime;
> Gentlemen and ladies, in the Christmas time."

There was silence in the hall for a moment and then the squire spoke out with a cheery welcome, for he heartily appreciated the amusement.

"Bring in your gallant crew. Ho, there, children, move to one side and give them room for fair play." This latter to various groups of merrymakers in the hall.

The whist players dropped their cards, the hall occupants withdrew to either side, and the elderly parties around the squire ceased their conversation to give full attention to the antics of these new merrymakers.

The herald bowed to the squire and company and waved his wand, and in capered a queer, uncouth figure in mask and flowing wig and whiskers. The young children burst into peals of laughter at his grotesque movements, and he had to uphold his authority and gain silence for himself by thumping the floor vigorously with his tall staff. He had a right to demand attention, for he was Father Christmas; his round, cheery face proclaimed it, even without his speech which he proceeded to make.

> "Here come I, old Father Christmas,
> Welcome or welcome not,
> I 'ope hold Father Christmas
> Will never be forgot;
> I bring the cold of winter time,
> That kisses red the nose;
> I bring the snow, the rain, the frost
> That bites and stings the toes;
> But, then, I'm welcome anyway
> Because I am the seer
> That brings the nuts, and cake, and pies
> Of happy Yuletide cheer."

Father Christmas executed a few joyous capers, but was interrupted by the herald who, with a little fear on his countenance, stated:

"Father Christmas, thee must stand aside a bit for I think I see an enemy of thine and of our good Christmas cheer a-coming."

Father Christmas moved aside with a shake of his hoary locks and muttered:

> "Ah, 'tez the Saracen, I fear,
> I would our bold St. George were near."

All eyes were fastened on the door through which the valorous Turk, in his green turban, was entering, his face a little more ferocious by the wound received from St. George's sword in the contest on the public road. The Saracen has some difficulty in expressing himself in good English, but that was to be attributed to his Turkish training. Flourishing his sword he began:

> "Bally, bully mally can
> Hodak 'ee St. George ann,
> Baresesh tally man,
> Abdul caliph Hassan!"

> "Pray, speak in English, brave Turk,
> Let's 'ear what mischiefs in thee lurk."

The herald had spoken in response to his heathen jargon, and the Saracen scowled upon him hideously and answered:

> "'Tis plain 'ee cannot understand
> The language of the Turkey land
> And so I'll tell as plain I can
> In the words of the Englishman.
> Here come I, a Turkey snipe,
> Come from the Turkey land to fight,
> And if St. George do meet me here
> I'll try 'is courage without fear."

The Turk stalked around in brave manner, when a new arrival, the redoubtable St. George, entered. A cheer went up from the younger element of the squire's visitors, and even the whist players clapped their hands, for the Turk was no favourite, and did they not love St. George, the patron saint of England? St. George bows to the spectators, and by his speech does not appear very modest over his great victories.

> "Here come I, that St. George,
> That worthy champion bold,
> And with my sword and spear
> I won three crowns of gold.
> I fought the dragon old
> And brought him to the slaughter,
> By that I gained fair Sabra,
> The king of Egypt's daughter."

The Turkish knight drew his sword and with a warlike pass at St. George, hurled his defiance:

> "St. George, I pray, be not too bold,
> If thy blood is hot I'll soon make un cold."

The squire smiles, for there is a strong Cornish accent in the Turk's tone, notwithstanding his efforts to conceal it. But now St. George also has drawn his sword and with the threat,

> "Thou, Turkish Knight, I pray, forbear,

I'll make thee dread my sword and spear,"

the contest begins.

The servants have opened the door leading to the kitchen department and now stand crowding in the entrance. Little ones that had been taken to bed by their nurses were brought down to see the fun. Fair play and a clear field, the squire had said, and so the centre of the great room was theirs. And how they did fight! Surely no earthly battle was like it. In no battle was so much blood shed and so many hard blows delivered, at least so thought the Turk in reference to the latter, for he was battered from head to foot with side blows and over cuts, jabs, and slashes, until he ardently wished for the time to come when he must fall down dead.

The squire and the others applauded when a good blow was given or one neatly parried. The Turk at length steadily gave way, to the delight of the little ones among the spectators. One little maid in her exuberance of joy danced up and down clapping her hands and saying, "The old Turk is going to be whipped, and I'm glad." At length, under a shower of blows, the Turk fell to the ground amid the plaudits of the onlookers. St. George bends over him to see the extent of his wounds, and the Turk whispers:

"Ande, I guess I 'ad better stay killed this time."

But St. George is inexorable. Standing erect he speaks:

> "He lives, he breathes, he speaks,
> Now in the name of Elicompane
> Let the man rise and fight again."

The Turk arises on one knee and continues the conflict, but not for long, as he is again stricken down and becomes at once a suppliant.

> "Oh, pardon me, St. George,
> Pardon me I crave,
> Pardon me this once,
> And I will be thy slave."

Bold St. George had no idea of mercy toward the Turk, and so he spurs him once more to the conflict.

> "I'll never pardon a Turkish Knight,
> Therefore arise and try thy might."

Again the contest raged, the Turk, seeking to save himself as much as possible from the onslaughts of St. George, fights with a good bit of desperate valour, but down he goes again. St. George shakes his head as if it were all over and then cries:

> "Is there a doctor to be found
> To cure a deep and deadly wound?"

Why he should be so solicitous for the welfare of the Turk as to seek a doctor can hardly be told, unless for the pleasure of fighting with him again. The doctor is not long in appearing from the hall entrance. With three-cornered hat perched above an enormous wig and painted face, there was a professional air about him.

With a leer and a funny grimace at the crowd he began his doggerel speech.

"Oh, yes, there is a doctor to be found,
The best old doctor in the town,
On my back I carry my pack,
Of pills both white, and brown, and black."

St. George stalked toward him and asked, "What can you cure? Can you cure this man?"

"Cure? I can cure the palsy, and gout,
If the devil's in him, I'll soon pull 'im out."

The spectators crowded forward. Could the doctor cure the slain Turk? Oh, yes. How wisely he goes about his work! He tries one remedy after another, but of no avail. The Turk had told St. George in their last encounter that he was going to fight no more. He wasn't going to fight again, but to sham being dead, and then they would have to bring on the other players. He was shamming wonderfully well, until even the squire thought he was possibly badly hurt. The doctor knew different, however, for he had been posted by St. George, and so he drew from his pocket a bottle of exceedingly strong smelling salts. He had purloined it from his mother's bureau. This would make him well, he averred. St. George had kindness enough to hold the Turk's head down, while the doctor was administering the dose. Three great strong whiffs entered the Turk's nostrils, and seemed to enter every part of his head like the stinging of a million hornets. He would have gotten up then and there and fought the whole crowd had not St. George held his head, and the doctor thought he had better have the full dose.

"Achew! Achew! Achew!"

St. George let go the Turk's head, and the doctor nimbly stepped aside; the Turk with all the wrath of his race in his face, grasped his sword and fought like a demon for a few moments. His being killed three times seemed to increase his power. Then the natural superiority of Ande in the use of the sword began to assert itself, and the Turk thought that the sooner he fell the better, and accordingly did so. The old doctor slowly advanced and shook his head, as if all his skill was of no avail to resuscitate the slain Saracen.

"Ashes to ashes, and dust to dust,
If man can't cure 'im, old Nick must."

The doctor waved his staff, and in capered the dragon, a sort of hobble horse made of hoops under distended canvas, and worked by an inside performer. The great snapping jaws and staring eyes scared the little ones, but they laughed when they found it was only the slain Turk that he wanted. The unfortunate Turk, grasped by those rigorous jaws, was dragged from the hall.

The entertainment ended with the passing of the Christmas box, into which each one threw an offering, and as if in thankfulness for the amount the Christmas band, Turk, and dragon as well, mingled in a ludicrous dance, after which the whole crew was regaled with hot egg-nogg and cake.

In the midst of the conversation and laughter new sounds penetrated the hall from without.

> "Angels from the realms of glory,
> Wing your flight o'er all the earth,
> Ye who sang creation's story,
> Now proclaim Messiah's birth."

Some of the hall occupants rushed to the hall windows to see the singers. There in the pale moonlight were singers from the parish church and neighbourhood. They were singing, accompanied with the music of clarionet and serpent players. After the anthem the squire sent the old steward out to bid the choristers enter. He did so by saying to the choristers: "The squire wants hall hangels to come in." They entered and continued singing.

In the midst of the singing the Turkish knight leaned over to St. George and muttered:

"Ande, I'll be a Turkey snipe no more, when thee art St. George."

"Why?" said Ande, "and for goodness sake why do 'ee call it 'Turkey snipe'? Did 'ee notice the squire smile? A Turkish knight, you mean."

"Aye, I forgits the name; but 'ee nearly beat my insides out with thy old wooden sword, so 'ee did,'" growled Tommy Puckinharn, softly.

Ande gazed at the Turk's melancholy countenance, and chuckled in amusement.

"It was all in the play, Tommy, and if 'ee didn't fight so hard and I didn't cut and slash as I did, perhaps we wouldn't 'ave the cake and good stuff that we are eating here now," said Ande, at which reply Tommy seemed some mollified.

The "curl-singers" had finished their anthems and were regaled in the same manner as the Christmas players, and there was a lull in the amusements, when the great knocker on the hall door sounded the presence of a new visitor.

CHAPTER XIII

THE CORNISH DROLL TELLER

"Seest thou not my harp?
Emblem of my peaceful calling."

—Harper Ballad.

A servant opened the hall door and ushered in an old man, slightly bent under the weight of a harp under its green covering. He was clad in the ordinary garments of the time, except that he still clung to the long stockings, knee breeches, and low silver buckled shoes that were now generally being discarded by the gentry. From the hue of his hair, that was of an iron-grey and thick and wavy like his beard, and the slight stoop to his shoulders, he must have been in the neighbourhood of fifty years of age. There was a trace of humour around the corners of his mouth, and much fun-light in the gleam of his twinkling eyes that seemed to belie the tragic nature of his heavy beetling brows.

"Uncle Billy! Uncle Billy!" shouted some of the younger ones, in glee.

"'Tis Uncle Billy, the droll teller," said the squire to one of his eastern friends in a side tone, and then to the new arrival, "Welcome to the Manor Hall, Uncle Billy, and to our Christmas cheer. Come nigh the fire and get thy fingers loosened up, for we must have a tune to-night."

Uncle Billy, the droll, sat himself near the yule log and, while he warmed up his cold hands, entered into conversation with the squire and one or two of his elder friends.

The droll teller of Cornwall was a privileged character in the olden times. Somewhat embodying the profession of the minstrel and the story-teller, he was always assured of a ready welcome. For ages the western part of Saxon England terminated at the River Tamar, and the people west of that stream, girt with hills and wild moors, had little communication with the outside world. Hence when the profession of the minstrel began to decline in the days of Elizabeth, this section gave it a ready welcome and asylum. The lack of railways and newspapers gave the droll the profession of a news courier, and at any house he tarried he was regarded with favour and reverence. How they stood around him in the evening hours, in cottage or hall, and listened with eager interest to the news of the great outside world, and how with awe upon their faces they listened to the tales of Tregeagle, the giant Cormoran of St. Michael's Mount! Many knew the tales, but none could tell them with the vivid realism of the droll, and then how the eyes of the youths would flash at the tales of King Arthur, the greatest king of the Cornish line.

Of all droll tellers, Uncle Billy was the most loved and the most famous. He could enter into the cottages of the common people and be one of their midst, speaking in their own dialect, or could associate with the gentry speaking in language as good as their own, and at times better. He was not only gifted with oratorical and musical power, but also had a fund of information in legendary lore and was as familiar with the tales of Rome and Greece as a university scholar. Some even went so far as to say that he was a scholar of Eton College when he was a lad, had been disappointed in a love affair and had drifted away from all who knew him in consequence. At times, after some legend told with great power, some of his friends among the gentry would remonstrate with him on his wandering life and offer to assist him into some greater sphere of usefulness, in better keeping with his education.

"Sphere of usefulness," Billy would respond. "What profession is more useful than that of the minstrel, or as people call me, the droll? I have brought happiness into cottage and hall and wiped the tears from sorrowing eyes with fun and laughter. I have made the youth's heart burn with high purpose to emulate the heroic deeds of old, and I have implanted thoughts of soberness in the giddy headed. What could be more useful? And could I have a happier occupation were I in the position of a servant? No, I prefer the old independent life of the droll; and as for my high education," Billy would always stop here, and with a funny twinkle in his eyes and dropping into the language of the country clout say, "I beant much of a scholard."

"Well, Billy, give us a song," said the squire, seeing that the droll teller had become sufficiently thawed out to finger the harp.

"Or a story," said a relative of the squire.

"Tell us of the oxen kneeling on Christmas night," piped in a young, shrill, boyish voice.

"Les have Duffy and The Devil," said one of the "curl" singers.

"Or the Cornish Tale of King Arthur," said another.

"Well, well, one at a time. Suppose I sing ye one of the old Christmas songs first," responded Uncle Billy, and tuning up his harp he swept with rapid, light fingers the opening bars of "The First Good News That Mary Had." This was followed by "I See Three Ships Come Sailing In," and was greeted with great applause at the close.

The old butler brought in a steaming bowl of egg-nog punch which he placed on the table near the harper's chair; after refreshing himself the droll began the tale of Duffy and the Devil, telling it, as was his custom, partly in verse to the accompaniment of the harp, and partly in prose.

THE TALE OF DUFFY AND THE DEVIL.

An old bachelor squire of Cornubia's race

Was the master of old Lovell Hall;
He'd a jolly round face, and the fox he would trace
Over moor and through dale in a glorious chase,
But of women he would none at all.

Cider making was nigh and in Buryan church town
For more hands he was seeking one day;
Words and blows did resound, and with her swing-tail gown,
Old Janey was beating her stepdaughter around,
In her cottage, that was by his way.

"Hallo, what's the row," said the squire, as he dis mounted and entered the cottage. Being a magistrate, he thought it was his duty to settle all quarrels, but he had scarcely got within when he was sorry he had meddled. Old Janey had been using the skirt of her gown to carry out the grate ashes, and beating Duffy, her stepdaughter, with the gown afterward; there was such a dust in the air that the squire went into a fit of coughing.

"'Tis Duffy," said old Janey. "She can't knit nor spin and does nothing for her living. She's that lazy, your honour," and Janey, the dust settling a bit, dropped a curtesy to the squire.

"'Tedn't so, your honour," said Duffy, as the tears gathered in her blue eyes. "My knitting and spinning is of the very best."

Well, the upshot of the matter was that the squire took Duffy home with him to Lovell Hall, and the hall housekeeper sent her into the attic to spin. Old Janey was glad to get rid of her stepdaughter, and Duffy was glad to get away and, though she had told an untruth to the squire, it didn't bother her much, until she found herself surrounded by the wool sacks in the upper part of Lovell Hall. There, casting herself down on the wool sacks, she said: "The devil may spin for the squire, but I can't and won't." Scarcely had she said this when a voice was heard:

"A bargain! A bargain!" said the voice loud and clear
Of a neat little man in garb black;
"But remember, my dear, since ye've called me here,
If ye can't guess my name, I'll have 'ee in a year,"
And he brought his tail down with a rap.

"All right," said Duffy undaunted, and tossed up her head in disdain, and then fell to lolling on the wool sacks and idling and singing away the whole day. In the evening the little man in black handed to her the result of his day's spinning and she descended with it into the great hall below.

"Zounds! What a liar old Janey was," said the squire, as he viewed the fine amount of spun yarn, and casting a favouring glance on Duffy he said she was the finest spinner in Cornwall.

The next day Duffy took the yarn with her to the attic to knit the squire's hunting stockings, and the little man, true to his contract, performed the work for her and soon,— —

The stockings were finished, and knit strong as leather,

Squire Lovell was filled with delight;
With dogs all together, in all sorts of weather,
His old shanks were sound in furze, brambles or heather,
Whether hunting by day or by night.

But now came a worrying time for the old squire, for the lads from the whole country around had heard of Duffy's fine spinning and were not indifferent to Duffy's charms. The squire feared that she would marry one of them and then he should lose his fine stockings, and so resolved to forestall such a dire thing by marrying Duffy himself. They were married in the old parish church before a great assemblage from far and near. The old squire's heart was full of glee as he gazed at the young, disappointed men around him. "Ha! Ha!" thought he, "she soon shall be mine." But no sooner had he thought this than there was a terrible, distinct voice echoing the same thoughts.

"Ha! Ha! She soon shall be mine!" blood curdling and dire,
Echoed a voice; the people were still,
And from window of choir gazed the black man in ire,
Yet knew that the end of his compact was nigh her,
When she must be subject to his will.

The people in the church heard the voice, but no one knew who had spoken the words. The rector was indignant that the service should be interrupted and would have had the party, then and there, up before the gentlemen at the court if he could have found him. The supposition was that some jealous suitor had spoken, and the thing was soon forgotten by everyone but Duffy, or Lady Lovell, as we must now call her. She knew and was nigh to fainting had not the squire supported her with his sturdy arm. They were happy in their married life, for the squire loved his wife and Duffy had always a secret regard for him, but there was a dread in her mind that the words of the little man in black must soon come true. The year was nigh up and she had tried all plans to discover his name, but of little avail. She was nigh in despair when a person whom she had befriended relieved her of much of her anxiety. That person was old Betty of the mill, who was commonly supposed to be something of a witch.

She carefully inquired of Lady Lovell when the squire went on his next hunting trip, and having ascertained the time to the very hour, she obtained from her a jack of the squire's best beer.

That day the squire went hunting far from home and even at nightfall returned not to Lovell Hall. As the hours of nightfall came on, the dogs, one by one, came back all lathered in foam, but no Squire Lovell. At ten o'clock came the squire and he was visibly excited and seemed bubbling over with laughter.

"Duffy," said he, "I have had as great a lark as I have ever had in my life. I hunted all day over all the moors and downs, Trove, Trevider, Lemorna and Brene, and didn't catch a thing. The mare was tired out and so was I, when up jumped as fine a hare as I had ever seen, from a hedge along the road-side. She was away and so were the dogs instantly, and I followed. What a chase! This way and that way she doubled, and at length entered the mouth of Fugoe's dark cave."

In went the dogs and in follow'd I, water dripping,
Mud flying, dogs yelping in full cry,
Owls wheeling, bats flapping, the place was nigh sick'ning
And black as the night, but the pace was now quickening,
When a singular sight caught my eye.

We had gone nigh a mile when the dogs turn'd to flight,
For Alack! On the farthermost shore
Of a lake was a light of a fire. What a sight!
There was old Nick a-dancing with all his might
With witches; there was more than a score.

"And there was old Bet of the mill a-thumping and a-beating her crowd, giving music for the dance, and, as I live, by her side was my best jack of beer, and each time old Nick would come around he would take a drink. The old witches sang as they danced,"

"Here's to the devil,
With wooden pick and shovel,
Digging tin by the bushel
With his tail cocked up."

The wild dance and frolic grew fast and furious,
Brighter blaz'd the fire-flames, blue and hot,
Then Nick in full chorus, with witches, uproarious,
Shouted and sang like the spirit of Boreas,
"My name is Terrytop, Terrytop."

"Aye, and he kept shouting it as if he had lost his head with the drinking of too much of my beer. Then he jumped among the old witches, and such a sight!"

He kicked the old witches and Bet the old dame,
'Till I laughed out aloud at the lark,
Then he whirl'd and he came, in a reel, through the flame,
"Go it, old Nick," said I, "you are worthy your name,"
And then—in a moment—'twas dark.

And away galloped I, with the mare at full speed;
With a din, the whole crowd followed fast;
With old Nick in the lead, over moor and o'er mead,
But I distanc'd them soon, for the mare knew my need,
And now here I am, Duffy, at last.

"Why doesn't 'ee laugh, Duffy?" said the squire. Duffy, who had turned pale at the mentioning of the little man's name, now regained her good spirits and laughed merrily and long, for she knew she was safe. The squire stretched out his limbs in weariness, for he had hunted far and wide and felt the need of sleep, so he soon retired. But not so Duffy, for she knew that in an hour or so the little man in black would come to claim his prize. First she said the Creed, and then she prayed, for she had resolved to become an exemplary woman could she escape the consequences of the rash vow she had made a year before. Then in the midst of her devotions there was heard the wild neighing of a horse without, and then the door, though shut with bolt and bar, opened, and in stepped the little man in black, bowing low, and yet with a cunning leer in his eyes.

"I 'ave come for 'ee, Duffy," said he, "unless"—and he paused,—"unless ye can guess my name."

"Terrytop!" said Duffy, with a confident look on her features.

"Correct, m'lady," said Terrytop with a sigh of regret, and then with a sweep of his tail he was gone.

The droll ceased his tale and was greeted by a round of applause, for it was not only the story, but the manner of the harper, at one time frank, ruddy and jovial like Squire Lovell, at another time with a cunning leer like the man in black, at another time disdainful or tearful, fearful or glad, according to the mood of Duffy, that drew forth the appreciation of his auditors. He calmly sipped a bowl of punch, while the auditors entered into conversation, though expecting more tales when the harper had rested himself.

CHAPTER XIV

ST. GEORGE AND FAIR SABRA

Blest as Immortal Zeus is he,
The youth who fondly sits by thee,
And gazes at the witchery trace
Of gladsome laughter in thy face,
The music of thy voice to hear,
The incense of thy presence near.

During the recital of the droll's tale where was Ande? Generally, he was interested in the tales of Uncle Billy, the droll, but this night he had eyes and ears only for the squire's daughter.

The latter was in her element. She was young, but the death of her mother had long made her the mistress of the great house. The presence of the guests inspired her to do her utmost as hostess, and she was not unequal to the task. The earlier part of the evening saw her flitting about, a fairy figure in lace and ribbons. During the entertainment of the droll she was at leisure, and sat on one side at a little distance, entirely engrossed in the narrative. Here it was that Ande found her.

"And is St. George welcomed by fair Sabra, the King of Egypt's daughter?" he said, as he sat himself near her.

In those weeks intervening between the squire's repa ration and the Christmas period, Ande had been a frequent visitor at the Manor. The squire could not easily forget his prejudice against the name stained with treason, but he was generous enough to smother it in the light of the youth's brave conduct in the runaway, and wished also to make some amends for the injustice of placing him in the stocks.

So the lad was found frequently in the neighbourhood of the Manor. The Manor walks were familiar to him. He had often assisted Mistress Alice in her garden work in her own favourite plot, and a warm and strong attachment had grown up between them. The old squire occasionally nodded to him and smiled, but beyond that there was little friendly conversation between them.

But to the squire's daughter how useful he became. Was there any work that would soil her dainty fingers? Ande must perform it. Was there any task that seemed too hard for her? Ande was in requisition. Once she had hurt her finger over a rose bush. It was Ande who heard the faint exclamation of pain and who flew instantly to her side, and how tenderly and with what a vague thrill, as if he himself were hurt, did he proceed to extract the jagged thorn. It was his own handkerchief that bound up the wound, and with what gallantry he had requested her to keep it as a remembrance of him. He knew not that that piece of linen was stored up among Mistress Alice's special treasures. She knew that her womanly intuition at the gate of the Primrose Cottage was true. This youth did love her, and it was not displeasing to her; but she knew something else. She was gradually knowing her own feelings, that she cherished a deeper sentiment than friendship for this brave youth who had saved her life. The thought of this sentiment would send the crimson waves o'er her countenance when she dwelt upon it, for a moment, in her own pretty rooms. She would not have him suspect such a thing—not for the world. She knew her father's hatred for treason, his strong loyal sentiments. No, she dare not think of it too often. Her father had revealed his plans for her future—the marriage with young Richard Lanyan. But she had neither acquiesced nor refused. Master Lanyan was a welcome visitor to the Manor, and she treated him well as her father's guest.

Lanyan and Ande had met once in her presence at the Manor. There was a gleam of hatred in each eye. This was the son of the hated family that had deprived the Trembaths of their rightful possessions, and now Ande could perceive the marked favour with which he was greeted by the old squire, and had a dim consciousness of the squire's hopes. It was as much as Mistress Alice could do to so conduct herself as to offend neither. Lanyan, after the first quick, sharp glance at Trembath, paid little heed to him. Calmly and tranquilly he ignored him and devoted his attention to Mistress Alice, taking the conversation into such scholarly, Etonian themes that Ande, finding himself out of his depths, was constrained to silence and soon moved homeward with bitter feelings within him.

He had not come near the Manor for a week after that, and somehow or other Mistress Alice had a foreboding that something was wrong. Did it pain her? She would not acknowledge that it did, even to herself. But how graciously she treated him when he did return. So had affairs been before the Christmastide, and on account of it there was not that strangeness between them that existed at the first.

With the remark above mentioned, the Knight, St. George, seated himself near Alice. She smiled pleasantly and responded:

"I am afraid fair Sabra and the King of Egypt are too far remote from our locality and times to be mixed up with us. I must congratulate you, Ande, for your able impersonation of St. George. By the way, who is that Turk that so murders the king's English?"

"Thomas Puckinharn, one of the village lads. He is a good fighter, but a blow or two harder than usual saps his courage. I had hard ado to make him fight at all," and he related their practice upon the village road and the strategy of allowing Tommy a squire as a balm to heal his wounded feelings. She laughed at his droll manner of reciting it, and her laugh seemed to be music to his soul and to quicken the beating of his heart within.

"Why," she was saying, "did you beat the Turk so savagely? I must confess I never saw a real battle, but I imagined I saw one all the time you were fighting. You beat down his guard and struck him over the head and shoulders, until I trembled. I believe you would make an excellent knight, had you lived in their times," and she shook her elfin locks in approbation of his fighting prowess.

"Well, I thought I was fighting for fair Sabra, and the reality of it seemed to put greater strength into my arms. A knight always fights more bravely in the presence of his lady."

"It must be nice to have such a brave knight. And who is the lady?"

"One surpassing fair and worthy of the crown of Egypt. One whom I have served, as a knight always serves his lady."

"I suppose you mean me," said the maiden, with a flush, and yet with some gaiety in her tones. "Well, be it so. You shall be my knight and defender and shall wear a pledge of your valour as a remembrance," and she plucked a hothouse blossom from the knot at her breast and presented it to him. "Fight bravely in life, and you will be a true knight."

"That I will," said Ande, as he received the flower, "and I shall remember this Christmas eve, throughout my life, as one of its best days. I shall even remove the stain of treason from our name. Treason that is so hateful to me!"

"I trust you may," said the girl, earnestly. "It has been a hard burden to bear. And with the ideas of our times, it is hard to advance under it to positions of honour and trust. But I believe you will succeed."

"You do not believe, then, in the current report, held true even by your father, of the truth of the accusation that has always clung to our name from my grand-father's times?"

"Knowing you as I do, no. If your father and your grandfather were at all like you, they could not have done what current report states. No. I do not believe it."

"I am glad that you do not believe it. It gives me courage to succeed." There was a light in the eyes of St. George, a gleam of genuine pleasure.

"The removal of that stain, which you have often told me of, will remove, perhaps, many barriers of which you are ignorant. My knight must do it."

"I am that knight," said Ande, warmly.

"The knight that I should admire would be one that will not despair at a few difficulties."

"I am that knight," eagerly.

"He must be truthful and scorn a lie."

"I do, from the bottom of my heart."

"He must be a worker, and brave and courageous."

"My principles exactly."

"He must not be satisfied to be an ordinary knight. He must be a leader."

"My ambition," emphatically.

"He must be an exceptional man, noble, upright, a defender of the weak, and—and—and—must be my knight, and no one else's." Her eyes were shining darkly with a happy gleam, and there was a glow on her cheeks that made her a thousand times more attractive to the enthralled soul before her. Her countenance was close to his. Ah! The magic of its influence!

"I AM THAT KNIGHT," SAID ANDE, WARMLY

His heart was beating so tumultuously he feared all heard it. He knew then and there the reason of his interest in her. Those vague feelings, which he had not taken the trouble to analyse, burst suddenly upon him like a revelation. He loved, yes, he knew it. Heretofore he had gone on blindly, driven by the subtile promptings within. Now he understood his own heart. There was a pang as he thought of the stain on his name, and then a joyous bound of his heart as he thought she believed in him, in his ability to eradicate the blot. She had called him her knight. He would be so. But then the thought of Master Lanyan emerged from the depths of the past, the squire's favour, and that scene when he was so contemptuously ignored by the haughty, young Etonian in the gardens. He had thought then that his hatred for him was due to the injustice to his family; now he knew. Her features, so close to his own, were the most prominent thing in the world to him then. What cared he for the twanging harp of Uncle Billy, the droll. He was ordinarily interested in the tales of Billy, but not now. That last sentence of hers of being her knight and a knight of no one else, sent a thrill through him. He longed to kiss her, then to throw himself at her feet and pour out the adoration of his soul. But he knew his situation and he simply said, "I am your knight, and no one else's."

Then the thought of Lanyan again came to his mind, "And since I am your knight and belong to no other, it is but fair to ask you to have no other knight," half doubtingly.

"Queens and ladies of old always had many knights to do them service," in mischievous, jesting tones.

Ande's heart died within him and the light left his features.

"And you intend to have many knights?"

"Perhaps."

"At least not Master Lanyan," fiercely, in an undertone.

"My knight must not be a dictator."

"But I must know," persistently.

"You are impertinent," with some dignity.

"He and his are the enemies of my house," doggedly.

"And the friends of ours," quickly.

"But he is an enemy of your knight."

"I will not be catechised." There was the gleam of a tear of vexation in her eyes and a quiver in her voice, that sent the militant spirit in the breast of Ande headlong in defeat. She turned her face from him in an effort to hide her feelings. An agony of remorse swept o'er his soul.

"I have hurt you," he said, timidly.

No answer.

"What have I done. I am a brute and a coward. I am not worthy to be called your knight," exclaimed Ande, in remorseful self-reproach.

No answer.

"Look at me, please. Speak to me," pleadingly. "You will not. I am the worst coward living—to hurt the feelings of the best of women," in doleful misery.

"You are hateful and unjust." An answer at length from the hidden face that made his countenance blanch and pierced even within, but he answered humbly:

"I am. I have been hateful and unjust to you."

"No. Hateful and unjust to yourself." The face again came into view and, could he believe it,—yes,—the tear was gone and the fun-light was twinkling in merriment.

"How?" in bewildered discomfiture.

"When you called yourself a coward and the worst of ones, you were unjust to yourself and hateful to yourself."

"I suppose you are right," humbly.

"Don't look so doleful; you may be noticed. I would have my knight cheerful and happy."

"And you are not angry?"

"No," and she shook her elfish curls and smiled.

"And you will have no other knight but me?"

"You must not be presumptuous," seriously.

"Mistress Alice, it is not presumptuous for me to speak to you on a subject that is dear to me," said with great earnestness, his eyes devouring her face. "And specially so here in the hall of my ancestors. Do you see the coat-of-arms o'er the mantelpiece, engraved in the oak?"

The girl was relieved by what she thought a change in the conversation. She brightened into new interest.

"Yes, and I wondered ever since a child what was the meaning of the horse with his rider surrounded by the waves of the sea. Oh, do tell me, please!"

"That is the coat-of-arms of our family. The earliest records speak of them as occupying the Lyonnesse country, which is now under the sea beyond Land's End. Sir Trembath, the head of the family, was overtaken by the flood, that happened about in the eighth century, and just had to gallop and swim his horse to the hills for refuge. He was the only one who escaped the inroads of the ocean. All the lands of his barony, together with others, and a hundred and forty parish churches, are now covered by the deep. My ancestry is as noble as any, and it is not presumption for me to speak to you on a subject that is very important to me. As my ancestry was then, so am I now. Mistress Alice, the last heir of the Trembaths needs a star of hope to guide him." He was speaking rapidly, although only loud enough for her to hear. The wild tempest of feeling was at length breaking forth.

"Listen," said the girl, demurely, "Uncle Billy is speaking now of the Lyonesse and Arthur."

The unruly tongue was silenced. Ande, though he listened, heard not. His eyes were on the squire's daughter, but seeing that she kept her gaze riveted on the harper, he grew moody and silent.

Whether she listened or not to the song of the droll is a question. Certainly there was nothing in the narrative of the droll, just then, to cause her cheek to glow with a damask hue.

The harper's song and tale was ended, and since the hour was late there was bustle and confusion to be gone.

"I have been unjust in dictating to you," said Ande, humbly.

"And I can have whatever knights I please?" archly.

"You are the best judge. But I would rather not," said he, with slightly woeful look.

"Then you choose to let me be my own judge?"

"To be sure."

"Then you are my knight. Master Lanyan is not and cannot be my knight. I choose so freely. Be upright, noble, and good."

Is it any wonder that the Knight of St. George departed with light footsteps. He was but a lad merging into manhood. Love was strong within him and flourished in keeping with the vigour of his youth. He knew not that she cared for him. Sometimes he thought so. He even dared to hope so when the doubts did not becloud his vision. It was something, though, to be her chosen knight. He knew by her last words that he was a closer friend at least than Lanyan. The thought lightened his spirits.

The Christmas players were the first on the way to the village. There was a chatter among them, some extolling the squire's generosity, others—the ability of the droll. Ande was silent. He was busy with his thoughts.

"Ah! The squire's maid gave 'ee as hard a drubbing as thee gave me. Edent it so?" said Tom Puckinharn, and he gave Ande a nudge in the side, as he whispered this in his ear.

"Ah! Get along, Tom, do!" replied Ande.

Tom was the only one who noticed the *tête-à-tête* of St. George and Sabra. Being a loyal friend of Ande, he prudently kept his own counsel. The remoteness of their situation, the voice and sound of the harp, the intense interest of the guests in the harper's entertainment, precluded any from hearing the conversation of that period.

Ande's dreams that night were very much confused. Now he was with King Arthur at Lyonnese; now against the dragon or the Turk; then on horse-back riding through the roaring waves of ocean, bearing in front of him the form of the fair Sabra, who appeared wonderfully like the squire's daughter. Then casting his eyes behind, he caught a view of the dragon, beating and lashing the waves into foam, in his rage, and somehow the dragon's head was that of Master Lanyan.

CHAPTER XV
THE HELSTON GRAMMAR SCHOOL

Three weeks elapsed and Master Ande Trembath had entered upon a new life. He was enrolled upon the list of the scholars of Helston Grammar School.

For four centuries the school had been the centre of education for the west of Cornwall. Gentlemen can point to it with pride this day, as they could then, as the birthplace of their early efforts and the inspiration of their ambitions. At the time of Ande's entrance it had emerged from the obscurity of the past into the foremost school of Cornwall. This result was due much to the energetic labours and talents of the head master, Rev. Mr. Trewan, M. A., a scholar of Oxford. Stern, yet kind and affectionate to the youths under his charge, he was universally beloved by his pupils. In his dealings with his pupils of whatever age, he was of the same opinion as Quintilian that "a child too disingenuous to be corrected by reproof, like a slave, will only be hardened by continuous blows."

Though the scholars loved and revered the head, yet the under-master, a certain Mr. Sherwood, received little or no affection from them. He was sharp-featured as a weasel, sarcastic in speech, a scholarly egotist, with the garment of dignity and a predilection to the use of euphonious words.

The new scholar, entering in the midst of the year, found himself sadly handicapped. In age and size, he should have been enrolled among the fifth form. His withdrawal from the parish school after the lamentable affair of the stocks placed him in no higher position than near the head of the fourth.

The head of the sixth, a certain William Jordan, a great scholar — almost a demigod — in the estimation of the lesser forms, and one of the school monitors, took Ande in charge after his examination, and courteously showed him around the school. The schoolroom with its row of desks and forms, the cloakroom, the dining hall, the library, the dormitory, all were successively inspected.

"This will be your sleeping apartment," said Jordan, as he opened a green baize door on the second floor. Within were several beds and other bedroom furniture. A few windows that opened toward the playground gave abundance of light.

The new scholar soon became accustomed with his new surroundings and set in to study with a zeal that surprised masters and pupils. He won the hearts of his fellows of the fourth by setting out a feast for them that first night in the fourth form dormitory. Mrs. Trembath had not forgotten a hamper of good things, among them several bottles of mild herby beer. These she had sent in with his luggage. The feast was spread on one of the beds, and his fellows, after it was terminated, promptly voted him a trump and proclaimed him, then and there, "King of the Fourth Form."

The king accepted his title by giving an entertainment that night in a noiseless manner. With the aid of a little phosphorus he caused many uncouth and laughable figures to appear upon the wall, to the great wonder of the smaller fourth form boys.

Before he had been in the fourth a month he had made such progress that Master Sherwood entertained seriously the thought of his promotion, and indeed, did promote him at the opening of spring. There was great sorrow among the fourth when the news became known, as he had been of great assistance to them in difficult points in the various lessons. A fifth form scholar was not so accessible as one in their own form.

The fifth were not near so desirable a set of fellows as those he had left. There was a difference between being king of the fourth, both in learning and strength, and occupying the lowest position in the fifth form. There were two in the form that were prominent, but in a different degree. One, a certain Albert Tenny, the head of the form, who made particularly bright recitations; the other, Richard Thomas, the one who was stationed next to him, the son of a well-to-do farmer of the Lizard Point. Thomas was heavy set, elephantine in size and strength, and on account of the latter and a dulness in study was named by the boys King Dullhead, although they never mentioned the latter in his presence, or dire would be his vengeance.

There was not much of a contest between Dick, as he was called, and Ande, to see which should be the head of the tail end of the form. The very first lesson Ande went above Dick.

"I see," said Mr. Sherwood, with a sarcastic smile on his sharp features; "I see, Master Thomas, you are resolved to maintain your old position."

There was a slight laugh on the part of the rest of the form. Dick squirmed under the sarcasm and half audible laughter of his fellows, and looked down in dogged silence, growling something under his breath. Sarcasm and taunts had made him sullen and revengeful, and the laughter at his mistakes had made him more stupid and awkward. He would sit at his desk in an idle manner with his large flat feet sprawling over the floor in different directions. Ambition had left his features, if, indeed, he ever had any. How he ever made the fifth was a wonder. He had tried year after year, but never succeeded in raising himself above the foot of the fifth.

The crisis between Dick, Tenny, and Ande came about in this way. The form had started in on the study of Virgil, and thought it exceedingly hard after the simple, narrative discourse of Cæsar's Commentaries. Master Sherwood was not sparing in his assigning of lessons, and had assigned a few lines in addition to the regular, allotted portion. There was much secret dissatisfaction, and especially from Dullhead Dick. The thing had occurred once before and they had universally decided not to read more than the generally allotted portion. Ande had been the soul of honour on that occasion, had refused to read, and the Master had passed him over lightly as he was a new fifth form lad. To his surprise several of the fifth arose when called upon and recited the extra portion. Now, disgusted with the whole fifth, he refused to assemble with them to consider their grievances. The secret conclave was called and the decision made, but they stupidly said nothing to their absent member.

The eventful recitation came, and the close of the allotted portion read by Ande himself. Then he paused.

"Proceed," said Sherwood.

"If you do," growled Dick, who was next in line, "you'll take a licking after school."

The whispered threat exasperated the reader, and he proceeded resolutely on. Dick gave him a sly kick under the bench in his rage.

> "Æolus, haec contra; Tuos, O regina, quid optes
> Explorare labor; mihi jussa capessere fas est.'"

"Stop there," said the master. "You may begin, Richard Thomas."

"We haven't got any farther," blurted out Dick.

"Ah! I thought I assigned to the eightieth line."

"We only take thirty-five lines," persisted Dick.

"Master Thomas, will you recite?" sternly asked the master.

Dick made no movement, but sat in dogged and sullen silence.

"Very well," said Mr. Sherwood, "you may write out the next thirty lines and commit them to memory."

"I'll pay you back," growled Dick to Ande, as he gave him a fierce nudge.

"Tenny, you may scan and translate."

Tenny, the head, did not dare disobey, although he had promised with the others not to read the extra portion, and even had not studied it. He, however, trusting in his natural ability, thought he could weather through. He began, but stumbled lamentably until Mr. Sherwood, incensed, gave his lines to the next, who made as bad a failure of them; and so it continued until Ande was again reached. Mr. Sherwood compressed his lips.

"Well, Trembath, we'll try you again."

Ande arose and scanned and translated in a truly commendable manner.

"Master Trembath, you have done credit to those lines," said Mr. Sherwood, well pleased. "You have saved the credit of the form; you may take your place at the head of the fifth."

The lads above were furious with jealousy, and burly Dick vowed threats of vengeance for his thirty lines.

The meeting was not long in appearing. Ande was on the Bowling Green that same evening, when Dick and a crowd of the fifth met him. The stupid and the bright had clasped hands against him; the bright ones out of jealousy, the dull ones out of revenge.

"Here's the red 'eaded Deane," said Dick, insultingly.

"I would just as soon be a descendant of the red-headed Danes, as an offspring of the Lizard barbarians[6], who, if history is correct, didn't know enough to walk upright, but travelled on all fours like a donkey," said Ande, coolly surveying the crowd.

Dick was in a fury of rage. The legend had been frequently poked at him and it always reached a sore part.

"Wilt fight," he roared, "and I'll show 'ee a donkey's heels." Dick, before the masters, tried the best English he could use, for he had tasted the scorn of Sherwood often, but in a rage, and before the lads, the dialect was good enough for him. Now, I suppose he meant that he would make Ande feel the weight of his shoes, but that worthy responded in sarcastic vein.

"No need to fight for that, for I see them already," and he gazed contemplatively at Dick's large feet.

Even the duller ones could not refrain from a grin of delight, but they were determined to have Ande whipped, and so arrangements having been made, they wandered out some distance from the Bowling Green to secure a place. The news had been carried to the fourth form, and the whole form came as his supporters. Now, the fifth were certain of Dick's victory, for in size, age, and strength he seemed superior to Ande. The fourth were exceedingly anxious, while Ande himself had no doubts of the outcome. Dullhead, though heavier and larger than the redoubtable Bully Bob Sloan, had nothing but brute strength, and even Bully Bob would have made short work of him.

"Art ready?" said Dick, and an affirmative answer being given, "then come on," and with a bellow, Dick lowered his great head and charged like an enraged bull. His antagonist caught his head in a vice-like chancery grip, and hitting him a playful tap, released him with a spin that sent him some distance back. Dullhead shook his head, as if he wondered what had happened, and then again charged. This time Ande side-stepped, and tapping Dick with his right, and crooking his foot, sent him head over heels.

"Dost see the donkey's heels, lads?"

The fourth roared, and shouted their applause.

Then was Dick's blood at fever heat. He must get the desired underhold for a wrestle, of which he knew some tactics, and so again came the charge, which was met with no love-taps this time. A straight, hard, left-hander caught Dick full upon the nose, and then, crash, another upon the eye. Dick, dazed, still came on, for he was the soul of courage. This kind of fighting was new to him, however. To be hit again and again, without being able to get a grip on his foe, was maddening.

[6] Lizard Barbarians.—An old legend of the Lizard Point states that its inhabitants were so ignorant in olden times that they walked on hands and knees until some shipwrecked sailors taught them the art of standing.

Meantime, Ande's hands were playing a lively tattoo upon Dick's eyes, ears, and nose. At last, fairly unable to stand the punishment, Dick broke for his corner, but it was not in retreat; it was but to gain the impetus for a new rush, by which he sought to gain the desired grip for a throw. On he came, like a whirlwind, and then, no one knew how it happened, but there was a quick flash of an extended arm, and burly Dick went down as if he was shot, and laid motionless.

Some of the fifth rushed forward to assist Dick, but were withheld by the voice of his antagonist, who wished to know if any of the fifth desired to take up Dick's cause.

Not a one responded, and then he did a thing for which he was always admired, and rightly so. He had not forgotten his knighthood. He came forward and was the leader in bringing Dick to consciousness. Some, at his word, brought water from the river Cober and tenderly he chafed Dick's hands and forehead, until the unconscious fellow was fully restored.

"Much hurt?" said Ande.

"Hah—hah!" gasped Dick, as he opened his eyes, and caught his breath in gasps. "Not much—all right, soon."

Then followed more chafing and Dick was at length slowly assisted to his feet.

"No offence," said Ande, as he held out his hand, "you know I had to fight."

Dick took the outstretched hand, a little sheepishly, and shook it gingerly.

"No offence. Better luck next time."

"Come, now. Is there going to be a next time? I don't want to permanently cripple my hands by hitting such an ironsides as you are," laughingly.

Dick rubbed his great head tenderly, felt of his battered features, and then, with a slight smile: "No, I guess we've satisfied the code of honour."

Together, fourth and fifth, wended their way amicably back to the school grounds. Ande continued to hold his position as head of the fifth, and won the regard of all by championing the cause of the school against all outsiders. In the latter he was ably assisted by Dick, who, strange to say, became his most devoted and attached friend. Dick was a magnificent fellow physically, and there was a good bit of fine principle about him, but his strength, dulness, and awkwardness had made him heretofore a bully. Under the warm glow of Ande's friendship, new life and hope was implanted within him; he applied himself with diligence to his studies, and under his chum's fostering care, made progress. The two were now partners in the same study.

One night, when they were preparing the coming day's lessons, Dick looked up from his book.

"Ande, remember the fight we had?"

"Yes."

"Did you 'ave anything in your hand when you struck me that last time?"

"No. Why?"

"'Cause, I thought it was a club," and Dick grinned.

"I hated to hit so hard. But it seemed none of my former blows were having much effect. It was like hitting an elephant."

There was silence in the study room for the space of half an hour, and then Dick asked his companion to review him o'er his lesson. Ande did so, and was agreeably surprised; it was the best lesson that Dick had ever prepared.

"I'm much obliged," said Dick. "This hearing of a lesson helps wonderfully."

"Dick," said Ande, "a red-headed Dane is a pretty-fair sort of a fellow, after all. I say, he has some redeemable virtues."

"Yes, and I 'ave discovered something else."

"What's that?"

"A donkey has a head as well as a pair of heels," whereupon they both laughed heartily.

CHAPTER XVI

THE HURLING MATCH

"Toms, Wills and Jans
Take off all's on the sands."

—St. Ives' Hurlers.

"Gware wheag, yeo gware teag."
Fair play is good play.

—Ancient Cornish Hurler's Motto.

"Gware wheag, yeo gware teag," roared Dick, as he seized Ande by the shoulders and engaged in a playful wrestle, in which, however, he was worsted, for the latter, though taken by surprise, soon had Dick down on the sward of the Bowling Green.

"Now," said he, "is it fair play for a wrestle, or is there something else in the wind? What's up?"

"Can't guess, old fellow?"

"No, unless it's hurling, my elephantine infant. There is nothing that stirs your blood like that. Is it hurling?"

"Aye, you've got it," and tumbling up from the sod, Dick shook his huge frame and adjusted his neckerchief that had become slightly awry in the brief wrestling match.

"Who's challenged the school?" asked Ande, with a little trace of excitement.

"The louts of Breage parish. Their captain, a husky chap, brought in a challenge. Squire Vivian, Sir James Lanyan, and other gentlemen put up a prize of ten pounds and a fine hurling ball to the victors. The hurling ball has a silver plate on it, with the old motto engraved on it, and the school decided to accept the challenge. The gentlemen are anxious for the school to wipe out an old score against Breage that happened years ago in a match against that parish. They are going to elect a captain of the school team and so I hurried off to find the Dane."

"Well, here I am, my husky Ajax," and Ande, seizing Dick's arm, hurried with him up to the Grammar School.

At the school there was bustle and excitement. The schoolroom was crowded with sixth and fifth form boys, and the interest of the lesser forms was noticed in the babbling of many tongues. Jordan, the monitor, the sage of the sixth, presided, and rapped for order, and the mass of lads crowded to their respective places. In calm, even tones, he speaks.

"We know why we are here. The captain of the Breage hurlers has just left us with our acceptance of the challenge to a hurling match. For the glory and honour of the school, and to wipe out an old score against us, we are going to play them, though they have forty stout fellows, and we are a little deficient in number. We are going to make up in training and zeal what we lack in number, and we are going to win the prize. But a great deal depends upon the captain we elect to lead us. He must be skilful, active, resourceful. In the election we must not be influenced by favouritism, but by worth. The sixth has heretofore always had the captain, but in this match I would recommend that the fifth be eligible also. If there is no objection, we will proceed to elect a captain from the sixth and fifth."

There were a few murmurs of disapproval from the sixth, but no open objections, so the election proceeded. Jordan was wise in his bringing in the fifth as eligible to the captaincy, for in that form were the best hurlers, the strongest, the most daring.

In the first ballot there was a scattering of votes, but the chief candidates were Ande and Dick, the latter on account of his experience and strength, the former on account of his activity, mental and physical.

Once more the ballots were taken and Ande won. There was a cheer, in which Dick heartily joined, for he had been urging the lads from the beginning to choose his friend.

And now began the enlisting of the team. To even up the deficiency in numbers, several of the town's expert hurlers were admitted.

The next evening, on the Bowling Green, began the practice and training. There was wrestling, running, tumbling, jumping, and kindred exercises to improve the agility and endurance of the crew. Three times a week there was a long run to Porthleven, and even to Breage and back, to improve the wind of the team, and get them more thoroughly acquainted with the ground. Dick and a few others needed constant practice to improve their quickness and activity.

The eventful day came at length, in the beautiful month of April, and forth from Helston sallied the hurling crew, followed by a hurrahing company of spectators. Halfway between the parishes the Breage men were lined up, with the gentlemen on one side to start the ball. Ande and the Breage captain consulted with the gentlemen about the rules.

"The object is to carry the ball, as soon as it is touched off, to your respective towns and hurl the same in through the open parish church doors," said Squire Vivian.

"Aye, us knaws that," said the Breage man, "but how about rules? Wrastling, passing, hurling, all to be allowed in the old style, or be there any changes?"

"All to be done in the old style unless you wish, both of you, to make modifications," said another of the gentlemen.

No modifications being advanced the captains returned to their stations and began to arrange their men. Then Ande anxiously consults with Dick and the other leaders of his side. He is once more outlining his signals. He has a small boatswain's whistle. One blast signifies close up on the ball; two sharp blasts means scatter out in the rear; three blasts, in quick succession, call the attention of the dogs to expected action on their part. Jordan nods his head gravely, as he listens to the captain, Dick shakes himself like a great mastiff, as if he would rather be engaged in active play than listen to rules. The gentlemen are sizing up the players and putting bets on either side, according to their fancy.

The heavy players, with Dick in the centre, are well up in front. There are some twenty of these, and they will make their weight and prowess felt ere the game is over. Back of them stands the captain, and back still beyond him, some ten players of lighter build, upon whose quickness and agility depend much. But who are those some two hundred yards farther back on the road to Helston? They are lighter players from the fourth and third forms, hard as pine knots, trained to perfection in fleetness of foot, and able to dodge and race like hares. They are the captain's latest addition to the efficiency of his team. They are to serve in the capacity of "dogs," as Ande calls them. They are to watch their chances; not to engage in the scrimmages where weight will tell, but to grasp the ball when opportunity comes, and speed with it to their own goal. Notice them playfully wrestling with each other, filling in the time until the game opens.

The Breage men are not thus trained or lined up. They depend more upon individual action and weight of their numbers than tactics. But now there is a movement up in front. The players are all in position.

"Are you ready?" shouts a gentleman, preparatory to casting off the ball. He is standing to one side, in front of the other gentlemen and spectators, and is holding the new hurling ball in his hand.

An affirmative answer is given from both captains, and up goes the ball in the air, midway between the two contesting parties. The next instant there is a charge of both heavy brigades for its possession as it descends. An outstretched hand catches it, and then there is a furious heap of wriggling arms and legs, and then who is it that is speeding away towards Breage, with a shout of triumph on his lips? It is the Breage captain. He is fully determined to race at that speed the two miles intervening between him and his own parish church, and he is going to hurl the ball, now in his possession, in through the Breage church door, and thus win the game. But not so fast. Two miles is quite a stretch, and there is some one on his track. Out from behind the mass of prone players leaps a form, like a horse and rider from the clouds of battle smoke. In one bound he has cleared the heap of wriggling bodies on the ground, and then, with the speed of a greyhound, he is after the Breage man. Will he overtake him? Oh, yes. If he can't, no one else can. Dick and his sub-lieutenants rest from their exertions. They are confident that the ball will be back ere long. A cheer goes up from the heavy brigade of the Helston players.

"He has him!"

"He has downed him!"

"He has the ball!"

It was true. The school captain had leaped on the back of the runner, and with a cute, wrestling trick brought him to the ground. The ball flew out of his hand and was possessed the next instant by the Helston captain, who was now returning with full speed. But now a new obstacle presents itself in the shape of the great mass of Breage players. Will he charge through them, elude them? No, there are too many for that. There are two shrill blasts on the boatswain's whistle, and along the Helston road, in the rear of their heavy brigade, scatter out the school men. They understand the signal and are ready to catch the ball. Then, just as the Breage men are upon him, out goes the hand, and with the full force of his muscular right arm, the ball is hurled full a hundred and fifty yards, over their heads, on the way to Helston.

A member of the light brigade caught it and was racing the next moment with might and main toward the town. There is a whoop and hallo among the dogs, as with their best efforts they strive to keep ahead of the runner, to be ready for an emergency throw, should he be overtaken. And now, in the rear, great Dick and his warriors of the heavy brigade get in their work, and work it is. It is no easy task for twenty or thirty fellows to stop and hinder the forty husky Breage men that are resolved to overtake the runner. Dick is in his element. He has profited by Captain Ande's training. In a twinkling he has thrown a half a dozen players to the ground, and is preparing to actively hinder others. The Breage men are swearing under their breath. But "Old Ironsides," as the boys dubbed Dick after his memorable encounter with Ande, could not handle all, and some there were that escaped around the wings and were speeding after the Helston player. It is Ande, the captain, who sees the danger.

There is a sharp blast on the whistle, the signal for the heavy brigade to close up on the ball. The light brigade are no match in a scrimmage against the great Breage men. They must have the assistance of the heavy brigade, and away go the heavy first line men, Dick lumbering along in a clumsy gallop, yet with considerable speed.

Three sharp blasts on the captain's whistle, and the dogs prepare with alertness, for action. And it is time, for a Breage man has seized the Helston runner. He promptly hurls on the ball. It is caught by one of the dogs in front, who sets off with it at full speed, accompanied by his fellows. These young striplings have not raced over moors and downs in the game of fox and hounds for nothing. See how he runs, dodging the great Breage men, who are now almost upon him. Ah, he is caught at last, but the ball is in the hands of another dog, passed to him rapidly in the time of danger. But now the light brigade are also among the dogs, and the heavy brigade is following up fast in the rear. The Breage men have been split into two factions, fifteen of them in front, among the light brigade, the others still in the rear of the heavy brigade men of the school team.

The second dog is caught, but he has time to hurl the ball to a light brigade runner near him, who as promptly hurls it on to the light runners ahead. One of the dogs seizes it and instantly diverges from the road to the fields. He realises that he has a much better chance among the hedges and fields than on the highroad with the big runners of Breage. Over the hedge go the runners of Breage. A little farther on the Helston light brigade men also leap the hedge and seek to hinder their progress. The heavy brigade follow suit. And now follows a battle royal. Helston and Breage men are close on the ball, and the Breage men are battling hard, for the town of Helston is but a scant quarter of a mile distant.

A crowd of sightseers line the road and hedges, for is not this for the glory of Helston and her grammar school? Labourers, with their shovels on their shoulders, farmers, with their produce, all are anxiously watching. They have come to see the ball brought in. They know it will be victory for the school, now it is so near.

Bravos, hurrahs, sound on all sides. The dogs and light brigade men are jubilant with expectation. The brook, or river Cober, is in sight. Could the runner make the bridge, or even dash through the flood, victory seemed sure. But no, there is a swift Breage man on his track, and bids fair to overtake him. He has him, and he hurls the ball toward town.

It was an unlucky throw, for splash!—it is in the river. Nothing daunted, a light brigade man has leaped in after it, and then a Breage man on top of him, and then others, until the little stream is choked with wrestling bodies, heaving, gasping, and the air is full of spray.

"'E 'as it! Bravo!" shouted the enthusiastic Helston spectators.

"Now, clear the way for un!" shouted a town beadle, as he made the people stand back to give the runner a clear track to their own town.

To their dismay and open-mouthed chagrin, it was the Breage captain that leaped out of the stream, ball in hand, and charging like a bull through the light brigade men, he scatters them right and left like chaff before the wind. With a whoop and hallo, the heavy brigade strive to block him, but he makes a detour, leaps another hedge, and is speeding through another field. What matter brambles or thorns, the game must be saved for Breage.

"Ah! dear! dear! us thought 'e was our man, but it 'twas t'other side," said some Helston labourers, as they gazed after the rapidly receding players.

"Ah wadn't fair, so ah wadn't," said others, disconsolately.

"Us may as well go back to market; the day is lost for Helston," said several farmers, as they turned from the scene.

"Man alive! Did 'ee see 'ow 'e runned. Ah runned like a white-head."

With many similar expressions, the crowd of spectators melted away.

But follow the runner of Breage. By leaping successive hedges he has distanced the pursuers, but he is some degree out of his course, and makes obliquely for the highway. The Helston players perceive his purpose, and gain the highway first. Here they can make faster progress. By the time the Breage captain vaults the hedge with a few of his fellows, the van of the Helston crew, their captain in the lead, is but a hundred yards in the rear. And now comes a race with fair footing. The heavy brigade is closing up fast, and the light and dogs running rapidly in the rear. He is overtaken at last, but the ball is hurled onward to Breage. A Breage runner seizes it and speeds rapidly onward. It was now Breage's chance, and they were doing their best. Ande blew his whistle valiantly for his men to close up on the ball. And close up they did, running with a will. The course again diverged from the highway and approached near the coast. He is downed at last without chance to hurl the ball. Quickly on top of him pile the other runners in the lead.

"Off of me; I've lost the ball!"

It was the Breage man underneath who had shouted, and the five or six players on top of him slowly arose, gazed at each other, then for the hurling ball, but it had disappeared as if by magic.

The players arrived one by one, panting hard with their exertion, but the ball was not found. A new ball was forthcoming for the emergency, tossed off by a ploughman, and the fierce contest renewed. All the remainder of the afternoon the battle went on, victory favouring, smiling, on one side, then on the other. The players showed the effect of their hard usage. The dogs were torn and bleeding with brambles and thorns, and of the hue of earth from their constant contact with it. The larger players were also battered and soiled, but they only played the harder. Sunset was approaching and gilded the western heavens with hues of scarlet. The ball was once more stopped within a quarter-mile of Helston. The brook, or river Cober, had been passed. The heavy brigade, the light brigade, and even the dogs, were mingled in one great heap with Breage men. Who had the ball was a mystery. A Breage runner had it when he went down. It was Dick who downed him. The Breage men were desperate, the school men determined. Tenny, Creakle, Jordan, and others resolved that the ball should not leave them thus close to victory.

But suddenly the great mound was heaved and tossed like the earth undulated by an earthquake.

"Pin 'im down! Hold un!" roared the Breage captain. "E's their man, and 'e's got the ball!"

The dogs and lighter men nimbly stepped aside to make way and assist their own runner. The Breage players made a last futile effort to hold the runner down.

"'Old un! 'Old un! damme, can none hold un!" shouted the Breage captain, in wrath at the apparent weakness of his men.

Frantically the Breage men piled on the heap, but of no avail, for there crept at that moment from the mound a great hulking form with the ball. He was on his feet the next instant and speeding away toward town, cheered on by the dogs and light brigade and spectators.

The Breage captain, with an oath of rage, hurling to right and left, like feathers, his own and the school men that impeded him, leaped upon the brawny runner's shoulders and sought to bring him to earth; but though hampered, the Helston runner strode on.

Now, like the phalanx of an army, the school men spread out, and with blocking tactics, withheld those that would follow. On went the runner, unimpeded, save by the human burden on his shoulders, the Breage captain, who in vain sought to drag him down. The ascent to old St. Michael's was reached at last, and up went the runner, striding on. It was harder progress now, but the open church door was near. Another few yards and the game was won. He is there at last. The runner's arm shoots out. The Breage captain strives in vain to catch and deter the aim, but the ball is gone, flung with unerring hand straight through the open tower door. The victory was won. Helston school had wiped out the score against Breage.

What cheers and what bravos resounded on all sides! The bells of old St. Michael's pealed out in concert with the acclamations of the people. The Breage crew were humiliated, especially the captain, but on every other countenance there was the gladness of victory won.

A feast was held in the school that night on a part of the prize money. Jordan was master of ceremonies. Around him clustered the warriors of the day, their garments, wet and soiled, now changed to clean and dry. With his arm extended for silence, he exclaimed:

"Who saved the day and brought in the ball with the Breage captain on his back? Who saved the game?"

"Dick Thomas!" was the roaring answer.

"Here's a huzza for Old Ironsides!" shouted another.

The cheer was given and the toast followed, and then they sang, "For He's a Jolly Good Fellow."

"A speech, Dick," shouted some one.

Dick arose and there was more cheering. "Well, I don't know whether old Dick Dullhead can make a speech."

Here there were protests of "No Dullhead any more, but Old Ironsides."

"Well, I want to drink a toast and I want you all to drink the same. Here's to the fellow that made Dick Dullhead a name and fellow of the past, and made me Dick Ironsides instead. Here's to the one that trained all of us so faithfully and well that each one of us had the swiftness, strength, and endurance to win the game. Here's to the fellow that so trained me that I was able to carry both ball and Breage captain to the goal. Here's to our valiant captain, Ande Trembath."

There was a storm of cheers as they responded; but where was Ande?

Though he had been missed since the regular ball had disappeared, yet every one had supposed him among the crowd somewhere. Now calls for the captain were on all sides, but he was not present.

The majority, believing that he was out, but would be in shortly, kept up the feasting, singing, and speaking.

Dick, after an inquiry here and there, went out and disappeared in the night.

CHAPTER XVII

PRUSSIA COVE. THE SMUGGLERS' BATTLE

> "Seventy years since, a native of Breage called 'Carter,' but better known, from a most remarkable personal resemblance to Frederick the Great, as the 'King of Prussia,' monopolised most of the smuggling trade of the west. He chose as the seat of his business a rocky cove two miles east of Marazion, which continues to bear the name of Prussia Cove." —*Robert Hunt, F. R. S.*

Where was the captain of the Helston hurlers?

The last time he was seen was on the cliff when the prize hurling ball disappeared. He had disengaged himself from the tumbling contestants when the ball escaped from the hand of the prostrate player, and saw it roll swiftly into a neighbouring ravine that led downward, like a funnel, to the sands below. Like a meteor he was after it and was out of view before any of his fellows noticed his absence. Down the narrow pathway he plunged with reckless steps, intent only on possessing the ball and had just grasped it, when crash! a part of the footpath gave way and down, down, down, he slipped, faster and faster. He saw the ground and pebbles fly past him upward as if endued with the power of ærial flight. He grasped futilely at the flying shrubs and boulders and then came the sickening sense of flying out into space over the cliff edge.

Then there was a shock, a sharp pain and, —all was a blank.

When he returned to consciousness, he was on a cot with a rough, kindly face bending over him.

"Drink, m'lad, it'll do 'ee good. Clunk un all down."

He felt something at his lips and mechanically swallowed it. The liquor, or whatever it was, revived him in a short time and he sat up.

"Where am I? Am I hurt?"

He slowly placed his hand to his head and felt a bandage around it.

"Ah, I remember now. I fell in the hurling game, but I still have the ball." Ande gazed around and found himself in what appeared an ordinary fisherman's cabin, rough and uncouth, but still comfortable. Fishing tackle hung here and there and there was an odd, fishy smell. A few cheap prints hung on the wall and there was a window through which a glimpse of the sea was visible.

"Why, bless 'ee, young sir, I thought 'ee would never come round, so Ah did;

Ah was holding my breath to see whether 'ee was mazed by the fall or 'ad come round, and I'm glad 'tez the latter. But, bless 'ee, what a fall! Damme, it was worse than a blow of a cutlass."

It was the voice of the attendant who had been bending over him; he was to all appearances a simple fisherman, clad in rough fisherman's clothes, and with a shaggy crop of hair that needed much the barber's art.

"And what place is this?"

"This es Prussia Cove."

A revelation dawned upon the mind of the captain of the Helston hurlers. He had often heard of Prussia Cove and its famous smuggling hero, Captain Carter, who, on account of his great resemblance to Frederick the Great, was named the "King of Prussia." Many a keg of brandy and bale of silk and lace found its way into the neighbourhood of Helston through him. Many a landlord and poor peasant profited by this illicit trade. But smuggling was not esteemed a crime by the people. The government, by imposing duties on imports, was viewed partly in the light of a tyrant and justly to be opposed and hoodwinked. The people loved the smuggler better than the king. Even rectors of the church considered smuggling an honourable occupation and the smuggler a brave citizen seeking a livelihood. The government itself was not bitterly opposed to it, at least such was its position until after the Napoleonic wars, for by smuggling a hardy race of seamen was bred that laid, primarily, England's prestige on the sea.

The lad, like many others, felt a kindly interest in them and looked for their welfare.

"And you are the King of Prussia?"

"Not 'zackly," said the man with a smile; "I'm just 'is prime minister on land."

"The watchman?"

"Aye, and I saw 'ee a-tumbling down the cliff just now and brought 'ee in. I thought 'ee was done for, sure."

"And the King?"

"Is out on the King's highway taking a walk."

"By which you mean that he is out on the sea, and is expected home to-night?"

"'Zackly so."

"I'm much obliged for your kind care; and now I feel able to stand I'll have to be travelling after the boys, for it's getting dusk."

"I think 'ee had better stay, at least until the King comes, for 'ow do I know but what 'ee favours the coastguard."

There was an anxious and cunning look in the watchman's eye.

"Well, just as you say; I'll stay."

The adventure of coming in contact with the watchman and the idea of meeting the celebrated King of Prussia harmonised with the lad's daring spirit and he was not loathe to remain.

"That's right, better so, and 'ee'll see a fine sight," nodded the watchman, relieved of much of his fears. "And now I suppose 'ee'rt hungry, leastways I be, and we'll 'ave a bit of scrowled pilchards and say biscuit."

The watchman set about the little cabin preparing the evening meal for himself and guest and became quite communicative. Exploits of the King of Prussia, his smuggling trips, his hairbreadth escapes, his great courage, all formed the burden of his tales. Ande listened and felt more and more the desire to meet this hero of the smuggling trade. The supper was ready and together watchman and hurling captain fell to with a will, the latter eating with the gusto that the hard day's game naturally brought.

In the meantime the night settled in dark and stormy. For some time there had been dark, leaden clouds pendant upon the western horizon and a low, weird murmuring, increasing to a sullen, muffled growl as of many beasts, mad with hunger in a jungle fastness. With the increasing wind the leaden mass burdening the horizon rolled steadily inward, a roof of tumbling blackness, now still, then rolling on, and fretted here and there with jagged gleams of lightning. There was a crashing roll of thunder like the peal of many guns.

"Hark!" said the watchman, raising his fork in midair; "just as I thought, a storm a-coming; so much the better for the King. A storm brings a clear coast, and yet I wish the captain was ashore, for there's going to be uncommon 'igh wind."

More thunder and more violent wind, and the waves along the shore, that generally rollicked and played with boulders and companion cliffs, began to rear their foam crowned heads and bellow back in harmony with the thunder tones above, beating the defiant rocks with a scourge of green watery thongs. The seagulls were silenced by the increasing roar and sought safety in the crannies of the cliffs. And now the full force of the storm was on, and even in the retired cove was its power felt, for the small window panes began to rattle and vibrate as if moved by a spirit of unrest.

"'Ark!" said the watchman, as he pushed back his chair and arose hurriedly. There was a sound of a solitary gun at sea, heard in the lull of the wind, and then through the window was seen the shooting course of a rocket, comet-like, athwart the stormy sky.

"Ah! The King is coming in, and 'ard pressed too. Damme, the government dogs are after 'im. Now there was a time when a man could earn a decent living without 'aving 'is lugger sent to Davy Jones' locker, but now—damme—there's another gun! Les out and give 'im a light! Bear a hand there with that lantern."

The watchman jerked an oilskin on his back and a sou'wester on his head, and casting a hasty glance at the cabin, turned and bolted through the door, closely followed by his companion.

Without the storm was not much felt in the sequestered cove, although there were occasional blasts of wind that penetrated the harbour entrance, terrific in force, and seemed to fairly take their breath on their exit. Above, streaks of twilight were still visible, and flying, scudding fragments of clouds driven on the blast. Then came sleet and hail that stung the face like needles. The lad staggered a moment almost blinded by the withering, hail-burdened wind.

"Avast a bit, lad," roared the watchman, and running back and securing an oilskin and sou'wester, "'ere, stow tha cargo in that," handing the oilskin, "and clap that on your main-top," handing the great sou'wester. Lights were stationed on both points of the narrow entrance and they returned to the beach where they awaited. There was a fascination in the great waves and breakers, hurling themselves from the gloom like vast mountains of green darkness toward the cove's entrance, where they would shiver themselves to pieces with a deep roar, augmented by its reverberating throughout the hollow length of the harbour.

Then as they watched, a higher wave than usual seemed to approach the entrance—nearer and nearer, larger and larger, until it seemed to fill the narrow cove's mouth from cliff to cliff, and threatened engulfment of cove and all in one watery grave. The wind ceased for a moment. The feeling Ande had was inexpressible.

"See!" he roared to the smuggler watchman, "see, it'll sweep the whole cove!" He was turning to bound up the cliff, when the watchman seized him.

"Avast, lad, 'tez only the lugger."

True, it was the lugger, that with shortened, bellying sails, rushed in like a thing of life, and so great was her momentum that there was danger of her beaching. The skipper was a skilful hand, and not new at his business, which he demonstrated by the quickness of his orders. A cry of command, and in a twinkling all sails were neatly folded and closely reefed. Another command, and gently the smuggler vessel drew in to the landing.

A scene of apparent confused activity instantly ensued. Kegs of brandy, bales of silk, and rich fabrics were hurled recklessly out on the sands, and numbers of hardy frames, springing from the very earth, bore them away in the darkness. There was a hollow boom beyond the entrance, and a solid shot sped in through the cove mouth, swept across the sand, and buried itself in the cliff beyond. There were oaths, loud and deep, from the husky, straining figures at work in the lugger and on shore, but they paused not. Ande's attention was concentrated upon one who seemed the chief, standing on the landing, giving orders, and, as he turned, he was startled by the intense resemblance of the countenance to a picture he had seen once of Frederick of Prussia. He was of ordinary height, a little inclined to stoutness, and had fair hair, and blue eyes that flashed under the light of the flaming torches; his regular, delicate features had great power of expression. With an oath, he saw Ande, and grasped him by the shoulder with a grip of steel.

"Who art thou, lad?"

The explanation of his supper companion, the watchman, was forthcoming, and with a word of apology the captain turned to other and more pressing affairs.

Again came the booming sound at sea,—this time closer—and another shot sped through the entrance. The revenue cutter was nearing the cove-mouth, but the smugglers were prepared for a grim resistance. Pikes and cutlasses were gleaming on all sides.

"Zounds!" muttered Captain Carter, "they'll be upon us in another moment, and that before we 'ave time to store the cargo. Up aloft, there, Jack, on the headland, and see if you can't beat off the dogs. Open on them with solid ball," he roared, after the watchman, who was already climbing the ascent. Ande, totally forgetting his injuries in the excitement, sped up after him.

Up, up, up, following the flickering light of the watchman's lantern, he went. And now the wind became more violent, the higher the ascent, until near the top he was scarcely able to stand.

"Larboard, port your helm, there!" shouted the voice of Jack, and he was seized by that worthy and dragged into a less exposed place. "No man could stand in a gale like this any further up," shouted Jack in his ear. Another step or two, and a sequestered place was reached, where were stationed two pieces of ancient ordnance, and Jack and Ande were speedily loading, and none too soon, for down below, the cutter's lights were seen a short distance from the entrance.

There was a flash and then a roar, and the ball was on its mission.

"Too high. Better luck next time. But I swear that I thought that 'ould 'a' gone amidships. I do think old Nick must a-turned un aside, I do."

"It's had some effect, for they are beating off," answered Ande.

"That's to get a shot at we. They're luffing. But we'll tap them first, I say. 'Ere, let's give 'em another."

Again was the flash and roar from the cliff, and Jack fairly chuckled, as one of the lanterns was snuffed out.

"Took a part of 'er taffrail that time."

But now the cutter was ready for action, and boom went one of her guns, and the next moment a ball struck the cliff below them, splintering the rock into fragments. Then again the cliff guns spoke, answered once more by the cutter's, and soon the action became general. The roar of the cliff guns and the revenue cutter's mingled with the howling blast, and made the night hideous with noise. Though so far above the sea, yet the spray of crashing breakers frequently swept over them as they worked the cliff guns, and it and the occasional flying sleet, at times, so dampened the powder that the guns had to be recharged.

Ande was in his element. Here was a real battle, and he paused not to think that he was firing upon a government boat. The wild soldier blood of his ancestors was coursing through his veins like molten fire. He had cast aside the sou'wester hat, as obstructing his vision, and truly he looked a martial figure with his bandaged head and flowing locks swept by the blast.

In the midst of the detonating roar, a figure bounded from the gloom behind them. Jack, with a sulphurous oath, swung his cutlass on high, thinking that some revenue men had landed and were charging, but Ande grasped the blade before it could descend. Although he cut his own hand badly in the act, yet he saved the stranger's life.

"Dick!"

"Ande!"

It was Dick, who, searching in the locality for his friend, was attracted by the noise of battle. He asked no questions, but stolidly set to work to assist in charging and firing the guns. At length the cutter's guns were fairly silenced; she had been beaten off and her lights were seen fainter and fainter in her hasty retreat out to sea.

"Now, stand by, men; one more shot to let them remember Captain Carter and Prussia Cove."

It was the gunner, Jack, who spoke, as he finished aiming the last piece. There was another flash, and away bounded the iron messenger. A moment and one of the lights of the distant cutter was quenched, as if the bay had engulfed it.

"As I'm a sinner, ef that didn't go straight through their cabin winders. And now, les down below and see 'ow fares the captain and the cargo."

They descended and found the King of Prussia in excellent humour. The whole cargo had been safely landed and concealed in numerous secret places, and even the lugger had mysteriously disappeared.

"And let's shake hands with our new comrades of the night," said the captain, as he grasped the hands of Ande and Dick. "You 'ave shown us your good will to-night, and ye had better now turn in and get a bit of rest afore morning, when, if ye are so minded, you can take the way back to Helston. But, mind 'ee, my lads, no word of to-night's affair."

Both accepted the generous invitation of Captain Carter, and weary with the double exertion of a hurling game and the smugglers' battle, they soon lost themselves in the land of dreams.

On the morrow they were awakened by voices in angry altercation without. The cutter had returned, but slightly damaged, and had landed a force in the cove capable of sweeping all opposition. But there was no opposition, nothing incriminating being found. Even the very guns on the cliff had disappeared, and the marks of numerous feet on the shore were partly obliterated by the tide. The lads, cautiously peering out from the small window, saw the King of Prussia angrily expostulating with the captain of the cutter. Prussia was clad in an ordinary fisherman's garb, and seemed what he professed to be by those garments.

"Damme," he was saying, "'tez a downright shame that my family and I, peaceful folks, have to 'ave our slumbers disturbed by the banging of your practice guns all night. Why doan't 'ee practice out at sea?"

The captain of the cutter was nonplussed, apologised slightly, and reëmbarked with his crew. Carter came into the cabin with a merry twinkle in his eye. The lads were convulsed with laughter.

"And now," said the captain, "I suppose it is time for 'ee to be going," and he pressed into their hands a small package, which later investigation proved to be a jar of currant wine. On the highway, Ande told Dick of his accident and his possession of the first hurling ball.

When they arrived at the Grammar School, they were notified to appear before the head. Mr. Trewan was seated at his desk, and looked at the two culprits very gravely, for to be absent all night was a serious offence. Then the grave look gave place to one of anxious concern, as Ande's bandaged head and hand caught his vision. Explanations were made, the fall over the cliff, the period of unconsciousness, and Dick's search the greater part of the night for his friend. The battle of the smugglers was not touched, as they deemed that treachery to their smuggler friends.

Mr. Trewan seemed touched by the accident, and the devotion of Dick, and let them both off without even a reprimand.

That night there was another festive scene, but in the fifth form dormitory instead of in the dining hall, and in it the currant wine formed a prominent part.

CHAPTER XVIII

THE DUCK CAVE ADVENTURE

"Ande, cocoa is pretty dry with such stuff."

Dick's great head arose from the hamper package which he was examining, and he flourished in one hand a roasted chicken. The hamper was one he had received that very day from home. They had ordered it brought into their study room, and, miracle to relate, it was done without the knowledge of monitors or small boys.

"What do you propose?" said Ande, as he, too, began investigation. Dick scratched his head dubiously and then his face brightened.

"Eggs."

"Old Ironsides is gone daft. Where does your majesty expect to get eggs, and if ye do get them, what are we going to do with them? Do ye think we are going to be egg-sucking weasels?"

Dick grinned, and, as he tried to set a dramatic attitude, flourished his arm, "We'll set forth the vessels of silver and gold— —"

"Avast, there, my lad," said Ande, imitating the tones of smuggler Jack.

"And 'ave a-blooming— —"

"Cough it out, my elephantine infant."

"Belshassar's feast. I have an idea."

"Whisper it not in Gath, publish it not in Ascalon. An idea," chuckling, "from an egg-regious Lizard philosopher."

"Egg-nogg," continued Dick, grinning.

"The very thing," said Ande, assuming a more sober tone, "but where?"

"We must first get outside of town," said Dick, soberly.

"No stealing?"

"No stealing."

"'Pon honour?"

"'Pon honour."

Forth they started, cautiously slipping downstairs and out into the street, where both darted away at a rapid pace. On the highroad that led to the little town of Prospidnic, the foremost paused, and puffing like an engine the latter caught up to him.

"Ande, remember the Truro champion footrace?"

Ande nodded.

"Well, I believe 'ee could beat the champion; you went so fast I nigh lost sight of you."

"Now, what's your plan?"

Dick paused a moment to gain his breath, and then spoke.

"Do ye remember the cave near the Red River? Well, the ducks from all around gather there. It's public property, being on the free downs. Eggs used to be there in plenty, but some snivelling squire's steward put a door on it and now tries to bag the industry."

"Art sure the squire didn't buy the section?"

"Well, if he 'as, the ducks that gather there are not his, and 'e 'asn't a mortgage on the eggs of futurity infinitum. The squire's steward is the robber of public rights and human freedom, and — —"

"Public eggs," said Ande. "Down with the tyrant, — *sic semper tyrannis* — and up with the eggs."

Onward they pressed at a dog-trot. It was evening and getting dusk when they reached the neighbourhood.

"You go in, Dick, and I'll mount watchman."

The door was the contrivance of a genius, for, while it was designed to hold out boys and men, yet a small aperture beneath favored the entrance of ducks and other smaller creatures. The cave was in the side of a hill near the Red River stream, and opened on the roadway.

"I'll go in as soon as I get un open," says Dick, as he wrenched at the latch. By dint of tugging and pulling, the hasp was loosened, and in went Dick, crawling on his hands and knees, the height of the tunnel not permitting him to walk upright.

"Hast found any?"

"No, steward must 'ave been here. 'Tis a most beastly place and nigh turns one's stomach," muttered Dick from the interior.

There was the sound of a horse's tread in the distance, and the sound of whistling approaching. Fearing that the open door would excite suspicion, Ande gently closed it, and the hasp being a spring affair, fell into place. Then, stealing cautiously behind a neighbouring hedge, he awaited the passing of the traveller.

Dick, having made certain and wealthy discoveries in the egg line, his bag full and certain pockets bulged to their utmost, was, in the meantime, cautiously returning to the exit, where, before he knew it, he had bumped with the force of a battering ram against the closed door. It would not yield to any of his efforts, and then, thinking Ande was joking him, he cried out in impatient voice, "Lemme out,

Ande, do, I got eggs a-plenty." Receiving no answer, he began butting afresh, and roared louder.

Now the horseman had approached and heard the infernal roaring and racket that seemed to come from the very bowels of the earth. He was a simple, unsophisticated countryman, with an appetite for ale and a passion for thievery that was well known to the community. Greggs, as he was surnamed, was not noted for his personal courage, and the loneliness of the place, even in daylight, the gloom of the overshadowing trees, and the dusk of twilight, was not calculated to make or add any more heroism to his nature. Within his breast, as within all countrymen of the time, and even still, in many districts, there had constantly been drilled the old beliefs in witches, fairies, giants, goblins, and a host of other superstitions with which Cornwall has been replete for ages. It was no wonder, then, that when he came within the border of the shadow, etched darkly by the trees, he whistled louder, and finally burst into singing a hymn tune, to let all wandering spirits realise that he was a godly fellow, kicking his steed all the while to hasten its ambling pace.

"Got eggs—lemme out—Ande—lemme out!"

The horse stood stock still, refusing to budge an inch forward, and trembling in great terror. In vain the fearful man began to belabour and kick his leathery sides; the animal would not go forward, but began to uneasily sidle around and around. The butting and bellowing of Dick still continued, with little intermission. Greggs ceased singing, the great drops of perspiration stood out in beads on his face, and with another frantic effort he kicked his horse's sides in an agony of fear. Then, as the butting was renewed with greater force, a cry came from Greggs's lips:

"Oh, Mr. Devil, 'ave mercy 'pon me!"

Dick was indefatigable in his butting and bellowing, but even his patience began to give way and he began to swear in a mild way.

"Damme, Ande, come take eggs!"

Each word was punctuated by a savage butt from Dick's great head on the door.

"Oh, no, Mr. Devil,—not that—Greggs done no 'arm," mistaking Dick's cry for the devil's warning "Damnation to Greggs."

Again came the stifled underground roar, coming forth with a muffled: "Take—(crash)—eggs—(crash)—damme—(crash)"—and a word beginning with h.

"Mercy, Mr. Devil, doan't 'ee take Greggs there. Ah, why did I leave the hangel tavern!"

"Damnation!"

"No, no, Mr. Devil."

"A beastly trick," roared Dick, still butting away.

"Aye, kind sir, I'm guilty of many beastly tricks."

"Ande, you deceiving cad."

"Yes, I confess I 'ave deceived dad."

"Here I am—beating m'head."

"Aye, I beat un on the 'ead, too," moaned Greggs.

"Like a thieving robber."

"Yes, Mr. Devil, I robbed un, but 'ave mercy. I promise to take un all back," groaned Greggs, in terror, still kicking his steed, that shied around and around.

"Come, take the bag, you wretched cad."　　．

"Aye, I promise; I'll take the bag back to dad."

"It's full," roared Dick.

"No, no, it was honly 'alf full."

"Zounds!" swore Dick.

"Pounds! No 'e wadn't; they were mostly shillings."

"Let me out!"

"No! Doan't 'ee come out. I promise, Mr. Devil—Oh!—--"

The last remark of Greggs gave place to a shriek of agonised fear. The door, under repeated blows of Dick, gave way, and out he rolled with his bag of eggs, looking in the darkness like a hideous monster come up from the deep. The horse, in mad terror, wheeled and galloped back to town; Greggs, praying and howling like a madman, hugging his horse's neck, let fall his basket in the way. Ande was rolling in the grass beyond the hedge, choking with laughter.

Dick was a picture of wrath, as he stood sputtering by the road-side. His clothes were foul, the natural result of crawling into a duck cave, and he was apparently sick at the stomach.

"What's wrong, Dick?"

"A beastly trick,—phew—ah, egg—phew—ah, in mouth,—phew—ah—addled—broke."

Ande roared and roared with shrieking laughter. Dick had filled the bag and his pockets, and finding one extra one, had placed it in his mouth for safe keeping, just before the latch gave way.

"Well," said Ande, "they aren't all broke, and the most must be good."

Dick, at first was very much incensed, but Ande, while he helped to clean him up at the Red River, explained how he had closed the door to avert suspicion. Dick was mollified when the description of Greggs's terrors was related, and laughed a faint laugh that partly brought back his good humour.

It appeared that Greggs had ill-treated his poor old father, and had robbed him of some of his savings. Taking warning from the supposed admonition of his

Satanic majesty, he afterward treated his father with the greatest consideration, refunding the shillings he had stolen. Nothing, however, could induce him to pass that way again, and the story getting wind and becoming much exaggerated, few would trust themselves in that locality after dusk.

"Whew! Look here, Dick." Ande picked up the basket and drew from it a small bottle of rye.

"The very thing we need," gasped Dick, "the egg-nog shall become punch."

"I don't know, Dick. You see, if we take it, it'll be stealing. The school rules are against it, and no matter how sparingly and temperately a fellow uses it no allowance is made."

"Well, if we give it back to Greggs, it'll do 'im more harm than it will us; then, we can send Greggs the cost of it, so it won't be stealing, and as to school rules, why, we are breaking school rules now by being away," said Dick, reassuringly.

"'Twon't do, Dick; the breaking of one law doesn't justify the breaking of another. We'll let it behind."

"Very well," said Dick, but at the same moment, concealed by the dusk of the evening, he slipped the flask into his pocket.

"You'll 'ave to 'cave' about getting the eggs in," said Ande, as they trotted along home, back to Helston.

"That's what's worrying me," said Dick.

"I have it," said Ande, and the plan seemed so feasible that he resumed his old bantering tone. "Dick, old lad, congratulate your friend on being a man of infinite resources. I have a plan, my Ajax of egg-hunting renown and Lucifer reputation."

"Huh," growled Dick, "we're getting near town."

"A rope—the hamper rope," said Ande; "that beast, Creakle, will be on guard within, or Tenny. I go in empty-handed,—see—you stay out below the study window, in the dark angle; I let down the rope,—presto—up come the eggs. You come in empty-handed,—see?" and Ande gave Dick a nudge.

Dick brightened up perceptibly.

"But 'ow to get you in with that pungent, ducky aroma, without exciting the blatant curiosity of Creakle, or the sharp smellers of Sherwood—um—das ist die frage. Whew! What a beastly odour."

Dick looked worried and down-hearted.

"But cheer up, Dick, you can't help it, and we'll get you in some how, never fear. The plan is sure to work."

The plan did work like a charm, and soon they were in the comfortable study, Dick clothed in clean garments, and the steaming egg-nogg and eatables before them. The evening's adventure, the terror of Greggs, the chicken, and other viands, made the evening pass pleasantly by. During the close of the feast, Tenny rapped, but was not let in.

"Now Creakle will be next," said Ande, "and we can't keep a monitor out. Away with the things!"

The things were hurriedly placed away, the Virgils opened, and with lexicons in hand, they seemed busily and studiously engaged when steps were heard advancing quickly along the corridor. The door was swung open, it being unbarred, and in stalked Sherwood and Creakle. The latter had a cunning twinkle in his eye; the former with grave, severe countenance.

"Gentlemen," began Sherwood, in stern voice, but he went no further. Ande looked up with a mild, reproving eye.

"I believe no student is to be disturbed in the evening study hour, except upon probable cause of misdemeanour; I believe that is an unwritten law."

"Quite right, gentlemen, excuse me," and Master Sherwood backed out, followed by Creakle. Humiliation is a poor word to express the feelings of the under-master. Creakle could be heard expostulating with him in the corridor.

"I saw them both, on the run out of town, and saw them enter on their return, and there was a smell of ducks, sir, on Mr. Thomas's clothes."

"Nonsense," said Master Sherwood, "how should it not be manifest to me also?" Sherwood had not thought of the possibility of Thomas changing his clothes.

Creakle still protested.

"Absurd! Why, sir, do you know you are accusing the head of the fifth?" said Master Sherwood, exasperated. "Do you know your misplaced zeal has involved me in censure that was just, and a rebuke from fifth form boys that was, to say the least, humiliating? You, sir, should have known better. There must have been an upheaval of latent stupidity within you to thus bring disgrace upon both master and school. Sir, how will the public esteem our reputation when they are informed that master and monitor are banded together to disturb the study hours, and falsely accuse honourable students."

"I thought," began Creakle, humbly.

"You thought, sir; what right had you to think? You must know before recklessly accusing honourable students and bringing disgrace, not on me alone, but on the head."

Master Sherwood, in high dudgeon, went to his study, and Creakle, crestfallen, retired to the form room, where he had charge over the smaller form study hours.

"Now," said Dick, "that spying cad must be brought down to give him some sparks of honour."

"What's the plan?"

Dick, for the first time, refused to divulge to his chum his course, but divesting himself of his shoes cautiously slipped down to the cloakroom below.

That night, as Creakle was donning his gown, which he always left in the cloakroom, there arose a fearful uproar in the corridor above. Hastening upstairs with full speed, he tripped over an invisible something and fell with a crash to the floor. Instantly doors opened, lights appeared, and a confused sound of many voices, and in the midst of all, along stalked Master Sherwood.

"What is the meaning of this, Creakle?" he asked of that worthy, who was still on the floor, dazed with his fall.

"I fell, sir."

"You did, and pray why?" with biting sarcasm.

Just then he smelt the fumes of rye on the garb of the miserable Creakle, and his face grew dark with severity.

"You have been drinking, sir?"

"I have not," stammered the monitor.

"Don't give me the lie, sir; you are reeking with the fumes of an ale-house. Ugh! you putrescent miscreant! This is a case for the head. You will appear before him to-morrow. Such a disgrace! In what light will the public view this scandalous demoralisation? Outra geous, sir! This is the second offence to-night. I thought you were inebriated,—intoxicated—in short, what the vulgar tongue calls drunk, when you brought me a silly, drivelling tale of a misdemeanour of two honourable students, and now you make it evident by staggering around, sprawling, and destroying the peace and sobriety of the school!"

"I—I—I am not drunk."

"I call you all to witness the state of filthy inebriety of this fellow," said Sherwood, with cold dignity.

"What do you say, sir?" said the tutor to Dick.

"He smells horrid, sir," said that worthy.

"Ah! You are all witnesses," said Sherwood, and then, turning to the dejected Creakle, "in with you to your study, and relieve honourable men from the abhorrent, filthy odours that assail decent olfactory organs."

Mr. Sherwood retired in dignified silence, and Creakle slunk into his study.

"Dick, what is the moral?" said Ande, after they had reëntered their study.

"The revenge of diabolical Ajax?"

"No, the moral is this: the man who takes delight in spying on others and revelling in their disgrace, even though he be a monitor, shall be beaten with his own stick."

CHAPTER XIX

CREAKLE'S REVENGE

"It's true; I heard it myself when I was over that way this last week," said Creakle, nodding his head affirmatively.

"Who was it told you?" said Tenny.

"A fellow called Sloan, a big, honest sort of a fellow in the employ of the Lanyans. He's a sort of an understrapper to young Master Richard, who will be graduated soon from Eton College."

"What did he say?"

"That Trembath's father was a traitor to the government; that he turned traitor in the late war with America, leastways he has not shown his face hereabouts since the war. Some think he is dead, and others think he was a traitor, and daren't show his face in England, but is living in exile somewhere in America. Sloan—I think his first name is Bob—told me himself that Richard and his father, Sir James, both believe that he was a traitor."

"No proofs but their thoughts," said Tenny, doubtfully.

"Well, it is the current belief of the whole neighbourhood, and then, there is strong proof of his grandfather being a traitor. There is no doubt about that at all. Bob told me that it was through the patriotism of Richard's grandfather that the matter was called to the attention of Newcastle, and Trembath Manor was confiscated."

"How? What was the treason?"

"Well, he was a soldier in the war of England against France, in the colonies. He was in Braddock's defeat, and after that battle he turned for the French. He was with them for upwards of a year or so, and no one knows what harm he did during that time. They say he consorted with the French of Quebec, was a spy in their employ, and was afterwards raised to some rank as an officer."

"A traitor to his own land and his own people!" exclaimed Tenny.

"Yes, and that isn't all. They say he became as bloody a savage as the Indians. I suppose he received a good reward from the French. Some say he was an aide of Montcalm."

"And how was he found out?"

"He was shot in the van of a fight between Armstrong's troops and the French.

They found his body and recognised it by letters from England. He had on a French officer's uniform and a commission in the French army in his pocket. They brought him home, and Sir Richard Lanyan brought the facts to the knowledge of the government, and the Trembath home was confiscated, and they were driven out. It served them right, I say."

"That it did," asserted Tenny.

"And here's one of the family, this Ande, that's lord ing it over us. I believe it was he that soaked my gown in that beastly rye and got me in such a scrape with the head."

Tenny smiled, for he had no love for Creakle, except as a tool.

"It was no laughing matter, I can tell you. The head nearly fired me," said Creakle, a little sullenly.

"Come, come, no offence. I have as much reason to dislike Trembath as you have. Didn't he sneak into being head of the fifth through meanness, getting up and reciting, when all the rest of the fellows had agreed to refuse to recite. He has been there ever since, but he never would have got there if he hadn't turned traitor to his form, like his father and grandfather to the government. Blood will tell."

"And, I say, we ought to let the fellows know, and pull him down a peg or two. Let him know his place among the sons of honourable Englishmen. He ought to be sent to Coventry, I say."

"Come over here and we'll talk it over with one or two of the fellows," said Tenny.

A little coterie of fellows of the fifth form were soon assembled around Tenny and Creakle, on the Bowling Green, and their nodding heads and colloquy portended mischief to the head of the fifth. Tenny had never forgotten the way in which he was shouldered out of the headship of the fifth form, and Creakle was burning with more hate since his late disgrace, which he blamed on Ande. Now, had it depended upon Creakle alone, nothing would have come of the disclosure of the stain upon Ande's name, but when Tenny took up the matter it was eagerly listened to. The latter portrayed in indignant tones the treachery of Ande's family to the government. Should they consort with him, after this knowledge? It was all well enough, as long as they did not know the family disgrace. But, now they knew, they ought to show their abhorrence of such conduct.

He ought to be expelled from the school, but they couldn't do that, but they could, at least, debar him from fellowship and keep him from the leadership in the form that he had always maintained. The son and grandson of a traitor shall not lead us in our sports. He was a traitor at heart, like his people before him, for had he not gained the headship of the form through an act of treason to his fellows, and his remarks of the injustice of the king also bore testimony. Such was the line of Tenny's sophistry, in which Creakle was a second.

One or two of the form demurred, with the remark that it was hard for a son to be villified on account of the errors of his fathers.

"I'll prove the contrary from the Bible," said Tenny. "Aren't the Jews to-day despised, and righteously, for their treason to their king, and doesn't the Bible say that the sins of the fathers shall be visited upon the children?"

"THEY SAY YOU ARE THE SON OF A TRAITOR"

The demurrers were overborne by Tenny's reasoning. Dick, being so close a friend of Ande, was not taken into the conference, but he was not so slow in taking in the cold demeanour of the students to Ande, and even to him self, in a milder degree. Henceforth there were no games in which Ande participated. If he sought entrance to a game, the game was instantly adjourned, and he found himself left more and more to himself. He, as well as Dick, was at a loss to know the reason of the altered manner of treatment. The revelation came to Dick.

He was going to enter a game of hurling on the Bowling Green, when Creakle objected.

"Why?" said Dick, in amazement.

"Because you are the friend of the son of a traitor. His father and his grandfather were traitors to the government, and he's a traitor himself," sneered Creakle.

"Who?"

"The Dane," said Creakle, with another sneer. "All the fellows have refused to have anything to do with him. He's been sent to Coventry. He's a traitor's son, and the blot of treason hangs to his name."

"It's a lie," said Dick, hotly; "he's not a traitor's son," and with a back-handed slap of his hand, he sent Creakle reeling.

"It's true," said Tenny, as he edged in among the other lads. "All the lads of his home place will tell you the same thing, and you'll be treated the same way as we are treating him, if you don't cut him."

Dick, scarcely believing his ears, hurried off to his friend, Ande, bursting into the study with a bound.

"Do ye know why the fellows have cut you and me?"

"No."

"Why, they say you are the son of a traitor. That your father and grandfather were traitors to the government. Creakle said so, and I give him a back-handed slap that sent him some feet. It was Creakle who told me."

"The contemptible dog!" exclaimed Ande, with a flash of the eye. "It's not true, though the circumstances look the other way. They were both honourable men."

"You needn't tell me," said Dick. "I believe if your father and grandfather were like you, there couldn't be a bit of treason in them. I told Creakle it was a lie, and then Tenny spoke up and said that it was true, and that if I didn't cut you the same as the rest of them are doing, they would cut me. They have sent us to Coventry."

"Dick, you 'ave been a good friend to me, and you did right in treating Creakle as you did, for I should have done the same. The old blot that drove me from my native village will drive me from here as well. It is the curse that has been on our family since my grandfather's death, but you have no hand in this. You had better cut me, or they will make your life here as unbearable as mine. I'll move into a study of my own. It is for your own interest that I am looking."

"Stuff! Let them send me to Coventry if they will. I don't believe there is any truth in the rumour, and we don't part like that. Didn't you save my life in the smugglers' battle, and I'm going to stick to you through all this Coventry business. Put it there," and Dick stretched his great hand across the study table and grasped the hand of Ande and shook it warmly. There was a grateful look in the latter's eyes.

"You have done too many things for me, to turn in with a rabble like that. You have changed old Dullhead into a brighter man, and made him Old Ironsides, and we'll let them know that Old Ironsides is going to stick to you. Why, Ande, you and I could clean out the whole crew in a personal fight on the Bowling Green, and—zounds! I'd like to do it."

"And they would gain their desires. We'd be expelled."

"Never thought of that."

"It's what would happen, though."

There was silence in the study for the space of half an hour, during which they laboured on the coming lessons. Then, it was Dick, who broke the silence.

"How did it happen that the idea of treason got out. I don't believe it, but I'm a bit curious."

"It's a long story, but I'll tell you some day, Dick, and let you see some documents that I have still in my possession. There's the gong."

A deep sound of a gong, indicating the dinner hour in the dining-room below, broke the silence, and they hurried forth to its summons.

After the discovery of Dick, and the encounter with Creakle, neither he nor Ande sought the games of the others. If they needed recreation, they took it in long walks along the sea-coast or in the country. The enmity of Creakle and Tenny was shown in many petty ways. They were not content with sending to Cov entry alone. Once, on their return, they found a placard on their study door with the sentence of, "The Home of Treason," written on it, but this did not stir the wrath of Ande as much as a later placard, a rude sketch of a soldier with red hair, hands bound, eyes blindfolded, and before him a file of soldiers with weapons presented, ready to fire, and near at hand a grave and a coffin. With a burst of passion, he tore it down and ground it under his heel.

"And how is my knight progressing in the tournament of the schools?"

It was in the gardens of Trembath Manor, and it was Mistress Alice who was speaking. She was clad in light spring garb that wonderfully set off her trim figure and brought out into greater prominence the wavy darkness of her hair, and depth of her eyes, that seemed deeper and brighter under the mellow sunlight without. She was standing near one of her favourite rose-beds, and near her was the tall form of Ande Trembath, the few months at school adding new dignity and age to his features. He was glad to be there, near her, and to be called "her knight," as she had called him on the last Christmas eve. He was home on a short vacation, and it seemed wonderfully pleasant to be with her in the gardens of old Trembath, especially after the dreary atmosphere of the school, rendered more dreary and wretched by the uncharitable spirit of his fellows of the fifth; to watch the dark eyes kindling and rekindling at some jest, and then the sober shadow at the recital of the escapage of the smugglers. He told her all, the merry adventure at the duck cave, the hurling game, and then the sending to Coventry. Yes, this was going to be his last year at the school. The curse of treason had followed him, and even his friend, Dick, was involved in the petty spirit of malice of the students. He was discouraged, and she knew it. His face betokened it as he related the sending to Coventry.

"Do you know that my knight has forgotten some of his pledges made last Christmas eve?" she said, and her eyes flashed once more, back from the sombreness brought into them by the Coventry recital.

"How?"

"I said that the knight that I should admire would not despair at a few difficulties, and my knight said that he would not."

"Neither am I," doubtfully.

"Your very tone indicates the contrary."

"You think it best to remain and stand all taunts and malice?"

"Assuredly; and will not that be the very best way to prepare yourself for the future battles. Is it brave to run away from a foe?"

There was a flush on the face of the youth.

"I see you are right. I shall stay and fight it out, and they will see who grows tired of the Coventry business first. You give me the same advice as Parson Trant. He said stand firm, and stick to the school."

"Parson Trant is generally right."

"And so are you."

"Of course, in this case, I am right, but at times, I suppose, I am wrong."

"For instance?"

"Well, my father has broached a plan that lies close to his heart. You know the Lanyan estate lies close to ours, and he is anxious for me to be settled in life soon."

A cold, icy hand seemed to clutch his heart and hold it in a vice-like grip. The blood forsook his features, for a moment, as he listened.

"And he?" interrogatively.

"And he was thinking how well the two would go together, and that Lady Alice would not sound so bad. Then it would place our family among the highest in the county. I thought at first that it was all foolishness, but I suppose he is right and I am wrong."

"No, no, no, you are right. You must not sacrifice yourself to a whim."

"No, I am wrong," pensively.

"You are right. It must not be," and then at the remembrance of Master Richard and Sir James, he flushed an angry hue and clenched his fists tightly.

"Must not be?" archly.

"Aye, it shall not be."

"Why?"

"Because I say it shall not be."

"Indeed, since when have I had a new master, or a master at all, for that matter?"

There was a rebellious tone in her voice, and a quick, tumultuous beating of her heart. To be told she should not do this or that was something new to her, the mistress of the Manor, and yet, his tone, his manner of speaking, that masterful way of asserting himself—she liked him better for it.

"I say it shall not be," doggedly.

"And why?"

"Because—because—because—I am your knight," he said, desperately, "and I cannot see any harm come to you, and your happiness wrecked by marrying such. If you only knew the Lanyans as I know them."

"Perhaps my happiness would not be wrecked."

"Ah, but it shall not be. It must not be."

"You have given me no reason why it should not. Should not a child obey her father?"

Her eyes were glowing mischievously.

"Alice, Alice, if you will not listen to reason, it is because I say so, and I—I—I—love you. Oh! Alice, I have wanted to tell you so long—but the stain of treason—but give me at least hope that if the stain be removed—and it shall—that I shall not love you in vain."

The hue of Mistress Alice's cheeks rivalled her own roses. She fought down the exultant, happy feeling within, and strove to be her former self; yes, even strove to be angry, but what woman is angry when told that she is loved.

"There is father. Calm yourself, or he will notice you."

Coming over the green terrace was the stout frame of old Squire Vivian, most unwelcome sight at this hour, at least to Ande. His question was doomed to remain unanswered. The squire greeted him in his bluff, cheery manner, asked him of the school and his progress. The excellent reports he had received from Master Trewan had inclined him a little more favourably to his *protégé*. Taking advantage of the presence of her father, Mistress Alice slipped away and hid herself in the privacy of her own rooms.

CHAPTER XX

EXAMINATIONS—ADRIFT ON THE DEEP

Examinations were coming on apace. The end of the half was near. Prizes had been established by gentlemen of the neighbourhood, and the diligent ones were striving for them with assiduous application to study. The sports of the students had little attraction for Ande now. Even had he not been sent to Coventry, he would have avoided them for the extra chance it gave him for work. He was determined to win the prize for general scholarship in the fifth. There were others working for the same goal, among them, Tenny, the former head. Tenny's ambition was of a double nature. Not only must he win the general prize, but also the silver medal for the best essay. The days sped rapidly by, and soon came the day of examination. The essays had been handed in to a special committee, some time previous, under various nom-de-plumes.

Most of the examinations were oral, and occupied some time. Generally, the master would put the questions, but at times one of the visiting gentlemen would throw in a question bearing on the special subject under consideration.

The contest of general scholarship in the fifth was manifestly between two students,—the old and the new head, and even after it was over, none could prophesy how the judges would decide. The decision came, after a brief pause and consultation.

The Reverend Mr. Trewan arose, and after clearing his throat several times began by complimenting the students.

"I am pleased to find the excellent form in which most of our scholars have passed this examination. The marks are far above the average of the half. I am glad to state that the whole form will enter the sixth at the next half without a single exception."

There was a little cheer from the mass of students.

"In reference to the prize for the general scholarship, there are two between which there has been a close contest. For quite a time one was in the forerank and the other close behind. Then the marks were even. Then the second forged ahead. Master Tenny," and the head paused to clear his throat, while Tenny flushed with gratification, "your marks have been admirable; they were far ahead of your average during the year. For quite a time you were ahead, then even with another, Master Trembath, then Master Trembath gained first place. The prize goes to him, however, who has the highest average of the whole examination, and I, therefore, declare Master Trembath the winner by four points; and the committee has given Master Tenny the highest honourable mention."

The master paused and extended twenty pounds to Ande, the prize for general scholarship. Dick was the first to congratulate him, and was followed by one or two others, notwithstanding the decree of Coventry. Tenny maintained his silence in bitter chagrin. He had hopes of the essay prize, however, the chairman of which committee now arose to report.

"We find," he said, after a little preliminary speech, "that six of the essays were most laudable, but out of them two were selected for their excellence—one on account of the beauty of the language, the other on account of its vivid realism and striking, rhetorical figures. The one written by Hector is admirable in wording and has many fine points, but lacks the realism and subject matter and thought of the other. We have decided that the silver medal goes to him who has adopted the certainly inappropriate and inapplicable nom-de-plume of Asinus Cornubiensus."

There was a pause, and the students at length, realising the meaning of the Latin nom-de-plume, which was the "Ass, or Donkey of Cornwall," burst into a roar of laughter.

"Certainly," resumed the gentleman, "this Asinus Cornubiensus has demonstrated a grasp of thought, power of language, and vivid description that belies his humble name, and renders him worthy of the prize. Stand up, Asinus Cornubiensus, and receive the silver medal."

Dick stood up, much confused, and received the prize. There was a cheer. Even Ande was astonished, and greeted his old friend with more respect. It is needless to say that Hector was Tenny, who was bub bling over with rage and mortification, to think that he was not only beaten in the general prize but also in the essay, and in the latter case by one whom he had always considered a stupid dunce, the worst scholar in the form.

The rest of the day was dedicated to the examinations of the sixth and the distribution of prizes in that form. Our two prize winners of the fifth wended their way out from the school and hied away from the town to one of their accustomed haunts, near the coast, high up on the cliffs. Here, throwing themselves down on the long grass, they watched, for the time, the active sea-birds and the flitting sails far out on the channel. At length, turning from the contemplation of these, Ande addressed his friend.

"Dick, what led you to choose such a queer nom-de-plume?" and he smiled.

"Well, I was always considered a dull'ead and never thinking I'd get the medal, I put down the name in a little disgust, thinking it to be the most appropriate one."

"What was the subject?"

"You can't guess?"

"No."

"Well, it was on that hurling game between Breage and our fellows, and I just played the game over again in imagination when I was writing."

"That accounts for its realism, no doubt."

"Did 'ee notice Tenny after the general prize was given?"

"No."

"His face was as wisht[7] as a herring."

"No doubt. I noticed him after the silver medal was given and he was green around the eyes."

"Serves him right," said Dick, "for sending us to Coventry on account of that tale of Creakle about your father and grandfather."

There was silence for a moment, unbroken save by the breaking of the waves on the beach beneath.

"Dick, you asked me once out of curiosity concerning that tale and I am now going to tell you and get your ideas. You have a better head than we gave you credit for."

"Fudge, Ande, your head would make two of mine, but fire away. I've been anxious for a long time to know."

Ande related the history of his family and the treasonable stain, while his companion listened attentively, and sympathetically. The tale was related to the finish.

"And the papers?"

"They were all confiscated except two, that are now in my possession."

"And your father?"

"He left a letter. You see the last letter that my mother received before father's disappearance contained one sealed, directed to me, which should be given to me when I came to mature years. It was given me when I came first to the Grammar School. Here it is," said Ande, as he pulled out of his inside pocket a long envelope that had been sealed with red wax.

"I have long since made myself familiar with its contents, but I am now going to read it to you," and opening it he read the following:

"Fort Malden, Canada, Sept. 10th, 1813."

"My Dear Son Andrew.—This letter is enclosed and sent in one to your mother, and is to be given to you when you are old enough to understand its contents. Whether I shall accomplish that for which I started to this blood-stained region or not yet remains to be seen. If not, and I should fall either in battle or a captive, you must faithfully carry out my request. Proctor has let hell loose upon the Americans and it has come back upon our own heads. I have no taste for this fighting side by side with savage Indians, and certainly Proctor is abusing his authority and position. He ruthlessly permits the savages to perform the most fiendish things imaginable, and has no respect for his word to a fallen foe.

---

[7] Wisht—sickly.

"All Michigan was taken by his predecessor, General Brock, but he was unfortunately killed and now this unscrupulous man is over us. It makes me blush at the name Englishmen must bear through him, and disgusts me with the present service. At the battle of Frenchtown, last January, the American general, Winchester, and his men were captured. They surrendered on Proctor's word that their lives and property should be safe, but Proctor returned to Malden and left the wounded and prisoners to be scalped and burned alive by the blood-thirsty devils, our red allies, who even dragged some through the streets of Detroit for sale. Detroit people remonstrated with Proctor, but he only shrugged his shoulders.

"The same proceedings were repeated after the attack on Harrison at Fort Meigs. The battle was as good as a victory for us. Our men were on both sides of the river Maumee. Our left was repulsed with a small loss, but our right was victorious, taking prisoners nearly six hundred men. Then the same savage atrocities began. Even Tecumseh, the great chief, was more merciful than our general. With an appalling yell he rescued an American prisoner from two of his followers and then insulted Proctor to his face.

"'Why do you allow such things when I am not here?' he said.

"'Your Indians can't be controlled,' said Proctor.

"'Go, put on petticoats; you are not fit to command men,' said Tecumseh, and with that he stalked proudly away. But those who heard it agreed with the bold chief. He's a good soldier, but no general, and his cruelty and indifference to his word of honour has made the soldiers sick of such service. On account of this, and Admiral Barclay's defeat to-day, Michigan is lost to us and even Canada may be taken away from the home government. The splendid opportunities that Brock placed in our hands are of no value on account of incapable Proctor and pusillanimous Barclay. The naval battle was won before it was fought. Barclay had six vessels and Perry nine, but what of that? Englishmen have conquered before against odds. But there was Barclay, keeping under the guns of Malden, casting down the spirits of his men with the thought of certain defeat, while the American ships were out in the open inviting him to the attack. The sailors and gunners begged him to attack, and even wept in humiliation at his cowardice. Tecumseh, with several thousand Indians, were on an island waiting to witness the encounter. Tecumseh rowed over and sought Proctor.

"'You said you were master of the waters. Why don't you go out and fight? The Americans are daring you to come out and fight.'

"The result of that battle is known, or will be known soon. Oh, for men like Nelson, and Marlborough, and Wellington!

"But to the point of my request. My father has a dishonourable stain on his name, though unworthy of it, I believe. I have travelled among the Shawnese, our allies, who were father's foes at Braddock's defeat. I was sent by Brock as an agent to the Ohio, and witnessed their dances and the Prophet's agitation a year ago. Ah, they were blood-curdling scenes. While there I talked with an old Shawnee about King Shingas and Captain Jacobs, father's captors. He said he was a sub-chief under Shingas and was in the ambush at the defeat, and from what I could glean from his description, father was among the batch of prisoners consigned to his charge. He knew not what I had in mind at first. He was so old that his hair had turned white or grey, an unusual thing among the Indians. He spoke to me of the greatness of Shingas and the suffering of the prisoners until I felt like shooting him on the spot, the hoary old sinner. All were not burned, for after running the gauntlet one escaped, snatching a club from an Indian in his flight. The Shawnee called him the Long Red Wolf, at least such is the meaning of the Shawnee name in English. From the red hair, length of limb, and swiftness of foot, it must have been my father, who was accounted the swiftest foot in old Cornwall when young.

"Now hark ye, son Andrew, among the papers of your grandfather, found on his person, was one overlooked by the King's officers. It was a rude map of the Kittanning region and the rough vale of the Lycamahoning. I send a copy with the same directions in Shawnese and English. The vale leads down from the Allegheny Mountains, and the river empties into the Ohio some distance above the old Indian town of Kittanning, as you can readily see from the accompanying sketch. I have learned from long association with the Indians that this region is rich in silver and lead, possibly gold. At least there are legends to that effect. The ability of the natives to obtain lead for their weapons and their silver ornaments testify to an eldorado somewhere in the region. Now father was much interested in mining and metals, as what Cornishman is not. I asked the old warrior of Shingas concerning the Indian legend of this eldorado and quoted the old directions in Shawnese, for I speak their language: 'On one side a plain, on the other a steep that a smart Indian can climb.' He gazed at my red hair and became silently suspicious. A bullet that passed through my hat on my way back to Malden told me my knowledge had made me a mark of vengeance.

"This is all I know. Connect this Indian eldorado with the

map found on father's body; explain how the French commission as captain was filled in with his own name, and how he happened to be in French uniform, and the problem is solved. If these could be explained I believe our family could raise its head once more among the loyal families of the delectable duchy,—Corn wall. I'll find this Indian eldorado and your grandfather's exoneration at the same time. They are both connected, I believe. If I fail you must take up the cause."

"Your affectionate father,
"THOMAS TREMBATH,
"Major——6th Royal Infantry.

"FORT MALDEN, Canada."

"That's what we were studying about the other day," said Dick, as Ande ceased reading. "De 'ee remember, Ande, about Proctor and Tecumseh?"

"Aye," said Ande, musingly.

"Are you going to take up the search?"

"Some time,—when, I don't know. What do you advise?"

"I should say after you get through with the sixth," said Dick promptly; "but, Ande, you haven't told me of Sir James Lanyan and Master Richard and——"

Ande gave a gesture of impatience and his countenance clouded over with anger.

"Dick," he said passionately, "parson says it's wrong, but I hate that family and I can never forgive them the wrong they did me and mine. When the time comes I will be terribly revenged upon them for the cruel slander and injustice that they, for the sake of capital, brought upon us."

Dick was silenced; he had never seen the pleasant face of his friend become so angry. A look like that of a demon had passed over his features at the very mentioning of Lanyan's name.

"Hist!" said Ande, and his countenance resumed its old expression.

Both youths listened, in their sequestered position.

"Remember, Penner, to 'ave the men 'ere within a half an 'our. See that each is well armed with pistols and cutlass. The cutter 'as been notified and is a-beating down the coast, and the paths be all guarded. This time we'll catch the hold Prussian fox or my name beant Penhall."

Gazing out cautiously, the youths saw, on the beach below, two men in seaman's garb.

"That's Captain Penhall of the coastguard, and his lieutenant, and they mean to surprise the King of Prussia Cove. We must give our old friend warning, Dick, lad."

"Les up and away."

"Hold on. Didn't 'ee hear the paths are all guarded."

"That's so," said Dick rubbing his head, doubtfully.

"Come, I have a plan at last," said Ande after a moment's thought, and he led the way cautiously at first and then rapidly inland. For a mile or more they kept up a smart pace, Dick following with some difficulty.

After a wide detour inland, they rapidly approached Prussia Cove. His plan was nothing less than to enter the cove by the perilous path from which he had fallen in the hurling game between Breage and the school. It was now twilight, and darkness was rapidly setting in.

"Halt!" said a quick, sharp voice ahead.

"On," whispered Ande, "there's only two of them. I'll take the right, and you take the left."

Dick grappled with his man and there was a moment of struggle. But the sudden impetus of Dick's rush decided the battle, for the coastguard tripped and, aided by his antagonist's bulk, fell. Ande was more fortunate, not suffering the other to lay hands on him. With a blow of his fist and a quick Cornish side kick he toppled him over.

"On!" shouted Ande and down the narrow pathway they rushed at breakneck speed. There was now no concealment. Shots flew after the two and Ande felt a sharp, quick pain in the left arm, but he gave it no attention. In a moment or two they emerged on the sands below, and their arrival was none too soon. The smugglers had already secreted half the cargo.

"The coastguard! They're coming!" shouted Ande as he rushed among the crowd.

Down the path was heard the approach of charging feet. From other paths the same ominous sounds were heard, all converging on the cove, and soon the head of the cove was dotted with black figures of guardsmen.

Now did Captain Carter show his courage. His men grasped desperately their pikes and cutlasses, and not even awaiting the attack of the guard, charged at the command of their king. Then followed a sanguinary battle. Shots, oaths, dull resounding blows, and groans made the silent cove a veritable pandemonium. In the midst of it a sail was seen gradually nearing the har bour entrance. The quick eye of Carter saw it. Flourishing his cutlass on high he roared:

"To the lugger, men, the hawk's at the entrance!"

The two youths, not knowing where to go, clambered on board, followed speedily by the captain and his men. The struggle continued to the very lugger's bulwarks, for the attacking guard were more numerous than their foes and felt loathe to leave them go. The appearance of the revenue cutter near the entrance also gave them renewed courage. They strove to follow after the captain and his men. A select guard of the smugglers was speedily appointed by the captain to repel boarders, and these did their work well, wielding boathooks and cutlasses with telling effect. In the meantime sweeps were gotten ready by the others and the lugger was under headway, slowly leaving the frenzied guardsmen of the government on shore.

A gun sounded from the entrance and a ball tore through the limp mainsail.

"Between two fires," muttered the captain with a smothered oath, and it was true, for the revenue cutter had stationed herself midway in the narrow entrance.

"Pull, my hearties, pull," shouted the captain, "we'll run 'er down, for we be heavier!"

The lusty fellows at the sweeps did pull, and with a will. The cutter's captain, seeing the intention of the smugglers, tried to frustrate it, and partly succeeded, but—crash!—the next instant the lugger's heavy prow ran athwart the cutter's bow.

"She's done for," gleefully said the smuggler cap tain, as the next moment the lugger glided into the bay. But Carter was mistaken, for the cutter though badly damaged, was not disabled. The blow was above the water-line and pursuit was kept up out into the channel. There was a light breeze blowing, the sails were set, and the sweeps were taken in. The cutter was steadily gaining.

"Can she catch us?" asked Ande of the smuggler captain.

"No," said the captain, pleasantly, "I think not. We are obliged to 'ee, lads, for your timely warning."

Ande wondered at his good humour and at his denial that there was any danger of being overtaken, when it was plain that the cutter was gaining. Evidently the captain had some plan, he thought; and he had.

"Port your helm!" shouted the skipper, and then at another command, more sheets were spread to the wind as if by magic, and away went the lugger staggering under a cloud of canvas, like a winged bird of the sea.

"Jack," said the captain to our old acquaintance of the cliff battle, "Jack, do 'ee think 'ee could wing that chap?"

"I'll try," said Jack, and away he rushed to the stern where a long brass cannon called "Long Tom" was stationed. The gunner sighted for an instant, then changed the sights and sighted again; then as if satisfied, he quickly applied the lighted linstock. There was a flash and a roar and the ball sped on its mission.

"A good shot, Master Jack, you've brought down 'er mainmast," said the skipper, who was examining the effects with a night glass.

He had hardly spoken when there was a puff of smoke from the cutter, then crash! the sound of rending plank, and a ball passed straight through the lugger at the water line. The next instant there was another puff of smoke and another ball crashed through close to the second. The cutter was avenged.

Captain Carter, with a pale set face, hastened below to ascertain the injuries, but returned in a moment. The lugger was rapidly filling and settling.

"Jack and I will give them a shot to pay for that while the rest of ye get ready the long boat," said the captain, sternly. But it was a fatal delay, for scarcely had

Long Tom been sighted e'er in a mad swirl of waters the lugger plunged to her watery grave—down, down, down, dragging, in her deadly, downgoing eddy, captain and crew. Ande had the sound of many waters in his ears, and kicked desperately to free himself of its deadly influence. Then, after an interminable time, to his joy he felt himself going upward, upward and upward. His lungs felt like bursting under the terrible strain. Could he hold out until he reached the surface? He made another desperate downward kick and joy,—his head shot above the surface—but—nothing visible but the dark, tossing waters and the pale stars o'erhead. Stay! There was a dark mass but a yard or so away and a form. He drifted nearer. He shouted and a hand grasped him and drew him up on a floating piece of deck timber.

"Dick."

"Ande."

Two simultaneous shouts, but that was all, as these two friends of school day life floated together on the loosened spar.

Then after a time:

"Didst see the captain or any of the crew?"

"All drowned, no doubt," said Dick.

Then there was more silence. Dick was a famous swimmer, but clung to the spar reserving his strength for the future; Ande was less expert in the swimming art and his wound and exposure was gradually weakening his grasp. It was now past midnight.

"Dick, do'ee think the cutter will pick us up?"

"Hardly; you see, she can't do much with her mainmast gone, and then the tide is ebbing."

Hours passed and the sickening sense of weakness became stronger and stronger, and that weary, pallid expression, the presage of unconsciousness, swept o'er Ande's countenance and remained there. It was Dick who realised it first, and he flung his own great arms o'er those of Ande, binding him to the spar with his own strength.

"Hold on. Don't give in."

"Dick, I was shot in the arm coming down the cliff, and I think that's what's making me weak."

"Weather it out until daylight and we shall be picked up. Some one is bound to see us."

"Dick, do 'ee think we did right in warning the smugglers?" asked Ande, weakly.

"Aye," said Dick, stoutly; "they were honest men trying to earn a living."

"Because,—you see—you'll get through all right, but I—I'm getting weaker every minute, and I can't hold out much longer—and a fellow thinks of these things when he hasn't long to live."

"Nonsense, we'll both pull through all right. Pluck up courage." Then as he noticed a piece of rope attached to the spar, "I do believe I'm still a dull'ead. Here we 'ave been floating in danger of falling off through weakness every moment and there is the means of our salvation."

He plucked out a knife from his pocket and severed the rope at the end from the spar and passing it around Ande and himself securely lashed themselves to the float.

"There, if we can't hold out much longer, we'll at least be on top of the water as long as this spar floats."

There was silence for another half an hour and then Ande said wearily.

"Dick, if you get back to land — and I don't, — you — remember me to mother and tell her I — died a Christian."

"Aye, aye, old fellow, but cheer up!" But the tears in his own eyes indicated that he needed his own advice.

"We must trust in God, Dick."

"Aye," said the other, as he reached over and shook hands earnestly.

"And Dick, remember me to her."

"Aye," said Dick once more. He knew for quite a time Ande's interest in the squire's daughter, and that "her" could mean no one else.

On they drifted, now on a swelling surge, then in a dark valley of water. Dawning light appeared in the east, but no land was visible.

"Cheer up," said Dick, "day is coming," but there was no answer. Grim unconsciousness had come at last. Dick, for another hour, battled with the terrible faintness, then the sea seemed to fade from his vision and — the sun arose beaming brilliantly on the world of tossing waters. Nothing was visible but the circling gulls and a stick of timber, and two unconscious, half-drowned lads.

CHAPTER XXI

AROUND THE TAVERN'S FLAMING GRATE

Around the tavern's flaming grate,
The rafting done and the hour late,
The raftsmen sit and laugh and sing,
Or 'bove the conversation's din,
Keep time with feet to violin,
On which the lively strains are played,
Of Devil's Dream or White Cockade.

"Right—Right—t!—Halt! Left—Left! Halt!"

Loud and clear rang out the voice of the raft pilot, so loud and prolonged that even the roar of rushing waters and the wild lashing of wind among the tree laden banks were not able to overcome the stentorian commands.

It was a rough night in the wilds of western Pennsylvania. The rain had descended steadily for three days, and now the Lycamahoning had arisen from its ordinary rippling tranquillity into a boisterous, turbulent onrushing tide. Raftsmen had been constantly busy throughout the winter, felling the gigantic pines and firs, squaring them with their great broad axes, and then with the aid of hickory saplings and pins and bows of the same tough material, lashing them securely one against the other, rafting them in for the cruise down the river to the Ohio. The first flood had come, and so violent was its nature that many a hardy raftsman had added additional bulyokes and hawsers to his rafts, fearing the loss of his winter's labour. The night had set in stormy and dark. The clouds that had covered the face of the heavens for the greater part of the week had grown in intensity, and had been belching down their floods with renewed violence. The wind had arisen, softly at first, and then augmenting into a small tornado, charging through the acres of treetops that added additional sombreness to the murky night, until beaten to madness with the invisible storm weapons and stung with the drenching rain, tree fought with tree, lashing themselves with their wooden arms into an agony of conflict.

"Who in the name of common sense can be running timber on a night like this? He is either a madman or an imbecile," so thought rather than said a horseman who had paused on the road to listen to the shouts. He placed his hand up over his brows, shielding his view from the drenching rain, and stared, from his elevation, out over the roaring stream. There was a flash of lightning, illuminating the yellow foam-flecked flood and out in the centre a raft, long and heavy, yet tossed like a feather on the rolling flood waves. There were two figures at the great rear oar, one of whom was the pilot, one figure in the centre with a coil of rope in his grasp, and at the front oar-running backward and forward, leaping on the great oar handle to jerk its cumbersome blade from the stream, running it back to the opposite side, plunging it in the flood once more, and with handle overhead pushing with might and main,—were six figures, seeming in the distance like the dancing forms of a puppet show, whose various motions were controlled by the dark form of the pilot in the rear. The flash of lightning passed away in a roll of thunder, and all was wrapped in darkness again.

"Left! Left!"

"Halt!"

"Left! Left!"

The raft was rounding a curve in the stream.

"Left! Left! Push! Push, with a will. More backbone to it, boys! Once more and a glass of toddy at Burke's for each man! Left! Left! Now then! Heave to it! With all your might! Halt! Don't let it pull you off! Hold on to her!" bawled the raft pilot.

"Again! Left! Left!"

"Halt!"

"Now then, Tom! Jump for it!"

"Run out the rope!"

"Snub! Snub!"

"There, ease up, Tom! Take the next tree!"

"All right," bawled a voice from the shore.

And slowly the great raft, a hundred and twenty feet long and forty wide, swung in from the flood after two trials had been made to break the speed. Closer and closer to the bank, away from the force of the current, until alongside she was safely secured with a double hawser, a prisoner under the guardianship and control of two massive oaks. The immense oars were swung clear of the water and their handles lashed to the centre -pieces. Up over the creek bank, stumbling through thick underbrush and over fallen trees, came the hardy crew and at length gained the turnpike. The weather in the meantime had grown colder and the rain changed to falling snow. The wind had fallen in its violence. Onward stumbled the crew, then at length up a slight elevation, through a covered bridge, and the lights, twinkling through many small windows, flashed before their eyes. It was the town of Burgtown, famed for its two rows of log houses, each having an upper story, and doubly famed for its renowned hotel of sawn timber and its hospitable but talkative host; famed also for the scholarship and mystery surrounding its founder. Scholarship and mystery! Yes, scholarship, for no one could withstand the logic of the Reverend Mr. Burg, and his tall, dark form, his deep eyes with their unfathomable look, was enough to awe even the stoutest. Mysteriousness? Yes, mysteriousness, for he had come in the night and had gone in the night. He was like Melchizedek in one respect, no one knew his father or his mother, no one knew his birthplace, and no one knew his end. There was a story rife among some of the town people that he had been guilty of some unministerial conduct in the neighbourhood of Standing Stone, thought it best for him to put the Alleghenies between himself and his old location, and had accordingly travelled with more speed than elegance to the Lycamahoning, where with the aid of a ploughline he had plotted and laid out the town. He was gone before the settlers that poured in became fully acquainted with him. Two years had elapsed since then and people remembered little of him with the exception of Peter Burke, the tavern keeper, and it seemed that Burke's knowledge increased with the years, and Burg became in the annals of his mind a demigod, a sort of modern Romulus, whose figure and deeds became larger and mightier as they reached into the dimness of the past.

The raft pilot, followed by his men, entered the door of Burke's place. The roaring fire of logs in the great stone chimney was most welcome to them after their night of toil. They made a picturesque group as they stood stamping the mud and snow from their long-legged logging shoes and brushing the great, soft flakes from caps and homespun wamuses. The majority of the eight were stout, ordinary-looking young men, with something of the air of the woods in their manner and appearance. The pilot was an exception. He was of medium height and stoutly built, with an intelligent face, lighted up with keen, sharp, grey eyes, that flashed in merriment in repartee, and that were even cunning and penetrating at times. He was the American product of the "canny" Scotchman, a Scotch American.

Along one side of the public room ran the rude bar counter with a few homely bottles and jugs, and near them, his rounded form a living advertisement for his wares, one eye smiling a welcome, the other, which was squint and cross-eyed, gazing unwinkingly, blankly, out of the window as if trying to penetrate the darkness, was the form of the tavern keeper.

"Supper for eight?" asked the tavern keeper.

"Aye, ye ken that," answered the raft pilot.

Peter Burke, with a rolling motion, tumbled off to a rear door which he swung wide.

"Supper for eight rafters," he bawled.

"Arright," squeaked a distant, feminine voice.

"Hallo, Hugh," said a deep voice from a corner near the flaming fireplace.

"Hallo yerself," said the pilot.

"What led you to pilot on a night like this, when the creek is getting higher and higher. I thought a raftsman ought to know that the proper time to raft is when the flood is falling, not rising."

"Not always," said the pilot, and then added, "Is that you, Bill?"

"Yes, it's I, sure enough."

"Well, you're schoolmaster and I'm raft pilot; every man to his own calling, and I suppose every man ought to know best what to do in his own calling; yet you'd criticise me for running timber on a rising flood."

"There are little things in all trades that most everyone ought to know. I was riding to the Burg when I heard your shouts on the raft and I wondered what ill-witted fellow was running on a rising flood on a night like this."

"Don't think it science, eh?" a little nettled to be called ill-witted.

"No. Every one ought to know that when the stream is rising it is higher in the centre than it is on the sides and when falling higher on the sides than in the centre. Hence by due process of ratiocination," — the school-master paused to give the large, scholarly word due emphasis — "you must run on a falling flood."

"That's what 'tiz to be a scholard," muttered the tavern keeper, admiringly.

"Aye, science and scholard," snorted Hugh Lark, the pilot; "and I suppose if you had a raft on a sand bar, you'd wait for a falling flood and jack it off with a hoisting jack, eh?"

There was a roar of laughter from the crowd of raftsmen, and Hugh smiled, his good humour once more restored.

"Oh, in that case it's different, but that's a single exception," said Professor Bill, in some humiliation.

"No single exception. Suppose ye had a raft tied up above the island or down under the hill, would ye run on a rising or wait for a falling flood?"

"I would most assuredly wait for a falling flood, and —"

The schoolmaster was interrupted by a chuckle from Hugh, and broad grins from his assembled men.

"I've no doubt that ye would, but you'd find your raft a-scattered all the way twixt here and Pittsburgh. Why, mon, there's ne'er a hawser made that can hold a raft in those positions in a rising flood. 'There are more things in heaven and earth, Horatio, than are dreamt of in your philosophy.'"

Professor Bill Banks, or Professor Bill, as he was commonly known, was silenced. The last remark and the quotation from Shakespeare had put him to rout. He flushed and kept his eyes on the fire. The raftsmen were delighted. There was nothing they enjoyed so much as a tiff between Bill and their pilot. Professor Bill was the most learned man of the neighbourhood. Since the exodus of the Reverend Burg he had held the pre-eminence. He was the leader, and there was none to dispute with him with any fair show of success except Hugh, the pilot. Hugh had invariably come off second; here he had achieved first honours. Hugh was well read in a number of subjects, but his knowledge was only such as he could find by perusing history, in which indeed he was a fair scholar, and the topics of the day.

"Was stuck, Hugh?" asked the tavern keeper, with some new measure of respect.

"Aye, yesterday the creek was full of floating timber and we stuck on a sand bar. There were no rafts behind to shove us off and we had to wait for a greater flood. We wouldn't have stuck if Tom, there, hadn't lost his head."

Tom, a great hulking fellow, looked a trifle sheepish.

"You see," continued Hugh Lark, "I was up at the crosscut and in making the bend, I was just gitting the raft pinted when he was afraid we'd strike and tear up. He bellowed like a bull, 'We'll strike, we'll tear up, some un run out a rope and tie up.'"

"It war pretty nigh striking, though," muttered Tom, in some apology.

"Nonsense! Why, there were fully fifteen feet of water on either side. How could we strike or even run out and tie up when we had nothing to run on but water? The rain had stopped for an hour or two and we were getting on fine. The flood was a-carrying us on with a good speed. The banks were slipping by as if they were running the other way. The front men were dipping occasionally, but they hung on to the oar. Then come the bend. I could see it a hundred yards before we come to it, the water a-swirling and a-twisting like a yellow ribbon and then disappearing from sight behind the trees. 'Left, men, left,' I shouted. Then Tom lost his head. He let go the oar, and the oar being too much for the other chaps, and being afeared of being yanked into the flood they let go too, and the next minute came the thud of grounding. I saw that it was a-coming and braced myself, hanging on to the oar. But the fellows in front, how they tumbled! They were around Tom in the centre, a-galleyhooting and shouting. I never had such a crew of numbskulls. When the grounding came they tumbled over each other like nine-pins."

Supper was announced and the hungry raftsmen wended their way to the eating department, a plain long room, ceiled with pine, and adorned with sundry prints of "Babes in The Wood," and "Red Riding Hood." The table was a heavy wooden affair, evidently the result of home labour; the provisions with which it was plentifully laden were of the class found in every woodsman's home, viz., pork, beans, corn bread, burr-wheat bread, and home-made syrup.

A split log, the level side up, the rounded side down, into which were inserted several hickory legs, served in lieu of chairs, and seated upon this, the hungry raftsmen fell to with a will.

Meantime the public room was occupied by the tavern keeper and Professor Bill Banks. Professor Bill was apparently thirty years of age. He had a high forehead, blue eyes, a mass of dark hair overhanging his ears, and a prominent Roman nose. The nose seemed to give great strength to his features, as also did his chin. He was clad in the customary tail coat, tight pantaloons with straps, neckerchief, and over all towered his tall "nail keg" silk hat. Professor Bill was attired for a special occasion. He was going to visit, ostensibly, the father of a certain rustic damsel, and had stepped in for his mail. The talk with the pilot nettled him, for in an argument he liked to show his superiority, as he was the recognised great man of letters in the place. The talk was not the only thing that disturbed and ruffled his feelings. His horse had inadvertently stepped into a washout on the road, and had fallen so lame that it was utterly impossible for him to proceed.

"Hear of Big Paddy's accident?" asked the tavern keeper, wishing to promote a better feeling.

"No," curtly said Bill.

"Ha! Ha! He!" cackled the tavern keeper, "it war amusin'."

"Come, cease those asinine cachinations and explain," said Bill, with some irritation.

"Yer a great scholard, Bill," said the tavern keeper, in some admiration at this flow of erudite language, "but when ye'd speak highly of me, I'd wish ye could use plainer words. Well, big Paddy and his uns are a-build ing a new church in the burgh, and they were all a-drinking of rye to make the work go lively. Big Paddy would always do the heaviest work. At last there war the heavy corner stone to lift off the wagon, and none could roll her down. Paddy were nigh full when the stone come. Ha! Ha! He!" and the tavern keeper went off into another cackle of laughter, his cross-eye blinking with tears of merriment, and his protuberant stomach laughing in sympathy. "Ha! Ha! He!" and he went off into another cackle that threatened to strangle him.

"If it's your whiskey that made him ridiculous, I do not wonder, for its the most catholicon panacea for the diminution of intelligence and propagating of blatant puerility and asinine imbecility extant. Witness yourself for an example." Bill was becoming sarcastic.

"So 'tiz, so 'tiz," said the tavern keeper, highly pleased. "I say, Professor, what a high larnt person ye are; now—do ye,—do ye think ye could write that daoun?"

"Why?"

"I could git it printed on a sign and it 'ould look grand-like. I'd be much 'bleeged to ye, Bill," said Burke, earnestly.

Professor Bill smiled good humouredly, and asked, "Well, about Paddy?"

"Oh, he looked at 'em all a-tugging at the stone, for it war a whopper, and then he ups and says, 'Let be, now, let the auld man have a chance,' and with that he grabbed a-hold of it. He pulled it off, but it war too much for him, and it come down kerflop on his foot. There war an uproar and the big paddies and little ones come a-running up and screaming and shouting: 'And are ye hurted now, Daddy? And—and—and are ye hoorted now, Pappy? And are ye hoorted now, grand-dad-dy?' Big Paddy war mad. 'Tare and hounds,' said he, 'trow a stun like that on a man's fut and ask if he war hoorted, ye spalpeens.'"

The tavern keeper went off into another cackle of laughter, and the schoolmaster feebly joined in.

The rafting crew now returned from the supper-room and gathered around the flaming open fireplace. Rafting stories followed each other in rapid succession, Hugh Lark seeming to have the greatest fund. Clay and corncob pipes were brought out from various pockets and soon wreaths of smoke began to dim the atmosphere.

"Hear of old Jim Handy's trip?" asked one after Hugh had told a rather exciting story.

"No," said Hugh.

"Let's hear it," said the others.

"Jim had ne'er been on the water and thought it would be a nice thing for him to go on a trial trip. He had allers said that the land war good enough fer him, and that he would ne'er trust himself to nawthing but solid land. Some of the boys up on the Big Lycamahoning, that were cutting timber fer him, up and began talking of the funny times they had down at the mouth, the dancing and the parties. And then they begun to talk of the ride down, just as easy as riding a good hoss. The old man had a powerful set of rafts to run, and he saw one after another go down the stream and the fellows cherry and 'parently enjying the ride. They got him so worked up over the ride, and the good times they had, that he decided to go, too, on the last raft. They told him that all he would have to do would be to stand in the centre and perhaps they could make a chair fer him to set on. The old man war tickled with the idea. On the river they told him they could put up a regular shanty on the raft and it would be like travelling in a coach, and then he would have a chance to see Pittsburgh. The old man had never seen Pittsburgh and it war the capping argument. Then some fool fellow told him of the dams and the going under the water five or six feet when the raft would plunge over the shoots. The fellows told him that they could fix that all right. They would make a high wooden horse fer him to sit on when they would take the shoots. That fixed him. Last week the raft war ready to make the trip. They had a slanting pole fixed in the centre, and a seat up at the top where the old man could sit in the dry when the raft would plunge under. It went all right till they come to the big dam. Then as they war making fer the shoot and were fairly in it, all the fellows at the front oar dropped it and run up the pole after the old man. The old man hollered to them that they would break it down, but they didn't keer. Up they went, and just as they were plunging under, the pole broke, and down tumbled the old man with all the others. The raft war oak and sunk dead, like lead. It went to the very bottom and then rose again. The old man hung on and so did the others, but he was mad, a-cussing and swearing and spitting water like a water dog. It war a sight to see."

The fellow burst into a laugh that was echoed by the others.

"If he had been a-riding that sixty-foot stick that you rode, Hugh, he would been scared worse, eh," said one of the rafters.

"Tell us the story, Hugh," said others.

"It were not much," said Hugh. "A sixty-foot stringer war torn off by one of the rocks in the Rough Water. I thought we ought not to lose it, and so gave the rear oar into the hands of my assistant and jumped for it. I landed clear in the centre of the stick as it slipped behind me. The raft was going faster than the stick. How do ye account for that, Bill?" asked Hugh, pausing in his narrative.

"Very easy," said Bill. "The timber stick did not give so much surface for the force of the current as the raft. Hence the raft went the faster of the two. But the stick?" inquired Bill, who was also interested.

"Well, I landed as I said in the centre of the stick, then slipped down on my hands and knees, and began to guide it. Sometimes it would roll and I would have to roll with her to keep on top. Then I had to watch lest I should get jammed against the rocks. I jumped off several times to avoid being squeezed, and swum back again. Once I got atween the stick and the rocks and she was a-coming for me. I dived under it, come up on the other side, and that's what saved me from certain death. I couldn't catch up to the raft and so I rode the stick all the way to the river, where the raft was awaiting for me. That was all there was to it. It was an exciting time, though."

There were murmurs of admiration from the assembled raftsmen and then more tales followed. Rafts torn up in the rough water, raftsmen drowned though expert swimmers, deeds of rescue, and things of a similar nature followed in rapid succession. The home distilled liquor was used sparingly, and finally the fiddle was brought forth and music enlivened the public room. White Cockade, Devil's Dream and others followed, the raftsmen keeping time with their heavy boots and sometimes by dancing. One of the younger raftsmen executed a woodman's fling in a creditable manner, encouraged by the handclapping of the others and the occasional shouting in tune with the melody "Heigh ho—de-do, de-do, de-do, de-do!"

In the midst of the revel the door was opened and two strangers entered. They had evidently been riding far, for their garments showed the trace of hard travel. The one who appeared to be the spokesman was tall, well proportioned, with a tangled mass of auburn hair, more tangled by the pelting storm without, and a beard trimmed in the Vandyke style and of the same hue as his hair. The other was a giant in size, standing fully six feet six inches, and broad in proportion. He had the dark hair and features of the Celt.

The tavern keeper was all hospitality. Room was made for them around the flaming fire log and their clothes, damp with the storm, were soon drying. There was a lull in the conversation of the raftsmen, the fiddle had been consigned to its place o'er the chimney piece.

"Can we get supper?" asked the one with the red beard.

The tavern keeper nodded and added, "Certain, and a good one at that," and going to the rear door he bawled to the cook, "Supper fer two gents."

"Arright," squeaked the distant, feminine voice.

"Our horses must be fed and stabled also," said the same gentleman. The tavern keeper gave the necessary directions to a tow-headed boy, who disappeared into the outer darkness.

"And 'ere," thundered the larger of the two strangers, as he opened the door after the boy, "see that you rub the horses down well and give them a good bed, and a warm mash."

The giant returned to the fire and stood before its pleasing blaze.

"You uns kin sign yer names when ye git warm." It was the tavern keeper that spoke, and the travellers, taking the hint, moved over to the soiled record book and added their names to the few already inscribed there. Peter Burke, tavern keeper, scrutinised the names carefully with his good eye, while the other seemed to be studying the appearance of the strangers. One of the raftsmen leaned over to Hugh and whispered in his ear that to be cross-eyed was a wonderful talent for the tavern keeper; he could read the names on his book and size up the people at one and the same time.

"You uns travelling fer?" asked one of the raftsmen.

"No, sir," laconically responded the red-headed one.

"Come from Kittanning?" said another.

"Yes, sir."

"How's election news down there, and what's opinion on John Quincy Adams?"

"Adams seems to be very popular, and Jackson has a good following."

"Adams will carry the day, no doubt," said the pilot.

"He'll not can do that," muttered some one in dissent. Whereupon there followed a small debate on the merits of the two candidates for Presidential position.

"Up here 'lectioneering?" inquired a third, turning to the strangers again.

"I calculate you are from the west, stranger," said Hugh Lark.

"You've struck it partly," laughingly said the red-headed stranger, and then apparently tired of answering questions, added, "We're here from Louisiana and are here prospecting."

Curiosity, instead of being appeased, was instantly aroused. A sharp look flashed into Hugh's eye as he scrutinised them.

"Wall," said the tavern keeper, "I allers said thar war something in these hills. What ye think 'tiz, stranger, gold?"

"No, we're prospecting for character."

"Karakter," said the tavern keeper, musingly, "I ne'er hearn tell of that metal afore."

"Don't think there's much about here?" asked the red-headed stranger, with just the shadow of a smile.

"Not as I knows of," and the tavern keeper rubbed his head in doubt.

Professor Bill snorted in disgust.

"Look here, stranger, we have more character, good sterling character, in this section than our dotard friend informed you of."

Peter Burke, tavern keeper, looked pleased at this compliment. To be called a friend of Professor Bill's and a friend, too, with that "high larndt word ahead of it!" If Professor Bill was a drinking man he would have set up a glass to Bill then and there free.

"Character, sir!" continued Bill. "We sent forth the most stalwart characters during the Revolution, though not from this immediate neighbourhood, yet from Western Pennsylvania—Captain Brady, the Indian fighter, and scores of others. Hugh Lark, there, can tell you of his father, Captain Ande Lark, the sharpshooter, who performed prodigies of valour in many a hard fought field."

"Aye," said Hugh, "'tiz all true."

"And didn't they hold the Britishers down at Concord and Lexington, Yorktown and Stony Point?" continued Bill.

"Aye, all ken they did that," said Hugh.

"And what was it for?" said Bill, getting oratorical. "The tyrant oppressed us; taxed us without representation; quartered soldiers on us in times of peace, and seized the patriots' powder and ball. Then, sir, the American eagle screamed in wrath and the noble characters, Washington, Putnam, Morgan, Green, Brady, Lark, and hundreds of others went forth to war, to battle valiantly for the cause of freedom and shed their blood for the rights of man. Even in the humbler walks of life sterling character was demonstrated. The ploughboy, the woodsman, the tradesman, the farmer, all left their habitations, and with their old flint-locks over their shoulders sped to the defence of their nation's life and honour. This country was won by the stout courage of the colonial fathers, and their stout-hearted sons to-day have within their breasts the same doughty heroism that dominated the republic in that day. Yes, but a few years ago, the War of 1812 made lucid that fact. Lundy's Lane, Fort Meigs, Thames River,—who has forgotten them? Character! The country is full of it, sir."

"So 'tiz, so 'tiz," interjected the tavern keeper; "Professor Bill's high larndt and orter know."

"And," said Bill, "should the tocsin of war sound once more, the temple of Janus be closed, and strife with bloody claws sweep like a dragon over the land, should even all Europe band together against us, send their fleets to harass our waters, their hirelings to devast our land, they would find how patriots could contend for the heritage of their ancestors, how they could battle against the iron heel of oppression, and victory again would ultimately crown the American arms. All, because of her brave characters."

"Thas so; Bill's a scholard and orter know," said the tavern keeper, nodding sagely.

"Patrick Henry was not the only one who said 'give me liberty or give me death.' The spirit of heroism is in the hearts of the American citizens. They breathe it in the very air. Mountains, trees, birds, and even the very beasts of the wild, proclaim alike the freeman's land. None can wrest it from us while there is a God and while Americans are true to themselves."

Professor Bill sat down amidst a round of applause from the admiring raftsmen, while the tavern keeper rubbed his hands in the keenest of pleasure.

"Bill," said one of the raftsmen, "ye'll hev to git that speech down fer the Fourth o' Jerly. That's the best speech we uns heard since the Senator talked in Indiana."

"So 'tiz," said the tavern keeper. "Bill's a scholard. I say, Bill, could yer write that daoun?"

"What's that?" inquired Bill.

"Why, about the eagle a-hollering like mad fer liberty and so on. Ye see, we uns are gitting a new brand of stuff with an eagle on it and it would look grand like to hev them words on, too."

"Aye, perhaps," said Bill with a smile, "but I wonder how they teach those events over in England. They must ignore them. Say, stranger, how do they teach in Louisiana those salient points of our national history?"

"What a scholard!" murmured the tavern keeper as he passed a drink to a newcomer.

"Concerning the salient points of American history," responded the red-bearded stranger, "they teach about the same as in this section, I surmise, — that is, local events are dwelt upon unduly and there is a tendency to glorify the victories and mitigate the defeats. The school children, there, know more about Jackson and the Battle of New Orleans than about Ross or Fort Meigs. In England the same thing obtains. Local events are prominent and the glorious things are magnified, while the dark, unhappy events are passed lightly over."

"Yes, so I thought. Now in this country, though, there is a tendency to do those things, yet national and international questions are fairly represented," said Bill.

The stranger shook his head in dissent.

"The very same thing is as prevalent in America as in England. The bright things are haloed and the dark obscured. The schoolboy gets but one side of the question at issue. History ought to be taught for the sake of truth and not for the sake of generating patriotism. Take the American Revolution. Children, here, are taught that England was a hateful tyrant, taxing us unreasonably, simply for the pleasure of showing the strong hand, and wantonly aggressive in destroying the patriots' powder and ball. Yorktown, Stony Point, and Saratoga are dwelt on. What American does not know those battles by heart and how feebly impressed on the American mind are the occupations of Boston, New York, Philadelphia, the Battle of Brandy-wine, the Long Island defeats, and the disasters in the South? Now a fair way would be to emphasise both sides of the war, the battles, and the causes. Causes are given in many American histories of the war, but they are American causes; the English are not mentioned. Would it not be foolish to war without a cause?"

"Well, what causes did Britain have for the war and her oppression?" said Bill, sharply.

"Many," said the red-bearded stranger, sharply. "Taxation, for instance, is not wrong in itself. The government of a country is supported by taxes. Britain sent quite a few armies to this country in the time of the French and Indian war to protect the colonies. Could the colonies, notwithstanding the bravery of her few colonial troops, have withstood the armies of France, Montcalm and the others, without aid? Hence the armies of Braddock, Amherst, Wolf and others. The home government was burdened with a debt that had been greatly for the protection and augmentation of the American colonies. Indeed, had that war not been; had Wolf not taken Quebec, the glorious United States would be only a narrow strip of country along the Atlantic seaboard. Even this part and other parts west of the Alleghenies would be French soil, and you would all be French citizens."

"The stranger must be a scholard, too," muttered the tavern keeper.

"And," continued the stranger warming up, "England, therefore, incurred a great debt and insured to America the territory to the Mississippi and even be yond partly. What benefit was this to the English citizen? Had he a right to pay it all? Ought not America a right to bear a part of the burden?"

"True," said Bill, thoughtfully, "but how about non-representation? Was it right to tax us without our consent?"

"Easily explained," resumed the stranger. "England herself did not have representation. Many parts, great cities, Manchester, Sheffield, and others had none. The House of Commons did not represent England. Was representation to be given to the colonies when it was denied to England herself?"

"Very true," said Bill, uneasily, "but what about oppressive taxes?"

"Not much oppression. Americans admitted themselves that it was not the weight of the taxes, which were small, but the principle of the thing. The chief taxes were stamp and tea taxes and taxes of a similar nature. The burden was laid on the rich, mostly. The labouring man had little occasion for stamped paper. In reference to tea, tea was a luxury and not a necessity at that time. Is there much oppression in that? And about the seizing of powder and ball of the patriots, that's nothing more than the United States would do should the State of Pennsylvania gather up powder and ball to be used against the national government."

"Well, why did the American nation arise en masse in revolt, if they were not overly oppressed," persisted Bill.

"The American people did not arise en masse," responded the stranger. "There were thousands of citizens, wealthy and influential, on the King's side, until toward the middle of the war. Would it have been so easy for the British to take Boston, New York, Philadelphia, and Charleston, if they were wholly in favour of Washington and the war? No. They would have burned their cities like the Russians did Moscow. Both sides ought to be taught in the study of history and a better grasp of truth would result. About non-representation, that was wrong and the Americans were partly justified in struggling against it. The English people are struggling for the same thing, to-day. They have no real representation, but will get it soon. It is much better, however, to win representation and liberty by peaceful means than by war."

There was silence for a moment, and then Professor Bill responded.

"Those are new ideas to me, and you have opened up a new channel of thought; but at least you will admit that our histories are substantially correct and fair in reference to the late war, the War of 1812. What right had England to prey upon our commerce and impress our seamen even though they were formerly

Englishmen?"

"The preying upon commerce was piracy upon the part of England——"

"Good and well said," affirmed Professor Bill.

"The impressment of American seamen—Americans must handle the subject carefully or——"

"Or what?"

"They'll be trampling on their own laws and government. England claimed once an Englishman always an Englishman, naturalisation notwithstanding. American law, that is based on English to a great extent, is somewhat the same. A citizen of the United States cannot throw off his allegiance and unite with another nation without the consent of the United States. Witness the case of Murray and the *Charming Betsey* in 1804, before the Supreme Court. In the case of Isaac Williams before the Circuit Court of the United States for the District of Connecticut, in 1797, it was decided that no member could dissolve the compact of citizenship except by consent of the United States, and there had been no consent on the part of the United States. These cases were of Americans who attempted to become citizens of the newly formed republics of South America. And yet we say England was wrong in taking American citizens, who had been formerly Englishmen, and had become naturalised Americans contrary to England's will. There is an apparent inconsistency in the matter, visible even to the dullest mind."

Professor Bill was silent and apparently in deep thought.

"You have travelled some," said Hugh Lark.

"Yes," said the red-bearded stranger. "My friend here and myself, during the last eight years have been travellers. We have been in Brazil and other American countries. That is why I remember the cases of the *Charming Betsey* and Williams. The decision of the United States in those cases still rankles in the hearts of the people of the southern continent."

The raftsmen and schoolmaster were eager for tales of adventure and strange countries, when the supper bell rang, and the two gentlemen disappeared into the long dining-room. After supper they retired, being thoroughly tired with the travel of the day.

"Who air those fellows?" asked one of the raftsmen.

The question was voiced by all in the public room.

The tavern keeper, obsequiously handed the record book to Bill, who read out for the benefit of all the following:

"Andrew Trembath, Esq., New Orleans."

"Richard Thomas, New Orleans."

"The one must be a lawyer," said Professor Bill, with a good bit of respect in his tones.

"Did you notice the silent one? What a giant in size he is? He'd make an oar fly,

I'll wager, eh, Hugh?" said one of the raftsmen.

"Aye," said Hugh, meditatively.

"The one fellow is a Cornishman," said Bill.

"Whas that, Bill?" said the tavern keeper.

"A native of the southwest of England, a section noted for its minerals and seamen."

"How do ye ken that, Bill?" asked Hugh Lark.

"Because," said Bill,

"By Tre, Tri, and Pen,
Ye may know the Cornishmen."

CHAPTER XXII

THE LYCAMAHONING

The sun arose o'er the eastern hills of Lycamahoning, a great disc of flame, fretted with the great solemn pines and oaks of the hilltops, and driving before it the opaline radiance of early twilight. Pine needles lost the sombre hue of night and glistened and gleamed with a richer emerald where the ever-shifting sunbeams touched and gloried them with light. Trees of oak and pine, a hundred and fifty feet in height, enveloped with interlacing branches hill and lowland, except where, oasis-like, the fields and cabin of some squatter dappled the general surface of woodland. A few clouds still remained on the western horizon, dark and threatening, but the day was propitious for fine weather.

Ande and Dick, for the strangers were none other, were aroused by the first, glancing rays of the sun that penetrated the curtains of their little window. Flinging aside the curtain drapery, they gazed forth delighted on the scene. Within a few yards of the house wall rolled the roaring, yellow flood of the Lycamahoning, a mighty torrent, sweeping beyond its natural bounds. Tree trunk and brush and what not tossed hither and thither by its rollicking mood, yet bore ever onward. It was an ambitious stream, for the banks could not hold it. The turnpike, beyond the bridge, was hidden three feet from sight, and tearing through the underbrush on either side of the public way was an ever-widening torrent. The town was on higher ground than the turnpike beyond and so escaped the damage of the flood.

"What a grand country, Dick, old chap," said Ande, surveying the scene with interest. "This is better than hot Louisiana or even the Mississippi prairies."

"Humph!" yawned Dick; "but not better than Brazil." Then as he ceased stretching his great arms over his head; "Just think of it, Ande, if we had not been picked up by that outward bound Brazilian ship, we would not be independent now. Ah! diamonds and gold! That's the country, lad."

"Softly, softly, Dick," said Ande in a lower tone, "we're not going to advertise our circumstances. A month or so here, then home to Merrie England."

"And right glad will I be," said Dick; "but let's down and see what this settlement in the backwoods is like."

Ande followed by Dick went cautiously down the steep stairway, that seemed squeezed between the great chimney and the farther wall and led out at the bottom into the public room. There was no one in the public room when they entered, and so they wended their way across to the door and thence out into the street, if street it could be called. The hotel of Peter Burke was at the head of the main and only street of Burgtown, and one walking straight from the front door of the hotel would pass down an avenue, prolific in stumps, midway between two rows of log houses. Back of the tavern and but a few yards from it rolled and roared the Lycamahoning, and but a few yards from the north end was the covered bridge. It thus stood with the homes stretching from it in parallel lines, like a captain at the head of his soldiers. Several citizens were abroad already with their axes and were busily felling a forest giant that, isolated and ostracised with a few others, waved its branches in the air above the middle of the main thoroughfare of Burgtown. Several raftsmen with Hugh Lark at their head were standing at the end of the broad porch gazing over toward the bridge and the rushing yellow flood, shaking their heads dubiously at it, well knowing that there would be no rafting either that day or the next. The flood was too high.

There was the sound of cracking and rending of wood from the thoroughfare, a swishing and snapping of branches, a cry of warning, then one of terror, and with a resounding blow the mighty, woodland giant sprawled its full length on the ground. With an exclamation Hugh Lark leaped into the roadway followed by the other raftsmen and Ande and Dick. They were soon on the scene. There pinned to the earth under the heavy tree trunk, unconscious, his brow streaked with blood, was a man, evidently the chief chopper.

Women from the neighbouring homes were wringing their hands in dismay, and then from a distant cabin came a woman's scream, a cry full of anguish, and then a flying form burst the crowd and flung herself down near the head of the unconscious chopper. With tender hands she mopped the blood from his forehead and kissed his pale brow again and again, calling by every endearing name to the unconscious one to answer her. Hugh Lark wiped the moisture from his eyes, as did many others. Then with the instinct of the leader of men:

"Run, Jack, and get the rope and tackle and block from the raft. Jim, go get the heaviest crowbar from the tavern, and the rest of you men get crowbars. Peter Burke, get to thy tavern as fast as your legs will carry you and bring a flask of brandy."

"Can nothing be done until the coming of the block and tackle," ventured Ande. "Is it too heavy for a couple of fellows to lift by main strength?"

The raft pilot shook his head. "Three men could not lift the butt of that tree, and more than three couldn't try, without doing more injury to Tom underneath. I only hope he won't die before the rope comes."

Dick had not said a word, but he now hauled off his coat, and placing his big arms around the butt end of the fallen tree began to exert his strength.

"The man is mad," muttered Hugh Lark to one or two bystanders, while they all looked and wondered.

The blood mounted to his face and forehead, crimsoning his features like the sunrise of a rainy day, and then the veins stood out like whipcord upon his brow and arms, but the tree moved not. There was a straining of the eyes of Old Ironsides until they threatened to burst from their sockets, a rigidity of the limbs that though motionless yet indicated that the giant was putting forth every atom of his strength. The spectators scarcely breathed. Then, even before the people were aware of it, the tree began to move, silently, slowly, almost imperceptibly, inch by inch, up from the fallen, injured chopper. There was a suppressed murmur from the crowd, then Hugh with a bound was beside the injured man, and with the assistance of Ande quickly and deftly hauled him from his perilous position. There was a shout from the tavern. The rope and tackle was coming, but there was no need of them. Then Peter Burke, his cross eye glaring at the bystanders, and his other fastened upon Hugh and the succoured one, pushed his rotund, sebaceous body through the crowd, and with one fat, trembling hand extended to Hugh the brandy. A swallow of the fiery liquor and the fellow opened his eyes.

"Hurt much, Tom?" asked Hugh and the chopper's wife in almost one breath.

"Not much. Pretty well shuk up. Yes—pretty well shuk up."

They assisted the fellow to his feet, and then to his cabin home, still muttering in his dazed fashion: "Pretty well shuk up! Yes—pretty well shuk up."

Hugh was relieved. It was evident that whatever injuries he had received, the shock was more than them all, and with rest he would evidently pull through it.

The clang of a breakfast bell sounded on the morning air, and the rafters and travellers trooped to the tavern.

The fame of Dick and his companion speedily spread through the neighbourhood. Dick, according to rough estimates, had lifted a weight of two hundred stone. Hugh Lark was the most affable of all. Tom, the injured chopper, had been a lifelong friend, and this aid to a friend in distress he could not forget.

"Ye'll come down and see my raft," said he after breakfast. "You have never seen a raft and it'll be interesting to see how it's put together, and how we manage it with the great oars; and then I have something to tell you that will be, no doubt, interesting."

Together Hugh and our travellers wended their way around the tavern end, and down the edge of the stream. They rounded a bend in the stream and there, riding in the comparatively quiet water of the eddy, was the raft of the night before. With a bound Hugh was on it, followed by the others.

"Ye'll notice the way it's put together. First we square the timber sticks after they are cut to proper lengths, then tumble them into the water side by side, and bore these holes with the augur three inches apart. Then we get the stoutest ash or hickory poles, green and strong, and lay across the top of them midway between the holes, and bind them to the timber with well seasoned hickory bows and wooden pins. Ah! I see you are trying the oar." This last to Ande, who swung with his weight the great oar blade from its fastenings, and shoved it to and fro. "It's not easy work in a strong flood, and especially in the Rough Water."

"The Rough Water?"

"Aye! That's a section of the stream in the Big Lycamahoning some fifteen miles from here, where in a course of ten miles the water rushes with the speed of a race horse. It's most dangerous because of the rocks and requires a steady head and a ready hand to pilot through. Yet I have done it many a time and had no accidents. I suppose, with the exception of old Pegleg, I'm the only pilot that can say as much," and then seeing the look of inquiry on the faces of his auditors he continued: "Pegleg is a one-legged pilot who feels as much at home on the bobbing raft as he does on the land. But," and Hugh looked at his auditors kindly, "I didn't fetch ye here for the sake alone of showing the raft. I wanted to get you away from the prying eyes and ears of old Peter Burke and the rest. Last night I felt little like saying much about certain knowledge that I have, but men who have favoured our village by saving the life of one of its citizens, and one of my best friends at that, deserve something in return. If you are prospectors, come to my place to-morrow evening and mayhap I can give ye the information that would be of value to you. But not a word to any others, and especially to old Peter."

"We'll be on hand, never fear," said Ande.

There was a crashing in the underbrush of the shore, and two or three of the raftsmen leaped on the raft.

"When do ye think we can safely start, Hugh?" asked one.

"In two days, not before. The flood will take that time to go down to a good rafting stage. In the mean time, boys, we'll go home; but day after to-morrow we start out for down stream."

All returned to the tavern where, after some conversation, the raftsmen betook themselves to their homes and Ande and Dick having mounted their horses, well rested with the night, pushed down stream, toward the west, on a rude, half-cleared mountain trail. The road wound itself in a sinuous line over hills and through deeply wooded glens, but always the roar of the stream was in their ears.

"What boundless forests these are," said Ande, as they rested their horses on the summit of a steep declivity and gazed o'er the rolling mass of treetops. "No wonder Professor Bill was so oratorical. This is the famous country through which Armstrong marched his troops in 1756 against Shingas and Jacobs, the Shawnese chiefs of Kittanning, and near this section, no doubt farther south, poor grandfather lost his life. It was a fatal mistake."

"Perhaps we shall find something in this section that will tell us of your grandfather."

"If we do, it will be in connection with the Indian eldorado, spoken of by my father."

They had pushed on rapidly and were now nearing the mouth of the Little Lycamahoning. The gleam of a great expanse of water between the trees ahead indicated their approach.

"That must be the Big Lycamahoning of which Lark spoke."

"Hist!" said Dick, "there are some wild geese on the big creek. Hear them gabble. There must be fully a score. It's fortunate we have our guns with us."

They were now fairly in the outer shadow of the trees that o'erhung the trail, and the stream, swollen by the flood to three times its natural size, stretched before them three hundred yards in width.

"You take the right of the group, and I'll take the left," whispered Ande.

Simultaneously with the crack of their own guns another sounded from the midst of the willows that fringed the shore. There was a confused "Hank—Hank!" from the frightened birds as they rose in flight. A second later, a light canoe darted swiftly from the willows, and an aged hunter, its only occupant, gathered up the five or six birds that were slain, placed them in his canoe, and rapidly paddled up stream. All happened so quickly that the canoe with its aged occupant shot around a bend in the stream and disappeared from sight before Ande or his friend could say a word.

"Cool robbery! let's after him," said Ande, and suiting his action to the word, he pushed his horse into the stream and swum to the other side, followed by Dick. The trail was struck again on the other side and up the stream they went at as fast a gait as the many stumps and fallen trees would allow. Several times they crossed the stream by swimming their horses. Two miles up stream the creek valley widened and the stream, winding around the base of a hill, formed a loop or peninsula of some fifteen acres or so in extent. Here, in a small, grassy clearing, a rude cabin of unhewn logs greeted their vision. It was a one-storied affair pierced with loopholes, and had a small window in the end facing the stream. The roof of heavy hand-made clapboards, weighted down with poles, was green with age as also were the mossy logs of its walls. The door, a heavy affair of split timber, was ajar and near it on a wooden settle was the figure of the hunter, a man of some seventy years. The hair of his head and beard were snowy white, but his active frame belied his years. He was clad in leathern breeches, heavily fringed along the outer seams, and moccasins of the same tough material. A loose, woollen wamus, the product of the settlements, served in lieu of shirt and coat. His coonskin cap was beside him on the bench and he was busily engaged in plucking the captured birds. The sound of trotting horses aroused him from his work and he cast a keen, scrutinising, blue eye on the approaching invaders of his little domain.

"I say, sir, we'd like to know why you appropriated our birds," said Ande.

"Aye?" inquired the hunter.

Ande repeated the question.

"I shot these birds."

"Well, we shot some too and you seized them all."

"Ye did shoot some?"

"Yes, we did; we were on the road at the fording and fired at them."

The old man gazed at them earnestly, and evidently believing their tale, said:

"I thought that more were killed with my shot than customary, and if ye fired at the same time that I did, that explains my not hearing the report of your guns. Ye are welcome to some of them."

"Oh, no," said Ande, somewhat mollified by the hunter's generosity and explanation. "We thought you were robbing us, but it was clearly a mistake."

"Will ye sit down; it's nigh dinner time and, if ye can eat with a lone old man, you're most welcome. Ye can pasture your horses in that bit of clearing."

The invitation was accepted. The horses were tethered out where they could nibble the grass, and they returned.

"Come from afar?" interrogated the old hunter.

"From Louisiana," said Ande.

"Here hunting?"

"No, prospecting."

The old hunter straightened up as if shot, and gazed at them as if he would pierce them through with those keen, blue orbs of his.

"What for?" suspiciously.

"Metal, either silver or gold," explained Ande, whose suspicions were also aroused.

"Do ye think ye will find it?"

"Yes, somewhere."

"Where?"

"Along this stream."

"And do ye have any aid to help ye in your search?"

"We have little but our own knowledge."

"And your home is in Louisiana?"

"No, we came from there."

The old man arose with the birds which he had finished plucking and cleaning, and was silent for a time while he placed them in a home-made oven for cooking. Returning to the settle he took up the conversation.

"Ye'll find naught here but woods and hills and coal."

"Have you been here long?" asked Ande, in turn becoming the inquirer.

"Nigh sixteen years."

"How does it happen that you, a hunter, should frequent this section, which is rapidly becoming civilised?"

"Well, the country is becoming more peopled the last year or so, but there is still tolerable hunting. There's black bear in plenty, and there's deer, beaver, coon, and wild birds, and then I have other reasons. This is nigh the place where my father was slain."

"Your father was a hunter, too, then?"

"Aye, aye, he hunted some. He hunted some," went on the old hunter, more to himself than his auditors.

"THE OLD HUNTER STRAIGHTENED UP AS IF SHOT, AND GAZED AT THEM"

"And did Indians kill him?" asked Dick, becoming interested.

"He was captured by Indians and — —" The old man shook his head and then:

"Dinner is nigh ready and ye are no doubt as hungry as I am myself." The trapper led the way into the little cabin. Everything within was comfortable as the life of the woods could make them. A rough oak table stood near the opened window, a pile of bear and deerskins in one corner near the fireplace indicated the place where the aged hunter took his rest at night, several rifles hung affectionately on the branches of deer antlers o'er the fireplace, and along the wall ran a slab bench cut from a split log, the rounded side down, into which was inserted the legs. The dinner of roast goose was soon placed on the table and the hungry men sat down and did full justice to the fare. The old hunter fell into a stage of taciturnity from which he could not be aroused. Toward the close of the meal the host again became talkative and pressed his guests, if they stayed long in the neighbourhood, to call as often as they liked.

"It's a bit lonely for an old man, and I like company at times," said he, as they were preparing to leave. They promised to come.

The horses were soon untethered and mounting they rode back to Burgtown.

"Dick," said Ande in the privacy of their own room, "I believe that old fellow could tell us something about father, possibly about grandfather. I believe he knows at least something about the eldorado."

"He looked most suspicious when you mentioned that we were prospectors."

"His father was a hunter before him, and surely the one or the other must have met him. We'll see as time goes by. We'll call upon him again and try to worm some knowledge out of him. To-morrow we'll get something, I believe, from Hugh Lark, that will bring us close to the mark at least, I'm a-thinking."

CHAPTER XXIII

THE RAFT PILOT'S HOME

"Here easy quiet, a secure retreat,
A harmless life that knows not how to cheat,
With home-bred plenty—the owner bless,
And rural pleasures crown his happiness;
Unvexed with quarrels, undisturb'd with noise,
The country king his peaceful realm enjoys."

—Dryden.

There was the steady tramp, tramp of horses' feet o'er the woodland trail and, by the moon's shimmering gleam that sifted down through the shadowy forest screen o'erhead, two horsemen could be perceived picking cautiously their way in the darkness of the shadow. In clear places, where the moonlight beamed unhindered, they pressed forward into a brisk trot and then again slowing down to a steady tramp as they plunged once more into some shadow. The road was uncertain, filled with pitfalls, stumps of fallen forest giants, and other hindrances that necessitated careful procedure. It was Ande and Dick on their way to the home of Hugh Lark, raft-pilot, and squatter on a ridge of hills, the watershed between the Great and Little Lycamahonings that poured their floods into the Allegheny River. The hoot of a night owl sounded dismally in the neighbouring forest and then, as if his call was the waving of an orchestra leader's baton, forth burst in full chorus hundreds of other birds of night, the most with the weird song "Whip-poor-will, whip-poor-will."

The effect was grewsome and Ande shivered slightly.

"Dick," said he, "I had a dream last night that troubled me much."

Dick was all attention.

"It seemed in my dream that I had found somewhere a pearl of great price and I cherished it as I did my own soul. In the upper Big Lycamahoning district I found a large, silver ingot. In seeking to grasp the ingot I lost the pearl, and I was filled with sorrow, and then the ingot turned into a diamond of the first water and I was glad. I awoke then, and the sun was beaming brightly in through the tavern window on my face."

Ande ceased speaking. Dick was silent for he was thinking, and, though a good, sincere Methodist, was slightly superstitious.

"God knows, Ande, what it all means, but it seems to me that ee'll lose summat and gain summat better."

Dick had spoken partly in the old Cornish dialect, which they frequently spoke when by themselves.

"Aye, I guess that's the interpretation," said Ande, thoughtfully. The way was pursued in silence for some time, unbroken save by the tramp of horses' feet and the whirring wings of some bird whose solitude was disturbed.

A mile or so was passed over and then through the trees ahead was the gleam of a light, and after a time they rode into Hugh Lark's clearing. The log house, two stories in height, loomed up darkly in the dusk of evening. The moonlight touched up its clap-board roof and the edges of its huge stone chimney, lighting them fantastically, and through the greased paper-paned window came the glow of a fire within, evidently from the great fireplace. There was the baying of a hound, and then the quick bark of a shepherd dog in concert, and then the door opened and the frame of Hugh was outlined against the inner light.

"Get back, you dogs! Back to your kennel, Shep, and you, Jack, over to the barn with you!" he bellowed, and the dogs, that looked most aggressive, slunk off at the word of their master. The horses were soon fastened to the rail fence and the horsemen approached the house to be greeted on the threshold with the outstretched hand of Hugh.

"Come in, mon, come in. It's a cauld nicht, as they ca' it in auld Scotland," and he grasped each man's hand welcomingly and drew them within and up to the great fireplace, for though spring had come, yet the nights were cold. Hugh had greeted them as a Scotchman can. Though a tolerably educated man, yet he loved to drop now and then back into his mother tongue. The pilot's wife, a comely dame but little younger than himself, sat near the light of the fireplace busily spinning. His two chubby children had been put to bed in the room o'erhead and the scene within was that of quiet, home comfort. Bunches of dried herbs and a few hams and flitches of dried bacon and deer meat depended from the rafters of the ceiling. A few common prints adorned the rude white-washed walls and o'er the mantle piece, supported by deer antlers, was an old-time flint-lock rifle of great weight and heavy bore. The pilot introduced his wife, who, having made the customary courtesy, resumed her spinning, the whir, whir of the wheel mingling with the cracking of the fire-logs.

Hugh drew forward two home-made chairs for his visitors, and Ande sat down, but Dick was interested in the great rifle o'er the mantle piece. Hugh noticed his concentrated look on the old rifle.

"Aye, ye are looking at a highly prized relic in that rifle. Test the weight of it, sir; notice the large bore capable of carrying a ball the size of a schoolboy's marble."

Dick took down the gun and examined it.

"That rifle could tell many a tale, Mr. Dick, if it could speak. It was my father's, Captain Ande Lark's gun. Ye ken that captains of sharp-shooters in the days of Washington carried guns. A gun was more use to them then than all of the swords made. Father fired the last shot out of it in 1794, when he was mortally wounded by Indians on the Kiskiminatas. It was this way," said Hugh, seeing the look of interest on the faces of his visitors. "After the Revolution, the nation was heavily indebted, and not even the efforts of Robert Morris could save the nation from financial ruin had not many patriots, among whom was my father, withheld their claims for service. Some speculating jobber offered to trade father a thousand acres of land, where Braddock met his defeat, for the com mission papers and his claims. Father accepted, and loading up his goods on a flat boat he floated down the river Kiskiminatas. He was attacked by lurking savages along the river side and, although he succeeded in bringing down several of them by bullets from 'Old Thump,'"—and the pilot waved his hand expressively toward the old rifle,—"yet he received a wound himself from which he afterward died."

Hugh Lark was silent and his usually pleasant face was sober and sad. There was a long pause, unbroken save by the puffs and clouds of ascending tobacco smoke.

"Light the lamp, Mary," he at length said.

Mrs. Lark arose from her work and took from a receptacle in the wall a species of lamp much used by the woodsmen. It consisted of a turnip, split, and hollowed out within. A stick, around which was wrapped a strip of oiled linen, was inserted upright in the centre, and the vessel having been filled with deer grease was ready for use. The visitors gazed at this primitive vessel, that at best gave forth but a dismal light and a far more disagreeable odour.

"Candles are too much of a luxury for us at present, so we still use the old turnip lamp. But to get down to business. I wanted to speak to you of prospecting."

Hugh poked the fire logs a little, and Mrs. Lark arose and brought in a pitcher of home-made cider and some drinking vessels, and then retired.

"Ye must ken that the Indians kenned more of this country than we do, having lived here longer," said Hugh, as he raked a brand from the fire and lit his pipe; and then without pausing for an answer he continued: "I have read much for a backwoodsman and know of how the spirit of jealousy has ruled nations as well as people. The same spirit of jealousy that led the Asiatics to conceal from Europeans their arts and sciences is within the Indian breast. The Phœnecians, so I have read, hid so truly their art of making their beautiful colour called Phœnecian purple that to-day we know nothing of it. The pyramids to-day are monuments of the lost sciences of the ancients. There is much wealth in the hills of the country, known to the Indian alone. Father thought the same as I did and was convinced of it by a wound he received in an Indian expedition with the famous Sam Brady. His wound was probed and the bullet ye see tied to the old lock by a cord was the one taken out of the wound." Both examined the silver bullet that was attached to the lock of "Old Thump."

"He found the mine. Then you know its location, Mr. Lark?"

"Perhaps we had best have an understanding first, before I say much more. If ye are agreed to give me a fair share with yourselves we will go ahead."

"We are perfectly agreed, and more. If you give my friend, Dick, a share, I desire nothing."

Hugh looked mystified at Ande and said partly in the Scotch dialect, "And ye're not after the siller yoursel'?"

Ande seeing that he must explain, related the tale of his grandfather's dishonour, and Hugh, with various nods and puffs, listened.

"Aye, I see, I see," said Hugh; "and ye think the unearthing of this Indian mine will bring to light your family honour. Ye said the other night that ye were prospecting for character, and we thought it was a joke on the tavern keeper," and Hugh's features relaxed into a smile. "But now for my tale. Indians appear here, from the Shawnee tribes in the west, every few years. They remain for a time and then disappear. Some say they come for hunting, some for to visit the graves of their tribe, but I always had my own opinions. Some years ago there was a great flood and we raftsmen went down to get the rafts in safer positions. I was busy piloting when I thought I saw something out on the waters. It was not a rock nor a piece of driftwood, and after I had almost wearied my eyes I saw it was the head of a man. I gave the oar to Tom, the fellow ye saved from the tree the other day, Mr. Dick, and flung out a rope. It fell nigh the fellow and we dragged him in, and if it wasn't a half-breed Indian, a Canadian, so he afterward told me. He was far from his tribe and people and had hurt himself in some scrimmage or other with a wild animal. After we got the raft safe in good quarters, we took him up to our place here and nursed him for many a day until he was ready to leave, and then he showed what stuff he was made off. He wanted to reward me for my kindness. By his directions I got some paper and a pen and drew off a rude map of the Big Lycamahoning region. After it was made he put his brown finger on a certain section and said, 'If white man know what under there they shoe their oxen with silver.' Here's the map," and Hugh took from an inner pocket of his woollen wamus a rude roll of paper which he spread out for their view near the old turnip lamp. Ande took out his father's map and compared it with the other.

"Ye have a map, too," said Hugh.

"The one sent me years ago by my father."

The two maps coincided in all the essential features.

"And now we know the place and the only thing that remains for us is to set the date of going on our search. The first night of the full moon would be best suited to our purpose. And there must be another let into the secret, for we can't get along handily without the use of the only canoe on the Big Creek, and that's Hunter Tom of the Loop," said Hugh.

"Who's Hunter Tom?" asked Dick.

"He's a queer old character, and has been in the neighbourhood of the Big Creek for the—well—as long as any of us around here, and for a great time longer. He's a hunter and has a cabin over in a little clearing alongside of the Big Creek."

"The very man we ate dinner with the other day," said Ande, and turning to Hugh he related the circumstances of their adventure.

"The very same man, and a better guide and hunter none ever saw," replied Hugh, emphatically. Good-nights were now spoken, and, mounting, the young men rode back to Burgtown.

CHAPTER XXIV

THE HUNTER OF THE LOOP

Several times had Ande and Dick visited the old hunter's cabin in the Loop, and there was a growing friendship between the old trapper and the young men. They told him quite a little of their travels, but never mentioned the mines of Brazil. Once the hunter mentioned that he had been a soldier under Brock and had been a hunter ever since. New hope sprang up within the breast of Ande. If this old hunter had been in the service of Brock and had travelled the American wilds for such a time he must surely have met his father. At length the question found utterance.

"You were in the service of Brock. Did you ever meet one of my name either in the army or afterwards. My father was in his service and possibly you may have met him."

"One of your name,—thy father? No, no, Mr. Ande, I know naught. None of that name has ever met me."

Ande, having received this reply, had not the temerity to push his inquiry further. He admired the old hunter for his kind disposition, and especially because he had seen service under Brock. He had frequently tried to get him to relate tales of battles and adven tures, but the old man was of a taciturn nature, a quality born in him by his years of woodcraft. But his taciturnity did not hinder their intimacy or his friendship. He had given them rare treats in canoeing; night after night they had dropped down with the stream to the shelter of willows, and secure from observation had quietly awaited the coming of the deer to slake their thirst at the margin of the stream. On one occasion he had taken them with him through the Rough Water, shooting the rapids with consummate skill, and pointing out to them the marks of interest, such as Pilot Rock or Shawnee Rock, Driftwood, the Sluice and others.

It was the evening just before the full moon when they made their last trip, still-hunting for deer. They had dropped down with the current, and had just secluded their craft beneath the willows when harsh, guttural, sometimes musical voices were heard on shore, at some distance. The old hunter placed a warning hand on the shoulder of Ande, and with the whisper of "Hist!" they listened. Bidding the young men be silent, and on no account to move from their position, the old trapper slipped up o'er the bank and in an instant was gone from sight. The same voices continued for the space of many minutes without interruption, and then, as cautiously as he had withdrawn, the hunter returned. With finger on his lip to indicate silence he cautiously dipped the paddle, and they moved silently up stream, skirting the willows in their journey. When beyond hearing distance he spoke in audible tones.

"The Shawnese are in the land. They must have come up from the Ohio."

"But they are peaceful, no doubt?"

"Aye, they are peaceful; but I always mistrust them. The cruelties they heaped upon my father and the cruelties that I have witnessed at their hands have always made them hateful to me."

"How do you know that they are Shawnese?" asked Dick.

"How do I know, lad? I have had more dealings with the Indians and the Shawnese than any one around this section. I remember the time I met Tecumseh and his brother, the Prophet, in the Ohio region years ago, and their language is as familiar to me as my own. The silver mine that the pilot was a-telling ye of was even then current among them, but more as a legend than as an active fact."

"The silver mine?"

"Aye, the silver mine. Haven't I searched for it, and found it not. I searched for it until I was weary, and then I gave it up. Of what value is silver or gold to me now. My friends are all dead, and I, myself, have not so many years to live that I should delve after the curse of earth. Two years after I left the old Dart I swore, on the receipt of news of the death of my dear ones, never to return, unless, — —" The old hunter was silent.

"Unless?"

"Not unless I accomplish my purpose here. I came not here as a hunter, lad, alone;—there were other pur poses, vain probably now." There was an element of sadness in the hunter's tone. "And yet I should like to see the old home once more. It is very dear to me."

> "'Ah, happy hills! Ah, pleasing shade!
> Ah, fields beloved in vain!
> Where once my careless childhood strayed
> A stranger yet to pain!
> I feel the gales that from ye blow,
> A momentary bliss bestow,
> As waving fresh, their gladsome wing
> My weary soul they seem to soothe,
> And redolent of joy and youth
> To breathe a second spring.'"

"Why, Hunter Tom, that's Gray's Ode to Eton College," said Ande with increased respect.

"Aye, sirs, ye are a bit surprised to hear an old backwoodsman and hunter quote that, but I have a right to it, for I was an Etonian, myself, in younger days."

The keel of the light canoe grated on the rocky shingle of the Loop shore.

Hunter Tom had insisted on going straight to his cabin on his discovery of the Shawnese. The young men waited until early dawn and then started for Burgtown. On the way they met Hugh Lark astride of his gray mare.

"Hallo! hitting the trail as usual! Well, we'll have a different trail to-night. We meet at Hunter Tom's place at eight o'clock and set out from there. See ye to-night," and Hugh was off up the trail.

"Hunter Tom is a queer character," said Ande to Dick, as they continued their way. "He's a combination of the old hunter and the scholarly civilian. It's a wonder we never heard of his scholarly attainments before."

"From what I have heard, he doesn't mix up with the people around here. What a marvellous woodsman he is, and how silently he approached the Shawnese camp!"

The log houses of Burgtown hove in sight, and they dropped all conversation as they rode up through the double row of log homes and alighted at the tavern of Peter Burke.

CHAPTER XXV

EUREKA! THE ELDORADO!

"So the boat's brawny crew the current stem
And, slow advancing, struggle with the stream;
But if they slack their hands or cease to strive,
Then down the flood with headlong haste they drive."

—Dryden.

It was still early dawn when Hugh Lark reached the hunter's cabin. Hunter Tom was cleaning his rifle and before the door was a pot of lead melting o'er a slow fire. A bullet mould was lying near by ready for use.

"Halloo, Tom!" said Hugh, as he dismounted.

"Good-morning," said the old hunter, a little curtly and yet with some dignity, for he liked not the unceremonious manner of Hugh, though Hugh was the only intimate acquaintance he had resident in the neighbourhood.

"Going hunting?"

"No," said the old hunter, a little more friendly. "I was down the creek and saw some Shawnese."

"Why, ye don't expect a brush with them in these days of peace?"

"I tell ye," said the old man, testily, "those were the enemies of my father and, peace or no peace, I trust them not unless I have Brown Bess ready and a quantity of powder and ball nigh at hand," and he continued his polishing and oiling.

"Well, we have some work and we would like to have ye along, if ye can go." The old man made room for him on the rude bench, and looked at him inquiringly. Hugh related the purposed expedition.

"And ye think there is a silver mine, and ye want me to help find it, and if I do I go fair shares?"

"Aye," and Hugh nodded. "Ye see there are two young chaps, travellers, prospectors; they say they know ye— —"

"Aye! ye mean the English travellers, Mr. Ande and Mr. Dick."

"Well, ye see they are prospectors and know the real stuff when they see it."

"So they told me," said the old man, nodding.

"Well, we want ye to go along and use your big canoe. I calculate between your intimate knowledge of the section and their prospecting science and my divining rod that we can get at the bottom of this. To-night will be full moon and we would like to start from your place for up stream about eight o'clock."

"Aye," said the old hunter, but he looked a bit dubious when Hugh mentioned the divining rod. Hugh was a firm believer in the accuracy of the rod that he had constructed. It was witch-hazel, curiously carved and with a bit of silver at the end of it. The principle, according to Hugh's statement, was like attracted like.

"Well, I'll go," said the old man, after some thought. "I warn ye, though, to take your guns with ye, for the Shawnese are here."

"Oh, they'll give us no trouble, but we'll take our guns. There may be a chance of shooting a deer or so," said Hugh as he departed. The old man shook his head, forebodingly, as Hugh's form disappeared down the trail. On his way back to Burgtown the pilot met the Shawnese, a full fifteen in number, great, strong, athletic fellows, but beyond a brief, cursory "Howdy!" and a glance they passed on.

At about seven o'clock that evening Hugh Lark rode up to the tavern of Burgtown. Burke, the tavern keeper, met him at the entrance.

"Going rafting, Hugh?"

"No. Air the two strangers here?"

"Been rafting?"

"No. Air Mr. Ande and Mr. Dick here?"

"But ye surely have more rafts to run, Hugh?"

"Ye ken well enou' that I'm not a-going rafting. How could I go rafting a-horseback. But perhaps ye think that I can get the gray mare to pull an oar, and I've no doubt that she could do that, for she has a heap more sense than some men I know that are not very far from me," said Hugh, exasperated.

"Yes, the mare has great sense," replied Peter, gazing at the animal with a bland eye. "I kalkilate you uns air going to find that mine, Hugh?"

"We are going a-hunting," said the nettled Hugh.

At this moment Ande and Dick came forth upon the long porch, and Hugh's anger was mollified.

"Are ye ready?"

"Yes," said Ande, and the next moment two horses were led around to the front by the stable lad and they vaulted into their saddles and prepared to leave.

"I say, Mr. Ande," —the tavern keeper had the habit of calling them by their first names, perhaps from Hugh's custom—"I say, air you uns a-going hunting fer thet mine?"

Ande gazed at the curious tavern keeper gravely and then responded:

"The primary intention of our nocturnal expedition is to reconnoitre the situation of the argentiferous fissures indigenous to this locality, the elucidation of which will be beneficial to us and of salient value to the community at large."

"Oh, I thought you uns were a-going to find the mine," said Burke, apologetically, and as they rode off he said, to himself, "Wot langwidge! wot a scholard! He beats Bill, but,—dang it, if I believe they're going fishing, though. They hain't no hooks or rods and who ever hearn tell of a man going fishing with a gun."

So saying, he went within.

The sun had gone down and twilight was creeping on, enveloping the earth with its soft hazy light, as the three rode over the lower bridge and o'er the trail to the forks of the creek. The moon was not up, but it was twilight still when they forded the Big Creek and turned up the trail to Hunter Tom's cabin. A short distance, and a glimmering light penetrated the trees and underbrush ahead.

"Some one on the trail," said Dick.

"No," responded the pilot, "'tis a light from Hunter Tom's cabin. The old man must be getting ready to start."

The light was dimmed by a brighter effulgence beyond. A rim of silver shoved itself above the neighbouring hills, and then a semi-circular disc, gradually growing in brightness and flooding hill and ravine with mellow light. Giant boulders and tree trunks were silhouetted against its rising disc, and on a tree branch just athwart the centre was, grotesque and huge, the figure of the lone bird of night—an owl.

"Plenty of light to-night," said Hugh.

"But not more than we need; the search will require all the light we can get," said Ande.

They arrived at Hunter Tom's cabin and dismounted. The horses were hobbled and turned out to graze in the clearing. Tom, hearing the noise, opened the door, and cheerfully welcomed them within. The hunter was clothed in his customary fringed buckskin and home-made moccasins, but in his belt, in addition to the usual hunting knife, was a small Indian tomahawk.

"Why, Tom, one would think ye were on the warpath," said the pilot, jokingly.

"Aye, and a warpath it may prove," soberly, and then seeing the look of the pilot concentrated on the tomahawk in his belt: "This tomahawk I secured in the Indian country of the Ohio in 1812. It is an effective weapon."

"But surely you don't expect a fight," said Dick.

The old man shook his hoary locks mysteriously and muttered, "The Shawnese."

By the light of the turnip lamp the pilot brought forth his map and spread it out on the rough wooden table. The hunter scanned it approvingly, and then:

"Where did ye get it, Hugh?"

The pilot related his experience with the Canadian Indian, and the hunter nodded his head as the pilot repeated the Indian legend and directions.

"I know the place so well that ye have no need of a map."

"Ye ken the place without a map?" said Hugh.

"Aye! haven't I searched for it full eighteen years ago, and ten years ago, before there was a settler in the region; I hunted until I was weary. If ye find no more success than I found, ye will have your labour for your pains. But we can try. The place where we will land is there." The hunter placed his knotty finger on a portion of the map. All crowded around the table.

The old hunter's finger was placed on the map at the mouth of a small stream. A moment passed in silent contemplation.

"And now we must be off if we would do much to-night." The old hunter's words aroused all to action. A couple of pickaxes, a shovel and a crowbar, that were in readiness, were shouldered by the pilot, and Dick, at the hunter's suggestion, took up an old tin lantern, pierced with holes and having a candle within, to be used in an emergency. The hunter carefully extinguished the turnip lamp and drawing the door shut behind him led the way to the canoe. The tools were placed in the stern and then the pilot, followed in regular sequence by the hunter, Dick and Ande, took their stations, and soon under the steady sweep of four stout paddles the canoe, though heavily laden, glided up stream.

The evening was still, save for the cry of some wild bird of night and the plash of some wavelet breaking on the shelving shore. Trees and shrubbery, underbrush of the shores, glided by slowly, and were swallowed up in the obscurity of the regions passed. Here and there with a skilful sweep of the paddle the pilot changed the course of the canoe to escape contact with some rock or sunken log. Now and then the hunter would give a sign of silence, and the paddles in their incessant sweep would be stilled into inactivity, while the canoe would drift for a moment until the hand of the pilot in the bow grasped some over-swinging tree branch and stayed her downward course. A moment of silence, in which the hunter strained his ears, would ensue, and then with a shake of the head he would give the sign to proceed. Once he insisted much to the protests of the pilot of going ashore. They drew in to the heavily wooded bank and he disappeared with no change on his immovable countenance. The pilot grumbled to himself at this unnecessary caution. The old man was in his dotage or had become filled with childish fear, thought he, and so he informed the others when the hunter was absent.

Who was going to hurt them? Not the settlers, for they were all safe abed by this time. Not that wandering band of Shawnese. It would be too perilous for them in these days of peace and in a section already vacated by their fathers to make room for the settlers. After the first hour the work of paddling became less arduous, the force of the current had abated, and they shot into a long stretch of slightly moving water.

"Still Water," said the pilot. "It'll be easy from now on until we reach some distance above."

"Aye," murmured the hunter; "but it'll not be still for long."

"No sign of rain; the sky up there is so closely studded with stars that there's not room for a cloud. There'll be no rain, or I'm no pilot. Haven't I piloted here for years, and before I came to this region I run as many rafts down the Susquehanna as any raftsman in the State."

The hunter raised his hand as if deprecating the sound of the pilot's voice, and then said in low tones:

"I have lived in the cabin at the Loop for nigh ten years, and have tramped these regions before my cabin was built, and I can read the stream as well as a scholar reads his book. In three hours what we call the 'Still Water' will be running like a mill race."

The pilot smiled a smile of superior wisdom.

"Look," said the hunter, as he dipped his palm in the water and drew up a little for the pilot's inspection. "The stream is turbid and discoloured, the first sign of the coming flood. There has been great rain at the headwaters. I can see it in the water; I can smell it in the air."

The pilot's smile left his features and he scanned the bosom of the Still Water and then:

"There's some truth in that."

"Aye," said the hunter, "and if we would get to the place we must paddle as strongly as possible. There's the swifter water beyond."

All bent to the paddles again with renewed efforts and the Still Water was soon passed, and the heavier paddling in the swifter water of the upper stream followed. Now they were in the shadow of some towering hill or under the dark tree boughs—that interlaced and formed a dark canopy overhead; now again the canoe shot out into a flood of pale moonlight. The latter the hunter disapproved and the pilot, grumbling, changed the course at times, avoiding the moonlight sections of the stream for the shadowy regions along the shores. At length the hills receded from the stream on the right and gave place to a gently rising plain, burdened with oaks and wild grasses, while the hills to the left seemed to be higher and more precipitous than those down stream.

"The place is nigh here," said the hunter.

They rested on their paddles for a moment in the shadow of a great boulder that stayed the downward drift of the canoe. Ande and the pilot instinctively felt for their maps and tried to refresh their memory in reference to the directions, but the dim light almost made it useless. Hunter Tom, in the meantime, was scanning the stream and shores and seemed to be ill at ease.

"The mouth of the little run is but a dozen rods up stream. Ye can put away the maps, lads, for I know the place." At the words of Hunter Tom both Ande and the pilot dropped their maps in the canoe, and all bending to the paddles while the hunter with his keen sight directed their movements, they moved on. Then came the babbling, rippling sound of a little run as it leaped, gurgling with delight, into the stream, like a child into the arms of its mother. The craft was turned to shore and soon grated on the pebbly beach. They stepped ashore and stretched their cramped limbs, while Hunter Tom tied the canoe to a swaying pine, and then pursuing his directions, they followed up the run. Ten yards up the run a divided oak was located.

"Now," said the Hunter, as he gazed around uneasily, "fifty yards due north."

Dick, having a pocket compass, now took the lead, following a course due north, and in the rear was the pilot balancing his divining rod, while Ande as closely as possible measured the distance. Hunter Tom, taking little interest in the affair, seemed to concentrate his attention on the trees, underbrush and regions around about.

"'Tis here, as near as I can calculate it, that the fifty yards end," said Ande.

"And the divining rod says the same, and it tells truth," said Hugh, the pilot, with a little triumph in his tones.

"My calculations, heretofore, located the spot a bit beyond," said the hunter, with the first interest he had betrayed since they landed. "Ye may be right."

Dick and the pilot grasped the pickaxes and set to work with vigour, while Ande used the shovel and occasionally removed with his hands some large boulder that impeded their work. The hunter seemed to constitute himself watchman and was incessantly on guard. The work went on for an hour, and considerable debris was removed when Dick's pickaxe slipped from his hands and disappeared from sight. With an exclamation he leaned forward and found that it had disappeared in an old excavation a few feet in depth. The excavation was widened and the pilot, leaping in, began to work with increased vigour. Hunter Tom now became as deeply interested as the others. It was at a spot that he had not investigated before. That old excavation must mean something, he thought.

There was the sound of a metallic click as the pilot's implement struck something hard. With an exclamation of "I've found it," he reached down and grasped something which he handed up to Ande for investigation. It was a small tobacco or snuff-box of ancient make.

"Time enough to look at that when we find the ore," said Ande, as he placed it in his inside pocket. The work was again resumed. The labour of excavation now became harder and Dick with his great strength took the pilot's place. At length a peculiar, grey, metallic substance rewarded their labour. A handful of small cubes and octahedral pebbles were passed up for inspection.

The tin lantern was lighted and around about clustered the pilot, Dick, and the hunter, while Ande held the handful close to the flame.

"The grey, metallic lustre looks like silver glance. It may be the blossom of sulphide of silver or sulphide of lead. We ought to have daylight for a better examination," said Ande; "now ——"

Crack! Crack! Crack!

Crack! Crack! Crack!

There was the whistling of bullets in the trees around them, and spiteful thuds as leaden missiles flattened themselves against the rocks. The lantern fell with a crash to the ground, perforated with a dozen bullets. The candle sputtered and went out.

"Quick!" shouted Hunter Tom. "'Tis the Shawnese. Aye, I feared it."

The pilot grasped his rifle and the prospectors theirs.

"This way! To the canoe!" roared Tom, and slipping from tree to tree, they reached the landing in breathless haste. Then came a yell that echoed through the hills, a yell—hellish and replete with rage. Trusting in their numbers, scorning concealment and fearing their victims would escape, the Shawnese charged after them. At the landing there was a sanguine scene, and now it was that old Tom showed the experience and skill he had gained in the Ohio region. Stationing himself behind a tree the old hoary-headed hunter fired, loaded, and fired again and again, and each time by the yell the bullet had found a mark. But the Shawnese were now close at hand and a hand to hand conflict ensued that was savage in the extreme. Hunter Tom seemed to be possessed with the fury of a madman. The presence of the foes that had tortured his father seemed to fill him with a wrath that was demoniacal. With clubbed rifle he beat back the foremost and sent him to the ground, lifeless, then with a swift turn he flung the useless weapon into the canoe, and with knife and tomahawk gave blows right and left. Swifter than a weaver's shuttle the bright weapons flashed in the pale moonlight. Nor was the hunter alone active in the fray, for Dick—great Dick, made more effective use of the butt of his gun than the muzzle by using it as a farmer would his flail. Ande and the pilot, for a time, had fired from a natural breast-works of boulders along the shore, but the proximity of the enemy was so close that they, too, were compelled to resort to the butts of their guns. At one time the pilot was down, but the dusky face over him went down a moment later under a crashing sweep of Ande's gun. The desperate valour of these few men was beginning to tell upon the spirits of their foes. One-third of their number were upon the ground, dead or helpless. There was a shout and a few unintelligible words among them, and then, as if in concert, they began to retreat slowly, followed by the impetuosity of Dick and Ande. Tom thanked his good fortune then for his understanding of the Shawnese tongue; he understood their plan to draw them from the shore and to give chance for two or three skulking forms to gain the rear.

"To the canoe! Back for your lives!" he shouted, and simultaneously rushed for the shore. Dick and Ande were either too confused by the yells around them or hard pressed in the conflict to give heed. Not so the crafty pilot. With instinct he seemed to understand the import of the retreat, and rushed headlong into the water after the canoe. The rope by which it was attached had stretched itself to its full length and the canoe had edged out by the force of the rising current. He had almost reached it when a shot rang out from the shore, and the pilot, flinging up his arms, plunged into the muddy tide. Hunter Tom who was next to him, tried ineffectually to grasp his falling form, but the next moment the swirling waters bore him away. There was no time for regret. The canoe was hauled in and Tom in its bow, with knife ready to sever the rope, looked shoreward for his friends.

Ah! What a scene! A sight that, though it filled the old hunter with alarm, yet thrilled him with admiration. Ande, apparently deeply wounded, was on the ground and Dick—did he ever appear so heroic? Standing head and shoulders above the tall savages, he seemed like a pine surrounded by scrub oaks. Nor was the giant Cornishman idle for, like a child's toy, the heavy rifle whirled and whistled around his head and shoulders. Death lurked in its sweeping circle. Nor was strategy of any avail. One sought to run in under his guard, while another was receiving the attack, but the attacking party went down under a terrific swing, while the stooping, swiftly moving strategist received, the next moment, a jolt from the end of the gun barrel that was as disastrous as the blow of the butt. Four had already fallen under those sweeping blows. Old Tom paused not for an instant. While some occupied Dick's attention in front, one or two were edging toward the rear, and should they accomplish their purpose the end was certain. With a cry of "Have at them," the hunter leaped from the canoe, beat off the skulking forms in the rear, and then reaching down he grasped the unconscious Ande, like a father would a child, and hurriedly placed him in the canoe.

"Back, Dick, lad!" he shouted as he pushed out a little from the shore.

Dick heard the call, and with another sweep of his weapon cleared a broader circle, but the rifle unused to the unnatural strain, broke at the lock. Flinging the shattered piece in the face of an advancing enemy he leaped to the shore. Two Shawnese, one a powerful built fellow, strove to intercept him, but there were other defences.

Crack! A shot rang out from the canoe. It was the trapper's gun that spoke, and one fell under that unerring aim. Crash! went Dick's great fist on the countenance of the other, and the dazed Shawnese sat down in a heap. Hunter Tom could have laughed then and there at the repulse of the latter, but there was not much time for sentiments of any kind. Dick had leaped into the stream after the canoe and was pushing toward it through the swift current. There were a few yells of disappointment on shore, and then a perfect fusillade of bullets hissed spitefully on the waters and crashed through the underbrush on the farther shore and then—like the falling of a forest giant that had felt the biting steel in its vitals, Dick fell. He struggled for a moment to reach the hunter's outstretched hand and then sank, and the swift current, now a roaring turbulent, gyrating mass, swelled to foaming madness by the rain at the headwaters, whirled his great body under the bellying bow of the canoe—and he was gone from sight.

With a quick sweep of the knife Hunter Tom cut the rope, and the canoe, freed, bounded away on the surface of the flood like a thing of life. Carefully pillowing Ande's head on his rolled up wamus in the rear, he lay down in the bow and with one hand over the gunwale, holding the paddle, he sought to guide the swiftly floating craft, while with his head slightly raised he kept a keen lookout for the bodies of Dick and the pilot. The Shawnese kept up a running fire on shore for the distance of a half a mile, when the fire slackened, and evidently the swiftness of the current and the gloom cast by the heavy foliage overhead had caused pursuit to be abandoned. The Still Water was reached and the aged hunter perceived with grim satisfaction that his prediction had come true. What was some hours before a still, softly flowing body was now a rollicking, turbulent mass that glowed with a yellow, dunnish hue in the moonlight. Onwards bounded the canoe, the hunter guiding it with unerring hand, now avoiding a towering rock, now bending with the full power of his muscles to guide the craft around a sharp bend in the stream. Fear of pursuit having long been left behind, he had arose to a sitting posture, and was lending to the onward force of the current the might of his own arms. No vessel ever scudded before a gale faster than the canoe on that eventful night. Once the sole, lone canoeist thought he saw the body of Dick floating before him on the surface of the tide and he redoubled his efforts to overtake him. The object was reached, but proved but a piece of driftwood, darkly dappling the yellow flood. With the first feeling of relief that he had experienced that night he saw the winding course of the Loop before him. Once more the paddle was brought into vigorous requisition, and then with a sigh of relief he turned the prow toward shore and the keel grated on the shelving beach. Tenderly he lifted Ande from the stern and laid him on the sward, then turning to the canoe he lifted it bodily from the water and, taking it a few yards inland, hid it securely in the underbrush. Then returning to his unconscious companion he carried him to his cabin home. Knowing that he dared not leave his wounded friend, and yet wishing to arouse the citizens of Burgtown, he went without, unhobbled the horses, and with a smart blow sent each galloping home to town. This done he returned to the cabin, barricaded the house, both window and door, loaded his rifle, and feeling secure, turned to resuscitate the wounded man. With a woodsman's skill he laboured through the long hours of the night until the dawn appeared, examining, with muttered commentations.

"Ah, a wound in the arm. It could not have been the last. A brave young man and fought like an old Indian fighter. Aye, another wound in the leg; 'tis only a flesh wound and will heal soon or old Tom doesn't know his art. And here's a slash of a knife in the breast. Ah! 'twas a cruel stroke, that. But none of them are strong enough to lay such a man out. He has the strength of a young lion and Tom will bring him through. But what's this?" In handling the unconscious man's head the hair had fallen aside and revealed the stroke of a tomahawk or knife. "Zounds! A ghastly wound that. It must have stunned him." With water taken from an earthen basin in the corner of the cabin he bathed the wounds, poured in some healing lotion and bound them up with a rude skill. Then, having poured a little brandy down his throat, he began to chafe his hands and wrists until, with the glimmering light of dawn, the light of consciousness returned.

"Where am I?"

"Safe here in my cabin, lad."

"And Dick and the pilot?"

"They are gone, my lad, the Lord knows where," answered the old hunter, and with his eyes glistening with tears he related the closing scenes of the fight, and how Dick and the pilot were shot and swallowed up in the flood.

"Poor Dick—I have lost in him the pearl, and my dream is fulfilled."

He sank back in weariness and closed his eyes. Suddenly the wounded man started to a sitting position and whispered with excited face:

"The Shawnese. Don't you hear them, Tom, Hunter Tom? They are stealing through the woods and around the house. I hear them. Give me a gun, and we'll defend the cabin."

The effort was too much, and he sank back again on the couch of deerskins in a semi-conscious condition.

Tom, too, had heard something, but it was not the tread of Indians. The next moment there was a shout without and the clatter of approaching horses' feet. 'Twas the settlers.

CHAPTER XXVI

THE RISING

"All parts resound with tumults, plaints and fears;
And grisly death in sundry shapes appears."

—Dryden.

There was great excitement in Burgtown. The old tavern keeper had found three horses without his door, standing there jaded, tired, in the early dawn. He recognised them as the animals of the pilot and the two prospectors. Around the tavern's long porch were assembled Professor Bill Banks, the town citizens, and several outside squatters, a motley assemblage, listening to old Burke's recital. The tavern keeper was filled with importance, for once he was the centre of attraction and seemed like a Fourth of July orator, so breathless did all seem to hang upon his words. His round body was swelled to greater proportions as he proceeded, in a roundabout way, to narrate what he knew of the affair.

"It war this way. The pilot, Hugh Lark, he kem a-riding up about dark last night and asked fer the strangers, whether they was to home in the tavern. He seemed powerful anxious to have them right away. 'Going rafting, Hugh?' sez I, social-like. 'No,' sez he; 'air Mr. Ande and Mr. Dick in?' 'Been rafting?' sez I. Then he fired up, mad-like, and talked about the grey mare of hisn being able to pull a oar as good as any raftsman. I had my doubts of that, though the mare has a heap of sense. But I thought he war joking, and I guess he war. About that time I up and asked whether he war a-going a-hunting for the mine. You see the strangers air pros—whatever it is—I mean they war miners, and we uns had the idee that they were a-searching for something of that kind. He up and sez, short-like, that he warn't and that they war just going hunting. 'Bout this time Mr. Ande and Mr. Dick come out, and their hosses were brought around, and they jumped on, and then I thought I would ask Mr. Ande, being as he war allers social-like. 'Air ye going to find thet mine, Mr. Ande?' sez I. Then he up, and in high larndt langwidge, told we uns about their going after some kind of fishes, but I ne'er hearn tell of a man going fishin' without hooks and with a gun and——"

"Come, cut it short," said Professor Bill, impatiently. "At what hour did they go?"

"'Bout seven o'clock last night, and——"

"And when did the horses return?"

"Well, if I do hev to say it——"

"Come," said Bill, with the authority of a leader, "when did they return?"

"Well—I kalkilate 'bout five o'clock in the morning, leastways they were here when we uns got up."

"And which way did they go?"

"Well, ye see, Mr. Ande, who is a great scholard and high larndt, he——"

"Egregious dolt! Vociferous driveller!" exclaimed Bill, in exasperation, "can't you say which way they went."

"Gosh, what langwidge!" murmured the tavern keeper in excessive admiration of Bill's explosion, but seeing that Bill was getting angry he answered quickly: "As I live, Bill, I think they went down creek to old Hunter Tom's, seein' as Hugh war fond of Tom. Leastways they went that way and——"

Old Burke's words were drowned in the commands of Bill.

"Every man get his horse and gun and we'll start in five minutes. Others can follow. We go to Hunter Tom's place. Perhaps some accident has happened. Fetch me some brandy, Burke; if they are hurt they may need it."

Rapidly the men collected, and under the able generalship of Professor Bill Banks forth they sallied. The tavern keeper watched them gallop down the town road and thunder over the lower bridge, and when they had disappeared among the trees of the farther shore he entered the tavern.

"Wot a scholard Bill is," he murmured as he endeavoured to write down his learned words. "Egg—egg—" he murmured, and then he slowly allowed his tongue to follow the twisting, uncertain movements of his quill pen. "It's no use," he said, as he flung down the quill; "Bill will hev to write her down fer me. Wot a scholar! He'll be a Congressman yit."

Bill and his men in a short time reached the hunter's cabin in the Loop. Tom, hearing the shout of familiar voices, flung open the door, and in a few, brief words narrated the adventures of the night. They had been up the creek, he said, and had been attacked by Shawnese. About the object of their night expedition he was silent.

The news of the presence of Indians in the neighbourhood was new to all but two of the party, who had seen them as the pilot had seen them on the former day. Bill, with the skill of a general, divided his forces. Two he told to remain with Ande in the cabin; some were sent down the river in search of the pilot and Dick; the remainder and greater number, with the hunter in their midst, were to take the trail up stream to avenge themselves on the remaining Shawnese. According to the hunter's account but half a dozen at the most remained. Tom was in little hopes of finding them, as by this time they had made good their escape; but Professor Bill was inflexible, and forth up the creek trail they started. Part of the expedition went in Tom's canoe and the rest, leaving their horses in Tom's clearing, started forth on foot. The place of the battle was reached after an hour or so, but little was to be learned. At the landing, with the exception of trampled ground and a few pools of blood, nothing could be seen. The bodies of the slain Shawnese were either buried or consigned to the flood. The neighbourhood was thoroughly searched, the woods and hills beaten by the scattering settlers, but Shawnese, living and dead, and even Dick's broken rifle, had dis appeared. Expecting the rising of the settlers they had decamped in haste. Disappointed in their quest they returned to the Loop.

There they waited the return of the party down stream while they listened to Hunter Tom's cursory narrative of the battle and the chief events. He told how they were surprised, but not for what purpose they had journeyed to that locality; how the pilot fought and slew a couple of the foe and afterward, rushing into the flood to reach the canoe, was shot down by an Indian bullet; how Dick, "the giant," as he was sometimes called by the settlers, towered a head and shoulders o'er the enemy.

"I'll wager he knocked them down like nine-pins," said Professor Bill Banks.

"Aye," said the hunter, "he did that; he handled his rifle like a farmer's flail, and every time he struck he threshed their top-knots out. Then, when I caught up the lad in yonder and took him back to the canoe, he cleared a wider circle for himself and leaped like a kangaroo toward shore."

"And they didn't dare stop him?" asked one.

"Not they? They couldn't. Aye, there were two fellows, one a stout one, good-sized, that did hedge in to cut him off, but one was shot down and the other— —" The old man allowed his weather-beaten face to relax into a grim smile of humour as the scene arose before him in mind.

"And the other?"

"Well, the other come too nigh to Mr. Dick's big fist, and he went down in a heap with the most astonishing look on his countenance that I ever saw on the face of any one. It makes me smile now when I think of it. Then Mr. Dick came leaping and pushing through the water. I had pushed out a little from shore and had my knife ready to cut the rope as soon as he could reach the canoe, when a hailstorm of bullets skipped across the water and Dick plunged under and I saw him no more. The rest of the tale you know."

The narrative was finished, but it was noticed by several that the old hunter spoke very little of his own achievements in that battle. And yet they knew that he had not been idle.

"And did Mr. Ande do much fighting?" asked Professor Bill.

"Fighting? Aye, he fought like an old Indian fighter. In all my experience with Indians, I have come across none who put up a braver battle than the young lion cub in yonder; aye, and fighting wounded at that, for he carries a wound in the chest that would have killed an ordinary man, and a wound in the leg, and another in the arm that would have made many a stout heart give in, but he fought on until he received that blow on the head that rendered him unconscious. Brave—very brave."

"And how about yourself, Tom?" asked one of the settlers.

"Oh, I killed a few," said the old hunter, simply.

There was a shout from down the creek trail, and the sound of horses' hoofs, and proceeding as rapidly as possible over the uncertain trail the band from down stream entered the clearing.

"What news?" asked Professor Bill, rising from his recumbent position.

"We found the pilot and he's living, but pretty badly hurt. He was pulled on a raft by the Pegleg pilot, and they put him off at a tavern further down stream."

A cheer went up from all the assembled settlers, and the wildwood rang with their voices again and again, and then when silence had come there were various comments.

"I thought the pilot was too tough to be put out by a single bullet," said one.

"I knew that ye couldn't drown an old water dog like him," said another.

"Did they get a doctor," said Professor Bill.

"Yaas," drawled one of the returned expedition, "they got a doctor and he fixed him up, but he can't be moved yet for some time, but he'll pull through, he said. We didn't have much time fer to talk with Hugh, for we uns wanted to see about the tother fellow and the Shawnese. We went all the way to the mouth of the creek, and there we learned thet five Indians were seen crossing the river in a canoe some hours before. Now, I remembers it, some of the fellows at the mouth said they seemed in a powerful hurry, and passed over the river in the early dawn, and were making their way toward Michigan."

"And Mr. Dick?" asked the Professor.

"Nawthing was seen of him at all. He must be drowned by this time."

There was a little conference between Professor Bill and the hunter about moving Ande to Burgtown, but the old man strenuously opposed it, and Bill acquiesced in his plan of leaving him at the Loop until he should recover. The setting sun saw all of the expedition trotting homeward to Burgtown, where the events of the day were gone over again and again for the benefit of Peter Burke, tavern keeper. In the mind of that worthy they were tabulated and placed on the same shelf in his memory as the records of Reverend Burg.

CHAPTER XXVII

THE SECRET OF THE SNUFF-BOX

It was in the late fall and the forests and wildwood had adorned themselves with their autumnal dress. Hills, mountains and ravines were gorgeous with mantles of scarlet, of brown, and of gold, while amidst it all several hardy ranges of pine seemed to resist the onward sweep of the frost, and triumphant in their vernal-hued robes, seemed to fling their plumy tops this way and that in contempt of their conquered brethren who wore the livery of the frost tyrant. Here and there several forest giants, weaker than their brethren, were completely denuded of their garments and stood mournfully shivering, trembling, sighing, in the faint afternoon breezes. The rocks and boulders of the Loop, once covered with green creepers, now were bare and desolate, except where a creeper, its leaves smitten to blood red hue, sought to lend its warmth to its cold, rocky, affianced one. The cabin of Hunter Tom seemed to stand out more clearly in relief against the general background of leaves and hills. The door was ajar and the window partly open, but it had no occupant. In a little glade near the cabin, and on a pile of bear and deerskins, was the form of Ande Trembath, apparently in a gentle slumber. Near him, seated on a rude, wooden bench, wedged in between the bases of two chestnuts, were the forms of Hunter Tom and the pilot, Hugh Lark. Hugh had recovered from the severe injuries of the Shawnese battle and had returned to his home and his pursuit of rafting. The old hunter, his hoary hair falling like a veil o'er his ears and shoulders, was engaged in cleaning "Brown Bess," as he called his trusty rifle, but he was not so intent upon this as he was in listening to the conversation of the pilot. It was their first meeting after the notable events of the previous spring, and Hugh was relating his experience.

"I don't remember much of the things that happened after the first few moments that I was shot. I was intent on bringing the canoe closer to land, and was just reaching out for it when I heard a shot and then felt a sting alongside of the head, and then I remember falling and hearing the waters buzzing around my ears like ten thousand bees. Then I kenned naething for, it seemed to me, quite a time. Then there was a time of dim consciousness, and I knew I was floating on at a pretty good speed, but it seemed I didn't care where I went, until at last I came to my full senses by a heavy blow that I got on the arm. I had been dashed by the flood against one of the rocks below the Still Water. Then I realised where I was, and tried to make for land, but the strength of the flood, or my own weakness, made all my efforts useless. I swept past the cabin there and soon approached the place where the Little Lycamahoning empties into the Big, and there I made a strong effort to get ashore, and did succeed in getting away from the violence of the current, but in the meantime I was swept onward past Pilot Rock and I began to hear the roar of the rapids of the Rough Water. I knew I could never get through that stretch of water alive, and had given myself up for lost, when old Pegleg with his raft hove in sight. There ne'er was a more welcome sight. I shouted to them and they heard me, and, as I swept by, they flung me a rope that I managed to grasp, and they hauled me on board. I was so done out that I couldn't speak until they put me off at the tavern, some miles down."

"It was a marvellous escape, and ye ought to thank God for it," said the hunter.

"Aye, I have many a time."

"I'm afraid we have seen the last of Mr. Dick."

"If he wasn't killed outright he must have been battered to pieces in the Rough Water, for I don't think there is a man living that could go through the Rough Water without some support. I have taken a stick of timber through, but riding a stick of timber and going through with nothing but your own arms is a different case. I have seen sticks of timber that have drifted through and been gathered in at the mouth of the creek, and the way they have been gouged and splintered in contact with the rocks was a caution. No man could be beaten around that way and live."

There was a pause of some length, during which Hunter Tom forgot his cleansing of the rifle, and there was a moisture in his eye, a faint indication of the sad ness that he had within him, and all the while the mellow autumnal sunshine poured down and around them through the crimson foliage o'erhead, and the birds of the neighbouring woods seemed to sing merrily as if jesting, laughing, at the solemn import of the pilot's words. It was the pilot who broke the silence.

"Is Mr. Ande nigh well?" with a nod at the slumbering form on the bearskins.

"Still weak, although his wounds have healed. I believe he came off the worst of any of us in the battle. But he's getting stronger. He was much worried about Mr. Dick and the maps being lost."

"Maps lost?"

"Aye. He said that both maps were placed in the bottom of the canoe before we landed. They may have been dropped out when I hauled the canoe ashore and hid it among the underbrush when I returned. The doctor thinks, though, he will be able to be moved soon, and then we shall have a search for them." Tom mentioned the doctor with a tinge of sarcasm as if in contempt of doctors and their medicine. "The lad was getting on well enough under my care, but Professor Bill insisted on calling in the doctor, and so I handed over the case to him, though the lad would have done just as well, if not better, under my own care."

"Do ye think ye can find the mine again?"

"Aye, perhaps, and yet 'twill be a hard thing. I looked o'er the ground when the searching party was with me. The oak and the stream can be found easy enough, but the place of excavation I looked for in vain. The whole hill is covered with loose stones and debris and should we find it, I doubt whether it will prove much more than a small vein of sulphide of lead. I might possibly find it again, for my memory is good, but I have sickened of the whole affair. What use is it to me?" There was a tinge of bitterness in the old man's tones.

"Ye were interested in it, though, years ago, for ye told us so."

"Aye, that was when I was younger than I am now. But my friends and family are all dead, and I am an old man. The rifle gives me all that I need; the spring that gushes forth from under the big rock gives all my drink; I am content to be as I am until God calls me hence; and then I shall go where there is no injustice and where traitorous friends shall be rewarded according to their due and all wrong righted; I am content."

The old man had finished cleaning his rifle; he entered the cabin and returned with a battered violin. Placing it tenderly 'neath his chin, he proceeded gently to draw the old bow across the strings, gently as if he was loathe to awaken the slumbering form on the bearskins near at hand. But the first, faint tones, quivering and like a child's cry, awakened the sleeper. He turned his eyes to Hugh and smiled a welcome and then extended his hand.

"Ah, Hugh, old fellow, glad to see you back and well. I heard that you had returned," shaking Hugh's hand as he knelt down beside him, "and wondered why you didn't come over and see your fellow soldier. Poor Dick is gone, though, and the maps are lost."

"And Hunter Tom says it's useless to try and find the mine," said Hugh, regretfully.

"It may be useless, but we can try. You know that it's not for the silver alone that I'm looking, Hugh."

"Aye, I ken well enou' that."

"Tom, could you play us something. You didn't know, Hugh, that Hunter Tom is a player. He can make the violin talk, and he has often made me cheerful when I felt sad."

Hunter Tom readjusted the violin, and forth upon the afternoon air, silencing the birds for a time and rivalling them in sweetness, pealed the tones of the old violin. It was a martial strain at first that seemed to swell and soar like some triumphant march of some hero returning from the wars. The stream back of the cabin seemed to roar in harmony with the melody, like the thrilling chords of some giant bass viol. The blood mounted to Ande's cheeks as he listened, and his eyes brightened. The pilot gazed at the figure of the old hunter with awe and reverence. If the melody was warlike and stirring the figure of the old man was more so; yes, it was imposing, like some old Viking, who had dared the deep and conquered it; the hunter's figure straightened, his eye flashed, and his hoary locks and beard, stirred by the breeze, appeared to roll away from his head and features like the dashing waters of some cataract from its rocky crest. On and on went the melody, soaring and wildly triumphant with its strong major chords. Then, almost imperceptibly, there was the change to the minor key, and then a number of changes from one to the other, and the effect was like hearing the distant murmur of crashing pieces of artillery. At times there would be a wild shriek from the upper chords and then the same repetition of booming artillery fire. The old man seemed to be giving a musical history of one of his own battles. Then, all of a sudden, all was in the minor key, soft and sorrowful. There was a wailing hopelessness in the tones. The old man's form ceased to tower at his full height, his head sank lower and more lovingly upon the violin, and the strains were like the requiem of a lost soul. The pallor returned to Ande's cheeks and Hugh bowed his head in his hands. The leaves o'erhead rustled in whispering sympathy, and here and there one would fall—a crimson tear from the eye of a giant.

The melody ceased.

"Tom, I didn't ken that ye could play like that. It made me feel that I was fighting the Shawnese again, and that I was knocking them right and left, and then it seemed to me that I was in the Rough Waters, hearing the noise of the rapids, and guiding a raft around the rocks, and then it seemed to me as if the raft was a-dashed to pieces and I was flung solitary and alone on the shore without a friend and without a baubee in my pocket to buy a night's lodging. It near made me greet. Hunter Tom, ye are a wonderful man."

There were tears in the pilot's eyes.

"I tell you, Hunter Tom, you should be on the stage. Play like that before an audience in New Orleans, New York, or London and your fortune is made. Whose melody was it?" said Ande.

"The melody is my own. Ne'er a note of it was e'er on paper; I composed it here in the wilderness and it's a history of my own life and my family. The end of the piece represents me now, a solitary dweller in the wilderness, an exile from home, with no friends but the great God above." The old man bowed his head in weariness, and then sat down on the wooden bench 'neath the trees.

"Ye have other tunes?" asked Hugh.

"Hunter Tom, you never told me that you were a composer and ne'er played that for me before. You have other melodies of your own; play them for us," said Ande.

"Aye, I have other tunes, and many of my own, but I'm not going to make ye sad with an old man's woes. I'll play ye 'Chevy Chase' and 'I See Three Ships Come Sailing In,' to make your hearts glad, and then I'll give ye some more of my own composition." The familiar airs, one after the other, in sequence, airs so delightful to the English ear, came forth from the violin under the magical touch of the old man, and all the while the pilot listened as if he was entranced, and Ande,—it seemed as if the green fields and coasts of England arose before him. Again he saw the Manor and the Manor woods, the Bowling Green of old Helston, and the gleaming, shimmering waters of the Lowe, and the rolling blue of the channel beyond. All passed before him again as if in a dream, and then there were faces that passed before his mind, Tom Puckinharn, Pengilly, and Tom Glaze, and the face of his mother, and back beyond all, a dark-eyed, youthful face, with dark curling locks deep on a broad brow, a countenance, merry, and with something of the joyousness of spring flowers in the gently flushing cheeks. There was an intense longing in his eyes as he allowed his imagination to roam at will. Ah, it was eight long years since he had seen her, and heard those words: "You are my knight." Would she remember him still? Was she married?

The thought gave him pain, and he drove it from him and thought of other themes. The Primrose Cottage arose clearly to his mind. Ah, he must get well soon and return to those haunts of boyhood, and to the dear ones of years ago. But what was that that the old hunter was playing? It could not be "Chevy Chase." The opening bars were swept off the strings with a master's hand. Soft at first and then with louder, more resonant tones. The old man was standing again, his head partly elevated, a look of hopefulness on his weather-beaten countenance. The pilot was drinking in, with eager ears, the melody, and sat motionless. The opening bars were finished, and the old hunter's voice rang out clear and with a wonderful pathos in the tones. He had sung before in other melodies, but never with such feeling as now. Ande rose on one elbow and stared excitedly at the old man. That song! Where had he learned it!

> "Blithe bird of the wilderness, sweet is thy song,
> Blithe lark of the wildwood, O, all the day long,
> A-singing so cheerily in the green tree,
> Thy anthem dispels gloom and sorrow from me;
> Thou sayest in thy song, 'What can sadness avail?
> Injustice shall fall and the good shall prevail.'"

Old Hunter Tom seemed wrapped up in the melody and utterly oblivious to all things around him. With a low plaintive interlude, he continued:

> "Yet bird of the wilderness, sad is our lot,
> Our home confiscated, our name a sad blot;
> The Cornish chief stricken at Prestonpan's fight,
> Wounded at Culloden for King and the right,
> And captured at Braddock's defeat in the glen
> Was——"

There was an outcry from one of the auditors, that interrupted the melody.

"Hunter Tom! Hunter Tom! Where did you get that song? Where?"

The old man had paused with the bow in midair, and with a vexed look at being interrupted, and then, seeing the flushed countenance and gleaming eyes of his patient, thought the heat was too much for him, and that his head was affected.

"The heat of the sun has affected his head, Hugh. Come let us get him in the shade."

"No! No! Where did you get that melody?" excitedly.

"I told ye that I was going to sing ye some of my own songs. It's my own song, lad," soothingly, "and now, Hugh——"

"Oh! God be thanked! My father! My father!" striving to arise to his feet.

"The poor lad is raving, Hugh," and yet with some pallor in his bronzed features.

"SWEET BIRD OF THE WILDERNESS, SWEET IS THY SONG"

"I am not raving! You are my father and I am your son!"

The violin crashed to the ground and was splintered on a projecting rock.

"No, no, you are raving, lad. I have no son. They are all dead, these many years."

"Mr. Ande," said the pilot, striving in vain to calm him. "Mr. Trembath——"

"What!" exclaimed the old man in agitated tones. "Is thy name Trembath? Thy father's name, lad?"

"Major Thomas Trembath."

"Of where?"

The old man asked the question with trembling, faltering lips, eager, yet fearful of mistake.

"Of Cornwall, and Major under——"

"My son—my son!" The cry that went up rent the air and startled even the birds o'erhead. Old Tom was down on his knees, his arms encircling his patient, and with streaming eyes uplifted to the heavens, he murmured fervently, "God, great God, I thank thee! Thou art very good." And then to his new-found son: "But they told me that mother and you were dead. The black sealed letter! Who sent it? It reached me after Proctor and Tecumseh's defeat at the——Ah! I see it all. Another scheme of Lanyan's! A curse upon their race! But no, I must be merciful since God has been merciful to me in restoring to me, in my old age, a son. Thy mother, lad?"

"Is well when I left home and there will be many happy days for her when we return! and as for me, I'm not dead, although the Indians did near finish me."

"And ye were all these years searching for me?"

"No; mother and I thought you were dead, and yet, at times, we would have hope of you still being alive. I was searching mainly for the honour of grandfather and to remove the stain from our name."

"A true son of your race," said the old man warmly and with pride. "Ye are just the same as I was at your age. I might have known ye for my son, and yet the letter of your death and your mother's death took all thought on that subject from my mind."

The pilot with a sense of delicacy, and wondering to himself, had withdrawn from the scene at the start, but was now returning. He saw them seated side by side on the bearskin, and seating himself near them listened with interest to the tales of both father and son.

Before beginning his narrative of his eventful life he turned to the pilot.

"Hugh, this is my son, Andrew Trembath, who with his mother I had long thought dead, and I must introduce myself also, for the Loop and the settlers of Lycamahoning will see me not much longer. Now I know that my wife is living I shall return to the place of my birth. I have long been known by the name of Hunter Tom, and unknown by any other. I am Thomas Trembath, once Major of the 6th Royal Infantry of England, and have been a soldier in three wars, the War of the Colonies against England, the Peninsular War under the great Wellington, and the War of 1812 under Brock and Proctor. The tale of my whole life would be useless, but it is but fair to my son to narrate the last one, and the history of my hunter life here. Ye must know that there was a stain of treason against our house."

Hugh nodded his head.

"I mentioned that to him the first night I spent at his home," interjected Ande.

"Well," continued the Major, "it was mainly for the purpose of removing the stain that I came to this region from Spain. I would have much preferred to fight under the Iron Duke and against the French than against the Americans, but the thought of once more being in the region where my father was shot, and possibly gleaning something of value that would remove the stain of treason, spurred me on. Our regiment was on board the *Royal George* and landed at Quebec, and from thence to the interior it was a weary march, only part of the time alleviated by canoe trips. At first we were under that worthy imitator of Wellington, Brock, and had he lived I have no doubt but what the war would have terminated differently; but he was slain, and Proctor, a stain on British generalship, was placed in his stead. My life was spent part of the time with my regiment and then, for some months, I was an agent of the government among the Indians of the Ohio. It was my purpose to glean from them, of my own account, news of my father. Possibly some aged chiefs would still remember the capture of my father, and would know something of his being found in French uniform with a French commission as captain in his pocket. Should he be guiltless of any treason against England these savages, being so closely allied with the French of that time, would no doubt know of it. Since they were our allies then and friendly, an affidavit from them might be of some service. An Indian's word is as good as another in a court of law. I overcame the natural repugnance that I had to them, and ingratiated myself with them. An old chief gave me much knowledge of my father's capture, but concerning the rest nothing was to be learned. Then I thought of the second plan. My father had a great knowledge of mining and metals, and, while he was resident with the Indians of the Kittanning region, learned the secret of a mine somewhere in the neighbourhood of the Lycamahoning. I resolved to discover the whereabouts of the mine and possibly solve my father's honour at the same time. I learned much as to its location, but nearly lost my life by my incautious repetition of the Indian legend, for on the way back to Malden I was slightly wounded by an Indian. From that time on we were busy fighting, and due to the conduct of our own generals we lost Michigan and a part of Canada. It was after the fatal battle of the Thames that I received the letter from home that filled my heart with sorrow and made me an exile. It was a cruel letter, stating that my wife and boy were dead. England had no more charms for me. I plunged off into the wilderness of New York and Pennsylvania, and after a few years worked my way into this region. I hunted for many years before I resolved to make it my home. The mine I searched for again and again, but met no success, and I finally gave it up in despair. Then I built the cabin here, and the rest of the tale is known to you both as well as myself. Though I have not discovered the honour of my father, yet I shall return to my old home and take up my former life."

The Major finished his tale.

"Ye have had a wonderful life, Tom," said the pilot, "and I'll be right sorry to see you leave, but I have no doubt that Mr. Ande has a tale to tell?" He gazed questioningly at Ande Trembath.

Ande, thus summoned, related the story of his life. The Helston Grammar School, the smugglers, and that long night with Dick on the waves of the channel, the rescue by an outward bound Brazilian ship, their adventures in Brazil, and their sojourn in Minos Geraes in the Sierra Do Frio district, were all successively dwelt on, but he mentioned not the wealth he had accumulated there.

"Mr. Ande," said the pilot, after he had finished, "do ye ken aught of the metal box I handed up from the old excavation that night?"

"The metal box? Why, it must be still in the pocket of my coat, that I have not worn since that eventful time."

The Major entered the cabin and soon returned with the garment. The box was still there, from the bulging appearance of the exterior.

"Father, take it out and examine it."

The old Major did so.

"Truly, an ancient specimen," said he, and then he started, for there on the one side was the engraved figure of a warrior galloping amidst ocean waves. He turned it over, and on the silver lid, in slightly worn characters, was the following:

CAPTAIN ANDREW TREMBATH

"'Tis the snuff-box of my father!" exclaimed the Major, trembling with excitement. "At last the secret of his latter life may be explained. God be thanked if it can!"

The box was opened and, crowding around it, they examined the contents. A few papers, yellow with age, met their vision. The first was extracted, opened, and spread out.

"A letter from thy grandmother to thy grandfather, son Ande," said the Major, and he read it with an agitated voice. The next, a small book, was taken out, and the Major turning to the fly leaf read, "The Diary of Captain Ande Trembath." The first part was a record of sundry things at home in the palmy days when Captain Ande Trembath was Squire of Trembath Manor, and the Major hurried over it, for he was interested in what was beyond. Toward the middle of the diary he paused, and began to read.

> "8th July, 1755. We are not more than twenty miles from Du Quesne, and in a day or so we will see the flag of our country planted on that fortress. So far no attempt has been made to hinder our march. The enemy must be demoralised."

"Ah, Braddock and his soldiers had great confidence," said the Major; "but see here is a great blank of many days." He hurried over the blank pages and again paused and began to read.

> "Nov. 30th, 1755. Quite a time has elapsed since writing.

> The glorious hopes of our army were shattered in a day by a few hundred savages. I was wounded and left on the field for dead. When I came to myself I saw an Indian face bending o'er me. It was Musqueta, a sub-chief under Shingas, and seeing me able to move and alive he promptly took me prisoner, and with a few others I was taken to the chief's headquarters, the Indian town of Kittanning. They told me the whole army was slain. Incredible fact! I was not able to write on account of my bonds. I learned their language and they had some idea of adopting me into their tribe. Indeed, Musqueta had lost a son, and no doubt it was on account of that that he spared me at the defeat, hoping to adopt me into the tribe as his own son. The thing was detestable to me, and I refused all offers of the kind. Then I was forced to run the gauntlet, but it was my salvation, for, seizing a club and leaping through the weakest part of their grinning line, I escaped by my running powers. The swiftest foot of old Cornwall can outstrip the savage."

"He must have been a swift runner," interjected Hugh.

"He was that, but we must see what happened after his escape. All this I knew before by my conversation with the Shawnese under Tecumseh when I was an Indian agent, but nothing more," said the Major, and turning to the diary he again resumed.

> "There was a shout and such a yelling when I escaped that it almost unnerved me, but I distanced my pursuers, and utterly left them in the course of a mile or so. My escape was toward the north along the banks of the river, but I had not gone more than a few miles before I encountered a small detachment of French troops. There was no getting by them at first, but at length I succeeded, after having first slain the French captain, their commander, which, since I could not avoid it, I trust God will forgive me. I accidentally met him in the wood, slew him, and since I could better make my escape in a French uniform, the whole region being French, I exchanged clothes. A commission was in his pocket, in which commission I inserted my own name for greater security."

The old Major paused and wiped the tears of joy from his eyes and murmured, "Thank God for that. Ande, my son, our family name may now stand forth as honourable and upright as any in the British Isles. He was no traitor. Here is the proof. We will depart for England and lay this diary before the authorities and get the signatures of Hugh, here, and the other settlers in testimony." The diary was forgotten for a moment, but the pilot was intensely interested in what followed.

"Read on, Tom, and let's see what happened, and how he got to this region," said he.

Major Trembath resumed reading.

"I arrived the same day at the mouth of a small stream coming from the east, where I found a canoe."

"Must have been the mouth of the Lycamahoning," said the pilot.

"Aye," said the Major, and continued:

"Up this stream I journeyed for fully ten miles when the force of the current became swifter, and I perceived that there were rapids ahead, and so once more took to the land, carrying the canoe, since it was a light affair, with me. I was anxious to place as many miles between me and the Kittanning region as possible. I am now fully forty miles from the enemy and deem myself safe for the time at least. Knowing their language, I discovered a secret when among them—the existence of a silver eldorado, and from remarks I surmise it must be nigh my present location.

"Dec. 1st, 1755. I have found the location of the eldorado. I shall remain a time and investigate.

"Dec. 25th, 1755. It is Christmas day, but I cannot keep it in the old style. I have laid in a supply of deer meat for the winter. In the spring I shall endeavour to find my way east to Standing Stone and be once more among the loyal people of the crown. Excavated two feet of the mine. It is either sulphide of lead or silver or both."

The Major ceased reading and ran over in silence a number of short entries, then paused, and then continued reading:

"August 1st, 1756. I shall work for a day or so yet and then taking some of the stuff east with me get it assayed. The hunting parties of Indians are becoming more numerous, and I cannot stay much longer concealed. In a few days I shall start for Standing Stone."

"The last entry," said the Major, as he closed the diary and replaced it in the snuff-box. "The subsequent events are as clear to me as if they were written on paper. The snuff-box, with its contents, was lost in the old excavation some time before my father left the neighbourhood. Later he left the section, and on his overland trip encountered Armstrong's troops, who shot him by mistake. The honour of our name is cleared."

Early the following spring a canoe was seen descending the Big Lycamahoning. Two occupants were in it, Major Thomas Trembath and his son. They were going to shoot the rapids of the Rough Water, and descending the river to Pittsburgh depart thence to the sea coast, and, to use the Major's own expression, "From there, home to Merrie England."

CHAPTER XXVIII

MISFORTUNES

"'Tis a downright shame," said bluff Captain Tom Lanyan, with some warmth, as he flung his grey hair back from the livid scar along his forehead, and stumped once or twice up and down the room in indignation.

"A shame rather to Miss Midget, herself, to refuse the alliance of a house like ours," snapped Mistress Betty.

"Now the old squire is in ill health and the estate is entirely within your power, brother James. I say it's a shame to pester the poor girl to marry Richard, if she doesn't want to," continued the captain.

"Very well," said Sir James with the slightest trace of a scowl on his placid features, "she shall not be pestered any longer, although many a girl would jump at the chance. I have changed my plans."

"Bless you, brother, you are more generous than I thought," and the captain's face actually lighted up with a smile, that was like the sunshine on a beetling, ragged cliff.

"I have changed my plans," continued Sir James, "I have another plan for Richard. Of what benefit is it to us to have an alliance with a fallen family. It would be much better to seek the Godolphin family. There is the daughter of Lady Godolphin, who will fall heir to the inheritance that a prince might envy, and I do not think the earl would oppose my purpose, for the fortunes of the Lanyans are ascending. With the Godolphins back of me, securely tied in alliance, I could demand anything from the government, and obtain it."

"I shall not marry the daughter of Godolphin," said young Mr. Richard, and his thin lips, so like his father's, closed in a narrow, determined line. "I shall marry Mistress Alice Vivian." Sir James's features flashed with anger. Richard Lanyan continued unawed. "The squire is in favour of it, and you were yourself some time ago. It remains only for the girl to be won over."

"Yes, I was in favour of it, but that was when the Vivians were in good circumstances. The old squire proposed it, himself, years ago, but times have altered. There shall be no alliance with the Vivians. Godolphin is friendly and is relying upon me for support in the House of Commons. For the last two weeks things have looked most favourable toward an alliance with the most distinguished and powerful family of Cornwall, and I am not one to slight the opportunities presented." There was determination in Sir James's tones.

"I shall marry Mistress Alice Vivian," said the son.

"You shall not," with a click of the jaws.

"I shall," with an answering, determined click. Richard Lanyan turned on his heel and left the hall.

"It will be so much better, after all," said Mistress Betty, echoing her brother's thoughts. "Our family might rival the Godolphins in time. Miss Midget will be sorry the day she ever refused. I must set myself to win Richard over from his infatuation, and I flatter myself I shall succeed. When did a woman ever fail?" Mistress Betty tilted her heavy eagle nose at an angle, as much as to say, you'll soon see how a woman's superior wisdom will manage it.

The old captain slowly shook his head as if in doubt.

"You may manage it, and I hope you will, but I would as soon attack a battery of artillery as try and turn a man away from the girl of his choice. I hope you will succeed, for the girl doesn't want Richard, and it is a shame to pester her and the poor old squire. I am glad the thing is settled, though, in brother James's mind, for you'll let them stay, brother James?"

"Squire Vivian must pay the mortgage within a week, when it comes due, or leave the premises. I already have a tenant for the Manor should he fail."

"But—Zounds! That's an outrage!" fumed Captain Tom.

"Nothing but a common procedure of law," asserted Sir James, coolly.

"Aye, it all sounds fine enough, and I suppose it must be so," said the captain, angrily shaking his head, and stumping up and down; "but 'tis an outrage all the same. The poor old squire will be driven out without a home."

"Captain Tom, don't be unreasonable. You know that Squire Vivian will not be homeless, for James intends to let him have the Primrose Cottage at a nominal rent," said Mistress Betty, championing Sir James.

"Aye, and the poor widow, Trembath, has already been driven from the Primrose Cottage, and whether she is in the Union Home, or elsewhere, no one knows. Is that just, James?"

"The Trembaths were traitors to the government," said Sir James, wincing a little under Tom's sharp shaft, "and beside I am not responsible for her loss of money by investment. I offered to loan her the money, and took a mortgage. How could I know that the investment would fail?"

"You advised her," said Captain Tom, bluntly.

"It was her own doing," said Sir James, sharply, "and besides it has all turned out favourably to us. We can't all be on top of the heap, Captain Tom; some must be up and some must be down to make room for those who get up. It's a law of nature, the survival of the fittest, and through it all the circumstances of the Lanyans are better now than they have been for a hundred years." So saying, Sir James turned on his heel and wended his way into the library, where he was soon absorbed in his London mail. Captain Tom called for his horse and rode off to

Helston, and Mistress Betty retired to her own private apartments.

Such were the scenes that happened two years previous to the discovery of Major Thomas Trembath by his son Ande at the Loop. At Trembath Manor was a far different scene.

"Ally, dear, draw the curtains and let me look out once more on the park," said the querulous voice of the old squire. A tall, young lady, with a sweet, though pallid countenance, arose to do his bidding. The curtains were withdrawn, and the bright afternoon sunshine flooded the sick man's bed chamber, and cast a halo of brightness o'er his features. But what a countenance! Time and sickness had wrought great changes. The old, hale, hearty, rubicund look was replaced by the pale, pained expression of suffering.

"Come hither, dear."

Alice approached the bedside, and the old squire, taking her hand, looked at her earnestly for a moment.

"I have fallen into the hands of a cruel master, my child. He who was my friend is partly responsible for my position. After all I did for him, working for his election to Parliament some years ago; for you must understand, dear, that had it not been for old Squire Vivian and some of his friends, Sir James Lanyan would not now represent our section. And how has he repaid it?" continued the old man bitterly, and angrily.

"Father," laying her cool hand on his throbbing temples, "you know the doctor says you must not excite yourself."

"Aye, I know. I know, Allie, but I can't help speaking of it. He inveigled me into schemes of his own making, purposely, I believe now, to ruin me, and get the estate and the mine into his own hands. A dastard! A selfish villain! And now he is going to foreclose the mortgage, and in a week, my poor Allie, your old sick father and yourself will be without a roof to shelter them. An ungenerous rogue!" said the old man with another burst of anger.

"Never mind, father, you have me, your Allie, left, and I'll take care of you," and she smoothed down his scattered locks and laid her cheek close to his. The action and words seemed to quiet the old squire for a time, and he kissed the pale cheek of his daughter.

"You are a good daughter. Has Mr. Richard Lanyan been here to-day?"

"No, father."

"Has his man—Bob Sloan—as untrustworthy as the villain, Sir James—has he been here?"

"No, father," endeavouring to soothe him.

"Aye, he is giving me time to think; you know his proposition, child," said the old man gently. "I shall not live long, and it distresses me to think of my child homeless when I am gone." He laid his hand, that once stout, brown hand, now pale and thin, upon the bowed head of the girl, who was silently weeping. "It may prolong my life if you accept Richard, and our home will be yours. Long ago, before I knew of the villainy of Sir James, I purposed in my heart your marriage to Richard. Now, though I know the father and his trickery, yet I think I know the son, Richard, and I believe him free from his father's faults. He seems a good young man and talented, and loves you, child, sincerely, and he may make up in kindness to you for the injustice done to me. Years ago, in my strength, I thought it must be so, but now I have learned many things by sickness, and I would not urge you against your will."

"Father," said the girl, raising her tear-stained face, "if it will make you live longer I will not oppose; I will freely and gladly consent. I will do anything to add to your life. Have you not been both a kind, loving father and mother to me?"

"Bless you, my dear Allie," said the squire as he sank back exhausted, and then, in a whisper, "'Tis better than doctor's medicine. Call Stephen Blunt—and write an answer to James Lanyan's letter that you will find in yon desk."

Alice gave the order and sat herself down at the desk to answer as briefly as possibly the epistle of Lanyan. It was soon written, and the next moment Stephen Blunt appeared. He came in looking more bent and decrepit than usual, for the sickness of his master was weighing heavy upon him.

"Stephen," said the squire faintly, "send one of the servants with that to Lanyan Hall and await a reply."

The taciturn, old steward took the missive handed him by Alice, bowed and withdrew. A great load seemed to be removed from the old squire's mind, and he slept peacefully for three hours. By that time the servant had returned with the answer. Alice would have rather read it herself first, but the querulous voice of the squire must not be resisted, and so she passed it unopened to him. He unfolded it with trembling, eager hands, and devoured the few lines written there. His countenance grew paler, and then flushed an angry hue, until the great veins on his brow stood forth like whipcords.

"What! What! It can't be so!" he shrieked. He crushed the letter in his hands with rage and was about to fling it from him, but the motion and passion was too much for him, and with a gasp he fell backward—unconscious. The crushed letter dropped from his relaxed hand and fell to the floor, where it remained unnoticed for the time.

"To the doctor, quick!" said Stephen Blunt to the servant that was in the room. The servant was down and out in a moment. The same horse that carried him to the Lanyans' was near at hand, and he vaulted into the saddle, and went tearing down the carriage drive.

With a shriek of "My father!" Alice fell to the floor in a faint.

"Carry her to her rooms! He is not dead! I will not believe it until the doctor comes," said old Stephen Blunt. The servants carried their young mistress to her apartments, while Stephen, murmuring many things to himself, bathed the squire's forehead until the physician came. In a few minutes there was the sound of clattering hoofs on the gravel of the drive-way, then a rapid step on the stairs, and the physician was in the sick man's room. A look and a touch sufficed.

"He is past help. It is as I feared—a sudden stroke of apoplexy produced by some shock." He picked up the crumpled letter from the floor, opened it, read it with compressed lips, and placed it in his pocket.

The news spread o'er the whole village with the rapidity of wildfire, and by night every man, woman and child knew and sympathised with the bereavement at the Manor, for Squire Vivian was generally liked.

The funeral was held in the parish church, and old Parson Trant preached the sermon. With his eyes wet with the flood of sympathy and sorrow, and his voice unsteady and quivering, he delivered to the hushed multitudes an address upon "How are the mighty fallen." He called to their minds the deeds of the squire and his open, frank, generous life in such a tender manner that many of the audience wept in sorrow as acute as his own. There was possibly one of that audience who felt more keenly than others, and he bowed his head down as if ashamed to meet the gaze of the people around him. It was Captain Tom Lanyan. His sorrow was increased with the thought that it was some action of his brother that caused the squire's death. None of the other Lanyans were present. Sir James had to leave to attend to some business in Plymouth, and, informing his lawyer to foreclose the mortgage on the estate and tin mine and secure a tenant for the Manor, he embarked on the first vessel from Falmouth. Mistress Betty was ill of same fancied ailment, and Richard was, no one knew where.

After the funeral there was much condolence offered to Mistress Alice Vivian, but no personal help, no one being aware that the Manor and even the home furniture had passed out of the hands of the Vivian family. But Alice knew, and with a sickening sense of loneliness and helplessness she passed out of the gates of the Manor on the evening of the same day of the funeral. She had packed up her little personal belongings and had forwarded them that afternoon to Penzance, where she in tended following on the morrow. With a heart full of unuttered grief she wended her way to the old parish church and churchyard to pay a last visit to her father's tomb. The sun had long since disappeared beneath the horizon, and the pale, glimmering moon flooded hill and dale with ghostly, limpid light, whitening the cornices of the old church tower in the distance, deepening the shadows 'neath the trees, and bringing into gleaming prominence the white monuments of the departed. The gates of the cemetery were passed at length, but there was no fear or terror in her heart. Why should she fear? The dead could not hurt her, and it was less lonely here than in the great, empty Manor house. The church door was not locked, and opening it she passed down the long aisle, the tile work underneath echoing hollowly to her faint tread. Near the altar was the tomb of her father. The moonbeams, penetrating the coloured windows, illuminated it with a soft warm radiance, so clear, that the lettering could be easily discerned. She contemplated the inscription with tearful, stony gaze and then read softly to herself:

RICHARD VIVIAN, ESQ.
Trembath Manor
"How are the mighty fallen."

It was the text of the funeral sermon that was inscribed below. There was nothing more save the dates of birth and death. Suddenly a keener sense of her loss and loneliness came upon her, and she bowed herself to the floor, giving vent to the first outpouring of grief—a grief that she had restrained until then. Sobs and cries, low, yet full of grief, shook and convulsed her frame.

"Oh, father! father! do you know how lonely I am? I am your daughter, your Allie, and you always wanted me near you. I am here near you, father, and yet I cannot feel your presence, for you are gone and I am alone." A great sob checked her utterance, and for a long time she struggled with her grief, murmuring incoherently, and, then arising, she dried her eyes.

"Perhaps he sees still, and pities my grief and solitude. Parson Trant said that the dead are more alive than the living—'I am the God of Abraham, Isaac and Jacob; God is not the God of the dead, but of the living.'" She quoted the Scripture passage softly to herself, and it seemed to give some comfort. "Yes, he must see and hear." A noise near the distant tower door startled her. She gazed that way, though not in fear. Who could be in these sacred precincts at night beside herself? she asked mentally. The noise was not repeated. It was some owl or bat, or perhaps it was a slight breeze that had moved the slightly opened door, she thought, and then turning to the altar she knelt down in prayer.

"O God, I have now no father, no friend, no helper but Thee. I am friendless, homeless, poor and lonely. Be my helper and give me strength. Be my father, O Thou who art above, and hold me in Thy protecting arms. Thou art the defence of the widow and the fatherless; be Thou the defence of the fatherless now and hold me in the hollow of Thy hand. O God, all Thy waves and Thy billows have gone over my soul. At one blow I lose all. Supported by a father's love, it is taken from me; reared in comfort, I am reduced to bitter poverty; surrounded by friends—yet to-day alone and helpless, and yet,—Thou wilt not forsake me, for Thou dost mark the sparrow's fall. I go a stranger among strangers in a strange land, yet Thou wilt not forsake me. Oh, be a light to my feet, a guide to my way, and a stay in my helplessness."

Some time more she spent at the altar in silent prayer, and then arising and casting a long lingering look at the silent tomb near her, she slowly wended her way down the silent and deserted church, and thence on and out of the cemetery.

Without she walked rapidly along the highway, when the figure of a man emerged from the shadow of the cemetery gate and followed and overtook her.

"Mistress Alice," he said, laying a detaining hand on her arm. She started and would have fled, but he restrained her. "You are out late; let me attend you."

"I asked not your escort, Mr. Richard Lanyan."

"Ah, but I choose to give it," said the young man, in a determined tone, and then added: "Mistress Alice, why will you not listen to reason? You know that you are friendless and poor and I would help you,—yes, lay down my life for you. I——"

"I do not require your aid. Why do you push your attentions upon me when you know they are unwelcome, and especially at this sad time?"

"Ah, but Mistress Alice, my love for you — —"

She gave an impatient gesture.

"Have I not often said that it is vain and useless. I do not wish it, and your father — —"

"Does not wish it, either," interjected Lanyan with an unpleasant scowl, "but that matters not; I wish it."

"But I do not, and I must not encourage you. I cannot give you what I have bestowed upon another." Her face flushed and then resumed its pallid expression.

Mr. Richard Lanyan was silent, but his facial muscles twitched with emotion, and his dark eyes gleamed with hidden fire.

"I say that no one shall take you from me. My father nor no one else shall stand as a bar in the way."

"I stand in the way, myself. My own heart is the strongest bar."

"If you will neither listen to reason or affection, there are other means," he said, threateningly.

"You are a coward and a miscreant, sir, to use such words to me."

"There are other means and — —"

The words were scarcely uttered when she was seized from the rear and a cloak flung o'er her head.

"The coach, Bob," said Richard.

"'Tis coming, sir."

There was the rattle of wheels and a coach stopped near them. The door was wrenched open and as he placed her within he finished the sentence, "There are other means, and he, whoever he is, will never get you, except over the dead body of Richard Lanyan."

The deed was done so quickly that the dazed girl had but time to utter a muffled shriek as the door slammed, and her subsequent cries were drowned by the rattling wheels and trotting horses.

Mr. Richard Lanyan, angry with repeated rejections, had made his master movement.

CHAPTER XXIX

TOM GLAZE TO THE RESCUE

"Oh, here's to the ale,
The merry King Ale,
It makes one jolly
Though home comforts fail;
We'll swing and we'll sing,
Merry as a king,
The tankard we love
For the joy it'll bring."

Chorus.

"Then swing tankard round
With ale pale or brown,
We'll clunk and we'll clunk
Till we clunk un all down!
Down! Down!

"King George, rich and hale,
Is naught to King Ale,
He reigns and cares not
For the poor man's wail,
But jolly King Ale
Makes sorrow to fail,
Huzza for the tankard
Of rud, brown or pale."

Loud and boisterous came the roaring voices of half-drunken tipplers from behind the green doors of an ale-house in the upper part of Falmouth. At the close of each chorus there was a thumping of tankards and fists upon the tables within that made the midnight hour a perfect babel of sounds.

"That's Tom Puckinharn's voice, I could swear to un," said a tall, well-built man, as he paused on the pavement without. He was talking to himself and evidently referred to one voice louder than the others, leading the chorus. A frown swept over his rugged features.

"Here I be following 'im all the evening from tavern to tavern and just missin' 'im at every place, and he a-spending his 'ard-earned money in drink and his poor wife, Susy, at home a-crying her eyes out. If it wadn't that I had promised Susy to fetch 'im home I'd wash my 'ands and disown 'im."

His thoughts were interrupted by the overturning of a table, the upsetting of chairs, the crash of falling tankards and voices in angry altercation within.

The stimulating effect of the ale he had imbibed had increased Tommy's natural proclivity to wit and repartee in the earlier part of the evening, and some of his shafts of ridicule had been directed at two young Scottish Highlanders, soldiers of Castle Pendennis on leave of absence. The petticoat men, as he had called them, had remembered him, and in the drinking chorus they took umbrage at the trifling mentioning of King George's name. There were angry words and then the ringing of steel.

The sounds stirred the man without to action. Pushing aside the swinging doors, a sight met his vision that tinged his spirit with righteous indignation. Chairs and tables were overturned; tankards were on the floor, with their spilt contents trickling away in sundry streams; Tommy's friends were huddled in fear in one corner, while unfortunate Tommy, in the grasp of the two half-intoxicated Highlanders, was forced to his knees. They had jerked him over the table and, with irate mien and with murder in their bloodshot eyes, had their sword points close to his breast.

With a quick bound and a blow the stranger sent the one Highlander reeling to the floor, and, with a Cornish side-kick on the ankle and a blow of his other fist, Highlander number two fell with a crash among the overturned chairs and spilt liquor.

"Ah! ye call yourselves sodjers and braave men, but thee'rt bubble-'eaded cowards for two of 'ee with swords to attack one unarmed man! Ah! ye drunken buccas! see if I don't report 'ee to your governor."

The two fallen Highlanders were either too inebriated with liquor, or dazed by the sudden attack, or dismayed by the threat of informing the governor of Pendennis Castle, to arise at once, and the stranger, casting a look of supreme contempt on them, grasped Tommy by the collar, jerked him to his feet and led him from the place. As they were going he could not but hear the admiring comments of two or three of the spectators.

"Ah! Dear!—Dear!—Man alive!—Did 'ee see un? 'Ow he knacked the sodjers down! 'Tez Tom Glaze, the Carnish champion!"

"The Carnish champion, the Carnish champion," went from lip to lip. The green doors fell to behind Glaze and Puckinharn and cut off the murmured admiration. Glaze hurried his nephew down one street and then into another before he suffered himself to speak the anger that was within him. Then giving Tommy a great shake to add to his soberness and intelligence, he began:

"I tell 'ee, Tommy, thee'rt a great chuckle-head and will wend up by being a brocken buddle if 'ee keeps on like this. Here I come to see my nephew, a respectable pilchard seller, and find un spending his time and money in taverns. Thee ought to be ashamed of thyself. Do 'ee call drinking and fighting a good time? Thee wert singing that ale would make 'ee hearty and merry and that sorrow would fail. I tell 'ee that ale brings trouble, and poverty, and sickness and broken health, and would 'ave caused thy funeral if I 'adn't come in when I did, for they sodjers had blood in their eyes. And thy wife at home a-crying her eyes out and without money. I tell 'ee I felt more like giving thee a skevern than I did the sodjers, a great chuckle-head, as 'ee art."

"Ah, Uncle Tom, doan't 'ee go on like that," said the crestfallen Tommy. "My head is almost mazed with the 'eadache; les go down to the kay [quay] and see if I won't feel better."

"Hark 'ee, Tom Puckinharn, let this be the last of thy drinking. Will 'ee promise?"

"Umsh—Yes—I promise."

"A man is always wuss off when he drinks. His money is gone, 'is time is gone, and 'is health is gone, and he winds by going into the Union Poor House. Now here I am,—I, Tom Glaze, champion Cornish wrastler and all round fighter, and I ne'er would be so had I took to drink. There was Jack Trewlan, champion before me, stout and strong, the champion of a dozen battles, and I thrawed 'im in ten minutes. I got an under holt and heaved 'im over my shoulders, and 'e went down like a bullock. Cause why? Cause 'e took to drink."

"'Ark!" said Tommy. "Wasn't that a woman's cry?"

They listened and the cry was repeated.

"'Urry up," said Glaze, "some woman in distress,—upon a foach if thee art drunk, 'ee can run a bit."

Away they went in the direction of the quay from which the shriek came, Tommy's uncle ahead, while he himself lurched along in the rear, like a distressed ship in a storm. They arrived at the entrance of the pier, and saw by the glimmering, flickering light of the lamp, at its head, a woman struggling in the grasp of a burly man. A coach swept by them at this moment and passed around the corner and up market street.

"Bring her along, Bob," cried a voice from a boat at the landing.

Bully Bob, for it was he, seeing the approach of newcomers, redoubled his efforts, when he received a blow that staggered him and he released his grasp. The woman ran screaming to her rescuers and Glaze placed himself in front of her. Bully Bob, recovering from the sudden assault, rushed in wrath at his aggressor, crying fiercely, "I'll eat 'ee up!"

Glaze grasped him with a quick, deft movement, and with a heave, threw him over his shoulder into the deep harbour water beyond. There was a cry of rage, and then a splash, and then the sound of oars in a long, steady pull, rounding the head of the pier.

"The fellow in the boat will pick un up, and I think they won't bother us nor the lady for the present," said Glaze.

"Why, 'tes Mistress Alice Vivian!" exclaimed Tommy Puckinharn, now thoroughly sobered. She had fainted under the excitement and he supported her with his arms. Glaze gazed at the countenance of the unconscious woman.

"THE DOOR WAS OPENED, AND THE GLEAM OF CANDLE LIGHT SHOT OVER ALL CONCERNED"

"'Zackly so; so it is," and he paused in some thought, and then, as though he had reached some conclusion, he relieved Tommy of his burden, and, followed by his nephew, he strode along to the nearest house, a small brown cottage, from the lower window of which gleamed a light. A rap on the door brought an answer, in the shape of a woman's quavering voice, demanding who was there.

"It's me, Tom Glaze, Mrs. Trembath." There was a pause within, then some hurried movement.

"Mrs. Trembath," said Tommy to his uncle, in some surprise. "Is that Ande's mother? How did she get here, and how did 'ee know she lived 'ere, Uncle Tom?"

"When she was turned out by the Lanyans, I got 'er this cottage," said Glaze. Further conversation was interrupted by the rattling of bolts within, the door was opened, and the gleam of candle light shot over all concerned.

Bearing his unconscious burden, Glaze, followed by his nephew, entered, and soon related his tale.

"Poor girl! Poor dear!" said Mrs. Trembath, as she chafed Alice's hands and then essayed to pour a little reviving cordial down her throat. The cordial revived her, and she opened her eyes, and then, in as many words as kind, motherly Mrs. Trembath would allow, she told her story.

"The young villain!" exclaimed Glaze, indignantly, as he heard of the doings of Mr. Richard. "I wish it was 'im instead of Bob, that I flung into the harbour."

"Poor child!" said Mrs. Trembath, as she drew the girl to herself. "The ones who afflicted you and defrauded you of your home, did the same to me. We are in similar circumstances, and you shall stay here until you feel better."

But Mistress Alice was far from soon being strong and well again. The long period of nursing her sick father, his death, the loss of the Manor, and the harrowing experience of that wild night's ride to Falmouth, were too much for her worn constitution, and she succumbed to brain fever. Throughout the long period of her sickness Mrs. Trembath would have been sorely distressed had it not been for the generosity of Glaze and Puckinharn. Glaze, as a friend of the old squire, having received his patronage, thought he was in duty bound to leave a sovereign now and then in Mrs. Trembath's hands, and his nephew, having taken the pledge, found he had many spare shillings and sixpences to spend in so good a cause.

CHAPTER XXX

THE MAJOR'S HOME-COMING

"Ande, son, we'll push straight on to the village; thy mother, lad, was always an early riser, and mayhap will have a light in the window," said the old Major, after they had eaten a light breakfast in the Angel Inn. Major Trembath and his son, Ande, had arrived three o'clock that morning at the Falmouth Breakwater. They had hurriedly left the ship and had taken the early morning stage coach for Helston, arriving there in time for an early breakfast.

"Shall we get horses?" asked the son.

"Horses, lad, what do I want with a horse? Have I not tramped scores of miles with the rifle over my shoulder, when I was a solitary hunter at the Loop. My limbs are as strong now as they were a score of years ago, and I doubt much, after these years of hunting and tramping, whether I would feel as much at home on horse-back as I would on my own feet. Then we must remember, lad, that though our name is untarnished and honourable, we are still poor, and it behooves us to be devotees of economy. Horses, no; they are not to be thought of."

Ande acquiesced, and forth in the morning twilight they started. What a happy two-mile walk that was! The Major related tales of his youth associated with the section through which they wended their way, and the son related tales as well. The incident of the duck cave and the scared Greggs was forcibly brought to mind as they passed the cave, and he told the story much to the hearty amusement of his father.

The activity of youth seemed to fill the frame of the old Major as he approached the proximity of the village. His steps seemed to lengthen and increase in rapidity. Then through the dim twilight the outlines of the village burst upon their vision, and then the Major strained his keen eyes to catch the first view of the Primrose Cottage. At length he saw it.

"It's there still," he cried joyously, and then added, "But no light. Thy mother is late in rising, lad."

They followed the roadway past the village and up the ascent to the cottage home. The hedges on either side of the little domain were sadly out of repair, and the Major noticed it.

"Things gone badly since I was in these parts, but we will soon have them on a better footing."

They opened the rickety gate softly, and then stole into the doorway. Then grasping the rapper, the Major lifted it and rapped hard several times. Then smilingly, with dancing expectant eyes, they stood back and awaited. What a joyful greeting, they thought. But there was no answer, nor even the shadow of a sound that greeted their own echoes.

"You try, Ande, lad."

Ande advanced to the door and rapped, but the same death-like silence prevailed.

"Something wrong," said the old Major. "Ah! what's that writing?" His keen eyes, sharpened by years of woodcraft, had caught the glimpse of a paper tacked to the upper portion of the door. In the happy anticipation of coming reunion they had not noticed it before. Ande tore it from its fastenings and brought it forth more closely to their vision.

"For rent,—James Lanyan," slowly read Ande.

"Some cursed doings of the Lanyans," said the old man weakly, and he sat down on the steps, for in his disappointment his strength began to fail him. Just at this moment a lad was seen passing, and Ande accosted him.

"Mrs. Trembath? Why—her's gone nigh two years ago. Sir James Lanyan got the place and sold her out."

"Where did she go, lad?" asked the Major, faintly. "No one knows that, sir."

The old man buried his face in his hands. His spirit, so cheery a short time before, seemed broken.

"Are the Vivians still here?" asked Ande, sharply, for there was an angry passion raging within him.

"Old squire died a year or so ago. The Lanyans got the Manor, and some says as how the old squire died of a broken heart, sir."

"And Mistress Alice?"

"Her's gone, too; no one knows where; the Lanyans turned 'er out."

"The black-hearted villain! Thief! Rogue!" roared Ande, his passion bursting forth beyond all bounds. The lad fled in affright at the dreadful words and the black countenance, that was in truth diabolical with rage. The old Major sought to calm him, but of little avail.

"For all that the Lanyans have done to me and mine, the dishonourable scandal on our name, the suffering and humilation it has caused us, and these last cruel and inhuman deeds, I will be terribly revenged on him and his!" Ande Trembath raised his hand to heaven and continued his invective. The hatred of a lifetime seemed to culminate in a torrent of expressions like these. Then there was silence.

"We'll go and see Parson Trant at the rectory, father," said Ande, and the old Major, seemingly with no resolution of his own, was assisted to his feet, and on they trudged.

The glimmering twilight had merged into dawn, yet there was a light in the parson's study window and his head, now thoroughly silvered, could be seen bending over his manuscript. The short walk seemed to revive the Major's spirits. They knocked and were admitted.

The old parson knew neither of them for a moment. Then Ande spoke.

"What! Parson Trant, and do you not remember me, Ande Trembath?"

"Why, Ande, my dear lad! This is a surprise! How you have grown! Why, lad, where have you been all these years? And this is your friend?" With his kindly, fatherly greeting, he shook hands warmly, and then turned to the other stranger.

"More than friend," said Ande.

"And do you not know me?" smilingly said the old Major, as he advanced with outstretched hands. The rector passed his hand o'er his forehead once or twice, as he scrutinised the stranger, and then, —

"What! Impossible! Yes — No — Yes, it must be he. My old friend and school-fellow, Thomas Trembath! Well, well, well, well!" and the old parson upset a pile of books in his eagerness to reach the Major. Tears of delight were in his eyes as he flung open the study door and called, "Harriet! Harriet!" His wife, a pleasant old lady, soon came in.

"Harriet, do you know these two gentlemen?" The genial old parson was smiling, and rubbing his hands in delight. "Ah, I thought you wouldn't. This is our old friend, Major Thomas Trembath, and this is his son, Ande."

"Goodness me!" exclaimed Harriet, as she cordially welcomed them, and entered into her husband's pleasure.

"And now come in and have a cup of tea. Breakfast is about ready?" said the parson aside to his wife, inquiringly, and receiving an affirmative answer, notwithstanding protests that they had already breakfasted, the Major and his son were ushered into the little breakfast room, where, over the tea table, the parson related the facts of Squire Vivian's sickness, and how both Manor and cottage had passed into the hands of the Lanyans. He mentioned the fatal letter that had caused the squire's death, and brought it forth, and mentioned both the disappearance of Mrs. Trembath and Mistress Alice Vivian. If ever Ande swore revenge in his heart it was during that narrative, in which all the brutal plans of Sir James Lanyan were revealed in a plain, unvarnished manner. Woe betide James Lanyan or his, if their paths crossed.

"I am glad he and his are not of my parish," said the old parson; "but now tell me of your experience and wandering."

The Major briefly narrated his wanderings, to which Ande added a short sketch of his own, with the exception of his good fortunes in the gold and diamond regions of Brazil.

"Wonderful!" exclaimed the old parson, and then as a sudden thought struck him. "But now you must find Mrs. Trembath, and I would suggest that you would find some news of her, no doubt, at Helston, for this is the Floraday. Ah! there are the bells of old St. Michael, now, and in a short time the town will be crowded with people from far and near to keep the old festival. You will get news of her from some one."

"That I will," said the old Major, as he arose from the table. "That I will; and if I fail there, I shall search through every town of Cornwall."

The parson insisted upon their going in his own carriage, but the very thought of news to be obtained in Helston made the old Major impatient of any delay, and he persisted in going on foot, and so with a friendly handshake, Major and son left the rectory for Helston.

"Hark'ee, son Ande, injustice shall fall yet and right shall prevail; I feel it," and the old Major strode on with renewed hopefulness.

Long before they entered the town it had put on its holiday attire. Homes were decorated, windows garlanded, doors swung wide open, and the bells of old St. Michael were booming and pealing in the festival which the abrasion of centuries could not obliterate. From the upper portion of the town came the pealing of fifes and rattling of drums and the drawling voices of old men mingled with the more melodious voices of boys and girls, singing the ancient Hal Lan Tow chant. Up in front of the Helston Grammar School stand the authorities of the borough demanding a holiday in behalf of the pupils, and when it is granted, according to custom, how the lads and young men pour out of the old dormitory, with hats tossing in the air! Vehicles, from the humble cart to the emblazoned coach of the gentleman, keep rolling into town, while every road and footpath is dotted with foot travellers. The streets begin to crowd more and more. Citizens in the finest broadcloth rubbed elbows with the humble fustian of farmers, and ladies in the finest brocades and silks pass, with kindly greetings, the figures of country maidens and women in humbler attire. Lads are blowing whistles, and others are shouting to their fellows. But now the noon hour has come, and from the head of Coinage Hall street come the rolling of drums, the signal for the commencement of the annual, festival, street dance. In front of the forming procession are the two town beadles with wands, fancifully and artistically garlanded with flowers. The wands are the emblems of their authority. They are the great men of the hour. Behind them are the drummers, the fifers, and the serpent players, with their instruments and forms so festooned with flowers and evergreen that it is almost impossible to see their features. They are in motion. The old beadles prance in a dignified way in front of the advancing procession, waving their wands and giving directions in the meantime. The music of the various instruments are pealing out in one steady strain, punctuated here and there with the sullen, "boom, boom—boom—boom" of the big drums, and the "rat a-tat-tat" and occasional roll of the kettle drums. Now they are dancing, hand in hand in the rear, to the first half of the melody. Now with a rattle of the lesser drums the second half begins. The gentleman with the second lady releases her hand and seizes the first and whirls her out of the procession in a circle and returns. The action is continued by the second gentleman and so on down the line. Then again the first refrain is taken up and the procession moves onward. They are followed by a great crowd of spectators. Now the beadles have disappeared. They have but entered one of the homes. The procession of merrymakers follow. The beadles emerge from another door and on goes the festival parade. Is that customary? Oh, yes. It is one of the customs of time immemorial, and the party owning any of the homes thus entered feels highly honoured. Through all the streets wends the dance and then it is brought to a close by a turn on the Bowling Green. Now follows a dance of the tradespeople in one of the inns of the town, while the gentry enter the renowned Angel Inn for a purpose similar.

A porter stands at the door of the hall above the Angel Inn to solicit sixpences to defray expenses. A dignified, aged man, with hair and beard neatly trimmed, passes in with the others. He is followed by another, a younger one, his exact counterpart in height and facial appearance. Both of them are well tanned by exposure, and their garments seem to be of foreign make. They are the old Major and his son, Ande Trembath.

"Bless my soul!" exclaims a rugged old fellow, stumping up with a slight limp in one limb. He stands in front of Major Trembath and stares at him; then passes a hand, rough and brown and heavy, through his grey hair, throwing it back from his brow, revealing a long, livid scar along the forehead.

"Bless my soul! You are my old comrade, Tommy Trembath, or my eyesight fails me. Is it not so?"

"I am that person," said the Major, smiling, and grasping the extended hand he shook it warmly. "And how is my Captain Tom Lanyan?"

"I am right well, and I can't say how glad I am to see my old comrade, once more, back in England. We all thought you dead. You haven't been on British soil the last eighteen years. Where have ye been wandering all this time?"

The Major related a part of his adventures briefly.

"The honour of our family is established, Captain Tom; my father was no traitor and the proof of it is in the hands of the government authorities at this time," concluded the Major.

"I always knew it; I always knew it," said Captain Tom. "I have always had my beliefs, and I'm right glad now that they have come true."

"Aye, I know it," said the Major. "You were always my stoutest friend, in the camp and out."

The two old comrades of the Napoleonic wars talked on and on, while Ande wandered from them, earnestly scanning the features of those he met, but none did he recognise. The violins, sweeping into the melody of the Floraday, announced that the dance was on, but he did not engage in it. He gazed here and there, vainly endeavouring to behold a face he loved. He was becoming wearied with his search, when, across the hall, he noticed an aged, veiled lady and near her another, much younger. It was the young lady that held him spellbound for a moment. His eyes were riveted upon her countenance that was in profile. There was a shooting thrill through his whole system and his blood seemed to be mounting in great billows to his head. He caught a fuller glimpse of her features, and then his heart gave one mad leap and apparently stood still for a moment. Could he ever forget that countenance, pale and yet beautiful as on the eve, in the long ago, when she had called him her knight. With a half cry he was up and pushing through the crowd, but, before he reached the other side, he saw them both pass out of the crowded ballroom. With a few, rapid steps and bounds he passed down the stairway, almost knocking over the porter at the door.

In the street without he missed the familiar figure, then his heart beat joyfully once more, for he caught a glimpse of her entering the Bowling Green. The aged, veiled lady was not with her. He hastened down the crowded street and entered the comparatively deserted Bowling Green. He swept a rapid glance around, but she had disappeared and his heart sank once more. Then he saw a flutter of lace amidst the leaves of a retired garden seat. She was standing when he reached her, but perhaps the record of his diary is better descriptive of the scene that followed.

DIARY OF ANDREW TREMBATH, Gent.

May 8th, 1829; *Afternoon.*

I saw my lady in the garden seat arbour, my lady Alice, the love of my childhood, the ideal of my waking hours, the vision of my wanderings, and the dream of my slumbers. She whose features were engraven on my heart by the memory of other years, and around whom clustered the fondest recollections of youth, was standing gazing at the setting sun that, as it sank in golden and roseate hues, painting the sea and sky with the glories of heaven, seemed likewise to retouch, with its refulgent beams, her curling raven locks and beauteous eyes with additional splendour. There was a faint flush on her cheeks in the midst of their pallor, like an early wild-rose nestling by a belated snowdrift. It seemed to me that she was much taller than formerly. So tall and majestic indeed was she that I was awed, notwithstanding my love that had been slumbering for years. I heard her murmur, meditatively:

"Ah, if he would only come,—my life, my hope!"

My heart smote me with despair and an icy coldness seized me; a lump arose in my throat that seemed to choke my breathing. My hopes seemed dashed to the ground, my idol shattered and a mass of chaotic ruin. I tried to withdraw, but had advanced too far, for she saw me and there was a slight additional flush on her countenance, and gentle recognition in her eyes. I advanced to the shadow of the arbour and bowed low, humbled with my previous thought, yet persistent and determined to know the truth once and for all.

"Mistress Alice Vivian,—Mistress Alice, I am Andrew Trembath, who has loved you all these years. You called me your knight once and gave me reason to hope that you were not indifferent to my feelings for you. But there was a bar, sinister and heavy, between us,—the stain of treason against our name. Now all bars have been removed; our name is honourable; no wealth is a hindrance. You have been my dream throughout my boyhood days and the star of my wanderings in more mature years, and I lay my hand and heart at your feet."

She answered not, and I feared to lift my eyes lest I should read what I half suspected from that brief, murmured exclamation I had heard, that there was another. Despair seized me at her continued silence.

"You were expecting some one?"

"Yes," she said, meditatively.

"And you love him,—him?" How bold was that question! I know not now whether I feared more her rebuke or the proof of my agonizing doubt.

"Yes," she said gently, and I thought pityingly.

I arose, staggered, and would have fallen but for the friendly support of a tree. Better to have perished with brave Dick in the floods of the Rough Water than to have my love thus wrenched from my heart and my cherished longing prove a vain delusion. I recollect the substance of my rambling, half incoherent apology for disturbing her. Oh! How empty heart, earth, life appeared then! The sun had gone down, and with it the sun of happiness for me! I turned to go.

"Ande,—Mr. Trembath."

There was something commanding in that tone that I could not resist. I paused and waited for her to continue.

"Is it not unseemly for old friends to part thus. Here, seat yourself with me in this arbour." I moodily did so. "I cannot say how glad I am to greet once more a friend of my childhood days. You have been a true friend to me." What a bitter mockery those words seemed to me. I was silent and she continued: "You have been a true friend and I cannot choose but to speak plainly. But tell me of your life and wanderings."

Little by little I told my story, but I could not refrain from my love for her, for one was so involved with the other that they could not be sundered. I told all with the exception of my fortune in the Brazilian mines. She seemed interested with the interest of a friend. I gazed at her after my tale was finished, and with the melancholy thought of what I had aspired to and what I had lost. She smiled, and I thought she was laughing at my presumption in laying my poor affections at her feet. It enraged me, and I arose to go.

"One moment," she said; "I have news for you; your mother is found and your father is with her, but I have other matters to mention."

This was the solitary joy that now filled me and life seemed brighter.

"I was expecting some one this evening."

"Yes," I said, the clouds again coming over my soul; "yes, I know."

"No, you do not know; I was expecting some one, and, as you rightly surmised, I love him."

"Aye," I murmured, for she seemed cruel, "and you could not love another?"

"No, no, I could not love another. You would not desire to see me unhappy and poor?"

"No," I said, doggedly, digging with my heel in the turf.

"Suppose I had the opportunity to marry," she said, mischievously, and with a merry light scintillating in her eyes, "to marry one who would give me wealth, happiness, love, and my old home, who took me on a long ride of twenty miles and told me of these things, would you say, 'No.'"

"No," I said, sadly, "marry where your heart directs you."

"But suppose he was Mr. Richard Lanyan?"

I bounded to my feet as if shot. Oh, what a demoniacal thing is hatred! Humbled and sad at the loss of her, the thought of one of that accursed race possessing her seemed like turning my blood from freezing coldness to boiling heat. My countenance must have been frightful; it terrified her. I could not speak. She trembled and drew away from me and hastily said, "But suppose I did not love him?" I was dumbfounded, and she continued, earnestly, while her eyes beamed with a new light.

"Suppose I did not love him? I was expecting him whom I loved—yes, loved from girlhood; I mourned him as dead, yet loved him more and more, and after many years I saw him at a Floraday in the Angel Inn ballroom. I saw him push through the crowd and I came here expecting him. I love him and could not love another,—and—and—and—Oh—Ande,—can't you see?"

Change darkness into sunlight and my feelings can be expressed. The full light of all seemed to burst upon my vision and dazed me; then as I saw more clearly, I recollect her stretching her arms toward me, and my leaping forward to clasp that wavering form.

Here the incident in the diary closes, and it remained for others to relate what happened afterward. They sat down again in the arbour and her head was on his shoulder.

"And you did love me, after all," said Ande, and the old, happy, boyish smile illuminated his features.

"I have always loved you from that moment at the gate of the Primrose Cottage, so many years ago. Forgive me for the doubt I put you in, but you looked so doleful at my first words that I could not resist the old mischievous spirit."

He leaned down and kissed her lips, and there was a long silence, unbroken save by the chirping birds and rustling leaves. A short time afterward thither came the veiled, elderly lady, accompanied by the Major.

"Alice, child, art here? I have found him, Major Trembath, my husband."

"Mother!" joyfully cried the young man, as he flung himself into her arms.

"How tall you are, son Ande," said his mother, after their first affectionate greeting; "yes, as tall as your father, and"—here she turned her gaze upon Alice—"you have found a sister along with myself."

"No, not sister, but my affianced wife," said Ande, proudly.

"And I can call you daughter in reality," said happy Mrs. Trembath, as she kissed her affectionately.

But now the Bowling Green became crowded with people. The ball was over. Gentlemen and tradespeople mingled in the sight-seeing of the great event of that memorable day—the wrestling. A space had been cleared and roped off in the centre of the Bowling Green, and soon forth came the gladiators, great, tall, muscular fellows, farmers from the country, miners from the tin mines, and seamen from Penzance and the Lizard Point. The men from the Lizard were great, giant-like men over six feet in stature. The spectators watched with intense interest. Jack Trewlan, anxious once more for honours, was among them, but went down and out of the lists in the very first contest. The poorest wrestlers were disposed of first, and then came men of the first class. Among the latter was a great Lizard Point fellow,—a veritable Goliath in size. Six feet, six inches he stood in his stocking feet and weighed fully two and twenty stone. The measurement of his chest was fifty-three inches, of his waist thirty-nine, of his arms—the right biceps—nineteen inches, the left—a trifle less; his limbs were in proportion to his other measurements. A wild cheer went up from the Lizard men as he stood forth in the roped arena. He had easily vanquished all his fellows,—the great Lizard fellows were as wooden men in his powerful grasp,—and he was entitled to do battle with the champion.

There was another cheer, mainly from the tin miners and farmers, as the champion of Cornwall, Tom Glaze, the victor of nineteen pitched battles, came forth to do battle for the twentieth time for the position he held. The champion was not near so tall or heavy as his opponent, but he was stoutly and toughly built; his muscles were iron-like with constant practice, and in his many battles he had gained that dexterity, cautiousness, tack and trickiness, that was characteristic and essential to a champion.

"A tough opponent, Tom," said one of the gentlemen.

"The bigger they are the heavier they fall," said Tom, and yet there was a little doubt in his mind as he sized up the Goliath before him. A moment they stood, their white duck wrestling jackets in relief against the background, and then they closed into action. The young Lizard fellow was cautious and wary. Tom Glaze seized his favourite hold,—the celebrated Cornish hug, and back and forth they wavered, but the young Colossus seemed to have his great limbs, like pillars, firmly rooted in the ground. Glaze was as agile as a panther, twisting and trying trick after trick. Once he nearly had him on the hip and a hoarse "Huzza" and "Bravo" went up from many throats,—but it was only a partial success. The young Lizard fellow now tried to bring into play his great strength, but every grasp was eluded. Glaze had not been champion so long without learning many things.

"At un, Tom, thraw un down!" cried the men of Helston and the miners to their champion.

"At un, lad, heave un over thy 'ead!" exclaimed the Lizard and Penzance men to their partisan.

"Wait a bit," said a Lizard man, with a knowing wink to a companion, "wait a bit, till 'e uses 'is strength; our man is only playing with un, I tell'ee."

"Ah, dear, dear,—us thought Glaze 'ad un then; but 'e's up again."

"Bravo! Bravo!" shouted the men of Penzance and the Lizard, and they fairly danced with delight, as Glaze went partially down.

"No fall!" bawled the referee.

"Ah was a fall, sure enough!" shouted an excited Lizard fellow; "I seed un."

"Seed un," snorted Tommy Puckinharn, who was near at hand; "thee doesn't mean to say thee seed un with they great, fishy eyes of thine, do 'ee?"

"Ah was a fall," persisted the Lizard man.

"'Twasn't," said Tommy.

"Ah was."

"What's the use of saying ah was when ah wasn't," said Tommy, philosophically.

"'Ere, 'ere, no fighting," said a town beadle, as he came up to preserve peace.

The wrestlers after a brief rest again approached each other. Now in a crouching position they circle around each other, each waiting for an opportunity for a good hold. Suddenly they spring forward like tigers. It was a collar and elbow hold; they tugged, strained, now pushing, now pulling. Determination is on the features of each. It is apparent that the young giant is exerting his strength to the utmost. He is slowly pushing Glaze backward. Glaze gave way slowly and then with a smile and a twist and a sudden jerk—

"Huzza! Huzza! Glaze forever!" bellowed the Helston men. The young Lizard giant had gone, like a crashing oak, to the ground.

"No fall," bawled the referee. The Lizard gladiator had but fallen to his knees and was soon up again, and the contest was renewed.

"Man alive! Did 'ee see un? 'E went down like a kibbel in a shaft," said one tin miner to another. The one addressed answered not, but kept shouting to Glaze:

"The Carnish ankle kick, boy! Kick un in the ankle, and poke un over!"

"Another case of Corineus and the giant Gog-ma-gog,"[8] said Captain Tom Lanyan to his friend, the Major.

"Aye, possibly," said the Major.

On went the wrestling match, with the advantage at one moment to Glaze, at another to the young opponent. Glaze seemed the better in agility and wrestling tricks, but his skill in these things were offset by the giant's strength and wariness. The crowd from a wildly shouting mass became silent, and were alertly watching every movement of the straining figures. They were at last becoming aware of what Glaze knew for quite a time. The champion had met his match. He knew it, for with all of his skill he was unable to overcome his opponent. But what was still more manifest was that the young Lizard giant, with all of his strength, could not conquer the old, wrestling hero.

The time was up at last, and there were stout huzzas for both as they shook hands. The decision went to Glaze, not on falls, but on points, as he showed the greater skill.

Then Glaze held up his hand for silence and began to speak.

"I want to congratulate my opponent on his stout defence, and say 'e's the hardest man I ever met in a wrastling match."

There was a roar of cheers, and then when silence came, he continued:

"Men, you knaw the decision is just as to points. My opponent could not thraw me, as 'ee have seen, and I couldn't thraw 'im. Now, I'm getting old for the ring, and am about going to quit wrastling. This is my last battle. I 'ave only waited until I could find the man I couldn't thraw, and now I've found un, I give to him the championship and all the honours of the position. What do 'ee say? Is it right?"

There was silence for a moment, and then, after the import of Glaze's generous offer became more fully understood, there was a resounding cheer that went up again and again. The people knew that, next to Glaze, there was none more capable or worthy of defending the championship of Cornwall than the young Lizard giant.

"Do ye know, lad, who the young Lizard chap was?" asked the Major of Ande,—but Ande was gone. Both wrestlers had been taken up on the shoulders of the crowd and carried, with various shoutings, to the Angel Inn. Ande followed, pushing and shoving his way through the crowd. When he entered the Inn, he shouted, "Where's the champion?"

"He's up in his room, changing his clothes," said the landlord.

[8] Wrestling match of Corineus, the Trojan, and Gog-ma-gog on Plymouth Hoe—"Polyolbion," Michael Drayton, 1563-1631.

Ande pushed his way up the stairs and opened the door of the room indicated.

"Dick, Dick, Dick, old fellow!"

"Ande,—why bless——"

The two friends were locked in each others arms. Then came a time of explanation. Dick had passed through the Rough Waters of the Lycamahonings safely. He who had breasted the breakers of the Lizard could easily take care of himself in the rapids. He was wounded, to be sure, and the struggle through the rapids had exhausted him, but he was picked up in the river and for some time was in the care of the good settlers of Kittanning; then he had returned.

"You must come back with me to see my father and mother and my intended wife," said Ande. Ande insisted, and Dick yielded. They passed out through the inn and down to the Bowling Green. There were Major Trembath, Mrs. Trembath and Mistress Alice Vivian, to each of whom Dick was successively introduced.

"What's wrong, Dick?" asked Ande. Dick was staring with all his eyes at the Major, and then he burst forth in answer:

"Why, bless me, Ande, if the Major and old Hunter Tom are not the same, they are brothers."

"The same, Dick, lad," said the Major, smilingly, and Dick again grasped his hand and shook it warmly.

"I never expected to see you and Ande again, and I can't say how glad I am that things have turned out as they have," said Dick.

He explained how he had returned to his people, who had long mourned him as dead, and how overjoyed they were to see him. He was now a prosperous, independent farmer of the Lizard, and was also preparing to enter the shipbuilding trade. "Thanks be," said he, in an undertone to Ande, "to the mines of Sierro Do Frio."

CHAPTER XXXI

ANDE'S REVENGE

——"A grudge, time out of mind begun,
And mutually bequeathed from sire to son."

—Tatian.

"Lanyan forever! Lanyan forever!"

"Trembath forever! Trembath forever!"

The old town of Helston was a roaring, gesticulating mass, and the shouting of bellowing partisans reverberated up and down Coinage Hall Street. Crowd met crowd, waving their respective banners, opprobious names were shouted, fists flung in the air, and a special force of officers were busy from early morn quieting unruly fellows, some of them more stirred by the spirits of the Angel Inn than the spirits of politics. It was the period of the election for the Reform Parliament. Sir James Lanyan had come forth on the old party platform, and, most unexpectedly, in opposition to him, came Andrew Trembath. The latter had made himself eligible by the purchase of the Primrose Cottage, thus making himself a landholder of forty shillings annual value.

Towards noon the crowds converged upon the Bowling Green, where upon a raised platform sat the Mayor, the town functionaries, the candidates, and their proposers and seconds.

The figure of Sir James was just as tall as of old; the same eagle nose and piercing eyes; the same easy, urbane manner and distinguished appearance. The Conservatives admired him. His wealth, astuteness, experience, all urged the necessity of his return to the forum of government. There was an easiness of manner in the very position Sir James occupied that augured well his own hopes of the coming election. Why should he not have hopes? The interests of the landed party were all back of him. The Godolphins and all their followers were in his train. Reform measures were dangerous in their eyes to the staid health, political, of the country.

On the left, Andrew Trembath was not so easy in his mind. Sir James was an old general, and he knew it; but within Ande's breast was the buoyant hopes of youth. Here was the first stroke of revenge against an ancient foe. Could Sir James be beaten in his cherished hopes, and that by an upstart of a hated family, the more triumph.

The preliminary proceedings were gone through rapidly. Sir James, with a good bit of wisdom, had selected as his proposer a retired country gentleman and as his second a tradesman of Helston, thus drawing from the sympathy of both classes. The proposer, however, weakened his cause by his interlarding his speech with many classic quotations, learned no doubt when he was a lad at Eton, and also by a most unfortunate mentioning of the stain of treason on the name of the opposing candidate. Sir James, himself, though he sympathised with his proposer, felt irritated that he should make such a blunder, and a slight frown passed over his placid features.

The proposer of Andrew Trembath was none other than the Reverend Mr. Trewan, headmaster of the Grammar School. In a short, neat speech, and with a few, withering remarks, he scattered the arguments of the proposer's speech in favour of Sir James. Then speaking of his candidate, Andrew Trembath, he referred to his being a scholar of his own school, his honesty, uprightness, and his grasp upon the problems that were stirring old England to her very centre, and closed with an able plea for the seating of ability, though that ability was young. There were strong cheers and many "hears!" from the crowd on its conclusion. But none of these preliminary cheers were so hearty as those which greeted the second, as he arose to greet the audience. And no wonder, for the seconder of Mr. Trewan's speech was the new champion of Cornwall, Dick Thomas. Sir James looked a trifle worried, for he saw the diplomacy in the choice of these. The headmaster of the Grammar School had weight, and Dick Thomas had the hearts of the commonality. The speech which he made was homely enough, and demonstrated that he was, as he said, more a man of action than one of words. But he was Dick Thomas, and Dick Thomas was a host.

Sir James arose with a look of relief on his features. He was a man accustomed to deal with the masses, and wished to offset, as much as possible, the blunders of his own proposer and the enthusiasm of the crowd over the speeches of the opposition. His speech was replete with smooth phrases, and the whole was conducted to the close with the arguments of a logician and the subtility of an old parliamentarian. He demonstrated that he had a clear grasp on the problems of the day, and the temper of the people toward them, but what he did not know was the growing popular estimation of himself among the masses. They were getting to realise that Sir James Lanyan was a "trimmer" and was more for Sir James Lanyan than anything else. He said in part:

"For upwards of a dozen years I have served the people of this section as their representative in the House of Commons, and I trust that, at this time, the confidence of the electors, that they have manifested so often heretofore in my experience and labours, will still remain with me. [Hisses and groans.] These are stirring times and the storms have swept over, again and again, the ship of state, threatening to founder her, and reduce the civilisation of the grandest and most enlightened country under the sun to a melancholy wreck and ruin, battered and beaten by every sea, and a prey of the pirates of Europe. To a careful observer, what perils threaten our country? The spirit of the old-time Luddites has again broken forth in the wrecking of machinery and ruthless destruction of property, and there is trouble and turmoil on every side that, unless checked by the firm hand of a Conservative government, will bring anarchy and ruin. In the midst of all these movements come our friends of the opposition with their so-called, universal panacea of Reform. Reform! Reform what?

"Would you reform the introduction of machinery? We cannot do it. If the people themselves could see the benefits of the oncoming flood of invention, they would not desire to do it. With the vision of a prophet I clearly see the time when business shall be enlarged, living become cheaper, wages higher, all on account of the increased output and increased commerce brought and caused by the introduction of machinery. Will this affect Cornwall? To-day, Cornwall has nothing but her farms, her fisheries and her mines, but with the advent of new machinery will come the spreading of new factories, until even within the 'Delectable Duchy' shall roar and sound the noise of spindles, giving employment to thousands of Cornishmen and their children. The increased wealth of the country will add to the price to be obtained for fish commodities and farm products, and there will be an era of prosperity for the hardy miner, fisherman and farmer such as they have never dreamed of before. Reform? Shall we reform the election laws and boroughs. The statement is frequently made that the election laws give unequal representation, and that there are members of the Commons not placed there by the people, and it is true; but abolish the present system and you will purloin from the nation the services of some of her stoutest pillars. If everything is to depend upon a wider suffrage and the throwing out of what has been called pocket boroughs, where would our broad-minded statesmen, who have, tempo rarily, not the support of the people, come in? Had it not been for a pocket borough, Burke, that Cicero of English politics, would never have entered the halls of legislation. Had it not been for the pocket borough, our most eminent statesmen, North, Flood, Canning, Plunket, Brougham, and others, equally indispensable, would not have gained a foothold in the parliamentarian halls. Sheridan, defeated at Stafford, found support in Ilchester; Grey, refused by Northumberland, was returned by Tavistock."

Here Sir James was interrupted by a rough, country lout, who said gravely that he had a question to ask of great importance.

"Well, my man," and Sir James flashed a keen look at him.

"I would like to ask," said the fellow with a leer, "whether m'lord could lend me half a sovereign?"

The absurdity of the thing gave the audience its desired fun, and a roar of laughter came from the crowd. But Sir James was not the man to be put down with the word of a buffoon. With a smile of sarcasm, he responded:

"Yes, my man, I can lend you not only a half a sovereign, but twenty sovereigns, when the cause of good government, which I represent, has prevailed, and then you will need no borrowing, but you will have so many, easily earned by yourself, that you will want to lend instead of borrow. The very reason that so many are out of half sovereigns to-day is because of the mob spirit and discontent stirred up by the element of so-called reform. I ask whether it was patriotism that stirred up the agitation for so-called reform? No. It could not have been that, for the best good of the nation, at the present time, requires peace and harmony."

Continuing, Sir James referred to the agitation of France that gave vent to Napoleon, and was interrupted here and there with various crys of "Tommy-rot!" and "Gammon!" from his opponents, and equally strong "Hears!" from the Conservative wing, and closed his speech with a strong plea for the upholding of the old line party.

He was not nearly so confident when he finished as when he began. He was beginning to realise that there was an undercurrent against him, personally. His agents had brought him word before of this, but he had placed it all down to the spirit of the reform movement. But now he was beginning to realise different. Dick Thomas and Ande's agents had not been idle in the period of the canvass. Sir James' conduct in reference to the Trembaths, to the Vivians, and his crookedness in politics, was fully aired among the voters, and those who could not be persuaded to vote against the old line policies, were moved, by the revelation of the unscrupulous conduct of Sir James, to abstain from voting at all.

There was silence when the new candidate, Andrew Trembath, arose to respond. Shaking back the tangled masses of auburn hair from his forehead, he opened his speech in clear, ringing tones. His introduction demonstrated that he had a tolerably clear perception of the issues of the day. He spoke feelingly of the popular agitation.

"These riots, this breaking of machinery, this tumult in many parts of the kingdom, to what is it due? To the spirit of reform? No. Rather is it due to the desire of the people for better conditions. The time has come when the voice of the people shall be heard, and that voice speaks in no uncertain accents. Too long has the government been in the hands of demagogues who have little to recommend them for election but corruption; and now all over this fair land of ours the people have arisen in their might, and demanded an extended suffrage. It is true, as Sir James has said, that great and good men have been returned from these pocket boroughs, but that single advantage can be offset by innumerable and inevitable disadvantages. These pocket boroughs are generally nests of corruption, held and dominated by some lord or landholder. The half a dozen or so good men that were placed in position by them can be offset by the hundreds of members that are fitter for Newgate than for the parliamentarian halls."

"Men like James Lanyan," shouted some one in the crowd.

An angry hue was on Sir James' countenance for a moment, but neither he nor Ande noticed the interruption.

"What right has a green mound in a grassy field or a hayrick to send a representative, while great and flourishing towns like Manchester and Sheffield have none?"

"Hear! Hear! Hear!" shouted many in the crowd.

Continuing, Ande took up, one by one, the arguments of the opposition, and tore them shred by shred, until not a vestige remained. Then he triumphantly drew from his pocket a perfect arsenal of facts, culled from Sir James' speech of years ago, when, turned down for a time by his own party, he sought refuge in the ideas of reform. The very facts used in his conversation with Squire Vivian, Captain Tom Lanyan and the others, when around the tea table in Lanyan Hall so many years ago, and which facts he used in a speech on the hustings at that time, were quoted now, and they were like arrows piercing his very soul. The Conservative wing were silent with consternation, and Sir James looked down, uneasily. Then turning to the record of Sir James in the Commons, he quoted how he had again and again voted against the will of his constituents. Then after a few, withering flights of oratory, which sent the Radicals wild with delight and chilled the Conservatives into icy stillness, he said:

"And now, members of the Conservative wing, you are going to vote for a man who has uttered sentiments like these, and acted in this manner. I need not speak to the members of my own party, I know their determination for good government, but to you Conservatives. You are going to vote for a man who has thus betrayed your sacred trust and thus surrendered your standards to the enemy. What does all his actions and speaking amount to in your minds? Just this, that though he is an experienced hand, yet you know not what he stands for. Like a vacillating weather vane, he is apt to be turned one way or the other as the interests of Sir James Lanyan may direct."

There was an uproarious "Hear! Hear!" from the Radicals, and the black looks that the Conservatives turned on Sir James were perceived by even that worthy himself. He shrugged his shoulders and took on his indifferent and placid expression. But Andrew Trembath was not through yet, for he continued bringing up clause after clause of Sir James' speeches, sweeping the audience fairly off its feet with a torrent of indignant oratory such as it had never before heard. All the poetry in his nature, all the passion of years of wrong heaped upon his family, burst forth then and there. There was no more applause from any in that assemblage, for they were all so enthralled that they hung upon each word uttered, riveted their eyes upon each gesture, and remained motionless like a painted throng. Then turning from indignant invective, he gazed lovingly over the Bowling Green and swept his vision around toward the town, and his eyes became misty with emotion.

"Helston! Dear old Helston!" he exclaimed, and he stretched out his arms to the town and people, and there was such emotion, tenderness and love in that tone that the crowd wept though they could not tell why.

Sir James' proposer had called him a foreigner in little touch with English ideals. He proved the contrary. He called vividly to mind the days spent as a school lad among them, the exciting days of the hurling match when Breage was defeated, and men nodded their heads and smiled as they remembered. Then sweeping into the closing address, he said:

"We need a strong and experienced hand at the helm in these perilous times, it is true, but far more do we need honesty, virtue, and manliness. Is youth, though inexperienced, yet with average intelligence, to be despised and condemned by the very fact of youth? Ask the rector or parish minister the names of the two most prominent lights in the expansion of religion, and he will say young Saul and youthful Timothy. Gray at thirty-four finished the most beautiful elegy in the English tongue. Milton began his career at a tender age. Shakespeare was but twenty-seven when his name became an authority on the drama. Napoleon, in his meteoric career, astonished and convulsed the world, yet he was a young man. What name more brilliant in English annals for courage and success than that of the well-beloved Wolfe of Quebec fame—yet he perished on the field of battle at the age of thirty.

"HE OPENED HIS SPEECH IN CLEAR, RINGING TONES"

"Civil government has also her young heroes. Need I mention the great name of Burke, who, at the age of twenty-six, won for himself a reputation for states-man-like judgment and skill that has placed his name high on the imperishable roll of fame. Need I mention Fox, and that other character who still lives as a blessing in the minds of Englishmen—still lives as the greatest diplomatist of the age—still lives in the agitation for liberty and fair representation that so pervades the country to-day?"

"Pitt! Pitt! Pitt!" roared the crowd.

"Aye, you have named him. Ask any bookman for a life of William Pitt, and he will hand you down a history of England from 1781 to 1806, for from twenty-one years of age down to the day of his death, his life has been a history of the empire. Is youth and inexperience to be despised? No! No!"

"No! No!" shouted the crowd, taking up the words of the speaker. "Huzza for Andrew Trembath!" And for the space of a few minutes the crowd let out its pent-up enthusiasm in wild gesticulating of hands and roaring of voices.

The speaker concluded with a peroration that was eloquent and passionate. Pathetic passages at times hushed that great crowd into silence, moved it to tears, and then again swayed it to applause, and when it was finished, and the speaker resumed his seat, there was silence for a moment—then, like the roaring of great guns in battle action, the throng, Radical and Conservative, sent up shout after shout, that reverberated again and again o'er the town of Helston, and caused the birds in the neighbouring trees to take refuge in flight. Such a speech had never been delivered from the hustings before. Old men shook their heads sagely, and muttered to each other that in a short time another Pitt would astonish England and the world, and that one would be from Cornwall.

Suffice it to say, that Andrew Trembath was elected by an overwhelming vote as M. P. for Helston.

Old Parson Trant met him the next day near the Primrose Cottage, and con-gratulated him on his election and bright, future prospects.

"I had a purpose in view," said Ande. "It was not so much my desire to enter Parliament as my antagonism to Sir James. I have had my first revenge, and there are others to follow."

"Lad, lad," said the old parson, as he sadly shook his head, "I like not that revengeful spirit, though you have had much provocation. There is a better way of revenge."

"What way?"

"'If thy enemy hunger, feed him; if he thirst, give him drink.'"

Ande said nothing, and the conversation, after a time, passed to other themes.

After his defeat, Sir James Lanyan gave his attention to speculation, but the ventures turning out unprofitable, he was compelled to sell Trembath Manor, through his solicitors, to the agents of a wealthy American traveller. But this was but a drop in the bucket of his financial reverses, and Lanyan Hall followed suit.

The purchaser of Lanyan Hall was Andrew Trembath, but the fact was unknown to any one but old Parson Trant, to whom Ande had confided the secret of his wealth. Subsequently the purchaser was revealed to Sir James, and the revelation seemed a crushing blow to him, for he sickened and began to sink rapidly.

"'Tis my second revenge," said Ande to old Parson Trant, and there was a grim, determined look on his features. "There are others to follow."

"Lad, lad, you must not go on in this way. Vengeance is of God. 'Vengeance is mine, I will repay.' There is a much better way, and you can do me, your old pastor, a favour, and render God a service at the same time." The old parson drew a pathetic picture of Sir James in his present condition, poor, helplessly sinking into the grave. To follow up any more of this revenge was hellish. It belied Ande's nature to continue thus, and if this revenge should continue, he, the parson, could not love him any more. There was one thing that would prolong Sir James' life, and that was the bringing back to him of his son, Richard, who was leading a wild, vicious life somewhere in London. This was the report of the physician. "He must be brought back to his father, who is calling for him. Who is better fitted for that mission than yourself, Master Ande? You are going to attend Parliament in a few weeks. Go a little before—aye, go at once to London, and take up this mission."

"I! I!" stammered Ande, in some astonishment and with a little of the old, angry feeling tingling in his veins. "You know what we have suffered—you——"

"But, Ande," interrupted the old rector, as he placed his arm around his shoulder in the same, affectionate manner as in the olden days, and with kind, loving tones resumed, "If Christ had felt that way to us, where would we be?" The old parson preached one of the most appealing sermons, then and there, that he had ever delivered. Concluding, he said, quoting the words of Scripture: "'Ye have heard that it hath been said an eye for an eye and a tooth for a tooth; but I say unto ye, resist not evil. Ye have heard that it hath been said, ye shall love thy neighbour and hate thine enemy; but I say unto you, love your enemies, bless them that curse you, do good to them that hate you,—that ye may be the children of your Father in heaven.' 'Be not overcome of evil, but overcome evil with good.'"

"Would it not be hypocritical to show kindness, when you are bitter with revenge within?"

"No; by showing kindness, even though you do not feel it within, yet nevertheless it has a healthy action on the soul. Do a kindness and you grow kind. We become what we do, my lad. Do it now, not because of your feelings, but because the Lord commanded it. And by and by you will do kindness to an enemy because your own heart commands it."

"I will go in the morning."

"And God will bless you, my son," said the old rector, as he parted from him and wended his way home. There, the parson mentioned the matter to his wife, Harriet, with some doubt as to the issue.

"I fear me, Harriet, it is like sending a fire-brand to quench a fire-brand."

Andrew Trembath was true to his promise, for that week saw him in London, actively pushing the search. Hearing of a midnight brawl, in which Richard was engaged, and which was publicly published in the newspapers, he sought that quarter, but Richard, fearing perhaps the police, had fled. His father had also heard of the brawl. It was the last of a series of crushing disgraces on the part of his son that sent Sir James into the grave. Ande did not give up the search, but Parliament convening, he was forced to give more time to other affairs.

It was in the early hours of the morning when one of the night sessions of Parliament adjourned, and Andrew Trembath, tired of the stupid, blocking tactics of those opposed to reform, was wending his way home to his rented quarters in Portman Square. The streets were deserted and he hastened along absorbed in his thoughts. A figure stole out from the shadow of some buildings in his rear. There was a quick leap, the glitter of steel in the air, and then Ande felt a stinging sensation in his shoulder. Like a flash he turned and had his assailant pinioned in an iron grip. He struggled to release himself, but to no avail. The knife dropped with a clang to the pavement and Ande kicked it from him. The light of a street lamp flashed on the would-be assassin's features.

"Richard Lanyan! You! You! You, who broke your father's heart,—you, the Etonian scholar,—you, base as you are, stoop to be the assassin!"

"Yes, curse you!" gritted the answer from between the clenched teeth of the writhing assailant.

"And why?"

"Because you have been the ruin of father, and not I. You occupy his place in Parliament. You took away Lanyan Hall. You took away the only woman I ever loved, and it is—revenge."

"Lanyan, listen to me," sternly, and still keeping his grip. Ande related in brief epitome the injuries he and his and the Vivians had received at the hands of Richard and his father, closing with the question: "Who has been the injured party? Your father's place I occupy because the people put me there. Your father lost Lanyan Hall because of his foolish speculations. If I hadn't bought it, some one else would. His death was mainly brought on by your own sottish conduct."

The eyes of Lanyan flamed with sullen passion, as he muttered, "I'll not endure this from you," and again made an effort to escape.

"Make another effort to escape and I hand you over to the watchman, or perhaps better still I could kill you where you are. What would the law and opinion say if I should? They would say it was good riddance of a rough character and in self-defence, and you see I have the strength to carry it out."

Lanyan paled a little, notwithstanding the brave heart he had, for he realised that he was but feeble in the hands of this man, his captor. He ceased his struggles and listened sullenly.

"But I have other plans," said Ande, gently. "I believe the fellow who won a prize at Eton is capable of better things. I place the best construction on your past actions. It was the ungovernable love for Mistress Alice Vivian that caused much of your past action."

There was no answer.

"I know that was the cause, and also the cause of your whole life being spent thus, and also of this last attempted deed. And I had been searching for you for months before your father's death, plunging into every slum and dive of London. I promised to bring you back to your father, and thus prolong his days. Your name was the last he called upon in his delirium. I tried to find you, but failed."

Ande released his grasp, for it was unnecessary. Lanyan was weeping in an agony of remorse and wretchedness.

"But still the hour is not too late now to begin again in right paths, and rear up your family name to its former, ancestral honour. You can do it."

"I cannot," groaned Lanyan, all hatred and vengeance apparently gone from him. "I cannot; I have no money, and to live honestly in a poor position— —No— No."

"I will help you. Come now, Lanyan, let us forget the past evils between our families. Oh, think how good God is to prevent you in the commission of a great crime, this night, that would blast your name irretrievably. God is better to us both than we deserve. He bestowed upon us these minds, these souls, and placed us in a beautiful world, and yet we abuse His gifts. Think, Lanyan, that you and I have souls to present upright and pure before the great God, the Father. It is a terrible thing to think that these passions, if we allow them to rule us here, by God's judgment, they shall rule us in the future. I confess that my hatred for you and yours has mastered me heretofore, but Parson Trant preached me a special sermon privately, when he asked me to seek you, and I have revolved it over and over again in my mind, and, with God's help, which I prayed for and received, my hatred is gone. If I had found you before, I should not have spoken to you in this way. I should have probably mentioned your father's desire to see you and left. Now it is different. Let the past be past, and here is my hand."

Lanyan grasped the hand extended to him and there was a wavering in his voice as he said:

"Trembath, you have a much better nature than I have. I must go."

"No, no," said Ande, detaining him, and he poured forth his plan, then and there, for the turning over of Lanyan Hall to Richard. This was conditioned on his reform.

Richard was to have possession of the ancestral place at a nominal rent, and when the rent would total the sum Ande had paid for it, the deed of complete ownership was to pass over to Richard.

There was silence for a moment.

"Come," said Ande, as he placed one arm over his shoulder, "don't on account of past ill feeling refuse this chance of making a man of yourself and uplifting, once again, your ancient family."

There was a period of inward conflict in the breast of the man beside him, and then, in resolute tones, he answered, simply: "I'll try. Forgive me, Trembath, for to-night's action, and for the injustice done by our family."

The two men shook hands firmly, and separated, Ande to seek a surgeon to have his wound dressed. But the wound gave him little pain, and what pain there was was wonderfully alleviated by the gladness of soul within. He knew that the best vengeance was forgiveness, as the old rector had said.

CHAPTER XXXII

CHRISTMAS IN THE OLD HALL

"Lo, now is come the Christmas feast
Let every man be jolly,
Each room with yvie leaves is dress'd
And every post with holly;
Now all our neighbours' chimneys smoke
And Christmas blocks are burning,
Their ovens, they with baked meats choke,
And all their spits are turning;
Without the door let sorrow lie,
And if for cold it hap to die,
We'll bury un in a Christmas pie,
And evermore be merry."

—Withers.

"Ah, this is like Christmas," said the old Major as he wended his way with his wife and Ande to Trembath Manor on Christmas eve. The Manor was to be reopened that night and the strange owner, through his secretary, had sent out invitations to the country around, and among those receiving invitations were the Major and his wife and son.

They passed through the gates, the old Major pausing a moment to scan the Trembath arms and remarking, "I am glad the new owner has not seen fit to remove our coat-of-arms from the gates."

"The drive-way is in better shape than it was in the days of Squire Vivian," said Ande, as the gravel crunched under their advancing steps.

"A careful and neat owner; it will do me good to meet him," said the Major.

Forth through the trees ahead gleamed the twinkling lights of many windows, only obstructed by the passing of forms within and the figures of many great holly wreaths. The great lantern in front of the double doors was gleaming brilliantly through its festoons of evergreen, and from the hall could be heard the sound of ringing festivity and jollification. The door was opened widely at the sound of the great knocker, and the butler footman, bowing low, ushered them into the great hall. Groups of elderly people were engaged at their favourite game, whist, at different tables, and down the long room were others engaged in sundry amusements. The panelled walls had been rewaxed and were glistening with holly and mistletoe. The large picture of Squire Vivian's father still smiled friendly at the picture of King George II on the other wall, and in the great open fireplace roared, cracked, leaped, danced and shouted with all the ecstacy of Christmas jollity the flames of the great yule log.

"Where's the new squire?" whispered the old Major to his son. He had hardly asked the question, before he started back in amazement at a sight he saw over the great, panelled fireplace. Two great oil-paintings, heavy in their rich framings, riveted his attention. He stared at them and then at the crowd of Christmas revellers, who, though now thoroughly quieted, yet had gleams of suppressed merriment on their countenances. What could it mean? Those pictures? Where had they obtained them? Was his mind affected? He knew that he was growing old, and as he dazedly thought of this, he hurriedly passed his hand through his whitened hair, a gnarled, brown bough in the midst of a snowdrift. The folding doors, separating the servants' hall from the apartment they were in, were thrown open, revealing the merry faces of group after group of servants. It was a tableau of suppressed excitement, broken at length by the voice of Parson Trant.

"My friends, we have gathered here not only for Christmas festivity, but to do honour to the dead and to the living." Pointing to the picture on the right, he continued: "Behold the picture of Captain Andrew Trembath. You are all aware of the terrible injustice done his memory. He was the most patriotic and loyal of Cornish gentlemen. His long war record amply testifies the fact. He was wounded at Prestonpans, and at Culloden, and did worthy service under Braddock in America. After that deplorable battle, he was captured by the Indians, escaped from them, slew a French officer, garbed himself in his uniform and for greater security in the enemy's country inserted his name in the dead officer's commission papers. He was accidentally shot by the troops of General Armstrong, the thought of treason penetrated the public mind and the estate of Trembath was confiscated. Yet, after all these years truth prevails. An old snuff-box, found in the wilds of America, reveals the secret, and though dead, Captain Andrew Trembath is once more honoured by the people as a faithful soldier and loyal subject of the King." Then, turning to the other picture, he continued:

"Behold the picture of Major Thomas Trembath, who served the King nobly in the Peninsular campaign, in the War of the American Colonies and in the Canadian War. He disappeared, due to an impression conveyed to him that his family was dead, and for many long years was an exile in the wilds of America. Then as a hunter he lived by the pursuit of game. To the place of his abode came his son, Andrew Trembath, and after a time became known to him, and through the finding of the records of the snuff-box, already mentioned, he is restored to his former honours,—friends and country. His life formerly was sad, now we trust his declining years will be full of sunshine, and I greet and welcome him as Squire Trembath, the rightful master of Trembath Manor."

"Welcome to your own, again, comrade," said old Captain Tom Lanyan, as he heartily shook the squire's hand.

Others crowded around the old squire, among them Dick Thomas, Tom Glaze, and numerous of the parish gentry.

The old squire and his wife were so dazed that they could not speak, and so they were escorted to the great armchairs in readiness for them near the great yule log, and one by one the Christmas guests came near and gave their greetings. When it was all finished, the new squire found his voice.

"I am glad, my friends, to be with you here in the hall of my fathers, but all this seems too wonderful to me to be true; yet I cannot help but believe what has been told me—but how has all this come about? Has the government——"

"There has not been anything wonderful about it but the kindness of Providence," said Ande Trembath, arising to speak. "Years ago, when a lad, I resolved to remove the stain of treason from our name. My life here and at school is familiar to you all. By a strange series of adventures my classmate, Dick Thomas, and myself found ourselves adrift on a bit of wreckage in the English channel. We were picked up by a Brazilian ship and after a weary journey were landed at Rio de Janeiro. For some time we laboured in the fields of planters, and then betook our way inland to the ridges of Sierro Do Frio. It was here that we laboured under a brazen sun for the space of three years. I cannot tell of all the various vicissitudes that overtook us there. At one time I was down with fever and, but for the help of Dick, would have succumbed to its ravages. At another time I repaid the debt by nursing Dick through a serious illness. Gentlemen, you have all seen him wrestle with Tom Glaze, but he was not the hardest opponent he met. He had the hardihood to win championship honours in a struggle with an immense Brazilian puma, or mountain lion. I do not remember whether Dick sprang at the lion or the lion at him. All I remember was seeing man and beast in a hideous mix-up, worse than any wrestling match I had ever seen. I ran to our cabin for a gun, but it was unnecessary, for when I returned, there were Dick and the lion stretched beside each other. He had choked it to death, but was so lacerated himself that it was months before he became well. In the midst of our work we were successful, both in diamonds and gold, and quitted the regions wealthy men. I deposited my wealth in the banks of New Orleans, and the charm of the hunting life still being on me, and being anxious to visit the place of my grandfather's death, we journeyed to the Kittanning region. The result of that Kittanning trip is now known to all England. I heard that the Manor was for sale, and secretly, through agents, purchased it. And now, father and mother, I hand over to you the title deeds of Trembath Manor and the Wheal Whimble tin mine as a Christmas present. I wish also to add this check on the Bank of England for the sum of fifty thousand pounds. A merry Christmas, and may you have many, happy years in the home of our people."

"Merry Christmas! 'Tis the merriest Christmas I have had in years," said the old squire with emotion, as he wiped the tears away, that would persist in gathering in his eyes.

Mrs. Elizabeth Trembath said nothing, but her bright shining eyes revealed her happiness as she gently pulled her son's head down and kissed him.

Here the thrumming of a harp was heard and a curtain was drawn from an alcove near by, revealing Uncle Billy, the droll, with an orchestra at his back. In the meantime Ande withdrew. The droll and his orchestra paused not a moment, but plunged, with voices and instruments combined, into the Hymn of the Lark.

The song was sung to its very end, and the old squire, as he nodded, said, "Yes, yes, it's true; evil fails at last and right prevails."

He had hardly finished speaking when the orchestra burst into strains of Mendelssohn, and down the great, hall stairway came a procession such as it had never witnessed before. First came a troop of little girls bearing flowers and scattering them profusely in the way. Then followed ladies. "Ah, the bridesmaids," whispered some one, and then followed by their respective attendants, in regular procession, came Ande Trembath and his affianced bride, Mistress Alice Vivian. Slowly they proceeded up the hall and took their respective positions before old Parson Trant. The orchestra gave one clashing peal of music and then was silent, and then arose the mellow voice of the rector in the marriage ceremony of the Church of England. At the words, "Can any man say aught why these two should not be joined together in holy wedlock," the voice of the squire was heard.

"There have been so many things happening on this Christmas eve, that I hesitate to interrupt the service, but have the laws of England changed in my absence. I mean that law that states that no marriages are lawful except those performed in a parish church?"

"The laws of England are the same," said Parson Trant, "but we have a special dispensation from the archbishop, dispensing with the banns, and allowing, in consideration of the return of Squire Trembath and the happiness of this occasion, the ceremony to be performed in the Manor of Trembath."

"Ah, that is different; my blessing and heartiest well wishes," said the squire, as he sank back in his armchair.

After the ceremony all adjourned to the dining hall, where an elaborate wedding dinner awaited them. During the wedding feast the old squire told of his many adventures, to which Dick and Ande added some of their own.

"It tells like a story-book," said Tom Glaze, in admiration.

"Or rather like a drama," said bluff Captain Tom Lanyan. "Wouldn't I have liked to have been in the Shawnee fight," and the tough, old, Wellington veteran rubbed his hands in delight.

"I have a bit of news," said Ande, as he drew a letter from his pocket. "Here is a letter from Hugh Lark in America, just received." He scanned it rapidly and replaced it, and then turned with a smile to his father and the company. "He says that he has given up the idea of the silver mine, that Professor Bill Banks has been elected to Congress, and that old Burke still thinks Bill is high larndt."

The voices of carol singers were heard without, and the wedding dinner being ended, they again returned to the main hall to enjoy the singing. The "curl" singers were followed by the old play of St. George and the Turk, performed by village lads. Then, in the closing scenes of the evening's festivities, Parson Trant pro posed his favourite hymn, and out on the evening air, echoing even far beyond the walls of Trembath Manor, the mellow voices of the trained singers, the piping of childish voices, the worn voices of the older parties, and the music of the droll's orchestra mingling all together, pealed the strains of Cowper's hymn:

"God moves in a mysterious way,
His wonders to perform,
He plants his footsteps in the sea
And rides upon the storm."

THE END.

Lector House believes that a society develops through a two-fold approach of continuous learning and adaptation, which is derived from the study of classic literary works spread across the historic timeline of literature records. Therefore, we aim at reviving, repairing and redeveloping all those inaccessible or damaged but historically as well as culturally important literature across subjects so that the future generations may have an opportunity to study and learn from past works to embark upon a journey of creating a better future.

This book is a result of an effort made by Lector House towards making a contribution to the preservation and repair of original ancient works which might hold historical significance to the approach of continuous learning across subjects.

HAPPY READING & LEARNING!

LECTOR HOUSE LLP
E-MAIL: lectorpublishing@gmail.com